THE BARSOOM PROJECT

Other Ace Books by Larry Niven

THE MAGIC GOES AWAY
THE MAGIC MAY RETURN (Ed.)
MORE MAGIC (Ed.)
THE PATCHWORK GIRL

Also by Steven Barnes

STREETLETHAL

LARRY NIVEN & STEVEN BARNES

THE BARSOOM PROJECT

ACE BOOKS, NEW YORK

THE BARSOOM PROJECT

An Ace Book/published by arrangement with
the authors

Ace books are published by The Berkley Publishing Group,
200 Madison Avenue, New York, New York 10016.
The name "ACE" and the "A" logo
are trademarks belonging to Charter Communications, Inc.
PRINTED IN THE UNITED STATES OF AMERICA

Quality Printing and Binding by:
ARCATA GRAPHICS/KINGSPORT
Press and Roller Streets
Kingsport, TN 37662   U.S.A.

CAST OF CHARACTERS AND GLOSSARY

Falling Angel

RICHARD ARBENZ: *Ambassador from Falling Angel; Charlene Dula's maternal uncle.*

Dream Park

MARTY BOBBICK: *Griffin's assistant. Plays as Hippogryph.*

ARTHUR COWLES: *Founder of Dream Park.*

ALEX GRIFFIN: *Security Chief of Dream Park.*

THADEUS HARMONY: *Dream Park Director of Operations.*

MITCH HASAGAWA: *Dream Park Security.*

TOMISUBURO IZUMI: *Dream Park R&D tech.*

CALVIN IZUMI: *Brother of Tom, deceased.*

SANDY KHRESLA: *Head of Dream Park Maintenance Division.*

CARY McGIVVON: *Alex Griffin's new assistant.*

MILLICENT SUMMERS: *Formerly Griffin's secretary. Now an executive in the Department of Financial Affairs.*

DOCTOR VAIL: *Dream Park psychologist.*

DWIGHT WELLES: *Senior computer tech for Dream Park; Game Master for the altered Fimbulwinter Game.*

Gamers

ROBIN BOWLES: *Professional actor. Actor in the Fimbulwinter Game. Talisman: caribou's ear, for hearing.*

CAST OF CHARACTERS AND GLOSSARY

CHARLENE DULA: *Gamer from the zero-grav habitat Falling Angel, and friend to Michelle Sturgeon. Talisman: a swatch of white fur, arctic seal, for invisibility.*

EVIANE alias MICHELLE RIVERS alias MICHELLE STURGEON: *Veteran of the first Fimbulwinter Game. Plays most of the game as a tornrait. Talisman: semi-automatic rifle.*

FRANCIS HEBERT: *Marine, Major in the reserves.*

AVRAM HENDERSON: *Gamer.*

MAZIE HENDERSON: *Gamer.*

OLLIE NORLISS alias FRANKISH OLIVER: *Professional Gamer and MD.*

MARTIN QATERLIARAQ alias MARTIN THE ARCTIC FOX: *Sorcerer or* angakok *among the Inuit. Actor in the Fimbulwinter Game.*

GWEN RYDER alias CANDICE alias KANGUQ alias SNOW GOOSE: *Professional actress. Married to Ollie Norliss.*

MAX SANDS: *Gamer. Professional wrestler under the name Mr. Mountain. Talisman: owl claw, for strength.*

ORSON SANDS: *Max Sands's brother. Gamer.*

TRIANNA STITH-WOOD: *Professional chef.*

KEVIN TITUS: *Computer programmer and computer gamer. Talisman: a crumpled skin crusted with black soot, for strength. "Soot is stronger than fire."*

JOHNNY WELSH: *Gamer; professional comedian.*

YARNALL alias THE NATIONAL GUARDSMAN: *Dream Park actor.*

Others

ANDREW CHALA: *Pan-African ambassador.*

CAST OF CHARCTERS AND GLOSSARY

KAREEM FEKESH: *Industrialist, suspected supporter of UMAF.*

ROBERT J. FLAHERTY: *Producer of* Nanook of the North, *1922.*

TOBY LEE HARLOW JUNIOR: *Alias of the person who disrupted the first Fimbulwinter Game.*

LOPEZES: *Legendary Game Masters, now semiretired.*

TONY McWHIRTER: *Computer whiz, incarcerated for industrial espionage against Cowles Industries.*

MADELEINE: *Mystery woman; a possible link to Kareem Fekesh.*

RAZUL: *Libyan ambassador.*

Glossary

AHK-LUT: *Leader of the Cabal; son of Martin Qaterliaraq, brother of Snow Goose.*

AMARTOQ: *A headless troll.*

ANANSI: *A space shuttle, the object of a terrorist attack some years earlier.*

ANGAKOK: *Sorcerer.*

BRANTA CANADENSIS alias Tuutangayak alias Canadian Snow Goose.

THE CABAL: *The clique of evil sorcerers.*

COWLES INDUSTRIES: *The parent company of Dream Park.*

COWLES MODULAR COMMUNITY: *Living quarters for Dream Park employees.*

FALLING ANGEL ENTERPRISES: *Industrial nation-state, off-Earth.*

FAT RIPPER SPECIALS: *Games modified for the re-education of substance abusers.*

HOLY FIRE: *Terrorist organization, precursor to the UMAF.*

INTELCORP: *The company formed by the partner-*

ship of General Electric and Falling Angel Enterprises.

INTERNATIONAL FANTASY GAMING SOCIETY: *The governing body supervising the world of Adventure Gaming.*

KOGUKHPUK: *The Burrowing Mammoth.*

LEVIATHAN IV: *Mining rig proposed for use in terraforming Mars.*

MARK CARD: *A widely accepted inter-Union credit card.*

OFFICIAL IFGS KAMA SUTRA: *A myth, a mere rumor. It doesn't exist. Forget it. Trust us.*

PAIJA: *Giant female demon.*

PEWITU: *Taboos.*

PHANTOM FEAST: *A Dream Park diet restaurant.*

RAVEN: *Progenerative force in Inuit mythology.*

SEDNA: *Goddess of the sea and of the sea's life.*

SEELUMKADCHLUK: *Where the sky meets the sea; the barrier between reality and the Inuit spiritual world.*

TERICHIK: *A gigantic caterpillar-like monster; the spirit form of Ahk-lut.*

TIN-MI-UK-PUKS, or THUNDERBIRDS: *Fabulous Roc-like creatures.*

TORNGARSOAK: *Sedna's lover, Lord of the Hunt.*

TORNRAIT: *Ghost who serves an angakok, usually as a source of information.*

UNITED MOSLEM ACTIVIST FRONT or UMAF: *A radical mideastern terrorist organization.*

USIK: *A weapon crafted from the pubic bone of a walrus.*

WINIGO: *Inuit Yeti.*

WOLFALCONS: *Hybrid creatures, half wolf, half giant bird of prey.*

THE
BARSOOM
PROJECT

PROLOGUE

Like a raging mountain, the Terichik rose screaming from a frozen, nightdark sea. Its many-sectioned, grotesquely wormlike body reared up; tons of water and ice thundered into the ocean with a howl like the death of worlds. The black night swirled wind-whipped snow through mist that tasted of salt. The Terichik's mouth gaped cavernously. Endless rows of serrated teeth gleamed as it shrieked its mindless wrath. Its breath was a cold and fetid wind.

The humans beneath it were warrior and wizard, princess and commoner. They were frail meat in the Terichik's path, brittle fleshly twigs tumbled in an angry storm. They scrambled for safety, ran back onto land, away from the sea. They fled past the wreckage of the shattered Inuit village: rows of crushed houses, a great stone lodge with its roof stove in, boat hulls splintered and scattered like insect husks.

Bulwar was the first Adventurer to die, and he died well. He was the greatest warrior among them, but foolish to think that his enchanted *usik*, the pubic bone of the sacred walrus, could stand against the Terichik. Even faced by a beast to dwarf ten killer whales, Bulwar roared defiance and sprang forward. His ice-caked black beard flagged in the frigid air. His mightily thewed arms coiled beneath the bear furs that lent him strength and courage. Bulwar had once been an ordinary man, a "systems analyst" in the white man's world. Here where the heavens met the earth, he was a great warrior, a great force for good.

His magic, his courage, his strength were not enough. The Terichik crushed him, savaged his body with fanged cilia. His screams echoed in their heads long after his body had vanished into its gaping maw.

The humans retreated. There were twelve now, people of the tundras and the people from the white world beyond.

They ran until the sound of rifle shots split their screams. Two more of their number fell, trapped in a withering crossfire.

Agile and lithe, beautiful Eviane rolled to safety behind an abandoned boathouse. Even as she hit the ground, she unslung the automatic rifle from her back and braced the butt against her shoulder.

She was a woman of flaming red hair and sparkling green eyes. Her mouth was generously wide, quick to laughter or rage. Now it was flattened into a fighting grimace cold enough to freeze the stars in the sky.

She peered along the rifle barrel and then glanced back over her shoulder. Her companions were holding the Terichik at bay. The sky shimmered with power, enchanted flame searing away the clouds. It was Eviane's task to break the back of the ambush, to send the minions of the Cabal howling back into the wastes.

The Terichik rose to blot out the moon and stars. Its screams shook the earth. Eviane's stomach boiled acid with fear.

Now was not the moment to shirk! Now was the time to concentrate, to bring her wit and skill to bear.

She sighted through the rifle scope. Through the driving snow, a black-speckled ridge of ice and rock leapt into relief. Somewhere behind it were the men who held them pinned and vulnerable to the awesome Terichik.

Her scope's crosshairs trisected a shadowed forehead. Eviane grinned: one of the Cabal's minions was about to join his ancestors. The painted face, the glowing eyes were almost an invitation.

She inhaled deeply, held that breath, and squeezed the trigger.

The rifle jittered against her shoulder. Snow sprayed to the Cabalist's left. He jumped in surprise. Before he could run she fired a second time. He threw his arms around his chest; his mouth gaped wide. Recoil pulled Eviane's gun barrel upward. The Cabalist's head exploded.

Eviane was shocked. Tickled in an odd way, but shocked. *Strange. Usually you just get the flash of red. This time they're using prosthetic makeup effects. Kinda gag-out, but Wow!*

Confusion reigned on the far side of the ridge, and the attack, the ambush, was breaking. It had failed! The enemy was in rout! Eviane came to her feet, howling victory, and her companions rose with her. Brandishing guns and spears they raced across the frozen ground. The night blizzard's shrieks matched their own.

Another Cabalist rose, his hands raised to the air in the sign of surrender.

Take no prisoners! She laughed giddily, and fired from the hip. The Cabalist doubled over, holding his stomach. He yelled something, something that seemed to take great effort to say, but the wind was too loud to make out the words. His face was twisted with pain.

Eviane fired again, and his body straightened out as if hit under the chin with a baseball bat. Twisting, he crumpled to the ground.

Eviane walked to her first target, moving more slowly now. She stared down at the body.

The wind's whistle was dying. The flakes of ice were settling to the ground. The air was warming, but she shook.

She bent down, examining the wound she had inflicted. The man's forehead was gone.

What incredible ... effects ...

As if they had a will of their own, her fingers touched the dead man, crawled to the ghastly hole above the still, staring eyes. They traced the edges—

The wind died. Sound became silence, save for the whimper of wounded and the growing murmur of the other warriors who approached with lowered weapons. Mute, the titanic shape of the Terichik writhed in the sky behind them.

Eviane stood, eyes wide, mouth open but silent. Finally, as with a terrible effort she screamed, and ran. She threw the rifle, the goddamned rifle, aside and hurled herself behind an upturned stand of boats.

She knelt there, whimpering, and watched without comprehension as the Terichik flickered and dissolved. As the moon disappeared from the sky above her. And the stars. And the distant mountains. All that had been heaven and horizon was now a blank white dome crisscrossed with enormous rectangles.

One building at a time, the abandoned Inuit village disappeared: the lodge, the smokehouse, the line of boats. The boathouse remained, but it was too far. Eviane whimpered and ran and hid again, this time beneath a heap of splintered wood and iron: the only remaining boat.

Over and over in an endless loop her mind screamed: *What is happening? What is happening? I don't under—ohgodohgod—*

And then even the wreckage disappeared.

Eviane knelt on a blank field of white. Around her, her companions threw down their weapons and began to gather around the two bloodstained bodies.

At the edge of the dome, a door opened. Men and women in crisp orange uniforms entered. They mouthed phrases about "effects breakdowns" and "optical difficulties" as they hustled away the warriors and *angakoks*, the princess and the commoners, separated the quick from the dead. Eviane remained on her knees, unseeing, unhearing, even when she was lifted up and carried gently but firmly to the exit.

The bodies were covered, belted onto stretchers, and whisked away. Only blurred imprints and smears of red remained on the artificial snow.

Finally, men came to pick up the rifle. They handled it with infinite care, as if it were a sleeping viper or a live grenade, something that might awaken to wreak new and greater havoc.

As if it was a thing of magic in a world of technology, or of technology in a world of magic.

Chapter One

THE BARSOOM PROJECT

"'In the beginning.' Three words spoken uncounted billions of times."

The narrator's voice echoed everywhere and originated nowhere. It filled the vast dark cavern of Gaming Area A with its rolling, resonant embrace. Alex Griffin peered into the blackness. Phantasmal carts danced about him in elaborate patterns, orange outlines in his infrared goggles. The carts glided through an endless, empty night, invisible to each other.

"Yet they have never lost their magic, never diminished in majesty. Ever have we looked back to the roots of our cultures, the origin of our species, the genesis of our planet.

"Come with us now, and peer into the past of our solar system, to the formation of our most distinctive neighbor—"

A darkened dome a few hundred meters across became a universe: the stars emerged.

Above and below, they flamed in primal glory. Never had the skies of Earth been so fully or brightly populated. Blobs and streams of dark matter moved across the stars, dimming them. Never had the stars made any noise at all, but now Griffin's bones rattled with the reverberations of the best sound system in the Western hemisphere.

One dim star abruptly flared brighter than all the rest. It was blinding... it was already dimming, while shells of lesser fire expanded from the supernova at ferocious speed. There were flame-colors in the shock waves.

Griffin chuckled quietly.

The thirteen hundred dignitaries gathered here by Cowles Industries and IntelCorp were in for a hell of a show. His chief deputy Marty Bobbick had a grip on his elbow. Marty's round face was soft with wonder, and his eyes gleamed.

"Though details differ, current theories agree that the solar

system originated as a cold cloud of interstellar gas. There were snowflakes and snowballs, protocomets, scattered through it. And so it remained until the shock wave from a nearby supernova disturbed its equilibrium."

The supernova had died to nothing . . . no, not quite gone. Griffin found it as a tiny blinking dot. Then the shock waves arrived with a rolling crash that owed less to physics than to Dream Park magic. The vast interstellar dust clouds bowed before it; flattened, then began to collapse and condense. There were hurricane shapes at the centers. The viewpoint zoomed in on one of the whorls as streamers began to separate, giving it the look of a carelessly spray-painted archery target. The great storm sparkled like a fireworks display. The center began to glow.

"Gravity and spin became the dominant factors. Stars began to form," the unseen narrator said, but Griffin found his mind blanking out the words. The illusion was so overpoweringly real that his chest ached for breath.

A new sun blazed forth, awesomely bright within its murky sheath of dust and comets. In that terrible light Griffin could see lumps condensing along the rings that surrounded the sun. The solar system was still murky; comets moved through the viewpoint like white bullets.

This was the big one, the project toward which Cowles had angled for over a decade, the beginning of the largest venture in mankind's history. And Griffin was part of it . . . if only as the security man who would keep these multinational billionaires from murdering each other. The 1,333 men and women taking their slow trips into the heart of the primordial solar system would be much more a part of it, if they chose.

And if they didn't, there would be no Barsoom Project.

And if there were no Barsoom Project, then . . . very soon, by geological time, there might be no life on Earth.

The turgid protostellar whirl was clearing now. Sunlight boiled away the nearer comets, leaving residues that would become asteroids; boiled the atmospheres from even the closer planets. The planets flashed and flamed from time to time as smaller bodies smashed into them. The viewpoint moved toward one such body, a glowing, cratered, lumpy sphere that grew clearer as its atmosphere dissipated.

Griffin wrenched his mind out of the illusion and brushed the controls before him in the cart. Of the hundred and fifty computer-driven carts gliding through an embryonic cosmos, he and

Marty had the only cart equipped with manual override. In case of emergency, he could reach another cart within moments. There was no reason to expect any such emergency, but . . .

He whispered to Marty, "Let's peek in on them." Marty nodded—he still had a death-grip on Alex's elbow—and Alex rattle-tapped instructions to the heat-sensitive vidplate before him.

It lit. It became a quad splitscreen, and in each quadrant a cart appeared. Each cart seated ten visiting dignitaries. At upper-left were intense, serious visitors from the United Kingdom. Only one, a rotund woman in her fifties, was smiling broadly, clapping with childish glee.

Upper-right held officials from International Labor Union 207, the energy people. The international unions were more powerful than some nations. Certainly they were prime candidates for the offer that IntelCorp and Cowles wished to make.

Chitchat broke off, heads swiveled right, mouths gaped. A gargantuan gas-sheathed snowball roared directly at 207's cart. A smaller comet grazed it. A tenor scream split the air as the comet flared blindingly and passed on the right.

They laughed and slapped each other on the backs, none knowing who among them had screamed.

Lower-left was the Pan-African coalition . . . members who were not currently embroiled in war.

What a mess. Africa was a jungle, all right. A jungle of artificially drawn lines, so complex that things might not sort themselves out for another century. National boundaries, tribal boundaries, industrial boundaries, and union boundaries all writhed and fluxed and left bloody tracks behind, year after year for the past century. Project Barsoom might straighten them out . . . might give some of these political entities cause to fix them in place. A reason to forget the past, for the sake of the future.

Lower-right, ten young Tolkien elves, inhumanly tall and slender, yelled and laughed and ducked a passing comet. That was IntelCorp, the company formed by the partnership of General Electric and Falling Angel Enterprises.

Wiser heads within those companies, understanding that massive success and massive inertia are two sides of a coin, had split off some of the best young minds from the GE think tanks. These maniacs were backed with a hundred eighty million dollars and linked with the creative whirlwinds behind Falling Angels, the rogue technological "nation" orbiting Luna. The zero-gravity laboratories of Falling Angels were responsible for the Tokyo-Seoul expansion bridge, as well as a revolution in high-tensile engineering.

The result was one of the most effective think tanks in history. They already held eight percent of the most productive patents issued in the past decade, and the best was yet to come.

The sun had dimmed. The solar system was finally settling down. The cratered sphere in the foreground was drifting closer. Its rocks had breathed forth a new atmosphere, pink in hue and not thick enough to block the topography . . . and as the orange-red sphere grew huge, clean white polar caps and a lacing of long gray-green lines were suddenly apparent. Two cratered moons rose over the planet's eastern curve.

There was laughter from the carts. *"In 1877, Italian astronomer Giovanni Schiaparelli observed a network of single and double lines crisscrossing the surface of the planet. Canali means 'channels' or 'grooves' in Italian, but the word was mistranslated into 'canals,' which implies intelligent design . . ."*

"Quite a show, eh?" Marty grinned in the dark: a new moon. "I want to sign up right now."

"Get out your Mark card if you've got the money. They'll be passing the hat pretty quick." Alex continued to look at Marty's black silhouette. "We haven't done any mat work for over a month. Have you been working the treadmill?"

"Sure. Well, not every day." He sighed guiltily. "Guess I'm gonna pay for that, huh?"

In about thirty-six hours Marty would be in his first Game. It was a Fat Ripper Special. The monsters chasing him would be slow, and that was as well. Alex's assistant had been muscular when Security hired him. Muscular, hell . . . he had come within one point of a Bronze in judo at Mexico's Pan-American Games in '36. By the time Griffin came over from Cowles Seattle in '49, Marty was soft, but still strong and skilled; he could wipe the floor with Griffin in a structured *randori*. Now Marty's weight was seventy pounds out of control.

They said these special Games would rip the fat right off you. And then they laughed. A week of waddling after orcs and dragons doesn't make anyone thin.

The IntelCorp cart (lower-right) held the reason that Marty would join the Fat Ripper. Charlene Dula stood seven feet zero, tall even for a Falling Angel. Her uncle Richard Arbenz was only an inch shorter, a double Ph.D. responsible for two of those lucrative patents.

Both were possible targets for terrorists.

The exact origins of the feud between Falling Angel and OPEC were lost in a welter of crisscrossed accusations. Falling Angel swore that it began in the infamous Anansi incident, when armed mercenaries had attacked a Falling Angel spacecraft. The United Moslem Activist Front were widely held responsible, although they had never been brought to task.

The UMAF had placed sole responsibility for the near disaster on a Brazilian industrial concern. No one believed them, and the organization had long since disbanded or been absorbed piecemeal into a dozen other pro-Arab organizations, especially the renegade Holy Fire group.

There had been other problems through the years—economic boycotts, military blockades, even reports of sabotage. It formed a thinly veiled pattern of hostility which had neither resolved nor escalated into open war.

The result was a highly effective war of nerves. At the moment, the battleground was the acid-ravaged stomach lining of one Alex Griffin, Security Chief of Dream Park. The industrial and political descendants of all involved parties were held in Gaming Area A of Dream Park.

Griffin tapped; the quad screen blinked and forty new faces appeared. Alex counted off Texaco, IBM, Aeroflot, and the Mitsubishi/Red Star consortium.

Mankind had come so far in some ways, and in others remained up in the trees, chittering and throwing rocks at each other.

If only the trees weren't so close together. If only the rocks were smaller.

Perhaps Barsoom would give mankind a second chance. There would be no room on Mars for the poor or ignorant. Human frailties would follow man to the stars, but some of the simpler motivations to violence could be left in the Cradle.

"—*Viking probes demonstrated that the Martian environment was not the haven for extraterrestrial life envisioned by Burroughs, Wells, and Lowell*." The viewpoint skimmed above tidy, spindly-towered cityscapes at the junctures of the canals. Alex glimpsed a street crowded with eight-limbed beasts, red- and ebony-skinned men, and tall, insectile green tharks, each group carefully avoiding all others...

Then the sky darkened nearly to black, cities and canals faded away, the great moons shrank to lumpish dots. "*Rather Mars is a barren desert, without sufficient water, oxygen, or hope to support any but the simplest life forms. Its atmosphere is far too thin to resist the fierce solar flux. Mars is lashed by ultraviolet radiation that would kill all but the hardiest microbes.*

"Despite the dreams of the past, there is no life on Mars. But there will be Martians."

The carts rolled across the surface of Mars. The landscape stretched to a razor-sharp horizon, too close, an endless plain of gray-red rocks and sand broken here and there by the rise of a weary-looking mountain.

A thin, lifeless wind whispered about them. Even with Marty seated next to him, Alex felt so unimaginably lonely that it shocked him. What was it? Subsonics? Subliminals in the light patterns? Whatever it was, it was eerily effective.

Mars seemed then a spinster sister awaiting the kiss of life, a bridesmaid to vibrant Earth, looking longingly across a two-hundred-million-mile gap, waiting, waiting...

Ever a bridesmaid, never a bride.

A light appeared in the sky, a moving, twinkling star crossing from east to west. It loomed larger and brighter, like some huge diamond, and suddenly it *blazed*. It was like a nearby sun when it touched the western horizon.

The ground shuddered. The sky shivered with the flash. It was as if an H-bomb had detonated. What stood above the horizon was not a mushroom (Mars's atmosphere wasn't that thick) but a rapidly expanding dome of flame. The dome's rim rushed at them, rolled over them with a roar. It passed, leaving them unharmed. Orange magma flowed forth where the intruder had struck.

"—life can come to this barren world, life in a flash of fire—"

A second comet streaked across the sky, and this one seemed to come straight at them, filling the sky, filling Alex's vision. Alex screamed with delighted terror as the world exploded. Suddenly the sky was pouring with sleet and rain. A billion tons of ice had vaporized—a thousand times the size of the comet fragment that exploded over central Siberia on June 30, 1908.

"—we can bring air and water to Mars—"

No poet had ever pictured Mars as female and Earth as male. *Too bad*, Alex thought. The Barsoom Project would get Mars with child.

As if by the power of time-lapse photography, the rain fell all around them now, utterly convincing. If Alex reached a hand into that, would it get wet? He did it. His hand remained dry in the midst of a torrential downpour. Marty stifled a laugh.

The rains passed. The small sun, filtered through a thicker atmosphere, seemed gentler now.

Perspective tilted until they were staring at reddish, sandy soil. Dust became gravel became boulders as the carts were zoomed down to a different level of existence. Alex found himself watching Earth-tailored bacteria at work.

The wriggling shapes became more complex; rocky soil broke under their attack; the rain turned fine Marsdust to mud. The expanding carts raced ahead of a writhing network of roots and emerged into a shrinking jungle of green plants.

Now the carts moved through a fall of Marsdust. Great bucketlike vehicles dropped out of the sky, each of a different bizarre design, puffing flame only at the moment before impact. Men erected the spiderweb-thin skeleton of a dome, then filled it in with rhomboidal panels.

The carts were semi-independent now. They would go where their occupants pointed them, though they remained out of view of each other. The central computer controlled them still, so that there was no chance of the invisible carts colliding with each other.

Griffin cruised closer to the dome. It seemed huge: bigger than Gaming A, big enough for a small city, an environment that could house an entire community of engineers and scientists.

"—there will be Martians. We will be the Martians. And you will be part of that process. This is the future. This is how it will begin."

Griffin accepted a glass of wine from the hand of an eight-foot indigo thark. Its four arms articulated gracefully. It delicately picked its way through the crowd, dispensing a seemingly endless stream of wine and beverages. For an instant he wondered how the illusion was sustained. Surely it was solid. Perhaps a human being within an external shell, the upper arms controlled by waldos?

This was futile. The magic of the Dream Park technicians should be accepted as magic, and there were more important matters to occupy his mind.

A brass-voiced Brit was telling half a dozen amused Americans that *"cannelloni* means 'pasta' or 'dinner' in Italian, but the word was mistranslated into 'noodles,' which implies intelligent design..."

Japanese investors chatted excitedly as they admired the Phoenix F1, the rocket vehicle IntelCorp had bet its roll on. It was a truncated cone, shaped much like its little brothers, the Phoenix variations that had served between Earth and moon for fifty years. But the Phoenix F1 wouldn't be just bigger. It would be fusion-powered. The kind of plasma torus that powered Bussard fusion plants on Earth would form the base of the beast; it would leak half-fused deuterium plasma to form a rocket exhaust.

Special Effects had been playing with the F1. Most of the model must be a hologram, but part of the base had children crawling all over it. No adult in the room was likely to live long enough to see the project's completion, but these children might. One day they would control Barsoom stock, and they would remember.

"A neat trick, eh?" The voice as a low grumble, and Griffin turned to see Harmony's face looming above him.

Alex said, "Good move, getting them to bring their children."

"We gave them all a week's free Gold Pass to Dream Park. What better way to make these people take the investment seriously?"

Thadeus Harmony was a bear of a man, with the shoulders of the linebacker he had once been. But time had sloped those shoulders, and a desk job added to the thickness of the waist. There was extra gray in Harmony's hair now, more lines in the blunt features, and a bitter twist to his mouth that hadn't been there a year ago.

In his first year at Dream Park, Alex had dived into the work headfirst, sometimes not emerging for weeks at a time. Harmony was the one who hauled Alex kicking and screaming from his desk to ski in Aspen or cast for shark in the Bahamas.

All Alex wanted was to return the favor. He had not yet been able to find a way. All he could do was watch a close friend turn into an old man before his eyes. The sense of helplessness was numbing.

With a sudden clankety-rumbling sound, the Leviathan IV model rolled up to them, and stopped. The demo version of the mining rig was only two-thirds the size of the actual unit, but at seven feet high, still impressive. A flock of children rode the vehicle like dogfaces riding a Sherman in World War II. The Leviathan chattered about its specs. Alex paused a moment to listen, and to watch the digging jaws and claws extend, watched the tank-treads and steel sides turn translucent as the whole thing went schematic: ore sample tank, three-man passenger cabin, minilab, communications, powertrain all detailed.

"Looks like a crab on rollers," Griffin said, walking on.

Harmony was silent.

The Security Chief waited a couple of seconds, and when no comment was forthcoming, ventured another comment. "Everything seems to be going well, don't you think?"

"Yes, everything," Harmony said. Griffin stopped. A flat note of disgust had taken root in Harmony's voice, suddenly growing strong. Harmony's eyes were tight and wary, and moved too quickly, as if looking for something to avoid.

"What's wrong?" Griffin asked, voice low. "Don't bother saying 'nothing.' Your nostrils twitch when you lie."

Not a trace of a smile. Harmony shook his massive head. "I have it on the best authority that nothing is wrong. The very best."

"Ah-hah. Well, I can accept that. But tell me."

"What?"

Nobody in earshot? "If there was something wrong—and there isn't, of course. But if you were listing the people you'd most like to watch sky-dive into a school of sharks, who might head the list?"

Harmony's face creased in a reluctant smile. "Ah. Evocatively phrased."

"Well?"

Harmony opened his mouth and shut it again. "Never mind, Alex. I've been told that what's done is done. 'Are you racing toward the future, or are you mired in the past?' That's what I was asked." Harmony smiled politely as a flock of chattering Japanese businessmen scuttled by. The instant they passed, his face went flat and bitter. "That's what they asked *me*."

Thirteen hundred guests milled around "A," poking into this, peering at that. They tended to form distinct clusters. The Arab delegation moved toward Griffin and Harmony as they inspected a 1/10 scale industrial complex, a computer-drawn hologram that pumped and hissed right down to the last detail. Its miniature lights made it a jeweled crown in the light of a Martian sunset.

Alex watched Harmony's face darken. Was it here, someone in this group of men? Who? His eye went to the tallest man in the group. Their leader, an industrialist named Kareem Fekesh, met his gaze. Fekesh was six feet of effortless elegance, darkly feline in a suit that made Harmony's Ralph Lauren look like a Salvation Army special. Fekesh inclined his head politely and turned back to his conversation.

Anyone else? If someone posed a clear security risk, Harmony would have spoken of it regardless of orders.

Whose orders?

The group from Falling Angel was nearby. Griffin directed himself and Harmony in that direction.

"Ambassador?"

Ambassador Arbenz inclined his head gravely. "You are the Security Chief?"

Alex nodded. "Alex Griffin. And this is Thadeus Harmony, Deputy Director of Operations for Cowles Industries. He used to be my boss."

"Kicked upstairs." Harmony's smile was purest porcelain.

Alex watched them shake hands. It tickled him to see Harmony looking up at the man. Arbenz said, "This is a great success, I think. To have collected so many different nations and interests at one place and one time. I wonder if any other organization could have accomplished it."

"Time will tell whether the victory is real or symbolic, Ambassador. There are greater things at stake than raw human ego."

"Nothing else costs so dearly."

"True enough."

A painfully thin and awesomely tall brunette came to stand at Arbenz's side. "Have you met my niece? Charlene, Thadeus Harmony, Alex Griffin."

The girl smiled shyly. She was pretty, in that elongated Spacer way. Alex saw her as a bit flat-chested and far too thin; but there was a basic sweetness and cheer to her as she said, "I'm so happy to be here."

"It's been a long eight weeks, hasn't it?"

"Yes, and only my second time down." She shook her head regretfully. "I built up my legs in the centrifuge and on the exercise bikes, but I've still twisted both ankles." She bent her legs experimentally. "My knee hurts."

"I hope you'll be all right for the Game."

"I've got two knees," she said, suddenly mischievous. "There's only one Dream Park."

"You don't know any of the other Gamers?" Where was Marty?

"I have a companion. We met through Compunet. She's a Gamer too, and we partnered on some frantic vid campaigns. I'm looking forward to playing with her here. Wow." Her eyes glowed. "I still can't believe I'm really here."

"I know the feeling." He'd heard it too often. Alex realized that he hadn't a whole lot more to say to Charlene.

Her hand pulled at his arm. "These effects. They're so... real. How do they do it?"

Alex winked. "Santa's secret. I tell you what—after you're out of the Game, I'll introduce you to the elves. How's that?"

"Fine. Thank you very much."

Harmony and Alex drifted away from the crowd, and Griffin could feel the tension reviving in his friend.

"Alex—"

Before he had a chance to say anything else, Alex's beeper trilled against his wrist. He said, "The office wants me. Shall I tell them—"

"We'll talk later," Harmony said.

Harmony's eyes were haunted. *To hell with the beeper* was halfway to Alex's lips, but he bit it back. What was going on here?

But the haunted look vanished as Harmony slammed the wall down. "Duty calls, Alex," he said sardonically. He winked as if someone had pulled a string behind his eyeball. Alex thought it was obscene. Harmony turned and vanished into the crowd.

Alex walked toward one of the side doors, pressed tabs on his watch and heard the lock beep in response. The door opened. With a last look at Mars—the past, the fanciful, and the future —he disappeared out the side door.

Chapter Two

THE PHANTOM FEAST

Gwen Ryder had been told about the Phantom Feast, but she still stopped in the doorway, bewildered.

It might have been a library. Half the walls were books, and most of those were tall and wide, heavily illustrated. Diet books and cookbooks and nothing else. Some were quite old, some quite recent. There were hundreds.

An old book, *The Beverly Hills Diet*, had been disassembled. Its pages papered one wall. Customers on their way out clustered around, guffawing as they read the funnier passages aloud.

Another wall was covered with fading photos of impossibly rich desserts—with a comparison chart showing how many New York Marathon miles it would take to burn off the calories. A double-exposure photo of anorexic, number-chested men and women staggering toward a ten-story banana split was stark and somehow disturbing.

It was 2:20, ten minutes before Ollie was scheduled to show up, and well past lunch hour. The Phantom Feast was still crowded. Old and young, cheerful or morose, singles and clusters, the customers all looked somewhat alike.

They were stocky, chubby, fat, or morbidly obese. Gwen was startled to recognize a famous middle-aged actor, Robin Bowles, cheerfully scrawling autographs for a handful of supplicants. She grinned, not because she collected autographs, but because he looked so *real* . . . and so comfortable. Six feet tall, maybe five feet in circumference, the huge, balding presence who had dominated so many vidscreens signed a last book and sagged back in a chair his own size.

No need to worry about little teeny chairs in the Phantom Feast!

Mazie Henderson waved from a table for four, without getting up. She was roly-poly, an oval woman with a round, florid face, but at five four she wasn't big enough for her chair. Her companion was bigger and a few years older.

Reluctantly, Gwen went over. The man got to his feet. It was the limit of his strength. Long black hair, full black beard, an ornate silver buckle the size of his palm. Mazie said, "Gwen, you know my husband Avram. Avram's a Magic User now." Avram smiled and pumped her hand once and sat down too hard. Worn out.

Mazie didn't look much better. Gwen's broad smile had no visible malice in it, she hoped. "Well! You must have enjoyed the East Gate Game. How about we take in a few rides? I've tried the Everest Ski Slope and it's—"

Mazie leaned toward Avram and stabbed a weary finger at Gwen. "Kill that for me."

"Dear, I haven't the energy."

Gwen laid an empathetic hand on Mazie's shoulder. "I but jested." Hallelujah! Maybe she could escape without a numbing barrage of anecdote. It might be safe to sit, after all.

In high school Gwen had become almighty tired of Mazie's Gaming stories.

That had been old-style Gaming. A dozen kids, or as many as could find the time, would gather in somebody's living room to play a two-day Game cassette. Interaction was limited to stiffly animated composite images: crude but effective. Mazie's living room had a monitor the size of a picture window. Gwen had liked it enough to graduate into real Gaming, Dream Park Gaming; but she had never come to love the Monday morning rehashes. Those were still as dull as somebody else's diet.

The waiter set a chopped-steak platter in front of Avram, gave Mazie a salad. She ignored it, but Avram dipped his fork into it. It looked good. Diet dressing, no doubt, but it was big and varied, all bright greens, reds, and oranges with no dairy products. Mazie seemed not to notice Avram's piracy. "I feel like I owe you a report, Gwen. After all, you talked me into it."

"Oh, no. You don't have to. Really. Actually, I was just waiting—" She started to get up. Her conscience was pulling her back even before Mazie's meaty hand closed on her arm.

This time Mazie had earned the right.

Last August Gwen had met Mazie for the first time in twelve years. Mazie was a mountain. Her new husband, Avram, was another . . . and he had been a Gamer, years back. They'd worked

Mazie in stereo, and they'd talked her into playing a Fat Ripper Special with Avram.

Mazie stabbed into her salad for the first time. She grimaced: *leaves*! In a Fat Ripper she should have unlearned that attitude. Mazie chewed, swallowed in haste, and said, "I'm three pounds down! A pound a day!" For an instant she showed some energy. "They ran it off me. We started off with Genghis Khan's army hot on our heels, and it didn't get any better."

"In spots," Avram said.

"Yeah. The Horde was tracking us. We were more worried about them than anything we might meet. Eight hundred of us, and thousands of enemy behind us. General Wisowaty said we wouldn't stand a chance if they caught up."

"Guide," Avram interjected.

Guide. General Wisowaty would be an Actor working for Dream Park within the Game. Whatever he said would be true in context, though it need not be the whole truth.

The salad looked good, and Gwen was tempted to order one. Gwen had no taste for a red vinegar dressing. Surely virtue had earned her an ounce of blue cheese...? She tapped her lunch order into the table's console.

Mazie rescued her salad from Avram, who pretended to sulk as he cut his Salisbury into inch squares. She chewed and swallowed quickly and resumed. "We were in strange territory. Nobody wants an army in his backyard. General Wisowaty was leery of farms, but we needed food. We were on short rations, of course."

"Of course."

"Gwen, Dream Park was starving us and working us, but they had us thinking about food all the time! I don't get it. We're supposed to learn how to lose weight on a Fat Ripper Special."

"You're supposed to notice your food. If you eat automatically, or for any reason that isn't nutrition, you get upholstered. The Fat Rippers teach you the difference between feeding your body and feeding your face." Gwen knew the lectures. She liked being plump, and Ollie liked it, and her doctor said her blood pressure and cholesterol count were inhumanly healthy. She hadn't gained or lost a pound in three years. The Fimbulwinter Game would be her first Ripper, but she was going in as an employee.

"Back to the East Gate Game. Did you have fun?"

Mazie thought about that. A smile flickered briefly. "Fun? I guess I must have. I didn't get killed out. I saved two other players because I saw what was coming."

"She saved *me*," Avram said. "I got killed later."

"We could see an Eastern-looking city in the distance. Towers like minarets, tall and pointed and lots of them, then the edge of a wall. We bought food at two farms not too near the city. Just enough to half-fill the carts . . ."

Where was Ollie? In the two years that they had been married, their mutual love of Gaming had made them the hottest pair of Gamer/Actors on Dream Park's list. Ollie had graduated medical school eleven months ago, and that made him even more popular. Doctors were needed in any Game, but particularly in Fat Rippers.

But their popularity also meant that they had less and less time to themselves. Mentally she counted off. It had been . . . eight days since the last time she and Ollie had shared free time and a water bed.

She flushed with warmth, and deliberately pulled herself back into Mazie's Game.

They always told it as if it had happened to them. In another age they'd have been locked up as crazy. It helped if you'd been in the Game, and of course some players were better storytellers. Mazie was not.

But Mazie was enjoying her tale. "The gates were rusty. The hinges weren't in good shape. The guards were kind of sloppy, but they whooped when they saw us and went running to tell everyone. The buildings were big and round, a little like turnips, with the minarets sticking straight up from the middle. The market didn't look like much when we got there—just goods in piles, and people coming with wicker baskets to get what they wanted—but an hour after we arrived there were hucksters everywhere. They weren't happy people, Gwen, but they sure wanted to talk. They helped us with the loading just so we'd have time to tell them about other places."

Between sentences, Mazie had managed to eat half of her salad. She cast a sidewise glance at Avram's steak. "Mind if I borrow a bit of this?"

Avram said nothing. His wife speared two rectangles with her fork, popped them into her mouth, and shoveled salad in on top. *Calories don't count if you steal them off somebody else's plate. I used to do that.*

"We bought another cart," Mazie said around her mouthful.

"A big one. We bought several days' worth of food for the troops and piled it in. They didn't bargain. We made out like bandits. The General wanted booze and opium for the troops, but there wasn't anything like that in sight. When Jeffrey asked one of the locals she just looked puzzled. We were afraid to push. And they wouldn't buy our spices."

A waiter brought Gwen's salad and a tray of crackers. Good-looking stud, but brisk; Gwen couldn't catch his eye. Oh, well, what difference did it make? She was an ancient married woman now...

A woman caught Gwen's eyes. She stood near the wall, pudgy as the rest, watching as the Beverly Hills Diet faded into the Jane Fonda Geriatric Workout and more general merriment. She stood out: she wasn't laughing, or even smiling. She seemed lost. Her straggling crimson hair and large green eyes made her improbably waiflike.

Green? Gwen knew she was too far away to see the woman's eye color. Had they met? Gwen suppressed the urge to walk over and ask if she needed help, and look at her eyes.

"—Avram set up a booth and started doing tricks. I got propositioned by a burly blacksmith type. I took him up on it, and that used up half the afternoon." Mazie's voice had the kind of wink-wink-nudge-nudge in it that left absolutely nothing to the imagination.

Avram didn't react at all. Mazie must have trained him to be civilized and modern about her peccadilloes. Gwen wondered how and where his passive aggression emerged. Ollie wasn't passive at all. Extramarital tactophilia—flirting—was part of their lifestyle, but any man who crossed a specific line was courting murder. Suddenly, and quite unspectacularly, Gwen's dislike of Mazie crystallized.

"—time I came back, Jeffrey and Carole and Blag were missing. Off getting laid, maybe. Blag and Carole came back around sunset. Jeffrey didn't. We thought we'd better get back to camp—"

Where had Gwen seen the redhead woman before? It came to her with a jolt: the dossier on the next Fat Ripper. Sure, she was one of the players.

Even in a static holo, there had been something about her that stood out, some potential for action, some suppressed energy that impressed Gwen. Or at least caught her attention. The back of her neck itched. She needed Ollie. His memory was better than hers.

"—what I said, Gwen?"

With a start, Gwen realized that for the first time Mazie had said something which required a response.

There was challenge in the way Mazie leaned across the table. That, and two words Gwen's memory fished out of the monologue, gave her the answer. "You chewed garlic, just in case. Because the villagers didn't want your spices. Were you already thinking vampires?"

Mazie slapped the table, and Gwen captured her salad before it jiggled over the edge. "Exactly! And Carole thought she'd seen gargoyles. The vampires lived on the heights, in the minarets. Come night, they started swooping down on us. We broke into the buildings to fight there. The doors weren't even barred. The people must have given up long ago."

Avram said, "I got my troop into the smithy—"

"We started a fire," Mazie said. "We thought it might help. My blacksmith, Hath-Orthen, he broke down and told us all about it. The vampires owned that town. The tops of buildings were theirs, and stairs didn't go there. They'd been there longer than anyone could remember. They kept alcohol and recreational drugs out, and anything else that might ruin the flavor of blood." Mazie's attention snagged on the forkful of salad she was waving in the air. She put the fork in her not-quite-empty bowl and pushed it away. "I have to tell you, something permanent happened to my appetite that night. I had to think of myself as *food* to figure out how to fight vampires. Garlic didn't keep them away. We decided they like flavoring. *Random* flavoring, *that* they don't like. And we couldn't count on any help. The locals wanted us to stay so twenty of them would live longer."

"Your order, madam?" The voice came from behind Gwen, but she didn't have to turn, just reach back over her shoulders and found Ollie's strong, chubby arms and wrapped them around her neck. One of his fingers unobtrusively brushed a nipple, and she felt a shiver of pleasure race along her bones. She leaned back for a deep kiss.

Mazie was polite enough to stop talking, but not enough to look away. She was staring at them when they broke for air.

Ollie was about five nine, and fifty pounds over the average. That was actually a great improvement: when they met, you could have added another sixty pounds to that estimate.

Ollie nodded to Mazie and Avram. He slid into the seat next to Gwen, still holding her hand. Gwen felt the tension leaving her in a wave, lost in Ollie's warm, wide smile. She sighed. "My lord and master."

"The Goddess who dances in my heart." He bent forward and kissed her again. "How ya doing?"

"Much better now." Her eyes flickered sideways, indicating Mazie, who had continued to chatter, as if frantic to get her story out before Ollie swallowed Gwen's attention totally—

"There were vampire sentries on the ground floors, and no light. First building we went into, we were swarmed! After that we rolled barrels of brandy down into the basements. First the brandy, then throw in torches, then wood. That worked. We turned the minarets into chimneys! But it took us till nightfall, and some of the vampires escaped the fire and some of our own started coming to life—"

Gwen squeezed her husband's hand. She half-whispered, "Boy am I glad to see you. Listen. Do you see that woman over there?"

He scanned the room, found Gwen's target just as the frowzy redhead sleepwalked out of the room, brushing past people as if they weren't really there. "Strange duck, but a recognizable breed indeed. Gamer. She's in our files for Fimbulwinter." He squeezed his eyes shut for a second. "Name . . . Eviane." He was delighted with himself, and bounced with pleasure. "Probably just her *nom de guerre*."

Somehow, miraculously, Mazie had managed to finish her story. She grinned and leaned back from the table. "I want to sleep for a week. With Avram." She stood, her lips curling salaciously. Avram heaved himself up, as enthusiastic as a steer at the slaughterhouse door. "I won't see you till we're back in Portland, right?"

"Right. Our final briefing is in thirty minutes. The Fimbulwinter Game starts tomorrow. I'm the shaman's lovely daughter." Gwen caught a flicker of disbelief in Mazie's eye. "Eskimos are allowed to have a little padding, my dear."

Avram laughed appreciatively, and Mazie gave him a polite shove toward the door.

Gwen dug into her salad.

Ollie watched the pair until they were safety out of earshot. "Another rousing Dream Park success?"

"Maybe. Avram's too torpid, but maybe he got something out

of the experience. Maybe if they ran him through again—"

"Which they can't. These Gamers don't nearly pay their own way. It's all for research, love."

"I know. And Mazie's a waste. She learns what to say and that's all she gets out of it. Saying the magic words won't take weight off and it won't teach her better habits, and it's hell on those of us who have to listen."

"My my. What a wonderful wait you must have had."

Gwen's wide blue eyes were moist and grateful. "My hero. Verily, you saved the maiden from the dragon." Her fingernails gripped the back of his hand, hard. "Claim your reward, dammit."

He sighed. "We've got about twenty minutes to make it to Gaming Central. Not nearly enough time to commit a serious indiscretion."

"Nor yet a frivolous indiscretion." Never be late to a briefing. "Tonight?"

"Sure, who needs sleep?"

Chapter Three

THE TOWER OF NIGHT

Twenty meters of Tyrannosaurus rex thrashed helplessly in the tar pit. Its gray-green hide sprayed blood from a dozen bullet wounds. It glared up at them and screamed the scream of the dying saurian—a sound very like the product of a Cowles Mach VIII synthesizer, to Max Sands's educated ear. It blended perfectly with the thunder of the volcano erupting at the south end of the canyon.

It would have been the perfect end to a two-hour mini-Game: the dinosaur, the tar pit, the volcano, the lithe and lovely cave girl who clung to his side like moist silk. One problem remained unsolved. Professor Deveroux's legs still kicked weakly in the tyrannosaur's mouth. This was, of course, no fun for Deveroux ("Remember, I'm a hologram! Don't try these stunts at home!") and no fun for Max and the rest of the team either. Deveroux still had the Time Key in his pocket!

Max checked his watch. There were only ten minutes left! The lava crawled toward the tar pit beneath them, toward the mouth of the cave where five Adventurers huddled in confusion.

"Jeez," Orson Sands wheezed. "We're up the creek now." At six feet four inches and three hundred and fifteen pounds, his twin weighted twenty pounds more and looked fifty pounds heavier than Max. The difference was that under his cushion of fat Max actually had considerable muscle, which made him an anomaly in the Sands clan. Orson's twenty extra pounds weren't muscle. Muscle didn't run in the Sands family. Nobody ran in the Sands family, which in part explained the proud and readily identifiable Sands profile.

Max said, "Any suggestions, Eviane?"

The short, freckled redhead shook her head without saying anything. She never said anything. Maybe she'd checked her vocal cords at the door. She was kind of cute, particularly if you liked them chunky. But ... standing or sitting, she seemed to wrap herself around herself. The space around her became armor. Max had to force himself to speak to her, and why bother?

Orson repeated his litany of grief. "We been screwwwwed." His face was red and puffy, as if he was about to roll on the ground and hold his breath for two minutes. The tactic had been awesomely effective when he was a plump, cute five-year-old. He had grown plumper than plump and less than cute in the past thirty years. Max was tired of the act.

The lava had reached the edge of the water covering the tar pit, and a feather of steam boiled up. The stench of sulfur grew chokingly strong. Flakes of gray ash streamed from the sky.

Eviane watched the lava with what Max couldn't help thinking was a practiced eye. Quiet she was, but she'd Gamed. That key—

They'd found the skeleton of a Tyrannosaurus rex, and the bones of a man within. Eviane's stick had poked among the bones of the right hand, just enough to disturb them, to spring any trap; then the left, just enough to expose a glittering key. Tapped the key. Tapped the ground at her feet. Reached among the bones and plucked the key without brushing a single bone, and before any other player had planned a move.

Alura, the lovely cave girl who had guided them, pulled at Orson's arm. "Must go."

"Oh, what's the poooint?"

"Orson, will you shut up? The point is that we came to play."

Eviane nodded approval, and said her first words in two hours. "This isn't right. They promised."

"Darlin', this whole thing hasn't been right."

"We go," Alura said in her best mock-Paleolithic accent. "We go, worship. Pray for help."

Orson pulled a face. "You've already gotten everyone else killed, you tryin' for a perfect score?"

Max smiled benevolently. "You're going to be a ball on the Ripper."

"I wish I hadn't come."

"That makes many of us, Orson." Max checked his watch. Eight minutes.

There were four players left: Max and Orson and Eviane and Kevin. Kevin Titus was a kid, and the only skinny one in the group. He was *really* skinny, painfully so.

In the two hours that the Game had been on, three of their four guides had been killed by various toothy carnivores. With the exception of the late lamented Professor, their guides had all been young, vivacious pidgin-English-speaking cave dwellers encountered on site. Max had chuckled quietly at the anachronism and followed the bouncing curves.

"They cheated," Kevin said plaintively. The kid was five feet of knees and elbows, sugarcube teeth, frizzy brown hair, and nervous energy. He was panting with exertion, though even Max had his breath back. "They said that everything made sense."

Eviane breathed hard, as if hyperventilation helped her memory. "They said that 'given the stated Game situation, everything is accurate.'"

"So they lied."

The lava was getting close. The mouth of the cave was growing warmer. "No. They wouldn't lie." She repeated that as if it were an article of faith. "Dream Park wouldn't lie. There's an answer."

"We go and pray! Gods must help," Alura said almost calmly.

"Have they ever helped before?" Max asked hopefully.

"No." Her shaggy blond head gave a mournful wag. Then she smiled ingenuously. "But maybe we pray wrong!"

"If Dream Park didn't lie, then they're idiots," Orson whined. "There weren't any goddamn cave people in the Cretaceous. Dinosaurs were dead for sixty million years before the first human being ever appeared. They blew it!"

Lava swept down the valley. The tyrannosaur's tiny eyes bulged as the water around it began to boil. It screamed piteously when the lava hit it. The scream reverberated through Max's bones, and a whiff of cooking lizard hit them in a blast.

Then the swamp was gone and the tar was exposed to the lava, and it all went up in a fireball. The Gamers threw themselves flat. The air whooshed, crinkling his eyebrows with heat. Max glimpsed big white bones before the lava rolled them under.

Damn! This is too much, too damned graphic, even for Dream Park. Thank goodness I haven't eaten since breakfast!

Lava filled the valley below. It percolated like a demon's cauldron.

"We're screwed, I'm telling ya. I want everybody's money back."

Eviane was looking thoughtful, if her slightly crossed eyes could be interpreted as a thoughtful expression. "Something isn't right here," she said.

A flat certainty in her voice caught Max's attention, and

Orson's too. *She may look like a flake, but there's somebody home in that head.* Orson's mood calmed in an instant. "What've you got?"

She shook her head. "It's . . . it's a puzzle. They always are, when they run over fifty minutes. There's a clue."

"What's the clue?" Orson said. "I haven't got a clue. I'm hungry and I'm tired, and we've got six minutes to live."

"Think about it. What's wrong with this?"

"Everything— Waitwaitwait." *Click*: you could almost hear it. In some ways the brothers lived in different worlds. Max made his living as a very particular kind of clown, Orson as a computer programmer. But when the puzzle-solver in Orson's head suddenly clicked on, Max vicariously shared the thrill. There was the brother he loved, the fastest question-crunching mind he had ever known.

"You're right. There aren't supposed to be cave people here. We found just one group, all about the same age. Everything else was right. All of the sauropods have been right for the era: we saw diplodocus and brontosaurus, but no stegosaurus or allosaurus mixed in."

Kevin slapped thin hands against his head. "So what are the cave people doing here—"

Max caught the joke, and his laughter drowned out the rumble of the volcano. "Unless they're time travelers too!" He turned to Alura, who had been cowering politely through the entire exchange. "Alura, take us to church!"

"This way!"

Behind them the sky glowed. The lava was filling the valley of dinosaurs, and in another few moments it was going to come roaring down the tunnel. The result was likely to use up all of his hit points in one hot second . . . so to speak.

They ran, or at least moved as quickly as girth and wind would allow. Kevin, a skinny little rabbit with barely enough meat to separate bones from skin, reached the chamber alongside Alura, way ahead of the rest. He was gasping, she wasn't. Max clamped his mind down on the fatigue, but when he saw the chamber, exhaustion and confusion melted away like snowflakes.

The structure might have been carved from limestone by the passage of water, or it might have been an enormous gas bubble in a mountainous, sludgy wave of primeval lava. Whatever had carved it had done one hell of a job. It was huge, a crystalline cathedral with indirect lighting. (And where did the light come from? Oh, give it up. Phosphorescence, bioluminescence, whatever, it was gorgeous!)

Stalagmites rose from the floor like rows of fairy teeth. Thick spiderwebs festooned the corners, strange, baseball-sized husks dangling from them; but the room still sparkled.

In the center, surrounded by a cone of light, was what Max knew they would find.

Orson clapped his hands delightedly. "That's it!" A platform with a metal post and a waist-high metal ring large enough for several adults to grasp simultaneously. "It's an advanced version of Deveroux's time machine."

"Another group came back, with their kids—like taking a picnic."

"Stopped to feed the dinosaurs—"

"Kids got stranded here, grew up with no adults." They were laughing and hugging now. Even Eviane had abandoned her vow of silence, and was whooping louder than anyone.

"Let's move!" Max said, checking his watch. He'd set it to count down. It gave him ninety seconds to end the Game.

Kevin and Orson examined the machine. Orson called, "It takes a key! Ev—Eviane?"

The only key still in the Game. Eviane tossed it underhand to Orson, who fitted it into a lock and turned it.

"Fits. It was drownin' fair, after all."

"Move it. We're about to have company, say a million tons of lava."

Kevin and Orson tinkered with the vehicle, fiddling with the buttons until lights triggered around the metal ring, and the air vibrated until it sang. Max felt the tingle all over his skin, and laughed and stomped delightedly. They were going to make it, they were—

"All right. Everybody gather around, and get ready." The room was heating up. The hair on his arms stood up away from the skin as the time machine's whir grew loud.

All five of them grabbed the ring, felt the electric trill as the power increased. The entire room began to vibrate. Alura released the ring with one hand to grab Max's shirt, pressing her warm little body against him. Max was terribly glad that Alura, unlike the rest of her family, was a real live unhologram-type person.

The entrance of the cave splashed with lava. For a moment fear filled his stomach, and a shrill whir filled his ears—

The room whirled, and there was nothing there, nothing at all. When the smoke and lava cleared, they were back in the clean, sterile Time/Life building.

The woman who called herself Eviane wandered out of the Time/Life building into the main thoroughfare. It had been a long time since she had been to Dream Park, although in another sense, Dream Park was with her wherever she went.

The facades of the rides and exhibits rose like a fabulous array of circus balloons. The hologram images rose thirty and forty feet into the air—Polynesian Paradise, DragonWorld, Fokker Biplane (duel the Red Baron!), the Ali Baba ride, the infamous Snuff Show (kill any of two thousand famous historical or contemporary figures!), and the hallucinogenic Little Nemo.

Some of the facades were pure delightful fantasy: the rosy cheeks of Snow White blended naturally with the Alpine splendor of the Ski Chalet. But there were also strong elements of the grotesque. Here was the face of a screaming South American Indian, with ants swarming . . .

Before her eyes, naked bone appeared.

The Marabunta Challenge. The threat of violence made Eviane's head spin. She stopped for a moment, leaned against a railing, and squeezed her eyes shut.

No violence. No pain. Just fun. Right? Nobody gets hurt . . .

It was self-defense. Plot smashed, the Cabal had been rabid for vengeance. The Terichik . . .

She opened her eyes, and when the film of tears cleared, she remembered to breathe again. The pain in her chest went away. Maybe she shouldn't be here at all.

She shrugged that thought aside. She had already met somebody nice, not even counting Charlene Dula. Charlene had been a miracle, a genuine seven-foot elvish miracle. But Max Sands was nice. Bright, cheerful. Curiously athletic for his size. And he seemed to like her. Maybe she should have gone with them . . .

The voice snapped back on her instantly. *How could anyone like you? You're a murderess. A crazy woman, and if they find you, they'll put you where the birds don't sing and the sun don't shine, and sleep comes in black capsules with little white bands.*

She swallowed hard, and forced her shoulders back and the voices into retreat. They grew quieter, but didn't go away. They never went away.

A little boy swiveled, and pointed. "Mommy! Wow! Look at

that costume the lady's wearing! She must be ten feet tall!"

Eviane turned and made herself smile. "Charlene!"

The hypertall woman picked her way through the crowd. It was true: she was grotesquely tall; she might have been another exhibit. Jewelry at her ears and throat had a high-tech look: medical monitors. But she carried herself with a grace and dignity that inspired respect rather than pity or shock.

Eviane ran to her friend, and hugged her. Charlene returned the hug for a second, then gently pushed the shorter woman back. For an instant, Eviane was overwhelmed by the variance in body type. With Charlene balancing on Eviane's shoulders, they could go to a masquerade ball as an exclamation point.

"How were the rides?" Charlene's voice was that of a cultivated child. "I wish that I could have been with you. Uncle wanted me with him at that Barsoom thing." She smiled in shy apology. "This was supposed to be our time together. I've made friends over the holo for years, but it's just not the same."

"Oh, don't worry. If it weren't for you I wouldn't be here in the first place. This is just the best time ever."

Charlene hugged her friend's arm. "I know I would have had more fun with you."

"The fun is in getting out alive."

They stepped aside to let a comical car cruise past. It loped along on jointed hairy legs instead of wheels. The "driver" had headlights instead of eyes, and fenders for ears. Charlene chuckled. "It's usually more crowded than this, isn't it?"

"Hard to believe, but true."

This wasn't ordinary Dream Park time. The Park was only half-full. This was a VIP week, reserved for people like Charlene, bigwigs and their families involved in the Barsoom Project, and people participating in the Fat Ripper Special . . .

She closed her eyes. The next thing she knew, Charlene was holding her.

"Eviane? It looked like you blacked out for a moment there. You didn't know where you were."

"It was the crowd. The noise."

Charlene looked unconvinced. "Right."

"Maybe I'm just hungry."

"Now, that I'll believe. Come on. Isn't it time for our briefing?"

"You bet."

• • •

Red-shirted acrobats juggled balls of fire bare-handed, with dazzling agility. The flame formed a stairway up into the sky, disappearing in a bank of mist. As exotic flute music played, one acrobat after another did hand-springs up the stairway and vanished.

The walls of Dream Park twisted and turned around them like the walls of a maze, every foot crammed with shops, exhibits, and concession stands, the entrances to rides and "experiences." To the north, like a great moon rising at the end of the street, was the gleaming dome of Gaming Area B.

They reached the restaurant, an ivory tower labeled "The Tower of Night," which rose from the middle of an Arabian bazaar. Eviane felt a little more at ease. Here, finally, would be people that she would be comfortable with. Gamers, Magic Users. Sorcerers. Keepers of the Dark Secrets, the same breed that she was . . .

. . . had been?

She got into the tube lift on the side of the tower, and pressed her hands against the tube as it began to rise.

And rise.

The cage moved at impossible speed. The sun was sinking behind the mountains when only minutes ago it had been midafternoon. Now they were above the entire arc of Dream Park, the hundreds of acres laid out in glittering array: conical towers and silvered spheres, twisting roller-coaster loops and the thousand hotels and motels crowding hivelike beyond, all shrinking, shrinking. Now she could see the entire valley basin, and as the elevator continued to rise, the lights of Los Angeles stretched out like strings of glowing pearls.

Neat! The illusion was magnificent. The cage was still accelerating. Around a black Earth, refracted light outlined the atmosphere in a bright circle that was still contracting. Eviane felt the chill of fear, just enough acrophobia to make things interesting.

Charlene's breath fogged the glass. "Wow." No acrophobia there!

Sunlight flared along one rim of the world, which had become a tremendous ball. Eviane wrenched her eyes away to look up. A structure was coming at her, a cluster of bubbles on the tower. The bubbles engulfed the car. The elevator stopped, and the doors opened.

Noise hit her like a solid wall, the cacophony of a hundred throats rumbling at the top of their collective voices. A flood of images rushed in on her, colliding somewhere between her ears.

Eviane wandered away from Charlene, meandering through the group. She felt both at home and alienated, able to float along on the periphery of the groups, skimming bits of conversations without the nerve to join in.

"I've never been here before," one Gamer was saying. He was about five and a half feet tall, black and pudgy. He juggled a drink in one hand and a four-inch saucer of little sandwiches in the other. He wore a quasi-military uniform that was too tight across the belly. His name tag said *F. Hebert*. "But from what I've seen so far, the whole thing is overpriced. Too expensive."

A stout, extremely pretty blonde whose name tag was stenciled *Trianna* attacked at once. She may have been overweight, but her self-possession and beautifully cut blue suit made her mass a deadly weapon. There was something else, too—a sense of leashed sexuality that Eviane found instantly intimidating. "If you've never been here before, what are you comparing it to?"

Trianna's target was overwhelmed. "Ah—other amusement parks, I guess."

"Do other parks really have facilities like this?"

"Well . . ."

She snorted in disgust. "The word I get, it costs more than you're paying. They charge it off to research and use it to make cassette games."

"Oh, that's—"

"But let's just assume they're taking a thousand percent profit. Then what? Nobody else has what they're selling. What have you got to whimper about? Pay or don't pay."

"Ah . . ." F. Hebert wandered away looking deflated.

There was a face all skin and bones, one gaunt visage across a sky of full moons. Kevin. She remembered him from the Tar Pits Game.

Fat Ripper, they call it; but we're not all overweight. Eating disorders. Substance abuse— That one black man was round of face but hardly overweight. Still, he had a twitchy look. She was guessing, only guessing, but who would he kill for a drink? or a cigar?

Eviane heard a ripple of laughter over in one of the corners of the room, and pivoted in time to catch a spherical dervish completing a complex pantomime. She knew that man. Who wouldn't? It was Johnny Welsh, one of the featured players on *Kodak Playhouse*. He was acclaimed as a brilliant comedian, but she remembered hearing that he had lost a lucrative television contract because the insurance company wouldn't issue a bond. Too much excess weight . . .

He was laughing now, and red-faced. She had seen him this way a hundred times. The rubbery red face and hiccoughing bray were as much a trademark as the famous profile. He was surrounded by a circle of admiring faces. "And if they wanted me to lose weight, then they should have stopped serving pasta in the commissary. Hey! If I look at one, it just cries out to me." He crouched down and squinted up at them, rubber face suddenly, absurdly reminiscent of a lonesome lasagna. "It says: 'Johnny! We're here! Don'cha love us anymore?'" Lasagna had an Italian accent.

Music blared in the opposite corner, and several couples were on the dance floor, moving languorously to the latest fusion of Indonesian and Latin music.

Eviane stood on the outskirts and tapped her toes to it, and felt a flutter of pleasure. Such a nice group of people. This is going to be fun! . . .

Unless something goes wrong.

Her breathing was going haywire, and she craved magic, magic in the form of a black pill rimmed in white. *There's no point to this. Let the past stay dead. What is there to gain?*

But I have to know. I have to know.

There were security cameras in every corner of the room. Information on eating habits, conversational patterns, and preferential interactions were being recorded on all Game participants. The data was carefully filed, collated, and processed in a hundred different ways. Computer programs weighed words and patterns of words. One special technician per participant annotated and corrected, planned and theorized as Game time drew near.

The information went out to nutritionists, psychotherapists, experts in aversive-conditioning behavioral modification, neuro-linguistic programmers, and the computer experts coordinating the effort.

And it went to one other desk.

At that desk a man watched, brooding. He frowned every time the camera crossed the features of the woman who called herself "Eviane." Her stringy red hair had once been well groomed. The padded body had been svelte, the confused, frightened eyes filled with purpose.

Dream Park accepted Gaming names, but demanded a real one as well: this woman had written "Michelle Rivers" in her file.

Lies within lies.

He held in his hand the picture of a younger, more slender, prettier woman, a picture summoned from a file eight years old. The label read "Michelle Sturgeon." There were differences, but the similarities were undeniable.

Beneath the picture of Michelle Sturgeon was a short psychological evaluation concocted by the Dream Park psych division. He traced it with a finger that shook.

Eight years before, Michelle Sturgeon had murdered one Dream Park Actor and severely wounded another. Her alter ego, the persona of "Eviane," however, was an Adventuress who had defended herself against evil magicians. It seemed that "Eviane" had become the dominant identity.

How had she gotten past Dream Park Security? The "Rivers" name shouldn't have fooled anyone.

"Came in with Charlene Dula. Okay, they wouldn't want Charlene irritated, they need her uncle's money in Barsoom. So no heavy security check?" He couldn't convince himself. "No, dammit. You couldn't stop The Griffin with politics. So what happened? Fekesh could have changed her records." The man's voice trembled. "But if he did, why? Because if Harmony and The Griffin saw the flag . . . hmm. He was afraid they'd use her. Somehow. So why the hell didn't Fekesh tell me? Damn, damn, damn." He opened a bottle of headache tablets and swallowed two of them without water. "Why now? I'll never get any sleep. What kind of game . . ."

He caught himself, forced the panic into remission. The office was empty, dark except for the light of the holoscreen. "Calm down," he muttered. "I can handle it. So she's back. It's not a trap. It's an accident. She doesn't know anything. I can get her out."

He scrolled Eviane's chart. He read slowly; he wasn't used to reading charts. "He's got to help. Fekesh. He's got as much to lose—" Finally he let out a sigh. "All right. It started in the Fimbulwinter Game. It can end there too. Kill her out."

He punched another button, and the screen went dead.

Chapter Four

THE PSYCHOLOGY OF ENGAGEMENT

An aroma of fresh-ground coffee wafted in the air. Alex averted his eyes from the urn as he stormed into his office.

The west wall blinked through the spectrum in its "alert" mode. The hubbub beyond quieted as the door closed. He circled his desk. When his weight hit the chair, the screen triggered.

Cary McGivvon, Griffin's new assistant, appeared on line. Her egg-shaped face was drawn with panic. "Chief—we've got a problem—"

"We've always got problems. If it isn't an emergency, it's a 'B.' Handle it yourself."

"It's an emergency."

"Isn't it always. Take a deep breath and talk to me."

Cary stopped and sucked air, flicking her head to get a few strands of brown hair out of her eyes. "Well, we had a punch-out. Delegates from Pan-African and the Libyan group. Everybody says the other guys started it. Chief, they're talking about walking."

"What is Psych doing?" McGivvon was a terrific worker, but a little on the emotional side. Why dump this on him? He had no control, or anything even close to it, over the actions of those zanies.

"Vail has already channeled them into the War-Bots scenario."

"Terrific. This is what he designed it for. I'll bet his black heart is tickled pink for the chance to run it." Alex's nose twitched at the pungent coffee aroma from the outer office. He would not walk out there and get a cup, nor would he ask someone to fetch one. Time to put a fan in here!

"What's the situation? Have they agreed?"

"More or less. Chala and Razul should be fighting it out now, but everyone else is twitchy too." He saw her beginning to relax now that she'd passed the problem on. He turned her off.

He still hadn't settled back into real space/time yet. The sounds and sights of the shaping of Mars played against the back of his eyeballs. If he closed his eyes even for a moment, blackness exploded into light.

Cary appeared in the doorway. He missed her mischievous expression, transfixed by the steaming mug in her hands. Was she going to drink that in front of him? Could she be so cruel?

"Looked as if you needed this more than me, Chief."

He stifled a whimper of relief. "You are an angel of mercy. Ten dispensation points. Shoot your husband tonight and move in with me. You'll still go to the front of the line on Judgment Day."

"Thanks—I'll save it. I may need it the next time my boss disappears for three hours and turns off his pager."

Touché. He sipped from the mug, then made a face. "Half-full?"

"Remember your ulcer."

He growled at her, and then drained the cup. Damn, that hit the spot. It was the taste he loved. Honest. The fact that decaffeinated coffee never tasted as good just meant that he loved the taste of caffeine. "Give me a minute to digest this. There wasn't any actual violence, was there?"

"You may want to look at the tapes yourself."

"Code them through, would you? And any updates on the Dula business."

Arrgh! There was just too much to do. The panoramic window behind his desk looked out onto the Little San Gabriel Mountains, but the touch of a switch could display any part of Dream Park that he chose. His fingers played on the keyboard, and the window divided into sections.

From an overhead camera in one of the cafeterias he watched a replay of a pushing-and-shouting match. Six of one group and ten of another, all Africans ... he recognized Razul, the Libyan Ambassador, so the other, bigger group must be Pan-Africa. They screamed in each other's faces, mixing languages, pausing to find a word but never finding the chance to use it. The language barrier was driving them berserk. Their interpreters kept trying to interrupt. Now security men and women moved among them, drawing the screamers aside ...

The incident had been neatly averted. Whoever was working security had done well, but could he have caught it quicker?

"Zoom." The screen zoomed up, and he had a clear view of Mitch Hasagawa. Good man on the floor, almost psychically sharp. Reminded Griffin a lot of Marty Bobbick, before Marty put in for desk operations. A good man in the field, a decent man in the office. Alex hoped that Mitch would stay in the field.

He zoomed the second window. It cleared and fogged again. Close-up of the Arab, Razul. Griffin remembered Razul; he had briefed his officers on the man. Razul was Kareem Fekesh's man. Despite Fekesh's staggering financial empire, the industrialist was widely rumored to be a primary supporter of Holy Fire, the radical political sect which had grown out of the United Moslem Activist Front in the teens. Nothing had ever been proven, but...

Holy Fire had openly threatened the life of Charlene Dula. Fekesh should never have been permitted within ten kilometers of the Park, but his influence had delivered most of the radical Arab sects, totaling billions of dollars of prospective investment capital. Money talks, and loudly enough to drown out the voice of a security chief.

"Don't disturb me for five minutes, Cary. I need to breathe."

"Got it, boss."

Griffin looked out over the valley. He stood, twisted his back until his spine crackled. The sun sat low on the horizon, and the mountain shadows stretched slowly toward Dream Park. There was too damn much to do, and it was all too damned important, not just for Cowles Industries, but for the human race. Africa might be a lesson for them all. Perhaps the lines of nationalism and factionalism and every other goddamn "ism" in the world had reduced the chances for this weary planet. Or not. Nuclear devices had existed for over a century, and only four of them had ever been used in anger. This could be interpreted as proof of divine intervention, good luck, a sign that the human race was growing up, or ominous portent, depending upon one's standing in the "half-empty, half-full" school of cocktail-party philosophy.

For most of recorded history, military technology had been the cutting edge of human knowledge. Only the leap to space called forth more of man's natural and intellectual resources. Project Barsoom was the most expansive dream in human history, big enough to create a world vision, to involve every world government. It would create millions of jobs and circulate hundreds of billions of dollars. It could be a rallying point, a place to start over.

The door behind him swung open ahead of Marty, who

bounced in talking around a mouthful of ham and cheese. "Quite a madhouse, Chief."

Can't get five goddamn minutes— Alex squashed the flash of irritation. "Getting madder by the minute. What now?"

"We've got the IFGS feed on line three. We need to take this one together."

"Why me, Lord?"

The question surprised him. "You've actually been through one of the Games. Chief, I need the input." Without waiting for Alex's approval, Marty leaned over his desk and tapped the vidfeed through.

The screen cleared; the pinched, aquiline features of Arlan Myers appeared. The man always looked like he had a wedge of lemon tucked in one bearded cheek. "Mr. Griffin," Myers said, with just the slightest hint of what Alex assumed was resentment. Where was Myers? New York? And what time was it there . . . ?

Oops.

"Sorry for the hour, Arlan," Griffin said solicitously. His imagination wandered, and he found himself wondering what Myers was wearing under the edge of the screen. Maybe the International Fantasy Gaming Society had summoned him out of bed. Better still, maybe Myers was the resident IFGS satyr, and something warm and pliant was waiting for him just off screen. Alex allowed a moment's fantasy about the official IFGS Kama Sutra. "We're going to be running that modified Fimbulwinter Game in a few hours. Have you had a chance to scan the Game tapes?"

"Of course." Arlan sniffed. "A basic modification of the Fimbulwinter scenario." For the first time a touch of joy appeared on his face. "Rather clever, actually. I worked on that one a few years back, when the Lopezes designed the control sequences." He shook his head reproachfully. "It's really too difficult for novice Gamers. I have to admit that I don't completely understand the method behind this particular madness."

The lower left screen cleared, and Dr. Vail appeared. He was sixty-four and looked thirty-eight, with that lean and leathery Californian healthier-than-thou look about him. His blue eyes always seemed feverishly bright and intense. "It looks like I timed this right. Mr. Myers, pleased to 'meet' you, finally. Your work on the Psychology of Engagement has been instrumental in developing our behavioral programs."

"Dr. Vail." Arlan inclined his head slightly. "What does my

little treatise on Gaming theory have to do with weight loss?"

Vail smiled. "You expanded Gaming theory beyond the mathematics of penetration, envelopment, and confrontation to the patterns of attention which influence an encounter. 'Rhythms of concentration,' you called them."

Alex leaned back in his seat, fingers laced, fascinated and totally out of his depth.

Arlan seemed pleased. "Yes, of course. Human existence is cyclical: circadian rhythms, Kreb cycles, the circular movements that the human eye makes even when trying to hold steady on a single point, these things are well documented. Mental focus exhibits similar cycles. Regardless of the level of intelligence or concentration, there are 'down' points in the cycles, perceptual blind spots, 'floating holes' where information simply slips through unnoticed. The more fatigued or single-minded we become, the larger the holes get."

"Yes. And you timed the engagements in the original Fimbulwinter Game to 'hide' some of the clues in plain sight, as it were. You took advantage of temporary blackouts due to fatigue or attention engagement. This idea forms the foundation of the Fat Ripper Specials. We hit the Gamers on every level except conscious/analytical. They think that the point of the Game is the exercise. The exercise isn't the medicine, it's the spoon."

"Nothing up my sleeve . . ." Arlan chuckled. "If my little postulations have been useful on a more practical level, I'm glad. Tell me: you've run several of the Rippers; why is this one a special problem?"

Now Alex spoke up. "Due to a security risk, it has become advisable for me to enter one of our people into the Game. This run consists of thirteen Gamers and up to forty-three Actors playing multiple roles. Most of the Gamers were on the waiting lists long before Dula was announced for the Game, so no problems there. Actors are all Dream Park personnel, and have been checked. The Park is closed to ordinary tourists, so we've minimized risks across the board."

"So what exactly is your problem?"

"I wouldn't want Mr. Bobbick killed out. I can't bend the rules to help him."

Arlan nodded approval. "Even in the best of causes, cheating is still cheating."

Marty shifted uncomfortably in his seat. "I've seen plenty of

Games. Watched 'em from the outside, I mean. It doesn't look so hard . . ."

Arlan Myers laughed heartily. "Oh, I can hardly wait to see your tapes. Appearances can be deceiving, Mr. Bobbick."

Griffin warmed, remembering his own Game. "I was wondering whether it might be permissible for Marty to take a look at the actual Game plans."

Myers reddened. "No, no, no! If he knows the answers, he will give them away."

"But if they aren't playing for points . . . ?"

"No! The other players will notice who is lucky, or who is successful, and rally around him."

Dr. Vail's blue eyes narrowed. "It throws the whole structure of the Game off. The Actors are highly trained to conceal their knowledge. You'd be surprised how much eye and body movement gives information away. In the last century a performer named Kreskin ran a mind-reading act you wouldn't believe, basically by observing body language."

"I agree with Vail. You could destroy the balance of the whole Game." Myers turned and looked at Marty. "What do you have, three hours until the Game begins?"

"Seven hours. Time difference."

Myers's lip curled. "Oh, yes. Well, that gives you enough time to read *I Made the Pits Too Big: Confessions of a Retired Deity.*"

"The Lopez biography?"

"Yes. That will give you an overview. I can give you a rundown of the Gaming rules.

"One. The duration of the Game will be three days, that is to say seventy-two hours."

"Two," he ticked off on his fingers. "The number of participants, thirteen.

"Three, the Wessler-Grahm auditing company has produced a variant on the standard Gaming tables for use in the Rippers. Even though they have no credit with the IFGS, they provide a means for Ripper participants to reference their efforts. This is new. In earlier Rippers there wasn't enough feedback."

"Competition is often valuable," Vail said. "Feedback always is."

"Four," Myers continued, "there will be a penalty of fifty percent of accumulated points in the event of a player's death, twenty-five percent of which will be rebated if the player returns to the Game as a *tornrait*, a helpful undead.

"Five, the Game will be conducted for sixteen hours out of every twenty-four—"

Dr. Vail interrupted. "Except that the programming will continue for twenty-four hours a day."

"Ah . . . yes. Six. Due to the nature of the Game, food and rest breaks will be subject to randomization and interruption.

"Seven. The usual quarter-moon symbol will indicate the presence of rest room facilities. That's all."

Dr. Vail smiled at Myers like a cat inspecting a bowl of cream. Griffin had the distinct impression that he was calculating Myers's body fat content from the thickness of the bearded cheeks. "Thank you, Mr. Myers. I think you will find that the adjustments we've made in the Game actually make it more interesting. I can't imagine any of our refinements—"

"Modifications," Myers corrected politely.

"Ah, yes. Refinements would interfere with security work. Mr. Bobbick, you may find that you are more tired than usual by the end of the last day, due to the fact that your brains are receiving constant input. We balance that with the distribution of food—"

"Excuse me?"

"Nothing but fruit or raw vegetables after nine in the evening. In that way your digestive system gets to rest while you sleep. Second, all of the participants will be wearing heart and blood pressure transmitters wired into the mesh of their underwear. These will be in constant operation.

"Well—I think that'll do it for the time being. You'll find everything else you need to know as the Game proceeds."

The two screens winked out. Griffin sipped the dregs of his coffee. "What do you think?"

Marty's face broke into a huge smile. "You know, for years I've been telling myself that I was going to do a Game. You seemed to have so much *fun* in the South Seas Treasure Game! But I just never did it. Now I've got the chance. I love it. I'll make you a little side bet—I outpoint everyone there."

"I've got a different bet for you. Lose twenty pounds within eight weeks, and we'll see about that raise."

"Aw, Chief, c'mon. I can still pin you two out of three—"

"That's the deal. What do you say?"

Marty waited a minute, then extended a heavy hand. "You're on."

Griffin pumped it solemnly. "Now, then. Is War-Bots set up yet?"

Marty rubbed his hands together. "Let's see."

Griffin punched a series of buttons, and the window cleared and—

Razul sat in a tiny cabin that pitched and yawed as he manipulated his controls. Each thundering footstep of the War-Bot reverberated to the core of his spine.

The enemy War-Bot came at him again, scarlet trimmed in black, two hundred feet tall. A thousand tons of mechanized thunder, with Andrew Chala invisible in the torso. It swung a gigantic fist that impacted like the direct strike of an avalanche.

Razul went down, and when he did, a row of buildings was crushed beneath him. Razul must keep the War-Bot rolling, must bring it back to its feet; but he was rolling across a park and into a block of apartment buildings, while families screamed and fled. Tiny nannies pushed prams at sprinter's speed, or abandoned them to die beneath the metal behemoth. He'd smashed the base of a building. It disintegrated. Concrete and screaming people showered his shoulders as he came to his feet.

"Have you never wished to fight a war all by yourself? Yourself the only general and the only warrior. No ally to betray you. No subordinate to ruin your plans through mistake or misunderstanding. War reduced to its basics!" Dream Park's fool of a psychiatrist thought he knew Razul's mind.

He was wrong. Razul had accepted the War-Bots challenge in spite of Vail.

He glimpsed his enemy through the wreckage. Razul and Chala had agreed to fight without missiles; but one could improvise. Razul clutched a mass of the concrete beehive and hurled it. It smashed through a shell of wall that was still standing; the scarlet behemoth behind it staggered, then came on.

By the sacred mountains of Allah! Dream Park's servants had violent, bloody dreams. He was a war all to himself, facing one monolith of an enemy now wading toward him through waist-high structures: a bank, some ancient business buildings that had become apartments. It was good, it was simpler than life, it was a heady experience. If only he couldn't hear the screams, he could enjoy the battle, concentrate on smashing Andrew Chala. They were little white English, antlike, insignificant; not his people at all.

Yet his battle with the black man, no matter what he did, no matter what crushing blow he dealt, continued to hurt the little people. He couldn't help but feel the shame and guilt associated, even as the exhaustion of moving the controls began to wear down his endurance. But the War-Bot was back on its tremendous feet, and Razul waded back into the park.

Sweat drooled down his face, and the sounds of screaming and wailing rang in his ears. Razul readied himself for the assault. His enemy's great black and red machine stalked toward him, nearly running now. If Chala maintained that speed he might be able to dodge—

Its right foot suddenly sank to the knee!

Razul screamed defiance and threw his machine forward behind its massive fist. Chala's behemoth was off balance. Its arms came around too slowly . . . everything seemed slow, the robots were so large . . . but Razul's fist plowed into the other robot just below the throat. The world rang like a million broken bells. Now duck, while the other's arms came around—

Where Chala's robot's foot had penetrated the turf, white light flared from underneath. Turf exploded upward. Razul blinked, dazzled, and fought the controls to avoid falling over backward. He could guess what had happened. Chala had stepped into the Chunnel, the vacuum subway that ran between Britain and France. A train must have impacted at meteor speed. Thousands dead in fractions of a second.

And his enemy's leg was off at the knee! Razul threw three missile-velocity punches. His enemy fell back and landed hard, and Razul had won.

He was crying like a baby as he struggled out of the cabin. War reduced to its basics. Smash things. Hope your enemy is smashed too. No honor in this, only fatigue and death and blood ruining the pretty parks. War reduced to its basics, oh, you sons of dogs.

He saw Andrew Chala climbing out of what was, after all, only the midsection of a giant red and black robot. Chala was sobbing helplessly.

We must keep war off Mars, Razul told himself. *We will. I'll have to talk to Chala . . . later.*

Chapter Five

CATCH IT AND YOU KEEP IT

"Move it!"

Max Sands ran as fast as he could, thundering along on thick, muscular legs.

What was...? Who was...? A moment ago he and the rest of the group had been ambling toward the embarking area. Then an alarm whistle split the calm of the corridor, and they broke into a stumbling, confused gallop. His heart hammered in adrenal overload. What had gone wrong? He'd heard rumors that mad Arabs were after Moon Maid. Had they...?

Max and exercise were ancient antagonists. He went into a kind of fugue state, where his body seemed to perform without his conscious intervention, a sort of automatic overdrive he had learned while apprenticing in his curious profession.

Just behind him, Eviane was puffing like a choo-choo, bouncing and jiggling, but keeping up. More: her face was grin-split with happy anticipation. Her elongated friend Moon Maid Dula moved as if walking on stilts, a continuous toppling run, unsteady but still making tracks.

The tunnel boomed and shuddered. Far off, he heard the rattle of gunshots.

The tunnel dead-ended at a curved metal door sealed with a thick rubber flange. Rows of fluorescent lights flickered around the edges. A cluster of Gamers were there ahead of him.

The guy who called himself "Hippogryph" was pushing against the wall, stretching his calves. Sweat streamed down his cheeks. His chest heaved. Hippogryph's breathing was a conscious thing: inhale through the nose only, slowly exhale... The guy acted like an outsider's image of a typical Gamer: big sappy permanent grin, constant quotes from Asimov and Chang, sly "in" references to Luke Skywalker and Frodo. Max read him as a Dream Park security watchdog for Charlene Dula.

Brother Orson stumbled, trying to keep up. A very large, conspicuously pretty blonde named Trianna Stith-Wood helped him right himself. There was strength in that woman's arms. She had a baby face, little pearly teeth, a smile you could use for a heliograph. He had heard she was a chef. Likely she was her own best customer.

Two more ran up. Francis Hebert was a short, dark-skinned, crop-haired career soldier, pudgy only by military standards. He ran easily; the bagel in his fist explained his late start. The second man was Frankish Oliver, a Gamer and a pure warrior, even though at this point everyone was still in street clothes.

A blast of cold air hit Max in the face, as if the air-conditioning units had suddenly gone berserk.

The door burst open, banging against the tunnel wall. A woman stood there, looking gaunt and frightened in a neatly pressed red uniform. The cords in her throat bunched as she screamed, "Hurry!" It was the voice that had shrieked panic from the intercom. "The Guard can't hold the cannibals back much longer!"

Cannibals? Max looked behind him. Two uniformed National Guardsmen, one black and slender, the other white and burly, were the ones firing the shots. The burly man fell, his hand clapped to a spreading red glow on his leg. His face distorted with pain as he tried to crawl toward the silver door.

Trianna, Orson, and Frankish Oliver squeezed through.

Charlene Dula started back. Max grabbed Charlene's arm urgently. "Wrong way!"

"But that man! He's hurt!"

Max pulled her toward the door. Hippogryph had her other arm and was following Max's lead . . . and staring hard at Max. Certainly he was Security; and Max had touched Charlene.

Charlene looked back over her shoulder; the concern on her face suddenly changed to horror.

From around the corner surged a horde of people in tattered clothing, bundled in rags. They grabbed the wounded Guardsman and dragged him away. His screaming grew acute, then stopped.

The second soldier bellowed at them. "Get that boat off the ground!"

The cannibals were bearing down on him when the soldier took a silver cylinder from his belt, pulled the pin and—

Finally Charlene seemed to understand. She eeled through the doorway. It was the curved thick doorway of an airplane, wedged half-open. Max feared he would tear skin pushing through after her. Hippogryph had similar trouble following him.

The soldier tucked and rolled as the corridor erupted into flame. The plastic structure ruptured from floor to ceiling, and what poured through was—

Snow?

A blizzard of powder and white flakes gushed through the cracks. Frigid air slapped his face like a giant frozen hand, sent him reeling back from the door.

The soldier scrambled into the plane, snow and sweat streaking his dark face. He turned and pulled the door shut. The floor lurched under his feet.

Max caught one last glimpse through the window. The entire tunnel was collapsing. Screaming, the raggedy man-eaters tumbled through the ruptured floor and disappeared.

"Strap yourselves in. We're taking off now!"

Max looked around, heaving for breath. He could hear a good deal of panting around him. Francis Hebert had had to pull Johnny Welsh inside. The comedian was red-faced and heaving, but recovering fast. Good lungs: a stand-up comic would need that.

Seats were four across, the fuselage constricted halfway back, where overhead wings showed through big curved windows. Max wasn't familiar with aircraft, but this plane seemed old: one of the smaller supersonic jets. Seats at the back had been ripped out and cargo was stacked nearly to the ceiling. The seats were already crowded. Nobody knew what was going on any more than he did, but they were moving. He settled into a seat next to Frankish Oliver, across the aisle from Charlene and Eviane.

Charlene's height forced her to sit knees to chest, and Eviane was helping her settle in. Charlene's voice was a frantic squeal. "Eviane, what's happening?"

Eviane smiled uneasily. "Seems to be the end of the world."

Charlene gripped her seat, silent, lips pressed thin.

Max admired the way Eviane helped her friend. In the midst of a whirlwind of panic and murder, she seemed to be maintaining control. Something had changed in the silent, withdrawn Eviane of the Time Travel Game.

There was a rumbling purr as the plane backed away from what Max could now see was a ruined airline terminal. The roof buckled under a crushing mantle of snow.

"We're very fortunate that the storm is dying," the stewardess said. She looked exhausted. "We're the last plane out of San Francisco Airport. I don't know what happened to the rest of them. I can only hope..."

Her voice trailed off, and she rubbed her eyes. They were red-rimmed and dark-circled, as if she hadn't slept in days.

As she buckled herself against the wall the plane lurched, bounded across the icy ground. The windows smeared with snow flurries. The plane tilted and went up at a steep angle. Snow-locked buildings and cars swiftly became toylike.

Max craned over Frankish Oliver to peer out of the window at the city below.

The plane rose, turning right. The long overhead wing swung back. Max saw the ruin that had once been the showpiece of the west coast. The rebuilt Bay Bridge lay broken and buckled, and snow partially covered a string of cars that stretched from Marin to Oakland. Ships were frozen in the bay, and the entire city lay under a blue-white mantle of ice. The light was dim; the sky beyond the folded-back wing was slate-gray.

Study Eskimos, Dream Park's instruction packet had read. He was beginning to understand why.

The passengers had grown quiet. A hush followed the *wump* as they eased through the sound barrier.

The stewardess switched her throat mike on. Her voice was a near parody of the countless airplane safety recitations Max had heard over the years. "The weather has continued to worsen," she said. "We can't go south. The airports in Los Angeles and San Diego are swamped. Texas and New Mexico are sealed; they're shooting unauthorized planes out of the sky. The Southwest just isn't prepared for this kind of weather. New York has done better. Its people and social structures have survived, while California is disintegrating. Since Canada commandeered the oil pipeline, that's no place for Americans. Alaska is our best bet."

The plane slid through gray clouds, and out.

Eviane hissed. Charlene frowned. "What's wrong?"

"The sun!"

Only fools look straight at the sun. Charlene caught it in her peripheral vision, glaring above an unbroken white cloud deck. "It looks fine."

Eviane stared at her, then looked out the window. "It looks that way from Ceres?"

"I...*Oh!* If it's right for Ceres, then...too small for Earth. Not enough light. What could cause that?"

Max cursed under his breath. Moon Maid was dead-on. Why hadn't he seen it? He tried to shake the cobwebs away. For the first time since the jumbled introductions at the Tower of Night, he had a chance to really look at the people around him.

One man stood and introduced himself, "My name is Robin Bowles. I owe you all, and I guess you don't know why."

The group went silent. Eviane canted forward. She whispered fiercely, "Robin Bowles, the actor? *He's* our guide?"

Max only vaguely recognized the name, but he knew the face from late-night movies, vidcassettes, talk shows, and tabloids. None of that mattered now. One of the first things that Gamers learned was that somebody along on the trip would have been briefed on the Game, the rules, the situation, the mission. When the "guide" spoke, you listened.

"It's been almost two years since the series of operations that saved my life." Bowles was a hair over six feet tall, and stout where many of the Gamers were merely chunky. His hair and beard were long and bushy, brown going gray. "The Red Cross had a severe blood shortage due to the blood bank terrorism of '54. Everyone was afraid. Infected needles, infected plasma— the entire system was beginning to fail. And the ten of you donated blood that saved me." He sighed. "It was a miracle, and there was no way I could thank you. I'd lost a fortune speculating on adverse-environment gear. I was betting on another oil strike in Alaska."

His face darkened, grim as a man staring into the depths of hell. "Then the sun began to die."

Six words, said without drama, without a roll of drums or a dimming of lights, yet Max felt the chill right down to the marrow.

Bowles paused to let the implications sink in. "It wasn't just that the sun wasn't burning. No fusion, no neutrinos, hell, that's news from the last century. But now the interior heat is going somewhere, somehow. Interior heat inflates a star, keeps it from collapsing. The sun is shrinking. The surface isn't any dimmer, but it's a smaller radiating surface. The Earth's insulation is down to half and falling.

"The weather changed, and suddenly the gear that had been a drug on the market became gold. The film industry in Utah and Illinois died overnight, but I was making more money on the gear than I'd ever made in holos. So I stayed in San Francisco, selling and manipulating sales, until it became obvious that the city was falling. It was time to move on. And I remembered you, *all* of you. I'd kept track of you. I found you, and offered you this escape. Thank you for accepting my offer." The sincerity in his thanks came through clearly. This was a man who was delighted for the chance to repay a fraction of what he owed.

"The plane is completely stocked. I own a wildlife research station in the north country. There will be heat, and food— enough to last a lifetime for us, and any children we may have. Beyond that . . ." The optimism slipped like a loose mask. "We all know what awaits us. Awaits mankind eventually. We can only hope that someone will find an answer. Some of you have technical skills."

He took a handful of manila file folders and moved down the aisle, passing them out. "These are personalized dossiers. Please correct any faulty information. We will have to depend on each other completely. We are a totally closed society."

He passed Max, and handed down a folder. Max broke the seal with his thumbnail.

Max Sands. 6'4". 295 lbs. Recreational therapist—whatever the heck that meant. Sounded sexier than what he really did. He'd never met the guy in the folder, but already liked him better than the one in the mirror. This Max Sands had stayed behind when the city began to empty. He cared for the sick who couldn't be moved. When the blizzard hit San Francisco . . .

He snuck a peek over at Charlene, wondering if she had taken a fantasy identity. She would have made a perfect Tolkien elf, but there were no elves in this Game.

Frankish Oliver's biography described an SFPD sergeant. A vital job, someone who had stayed behind during what must have been a long and painful exodus from the northern climes. Max closed his eyes . . . it was easy to imagine. The sun shrinking, the weather cooling. Panic. The beginning of the end for Man on Earth. And what was happening to Man in space, with their dependence on solar power?

He examined the men and women around him. These were the people he would have to depend upon for his survival. He envisioned himself learning to use snow tractors, working in hothouses, tending the reactor . . .

Max shook himself out of the reverie. *Stop being so clever. Don't even try to guess.*

Frankish Oliver was chuckling under his beard. "Isn't he good? Robin Bowles, under all that hair!"

"Last time I saw him, he was balding."

"Actor's ego. He's on camera now. He was Nero Wolfe in *Fer-de-Lance* and *The Mother Hunt*. They couldn't be paying him enough for this."

"He must want to lose weight for a movie."

Oliver looked at him, scanned him up and down. "So you're Mr. Mountain, eh? You look bigger on holovid."

"Elevator tights," Max said quietly. Dammit, he'd hoped no one would recognize him... "Listen—you're the only one who knows. Don't spread it around, all right?"

Oliver chuckled. "Well, all right, but I wouldn't worry about it. We're all playing roles here." And he turned back to his dossier.

Odd comment. Was Oliver a Gamer or an Actor? Best to watch him, see what he did, maybe do the same. He hoped Oliver could keep a secret.

Clouds were fragile veils that flashed past without leaving moisture on the windows. The land streaming below might have been a boneyard shrouded with cotton.

"Seattle," the stewardess said. "Totally dead except for scavengers. A few unfortunates who couldn't get out. And the frozen, unburied dead." The stewardess was talking into a tape recorder. She caught Max staring and her lips gave an embarrassed upward twitch. "I've been trying to make a record. It doesn't matter now. Maybe it won't ever matter. But I have to believe there is hope. Someone has to."

The mood in the room was grim. This was fun? This was supposed to be entertainment? It felt like a wake, a gathering to mourn the death of mankind beneath the marching glaciers. Suddenly Max felt so depressed that he couldn't—

There was a low rumbling in the engines, so low that he almost didn't notice it. Now he caught it and recognized it. Subsonics. The rumble died, and he began to feel a little better. Damn it, he knew that Dream Park was manipulating him with sound, with subliminal visuals, and if rumor had it right, with smells that impacted below the threshold of conscious perception. It didn't matter. As his mood lifted he suddenly felt buoyant, filled with hope and energy. He looked around himself in the plane, saw everyone sitting up straight, eyes tight with determination.

Bowles nodded. "I knew that I could count on you. Now listen to me." He spoke in an odd, measured cadence, suspiciously like a stage hypnotist Max had seen on holo once. "Sometimes we can do things for other people that we can't do for ourselves. If that's what it takes to get you through this, to help you survive, then that's what I want you to do." He scanned the room. Max felt a musical trilling sensation. It was similar to the thrill he'd experienced when he figured out the answer to the Time Travel Game: like someone using his bones for a piccolo. He felt like he could whip the world.

"We're going to survive. Each of us is going to go beyond his ordinary limits. Every one of us is going to make sacrifices. We're going to give up things that we love, to make a healthier situation for our friends, our family.

"I want you all to look into your hearts, and be sure that you have *permission* to survive. To win. Because if you don't have that, then no matter how much food we have, how much shelter or heat, you won't make it." Bowles made very deliberate eye contact with each of them in turn.

Max felt comfortable, drifting, warm. He sank into an ocean of comfort . . . and only when he bobbled up again did he realize that Bowles had been talking the whole time. "—help that is asked for, no matter what it is. Agreed!?"

"Aye!" The Gamers answered raggedly. Max joined in late, too embarrassed to admit that he hadn't the foggiest notion what he was agreeing to. But judging by the confused expressions around him, his lapse of attention had been more rule than aberration.

Something was being passed forward from the back. He sniffed sharp cheese and beef, and his mouth watered. Lunchlike substances! Waiting, he suddenly realized that the plane was shuddering, humming with stress.

"This is your captain speaking. We are running low on fuel, but there is nothing to worry about. The charts indicate a refueling depot just south of Bethel, within glide distance. We will land there. Please strap yourselves in."

The shudder eased: the plane had dropped back through sonic speed. Through the window he could see the ground looming close, a vast expanse of white dotted with a few rectangular dwellings. The wing had moved smoothly forward; flaps were sliding out to extend the trailing edges. His stomach crawled up into his throat, looking for a place to hide. There was a clutch of buildings ahead. The land humped to the left, a sharp black ridge, and beyond that were more oblongs on the white blanket. An Eskimo village?

The plane shifted about, outspread wings feeling the air. The craft tilted and dropped, gripped by a freak wind. Gamers gripped their seats with white-knuckled fingers.

Max glanced across the aisle. Eviane's bright emerald eyes were as wide as saucers, blinking rapidly as she peered out under the wing. The craft straightened and surged and touched down in a snow bed. Plumes of white spewed to either side. They slowed, sliding toward a pair of snow-shrouded refueling pumps.

Then it was as if a malicious hand clutched the wheels on the right. The plane lurched and slewed drunkenly, heaving Max against his seatbelt. It smashed straight into the pumps and ripped them away.

Half of the service station shell went next. A thick splinter of metal gouged into the hull of the plane, breaching the cabin. Max heard the clang and saw something ripping through the wall, slicing toward him at knee level. He pulled his knees to his belly as the jagged steel wedge slicked past.

The intoxicating stench of spilled fuel filled the air. The stewardess screamed at them. "Move! The emergency exits are middle and front. Take the left side exits only, but hurry!"

The passenger cabin dissolved into chaos. Everyone grabbed gear or friends or both. The copilot and pilot burst from the cockpit and reached the door ahead of the stewardess. They pulled handles; the side doors of the plane popped open, completing the cabin temperature's descent to zero. A chute hissed as it expanded.

The copilot jumped into the chute and disappeared from view. His voice came back: "Okay. Move!"

The pilot stayed to help Robin Bowles into the chute. Bowles let out a boisterous "yaah-hoo!" as he hit the plastic. He skidded to the ground and spun dizzily on the snow.

Max was next. He slid all of the way down on his butt, hollering every inch of the way. What a trip!

Passengers followed at four-second intervals. The inflated chute bounced and flopped behind him.

He counted heads. All out, except the pilot, the stewardess, and the Guardsman. They were throwing things from the open door. Half a dozen bulky items fell in a cloud: backpacks, then crates. What about damage? But they were in haste.

"I bought good stuff!" Bowles bellowed. "Falling Angels

stuff. Antibiotics made in orbit. Lines that'll hold six elephants. Foam-steel backpack struts. Hey, use the chute for that!" He caught a crate as it slid down the chute. "We may need those medicines."

The copilot was jogging around to the tail of the plane. His feet thrashed in the air as he pulled the tail ramp down. He yelled something undecipherable in the wind and excitement—

And then disappeared in a deceptively soft puff of fire. Yellow flame rolled up from the back of the plane like a flapping carpet, darkening to a roll of oily smoke.

Max was chilled. The man had been cremated in an instant. Killed out. One redundant guide, gone. It's only a Game, come on— Eviane was running toward the flame. The stew had her by the arm, was shouting at her above the howling wind. Eviane desisted.

The exit had become a rush, and he thought: We'll get clear, but what about the supplies? The food? Max made himself move.

Luggage was being thrown out of the forward door, and they scrambled for it, catching it as it fell, in a bizarre game of— what was it called? He vaguely remembered an ancient comedy routine entitled "Catch It and You Keep It!" (Announcer: "We're here atop the twenty-story CBS building, and our contestants are below us in the parking lot for the first round of Catch It and You Keep It. Johnny, what's our first prize? A Tappan gas range . . . ?")

Something soft slammed into his chest and sent him stumbling backward. He couldn't hold the belly laugh in even as he tried to catch his balance. They were stranded! Their food was going up in smoke! The copilot, fried! This was disastrous! This was tragic!

This was getting *really* interesting.

Chapter Six

SUPPLIES

Eviane watched Francis Hebert roll clumsily down the chute. He managed to right himself, and hit the ground running. The stewardess helped Trianna Stith-Wood through the doorway. For all her size Trianna managed somehow to express panic in a dainty, ladylike manner.

Eviane decided that she definitely didn't like the woman.

Crates of equipment lay scattered in the snow as Bowles and the pilot struggled to haul luggage from the cargo hold. The Guardsman left the chute three feet above the ground, hit the ground rolling, and took off with rifle held at the ready.

The stewardess took a last look into the plane, seemed to breathe a sigh of relief, and stepped out into the chute.

The plane shuddered against the ground, and an instant later the windows exploded, gouting fire. For an instant the stewardess was outlined in flame, her body a blackened silhouette against a yellow corona. Then she was gone.

The plane's death-cry flattened the hapless Gamers. Chunks of burning metal rained from the sky.

Eviane lay facedown in the snow. The snow just a few feet from her head flickered with gasoline flames, and glistened as it melted. A fragment of twisted steel lay just out of reach. It was hot. It would burn her if she touched it . . . wouldn't it?

It was all real. The mists were clearing . . .

She stood, and looked down and out at the survivors. Thirteen in all, passengers and crew. They moved toward Bowles, gathering into a tight clump to hear each other over a hammering, frigid wind.

The pilot yelled above the storm. "I'm sorry, Mr. Bowles. Made a right cock-up of that one. I think there must have been a bullet in the fuel tank. Where's Greg? Where's . . . ?"

The pilot gasped, eyes fixed on a smoldering, human-shaped

mass lying crumpled in the snow at least thirty feet from the plane. Ashen-faced, he ran toward it, legs plowing unsteadily through the snow, and at last stood silently above what was left of the stewardess. He removed his outer jacket and draped it over her smoldering corpse. His breath puffed little clouds into the air. He shivered, and wrapped his arms around himself, rubbing his shoulders.

After a few seconds, he rather guiltily took his jacket back.

Bowles threw a blanket over the stew's body. He said, "Grant, we've got to reach the lodge. Apologize then." He glanced up at the shrunken sun, which was a third above the horizon. "I figure we have a month of daylight left. It will just have to be enough."

"Then three or four months of night," the pilot said, "and after that..."

"Fimbulwinter," Bowles said. "Carbon dioxide freezing out of the atmosphere, maybe. Ah, well. Sufficient unto the day."

The wind was whipping the fire to death. Snow ran in blinding flurries. Eviane shielded her face as her cheeks began to numb. The Guardsman ran up to them, carrying his rifle at port arms.

"Supply store!" Bowles's scream competed with the storm's growing wail. He pointed into a white wall of driving snow. "Can't see it, but it's out there."

"Eskimo village, half a mile that way," the soldier shouted back. "They must have seen us come down. Probably on their way now."

Eviane picked up a box marked with a red cross. It was heavy. She trudged toward the cluster of buildings. The other Gamers followed her, carrying gear, leaving tracks like a colony of snow snails. The sky began to clear, the wall of white slowing to a flurry.

Charlene caught up with her. "Whew. Off to a start, aren't we?" Charlene lowered her voice. "You've Gamed before. What is happening?"

Game? This isn't a Game. It's...

It's...

Eviane shook her head, clearing the smoky strands that wove themselves tighter and thicker by the moment. A flicker of pre-science made her say, "I don't know. Let's just play it by ear."

"Ear?"

The door of the supply store was open a crack. Grant pushed against it cautiously with his fingertips. The pilot had just lost a plane, a copilot, and a stewardess. He might not be overwhelmingly eager to lose a half-dozen passengers.

The door creaked open, throwing a wedge of light into an abandoned store. As soon as Grant nodded, the Gamers crowded in, out of the freezing wind. Oh, it was stocked. Well stocked, in fact, with all manner of food, and suddenly Eviane remembered that the alarm Klaxon had sounded in the middle of breakfast. A line of portable stoves, several canisters of fuel: they could cook, too.

Orson Sands spread massive fingers, grabbing three foil packets of pork and beans. "Real men don't need Sterno," he proclaimed. "I'll suck 'em cold."

Kevin, the skinny kid, called from elsewhere in the store. "Clothing. Coats! Hats! It's cold out there, troops."

"Wait just a minute." Bowles seemed uneasy. He ran thick fingers through his beard, brushing out snow. "Why isn't there anybody here? Where in the devil are they?"

"I don't know and don't really care." Orson's teeth tore a foil packet's serrated corner. He spat.

"You had better start caring, if you want to stay alive very long," his brother Max said cautiously. Eviane's little pink heart leapt. Max was smart, and despite his girth looked like a fighter.

She remembered him, too, from the Tar Pits mini-Game. He was well over six feet tall, inches shorter than Charlene but three times as wide. He looked a lot like his brother Orson, barring his neatly trimmed beard; but he looked and moved more like an athlete. His belly didn't sag the same way. An ex-football player, maybe? His eyes were a luminous gray-black.

He said, "Orson! Even up here, would people just walk away from a store and leave the door open? All right, maybe they would. But we have an exploding airplane out here, and nobody has even come to take a look." His voice was patient. "It's another *puzzle*, Orson."

Orson said, "Aw, Max . . . yeah."

Eviane noticed Charlene watching them. She whispered, "Brothers. Interested?"

Charlene nodded judiciously.

"Me too. His name's Max."

The pilot was saying, "Vote! All in favor of checking to see what is happening around here, say aye."

"Aye!!" Six hands and voices were raised. Three belonged to Charlene and Max and Hippogryph.

"Opposed?"

Seven no's.

"The no's have it," Grant said.

The Gamers drifted among the shelves. Some were at the rear with Kevin and Hippogryph, choosing cold-weather gear. More were finding dinner.

Trianna Stith-Wood called, "Veal paprika!"

Johnny Welsh's head rotated 150 degrees. "Veal?"

Trianna rubbed the foil packet, winking. "I make a veal loaf to die for. Thyme, tarragon leaves, minced parsley, and tomato fondue sauce."

"Lady, you're killing me."

"There are worse—"

Bang.

The clatter of canned goods stopped. Another distant gunshot, then a volley. Orson Sands dropped the bag of freeze-dried pork and beans, eyes sparkling. "Puzzle, right." He and Max thundered through the door, the others crowding right behind.

They clustered outside, looking out across the choppy permafrost of the valley floor into the blizzard-shrouded ridge to the north. Had the shots come from there? It was the only decent cover . . .

"Come on, baby." Max Sands spoke again, and Eviane found herself drifting closer to him, craving an opportunity to watch more closely.

He was handsome, in a massive sort of way, and she liked the sound of his voice. Voices had always been it, for her. The sound of an announcer's voice on the stereo. Others seemed fascinated by the glow and depth of the video arcades, but she had always loved audio. Just the sound of a voice was enough . . .

And he had the Voice. Something inside her melted.

Captain Grant and Hebert struggled out carrying armfuls of bulky coats and hats with earmuffs, dropped them in the snow, and began sorting for something that would fit. Bowles emerged with a double armful of tennis rackets. *Huh?* Snowshoes. More of the Gamers were wearing coats now.

It was cold. Eviane picked through coats, chose one, found a hat with fold-down ear flap, pulled on thermal galoshes, all while listening with her whole body.

"Come on," Max Sands said. "Where is it? Give me another shot."

And they got it. *Crack! Crackcrackcrack*, and a thin, wavering scream.

They had their direction. The group straggled off across the snow, north toward the black ridge. A long way to walk, but the snow was packed hard; Eviane carried her snowshoes. She cast a glance at Charlene, saw the fatigue in her friend's face. They linked arms and struggled up the grade.

They were making good time.

Bowles lifted a hand and brought them to a halt before they reached the top. They followed his lead: dropped onto their stomachs, scuttled over the ridge like a line of crabs, and peered down.

It was night in the shadow of the ridge. Their eyes adjusted quickly.

Four armed men lay in an arc, facing a house that lay in partial ruins. It was burning, smoke and ashes boiling from the roof. Attached to one end of the house, a smaller shed—perhaps a smokehouse—had been blown apart as if by an explosion. Around the main door two . . . no, three bodies stretched out on the snow, in positions that only the dead could assume.

Eviane heard a whimper. After a long, startled moment she recognized her own voice.

She had seen this before. Been here before. Prescience.

One of the riflemen barked out a challenge. Eviane didn't recognize the language, but the meaning was obvious. She had heard it a thousand times in flatfilms and holos and even radio plays: "Come out with your hands up!" What had they tripped into? Was this the equivalent of the Royal Canadian Mounted Police? Were the people in the house desperate criminals? Eviane couldn't remember. She'd tried to forget, she'd fought to forget, and now, when it mattered, it was all gone.

Someone emerged from the smoky hell of the front door. His hands were high in the air, and he yelled something back to the attackers.

There was a guttural laugh, and a rifle barked. The man fell, palms slapping to his forehead.

Eviane closed her eyes. Her empty stomach curled into a knot.

Charlene's whispered laughter rang in her ear: "You're overacting. It's embarrassing. What are we supposed to do?"

She had no answer. Dreamboat's voice saved her. "Well, we know that they're not the good guys."

"We don't have any weapons," Hippogryph said. "We could get into a lot of trouble."

"We have flares," the Guardsman called. "Two boxes of them, and my rifle. Listen, with three flare guns we can convince them that they're surrounded. Goners. I say we give it a shot."

Hebert objected. "Flare guns? All right, they aren't that well armed—"

Impatiently Eviane snapped, "Lead on!"

After a few whispered instructions, the group spread out. Eviane was all elbows and knees as she crawled along the ridge, the curving sickle of snow that sheltered them from the war below. Just ahead of her, Dreamboat raised his flare pistol. Bowles slashed his hand in the air, and—

With a chorus of dull *phuts*, white streamers cut through the air. Suddenly a half-dozen smoking, parachuting flares were drifting from the sky like burning blossoms.

The men on the ground looked up.

"Ooooobleobleoble—" Charlene screamed out, her cry swiftly echoed by everyone else in the group. Eviane joined them delightedly—who could resist an opportunity to scream baby talk with a bunch of supposedly grown adult-type people? It was ridiculous, and silly, and somehow cleansing.

The men in the valley looked around in confusion, but the sound was coming from everywhere and nowhere. The Guardsman aimed his rifle carefully, and squeezed the trigger. One of the enemy went down clutching his chest. The remaining three sprang to their feet, and spread their arms. For a moment Eviane thought that they were asking for mercy.

Then the clouds parted.

No, they hadn't parted. The sky was slate-gray, threatening snow, but a northward wedge of cloud was brighter, widening, and—

Sky and land were flowing. Off to the north, the vast dim expanse of snow flowed to left and right, as if a folded blanket was being pulled straight. It was hard to see, because what was summoned into being was only new snowscape, no different from the old except that it glowed beneath a brighter sky.

The four gunmen hastened north, two carrying their wounded member. They didn't look back, not even when the Guardsman stopped gaping and fired after them. He fired three careful shots. Snow puffed wide of the gunmen.

"Damn," the Guardsman said.

A distant ridge of snow humped ahead of them. The four stopped, and one gestured wide-armed, his face lifting as the white mass lifted...and then the snowscape flowed, the path closed, the light dimmed. Eviane huffed as her legs gave out and dropped her in the snow.

They were gone. There remained only a bare field of snow, and four corpses to mark the place where, a moment before, a dreadful battle had raged.

Chapter Seven

THE QASGIQ

Eviane stumbled down the bank of snow, caught her balance for an exhilarating moment, then tumbled again. She wiped ice from her hair and snorted it from her nose as she came back to her feet.

The other refugees plowed furrows in the snow as they plunged down. Some rolled like pill bugs, whooping. Max and the National Guardsman both kept their balance all the way down. At the last instant Max lost his battle with momentum and plowed face-first to the bottom.

Charlene walked down fully upright, slowly, like an aged elvish queen, with Hippogryph alongside her as a dwarfish attendant.

Eviane's amusement vanished almost as quickly as it bubbled up. What was happening here? They had left the violence of the cities behind . . . and now this!

Something deep within her was untouched by the cold and the fear. Some voice whispered that it was all a dream, only a recurrent nightmare. Eviane shook her head violently. Such thoughts were dangerous.

She approached the burning lodge, cautiously avoiding the bodies of the dead.

Eviane had seen corpses before. A few more meant little. One of the dead men was heartbreakingly young. His eyes stared sightless, freezing in the terrible cold. His arms were outstretched as if begging for mercy, or trying to provide some small measure of protection for his people inside.

Charlene crunched through the snow behind her, whispered close in her ear. "Be careful?"

"Why?" Eviane asked, surprised with how damned reasonable her voice sounded. "We can handle it or we can't. If we can't, we're probably dead anyway. Let's go."

Charlene looked at her with what could only have been amazement . . . but Charlene hailed from an earlier, more benign world. Here the ice ruled, and only the strong would survive. Somehow Eviane would keep her friend alive until the tall girl had a chance to adapt to reality.

The National Guardsman jogged up beside them. Eviane scanned him appraisingly. He looked young and hard, jaw square and tight-curled hair cropped short. Good. An asset. There were bad times ahead.

Max Sands . . . she could trust Max. Despite the run, he wasn't really breathing hard. Hippogryph was no weakling either. But Bowles was bent over, hands on knees, panting. Stith-Wood was massaging her knee. Orson and Kevin were still back on the slope. Johnny Welsh hadn't told a joke in an hour.

Kevin of the pipestem legs: his padded clothing hung on him like a deflated balloon. He was puffing a little, but his smile was intact. The rest could survive a day or two of starvation, though they'd whine, but for Kevin they'd better find food. He'd build muscle-meat on this trip or die trying.

Smoke belched out of the front door as it creaked open. Fingers scrabbled on the inside, pulling weakly.

A man emerged. His broad Eskimo face was all planes and angles, the face of a man who has known starvation or terrible illness. His hands were lines and knobs. Only the eyes were alive. They were piercing, frozen blue, like chips of flaming ice.

He gasped for breath, and stretched the door wider so that a young woman could squeeze her way out. The girl fell to her knees in the snow, threw her arms around the young man's corpse. "Wood Owl," she sobbed hysterically. "Oh, you fool. Oh, my dear."

She was rounded, solid beneath her furs. So: it wasn't starvation which had stolen the fat from the old man's face. Years of illness might do that.

As the old man stumbled from the doorframe, the roof gave a sigh and collapsed.

His voice was as timeless as the howling wind. "We must find shelter. Come with me to the prayer lodge. Ahk-lut dares not violate that sacred place."

Eviane nodded as if she understood, and helped the girl to her feet.

The air grew even colder as they marched. The wind drove the snow until it was almost a solid curtain. The refugees stumbled on blindly, following the old man. He bent into the storm, pushing on step after painful step. Who could tell what the old man was following? Instinct or memory or the distant outline of white knife-edged mountains momentarily visible through the terrible gale. Except for those brief moments, they were in an endless, impenetrable shell of white, until Eviane could see only the stunned shadow of Johnny Welsh struggling ahead of her. One moment's lapse of attention, a single misplaced footstep, and she would be lost.

After a time the storm's fury diminished, and she could distinguish the alien landscape around her. There were no trees, although the snow was clotted in irregular lumps that might have been trees shrouded and drowned in white. There was no sign of life save for the line of silent travelers. Now that the wind was dying, she heard their gasping.

Charlene tapped her shoulder, whispered down from her enormous height. "How do they do this? It looks as if we can see for miles."

Eviane frowned. "We're on a hill. Sometimes I don't understand you at all."

Charlene stared, caught without a reply.

Eviane withdrew to a deeper, cooler place inside her mind. *Charlene had already begun to crack. Snow madness. Shock. It was to be expected. In a group this size they might lose half simply to fear and despair. Eviane must be strong for all.*

Eviane snapped out of her reverie as they approached a large, regular mound of snow.

The old man got down upon his hands and knees. He oriented himself to the mountains, then began digging in the snow. In minutes he uncovered a man-sized oval cave mouth. He disappeared into it like a seal diving into an ice hole.

Others followed. Eviane was sixth in line.

The floor of the passage was compressed and melted into an icy glaze. The tunnel sloped down for the first eight feet, then leveled out. She pushed her pack ahead of her, and nudged herself along with knees and elbows. The tunnel gave her only a foot of clearance to the sides, and if she had suffered from claustrophobia, this would have been sheer terror. Wiggling another ten feet brought her to an upgrade, where the lack of traction became treacherous. Hands grasped her pack from above and pulled. She hung on for the ride.

She emerged from a trapdoor into a kind of lodge. Fifty or a hundred years earlier, the lodge would probably have been constructed from wood and snow, but more modern materials made other options available.

Tubular plastic bladders filled with frozen water formed the rectangular structure of the walls. The ceiling stretched over nine feet high, and a conical sheet of clear plastic capped the roof. The air smelled stale, already warming with the scent of tired human flesh. The old man poked a long spear through a vent hole in the center of the sheet, knocking loose the snow.

In the middle of the room a blackened pit had been filled with branches, chunks of log, and tinder.

One by one the travelers came in out of the cold. Their collective bodies warmed the room. Outer coats were coming off.

The old man looked at them, and Eviane had a better opportunity to examine him in turn. He and the young woman were similarly attired, though the lower cut of her garment was more curved than his. The fur-hooded robe had been sewn together from a variety of animals. Eviane recognized squirrel and mink, and something that was probably muskrat. There were other skins, perhaps not native to Alaska but traded hand to hand from hundreds or thousands of miles away. Was that a poodle skin?

She didn't see any machine stitching in the older man's clothing. As the girl peeled off her external clothing, she revealed a pair of Jordache designer ski pants and boots. Girls will be girls. She was cute, in an Eskimo kind of way. Eviane flickered a glance at Max Sands. Yes, he'd noticed.

"Call me Martin Qaterliaraq," the old man said. "Martin the Arctic Fox. Your Christian missionaries named me Martin, long ago. They were good people, and I pay them the respect of keeping that name. But although my daughter calls herself Candice, to me she is Kanguq, Snow Goose. I serve the old ways." His face fell. Once more, he seemed impossibly ancient. "It is the old ways that brought you here to this place, and only the old ways can save the world."

Orson spoke into the silence. "What are you saving, exactly? From what?"

"Wait. We know the way to show you. You have helped us already, but we need more."

The trapdoor in the ground puffed again, and more people emerged. Some were Eskimos in traditional dress, furs and skins. Some of the frocks looked to have been made of fish skin, and others of waterproof gut. Some wore more modern cold-weather gear, perhaps even some of the plastic adverse-environment gear Bowles had mentioned.

Both men and women wore earrings hanging from pierced earlobes. As one wrinkled Mongol face passed close by, Eviane caught a closer look at his flat, rectangular earrings. Bits of ivory, glass beads, and colored rock were stuck into them.

The women were heavy but withered by time and environment. Many wore jewelry decorated with grotesque faces, grinning demon-shapes, snarling animals. Two had bone needles projecting through their septa.

Eviane counted a dozen men and women. One...two wore bloody bandages. Some were introduced by name, names that made Eviane's head hurt to hear them: Kitngiq and Pingayunelgen and Tayarut and even less manageable mouthfuls.

All had the characteristic padding of fat, the dark skin and epicanthic folds. There was a kind of vitality to them that made the excess poundage seem appropriate in a way her own never had. They carried it as if it was insulation above hard muscle.

When the room was three-quarters full, they arranged themselves around the fire pit in a circle.

With flint and steel, Martin started the fire. Smoke clouded the air, although it was almost magically drawn up through the roof.

Pouches were opened. Dried fish and meat went around the circle. Orson Sands sneered at what he was holding. "This isn't even diet food. There was plenty of real food back in the supply store."

Martin shook his head sadly. "You must learn to see as the Cabal see, if you would best them at their game. We must prepare you for the traditional ways, my friend."

"He doesn't mean Eskimo Pies," Max told his brother.

The pouch reached her hands. What Eviane pulled out had a texture like rough cardboard. She began to chew. It was stringy, with a smoked flavor.

"The Inua of the fish must be respected. They feed us and clothe us, quiver our arrows and seal our boats. Their eggs tan hides and the oil of their bodies lights our homes. Eat, and nourish your bodies, and give reverence to the Inua of the fish. Many of you will die before this is over, and then your spirits will mingle with those beings you have consumed. It would be best to make peace with them now."

The girl—Snow Goose—said, "Sedna is already gravely ill. Too ill to—" Martin glared at her and she was silent.

Eviane took Martin at his word, eating slowly, chewing until each mouthful was almost a liquid. (Sedna?) The atmosphere in the lodge was close, growing warmer. Her companions were having little trouble eating the peculiar food. Most of them must have tried stranger diets than this, from the look of them. (Did she know that name?)

When she stopped eating, she wasn't full, but the edge was off her hunger. She felt in a state of readiness, eager to hear the next of it.

Several of the older men and one of the younger went to the fire and threw on crumbled handfuls of powder. When they burned, they made a smell like tobacco and dust. The smoke grew thicker, the flame hotter.

The Eskimos were peeling off their external clothing. Soon they were all in underwear or twisted loincloths. The refugees looked at each other, in speculation or embarrassment or panic. Martin the Arctic Fox seemed half-starved, bones showing, concave belly... no navel. Qaterliaraq had no navel. Orson nudged Max, whispered.

The air grew thicker, warmer. Eviane was perspiring. No help for it. She stripped, and didn't stop until she was down to bra and panties. She folded her clothes into a careful bundle. The Eskimos weren't hiding themselves, and she wouldn't either.

Bowles and Stith-Wood wore their near nudity with ease, but Orson Sands held his shirt and jacket nervously in front of himself, trying to cover as much flab as he could. Kevin spread his thin arms before the fire. His eyes were half-closed in bliss, and his ribs were prominent.

Hippogryph, sweating freely, had kept his clothes on until he couldn't take the heat. Now he was undressing in some haste. He kept the bundled clothes in front of him, blushing furiously.

Max had stripped down to shorts without a tremor, but many of Eviane's fleshy companions were embarrassed. They shifted their considerable weight nervously from side to side like guilty children. Charlene tried to shrink into herself, shoulders hunched, arms hugging her knees, guilty grin... but she was relaxing even as Eviane watched. She was watching Hippogryph.

Hippogryph would not meet anyone's eyes. His ears were quite red. He was hunched as Charlene had been, yet he had little to hide. Beneath his quite Eskimo-like fat layer the muscle was solid. And what did Charlene think she was hiding? Elvish alien beauty, if she would only straighten up.

Behind her, Johnny Welsh whispered, perhaps to himself, "I wish there wasn't so much light . . ."

Bowles chuckled. "Steam bath scene, Take One."

Johnny relaxed; he smiled; his voice rose. "Gosh, Charles, wasn't it nice of the cannibal king to let us use their bathhouse?"

"We should hurry, Johnny. There must be a dozen tribes outside waiting for us to finish."

"They're probably here for the feast the king promised—"

Martin Qaterliaraq spoke again. "This is the sweat lodge, the qasgiq of my people. Mph." The old man pronounced the word *kuzz*-a-gick. "Here we dream our dreams and see into the world beyond. But Ahk-lut has t-t-torn the veil between matter and spirit. He would bring the chaos of his greed and fear into the world—mph—and destroy everything."

The other Eskimos nodded assent. But Martin's lips were twitching, and some others were having trouble keeping their faces solemn.

The trapdoor in the floor flapped open again. More Eskimos brought in handfuls of brittle driftwood and loaded them into the central fire pit.

Smoke curled up from the crackling wood and twisted through the ceiling. Watching it lulled Eviane into an almost hypnotic reverie.

The relaxation became dismay a few minutes later, when the air grew so close as to be almost unbreathable. Several of the refugees were choking and gasping for breath.

Then the smoke lightened. Pictures floated in a gray, misty ocean that merged into a gray, misty sky. Martin's voice was strong once again. "It was the beginning, and there were not yet people upon the Earth," he said. "For four days the first man lay coiled in the pod of a beach pea. On the fifth he burst forth and stood full-grown."

A man, a proto-Eskimo, stood naked in the mist.

A black shape emerged from the sky, grew wings and a head, became a gigantic Raven. In Eviane's mind the words of the ancient shaman and the images in the air melded together. The room around her receded from her awareness. She stood on an ancient beach, could see the oily gray sky, smell the protosurf.

The Raven covered a sizable patch of sky. It shrank as it glided to earth: perspective in reverse. It was man-sized when it touched the sand. It stared at the man, cocking its head to the side, and finally said: "What are you?"

The man stuttered in fear and confusion. The great Raven pushed its beak aside, and its feathers away, revealing smooth brown skin beneath. It became very like the man, not fearsome at all.

The man relaxed. "I know not who I am. I know that I hunger and thirst."

The Raven opened his hand. The flesh of his palm melted and ran, and formed beads which darkened to berries. The man took them and ate.

With the sweep of an arm that was also a wing, the Raven transformed the sea into a creek running at the base of a snow-capped mountain. The Raven scooped clay from the bank of the river and molded it lovingly. He set two blobs on the earth, and waved his feathered arms again.

Two mountain sheep stood inanimate for a few moments, then opened their eyes, shuddered, and ran off to the mountains.

"The Raven made everything that lives," Martin's voice whispered behind her ear. Shapes were flowing from the Raven's wing: reindeer, caribou, rabbits. The other wing swept out, square miles of glossy black shadow, and seals and whales and a thousand shapes of fish rained into the ocean.

The Raven was studying the man again in that odd, avian manner. He molded clay into another man-shape with a slightly different symmetry. He took long grass from the bank of the stream to cover the new creature's head. Its eyes opened, and it was woman. She stretched her hand out for the man's.

They walked away. As they passed over the land it blossomed, the stream ran with fish, and birds filled the sky.

Eviane snorted at the smell of smoke and was back in the qasgiq. Martin, half-visible in the smoke, was hunched over, talking as if to himself. "The Raven gave all sea life into the care of Sedna. All land life into the hands of her lover Torngarsoak. When these two are well, all creatures are fruitful and multiply..." And within the murk Eviane found herself deep underwater. Schools of fish streamed past a kneeling Eskimo woman with long, floating hair and a face not unlike that of Snow Goose. Playfully, she brushed her hands through a school of fish—

Her hands! Her fingers were stubs, chopped off just below the first knuckle.

Orson was whispering to Max: "—pretty typical myth pattern.

Sedna was a beautiful Eskimo girl who tried to escape an arranged marriage. Her father cut off her fingers. The joints fell into the ocean, became whales, seals, and so on."

And yet there was no sense of tragedy or regret in Sedna's beautiful face. Her eyes met Eviane's; her lips twitched in a smile. Eviane was warmed by the beauty.

Smoke swirled. Land again: ice melting, green sprouting. She watched men multiplying, expanding across the land. The land filled with children, laughing, growing, mating, spreading their villages and hunting lands out beyond the horizon.

The seas swelled, and suddenly Eviane was in the prow of a small, shallow boat, skimming across the waves behind a flashing seal. The seal was speared, pulled aboard. The hunters rattled quick memorized words, and for a moment Eviane was back underwater, and the woman with the stubby fingers cocked her head to hear the voices.

Eviane was on the ice, belly flat against the floe, as a walrus rose through a hole to take a precious mouthful of air. A spear flashed past her viewpoint—

She ran with her companions beside a river, stretching their nets. Nets heavy with salmon were pulled to land. Voices were raised in happy song—

She was surrounded by dancing children in the midst of a communal hall, a qasgiq. Naked bodies bent and twisted to the rhythms of a hundred unfamiliar percussion instruments—

She stood on the shore, and watched a strange and alien vessel approach across the water. It was large, larger than a whale, large enough to *hold* whales. Gigantic white billowing wings caught the wind and breathed the thing in toward the land. Men sprang out, hairy men with pale skin.

As she watched, with impossible, magical speed, they began to build. Suddenly houses of wood—more wood than her people had ever seen—began to sprout in tight clusters. The new men killed whales and seals until their corpses littered the beach like poisoned ants.

And when there were no more whales and seals, they dug the hills, pulling out the yellow metal.

And when that slackened, they drilled into the ground, and pumped out thick black fluid.

The quickly shifting views of white intruders spilling across the land were becoming blurred. Behind them Eviane could see the woman beneath the water, the Eskimo woman with mutilated hands. Sedna was sick. A pale mass with white, veinlike threads, a fungus or parasite, was spreading through her hair, across her cheeks and neck, down her shoulders. She hunched her shoulders and hid her face in misery.

"The people of the Raven watched the destruction of their land." She heard Martin's voice dimly in her mind. "The people learned the ways of the intruders and forgot their own. Sedna was ill with their sins. And the Raven circling overhead, watching his people seduced from the way of their ancestors, was not happy."

The Raven was a monstrous black shape, diving like a hawk. The earth's surface tore like paper. The Raven ripped his way deep into the world's heart. He emerged with claws filled with sticky orange-glowing magma. From that he made new shapes: children, boys and girls who glowed with force, whose faces were filled with wisdom and knowledge. They—*uh-huh!*—they had no navels.

Eviane watched as the Raven swept the magical children into his claws and swooped up, up until the entire globe of the earth was a hazy white arc beneath her, and her heart was in her throat. Then the Great Bird swooped down, and left pairs of children around the rim of the Arctic Circle. She saw them swiftly gather together the tribes of the People, and teach them to make fire with the fire drill, to skin and tan, to build houses of wood and stone and ice. The old ways. Sedna showed in double exposure: her hair was coming clean. Her head lifted, she sighed, she waved a languid stub-fingered hand that streamed flocks of seals . . .

Gone.

Eviane blinked her eyes, rousing slowly from the spell. The pictures were gone, and Martin the Arctic Fox was speaking again.

"The Great Raven made the new men to teach the old knowledge to our people, to give us back the spirit world we had lost. He dispersed us around the great circle of ice. I came here, to this land you call Alaska. My son is called Ahk-lut, and together we were powerful guardians of the Old Ways. For half a century we used the power to help my people. Then Sedna became sick again, and Ahk-lut formed other plans, other ideas.

"Through dreams, through chanting, he reached our children, the children of the children of the Raven. Gathering them from tribes scattered around the ice, around the world, he formed the Cabal. The Cabal seduced more than half of our children. They kept their secrets from their parents, and together they worked their magic."

An ocean of mist boiled away, and when it cleared Eviane was in a sweat lodge much like Martin's qasgiq, but larger, darker. Eight young men formed a circle around a smoky fire. They were naked but for leather pouches slung on thongs around their necks. Their skins were burnt dark red by the heat. Perspiration drooled down their faces and slicked their bodies.

An alien, evil sound coursed through the air, one she finally recognized as a chorus of low mutterings, malignant human voices joined in dark harmony.

One stood. His face was very like Martin's, leaner than a normal Eskimo face, with indented cheekbones and sunken eyes, as if he had not only Martin's genes but the old shaman's suggestion of deep sickness. He was shaven-headed. The dark eyes squinted in old hatred; the corneas looked milky. He reached into the pouch that hung from his neck, fumbling, and for a moment Eviane saw a tiny, withered pair of human legs in the pouch, and the rounded suggestion of a head. Then it vanished again, and Ahk-lut (who else could it be?) drew out a bar of chewing tobacco.

With dark, stained teeth Ahk-lut tore an enormous plug from the bar, masticated it, then spat a long, brownish stream into the fire. The flames leapt, and the smoke became a pillar of fetid dark green, masking and noxious.

"The young ones. Our children," Martin said. "They were trying to heal a great wrong, but they were impatient. They wanted it quick and easy. They've done a dreadful thing..."

The Cabal passed the tobacco from hand to hand. One at a time every man in the lodge spat tobacco juice into the fire, until at last the smoke within the lodge was so deep that she could barely see faces at all.

Ahk-lut turned, picked up a robe, and swept it aside. The lump beneath glowed faintly blue. Ahk-lut picked it up—it was heavy—swung himself around, and set it in the center of the fire. Sparks sprayed outward.

Firelight masked the blue glow, but set the irregular mass gleaming. It was polished metal, with shattered edges like curved daggers, and thick tubing twisted and torn.

Above the fire, a huge face looked briefly through the smoke. It was part bird, part man: enough of man to show its astonishment.

Each man reached into the pouch hung around his neck, and from it drew a handful of powders and bone fragments.

With each handful there was a brief flash of a shape that roiled within the smoke and then vanished again, like a walrus rolling at the water's surface before disappearing back into the depths. Here was a monstrous caterpillar, a writhing, multiarmed abomination. Smoke churned and became a killer whale with stubby human arms. It changed again, into the malformed corpse of a fetus pushing its flattened head against its amniotic membrane. A dead man clothed against bitter cold, face hooded, clothing and torso ripped open and empty. There were other, darker, bloodier images.

Higher within the pillar of smoke, the bird-face showed again. Its beak opened wide; it screamed silently, and faded, and *then* the shrill cry of a bird burst through the illusory smokehouse. The Cabal bellowed in triumph.

. . . When had they become nine?

Ahk-lut stepped into the circle, set his hands on a man's shoulders, and pulled him to his feet. Eviane saw that the man's arms and ankles were bound. He screamed like a bird. She saw, now, the suggestion of a beak in his pointed face.

Quite suddenly, the fire was out. An angular metal shape gleamed harsh blue within it. Shapes moved in the dark. A shadow occluded the glow, and fell into it—man-shaped, a bound man, writhing—and he was gone, and the blue glow was gone, and the firelight was the light of Martin's qasgiq.

Chapter Eight

THE MISSION

The fire was down to coals, and the smoke was thinning. Some of the refugees began to remember their half-naked state ... but there were larger matters to consider.

Martin said, "We believe that the Raven's children's children tricked their grandfather. They piqued his curiosity until he assumed human form to spy upon them. They cast their spells upon him, then upon the sun. The sun's death spells the end of your world, and the beginning of theirs."

"Martin." Within the smoky dark, who spoke? "What was the metal object that glowed blue?"

"That? A powerful talisman I traced when I was young. The Cabal has stolen it. It was a fragment of a thing that fell from the sky, in Canada."

"That was no meteor." Now Eviane recognized the voice of Orson Sands.

"No, it was a machine from Russia that fell before I was born. Talismans gain power from the distance they have traveled. I learned that this object had gone round and round the world until whatever held it up stopped working. So I sought it out. Now the Cabal is using it to throttle the sun."

Eviane heard herself saying, "They'll make the whole world into an Eskimo world." She wondered how she knew. "Cold. No crops, only the animals. We'd have to learn ..." Her prescient vision ran far ahead of her tongue.

Martin said, "Yes, you would have to learn. Ahk-lut would teach the white and black and yellow men our ways. Those who will not learn would starve. We have guessed that much. We can even guess why they have barred us from tending Sedna—"

"Sedna," Orson Sands broke in. "Shouldn't we know more about Sedna?"

"Ah, I forget. All who live at the rim of the world know Sedna, or Nuliajuk, or the Food Dish. Sedna has the care of the sea life that keeps us alive, fish and seals and plants and the very core of our lifestyle. She is the conscience of all mankind. When the sins of men and women take refuge in her hair, then Sedna becomes sick. If the sea dies, the land dies, and all men starve. Your people are starving now, and will continue to starve until Ahk-lut believes you are few enough."

"What about this Torngarsoak?" Kevin asked. "He's her boy-friend? Why doesn't he help?"

"He is a hunter, and roams the land," Martin said. "Hunters are often gone for months at a time. He may not know her plight."

"Okay, sins. It's a missionary word." Hippogryph spoke sharply, as if he were questioning a prisoner. "What do you mean by sins?"

Martin's lips moved, tasting his choice of words. "Abortion is a sin."

"Were the Eskimos practicing abortion?"

"You don't understand yet. Abortion of a creature's soul is also a sin. To kill a whale or a walrus without proper respect, this causes Sedna pain. Such sins breed in her scalp and hair and cause her misery. Then an *angakok* must visit her and soothe her and comb away the sins. Sedna can't comb her own hair, you know."

"But the New People fixed that. You taught the Eskimos the old ways again, right?"

"Yes," Arctic Fox said bitterly. "Sedna was growing healthy. Then she grew sick again. Our children, they didn't understand. How could they? We had no answers either! We prayed to the Raven, we tended Sedna, but Ahk-lut's secret Cabal had a quicker answer. Now their magic prevents us from reaching Sedna at all.

"We left the Cabal alone. Some of us thought their way might be right—"

"What, freezing the world?" Orson was shrill, disbelieving. "How would that help anyone?"

"They hoped to end the sins by forcing you to learn our ways. We couldn't fight them. They are too powerful, and they had the skyfall talisman. But then Ahk-lut demanded Snow Goose for his own. To take his sister in marriage would give him children who were closer to the blood of the Raven. They would found a new tribe, and rule the world.

"I refused. His forces clashed with mine. Ahk-lut used white man's guns from the other side of the circle. I was not prepared for that. My . . . foolishness has killed what remained of our warriors."

Max Sand leaned forward, hands on knees. "How can we help?"

Martin's voice was grave. "We have already sent out warriors, our children, beyond the veil of Seelumkadchluk, and none have returned. You are young and strong—and Ahk-lut will not expect to find white men in the world of spirits. Perhaps you can succeed where we have repeatedly failed.

"We can do some of what needs doing, but we cannot do all. Sedna must be tended, but we can no longer reach her with our minds. Ahk-lut has imprisoned the Raven, and we must learn how and whether he can be freed." Martin's eyes were on the fire, and he seemed reluctant to speak. Did he have a plan, or was he only reaching out in desperation?

"There is your tribe and my tribe," he said. "One tribe must spy on the Cabal. One must tend Sedna, remove the parasites, before famine takes all of the people of the white lands and half of us too. Which would you have?"

Hippogryph spoke. "What does tending Sedna involve?"

"You would have to travel to her, in the flesh, through the realm of spirit. Go to her in her home beneath the sea. Soothe her. Comb the parasites from her hair. Learn from her why she is sick, if she will speak, if she knows."

"Fighting the Cabal sounds like more fun," Max Sands said.

Eviane's voice dripped daggers. "Fun? It has to be done, but killing people isn't entertainment, Max."

His mouth dropped open, but he didn't speak. He remembered the Tar Pits Game, and the careful, single-minded way Eviane had gone after the key. She was a Gamer. He'd heard of the type. She had donned her persona like a second skin—like a body condom—and it wouldn't come off until the Game was over.

Hippogryph was speaking. "We don't know enough. We've learned as much as we're going to here, haven't we, Martin? Your skills have reached as far as they can?"

"Unfortunately true."

"I'd say let's find out what Sedna knows before we tackle the Cabal. She might know where the Raven went."

Max shook his head. "But—can't we follow Ahk-lut? He could take us right to the Raven. Free the Raven, he'll kick ass!

We've got guns . . . do guns work in the spirit world, Martin?"

"Of course. Why would a tool stop working?"

"Vote!" Bowles cried. "Hands up for Sedna!"

Hippogryph and five others raised hands. Orson's pudgy face was lined in concentration . . . and his hand went up to make seven.

"Hands to follow Ahk-lut!" Max's and Eviane's hands shot up. And Charlene's, and three others. Bowles had abstained, and so had Trianna.

They would go to Sedna. Underwater. Claustrophobia and sea monsters . . .

The sober, round-faced men and women around the sweat lodge nodded their heads as if at a prearranged signal. They rattled segments of bone, seal-hide drums, whittled-ivory percussion instruments, strange musical devices that produced a flow of sound like nothing in the modern world. Rattling, lilting, now strident, now coaxing, but always seething with urgency.

"You," Martin said, pointing to each of the refugees in turn. "You who are young must go, and right this terrible wrong."

"What happened to your own men?" Max asked softly.

Martin's eyes dropped. "They crossed the veil of Seelum-kadchluk, where the sky meets the sea. Some went to Sedna and some followed the Cabal. The most powerful of our *angakoks* carried the most powerful of our talismans. None have returned. We do not know why."

Kevin clucked, punching something into a little hand-held keyboard. "This bodes not well . . ."

Martin ignored him. "But your power is greater. You may find them as allies on the other side."

Or not. Eviane looked around at her companions. Overweight and soft . . . and youthful, with the exception of Robin Bowles, the man who had saved their lives in San Francisco. But they looked inspired. Could a dozen chubby but game neophytes match the unknown powers of these renegade Raven-spawn?

The fire had nearly died. One by one the old Inuit rose and began to dance around the coals. The walls of the sweat lodge shuddered with the low chants as they circled, their miming at first cryptic and then discernible as hunting and fighting movements.

An old, old man hopped around the fire in a crouch, as if perched next to an ice hole, awaiting a fish. Behind him, another grandfather cast a spear, and another raised an imaginary rifle to his shoulder, squeezed the trigger, spun and rolled on the floor in simulated death-throes before springing up and repeating the ritual.

Martin threw a handful of powders onto the fire. It flared to new life, and threw a ghastly emerald light against the walls. A handful of dull green embers floated down, were borne up by air currents, and then settled down again.

One by one, the old people sat. Snow Goose stood, wearing only a thin undergarment that might have been stitched from gut. Her body under it, although *zaftig*, moved with practiced grace. Eviane's hands touched her own body self-consciously. She wanted to move like that. She remembered . . . faintly . . . a time when she had.

The girl writhed beseechingly, beckoning to each of them. Max Sands jumped grinning to his feet and began to dance around the fire, too close behind Snow Goose for Eviane's comfort.

Eviane stood, embarrassed in her underwear. She gritted her teeth and began to dance, moving with the flow of the pipes, the rattles and drums. Even though the musical implements seemed like relics from another, earlier time, they blended together in surprisingly complex and precise rhythm.

One at a time, the others stood. The pilot. Charlene. The Guardsman. Hebert the soldier. Half-naked they danced around the fire. And as they did, Eviane felt her body pulse to the music.

Her sense of self, of midcentury mid-America, began to fade. There was no formal ceremony, no verbal acknowledgment or speech, but she knew that the Inuit had accepted them, had welcomed the refugees into their family.

The long shadows played upon the walls, and the music, the exertion, and the swirling smoke began to weave their subtle magic. The refugees took their place around the fire, twisting and hopping. Eviane gasped heavily for breath, blind to her exhaustion, unmindful of her ungainly heaviness, lost in the sheer exhilaration of it all.

For Eviane it was total ecstasy, the very best that life had offered her in a long, long time.

Chapter Nine

BAPTIZED IN COMBAT

The world was blind with snow as Max Sands crawled out of the qasgiq. The frozen ground was rough on hands and knees. Other Adventurers popped out of the tunnel to sprawl gracelessly on the snow.

The sun was a pale disk daubed in watercolors upon a paler sky. Tiny flakes of ice flurried like flower petals driven by the wind.

Max stretched his back. He was cramped and sore.

A ragged chorus of barks split the air, and a dog sled appeared around the curve of the lodge, driven by an old woman. The six dogs pulling the sled described a semicircle, slowed to a crawl, and stopped. The sled carried one soot-stained crate from the plane and an additional pile of equipment.

Bowles and the Guardsman went to the sled. The Guardsman opened a sheathed knife and went to work on the crate. A slat creaked in protest, then pulled loose with a long, thin whine.

"Yeah!" Max hefted out one of the rifles, checked its action—long-forgotten ROTC training flashed to mind—then passed it to Orson.

The rifles were relayed hand to hand like fire brigade buckets. When the last weapon had been distributed, the National Guardsman balanced a gun in one big fist, then brandished it overhead. "Is there anyone who doesn't know how to use one of these?"

Some of the refugees paused, then raised uncertain hands.

"All right. These are Remington thirty-caliber gas-operated semiautomatic carbines—"

Max sidled over to Eviane, ready to lend assistance. She didn't need any. As the Guardsman called out instructions she worked with manic intensity, with a mixture of dread and fascination that was almost alarming to watch. During a pause in the instructions she relaxed, and then looked up at Max, through

Max, as if he wasn't there at all. The bullets in her hand were blanks, and she was not his enemy; but there was something in her eyes, something in the way she gripped the gun that made him feel queasy.

"—we don't know what we're heading into, but we do know that it's dangerous: we don't want to lose any of our own." There were sober nods of agreement from the others, but Eviane stared fixedly ahead, her eyes on the snow-blown horizon, or beyond.

Damn, she was really into this. Had she Gamed before, in the real Games? Once her hands closed around the rifle she didn't seem to want to release it. Her reluctance created a neat topological puzzle as she tried to pull on her backpack.

"Need a little help, there?" Max volunteered. "Why don't you let me hold that?"

She clutched the rifle defensively for a moment. He watched her face tighten and then reluctantly relax. "Yes. Thank you very much."

She handed him her rifle. She shrugged into her pack, bent, and fastened on her snowshoes. "Check me, will you?"

"Nothing looks broken from here. Maybe a closer look." He ran a finger along her shoulder.

A smile struggled with her businesslike expression, won for a moment, then fluttered nervously and died. "You're nice," she said shyly. "I hope we make it out of this."

"Stick with me, kid," he said, giving it his best Bogart. "I'm strong enough for both of us."

She took the rifle, twirled heel-toe, and was gone.

He knew he was pushing it. Bulky, flirtatious, helpful Max Sands. Some women seek a nonthreatening man. He could usually tell, but he couldn't tell with Eviane. Maybe she didn't know herself.

He could switch out of that "harmless" mode. He could do a Jekyll-Hyde and become "Mr. Mountain," but he didn't want to. God, he was tired of Mr. Mountain and his lavender leotards. Distantly, he heard a playful announcer singing about "purple Mountain's majesty—"

With a little help from Dream Park's magic, he just might retire that role forever.

Snow Goose knelt by the lead dogs to hug a muscular light gray husky with reddish highlights in his fur. They nuzzled each other like old friends.

Max hunkered down next to her, scratched the back of the dog's neck, peered out toward the horizon. The weather was clearing a bit, but a curtain of snow rolled across the horizon, reminding him of an Arizona dust storm.

Snow Goose said, "This is Takuka, the Red Bear."

"Hail, O Bear."

Red Bear sniffed at Max, found him mildly unobjectionable, and then turned back to adoring Snow Goose. She said, "He and Otter are our last lead dogs. All of the others just ciphered. Disappeared. Lost."

As if on cue, Red Bear whined disconsolately.

"We'll get 'em back. We'll get everyone back."

She nodded silently, then stood.

Most of the gear had been tightly packed onto the sled, then bound with tarps and oilskins. Antibiotics, coils of thin line, hard-weather gear, food. The dogs came to attention, shuffling and whining at Snow Goose impatiently, as if awaiting a signal.

Martin the Arctic Fox emerged from the qasgiq tunnel. Old age and despair seemed to have filled his joints with rust: his neck virtually creaked as he scanned them. He pulled a bag out after him.

He pulled out a fistful of little leather pouches on leather thongs. "Hang around your necks," he said. "You are *angakoks* now."

Again he reached into the bag. "These are things of power," he said. He pressed a bird's foot into Max's hand. Max took it, grimacing. "Owl claw. Give strong fists."

He gave a withered Caribou's ear to Bowles, who smiled and bowed. "Make you quick of hearing." He pulled a crumpled skin from the bag, opened it to show that it was crusted with black soot, and gave it to Kevin. "For strength. Soot is stronger than fire." For Charlene he had a swatch of white fur. "Sealskin. Hide you." Kevin whipped out his little computer and entered the new information soberly.

He moved along the Gamers until the bag was empty. Then Martin spoke to them all. "You from the hot countries are our final hope. If you cannot prevail, all is lost. I trust the Gods will grant you victory. Seek the Thunderbirds. Only they can take you to the underworld."

Snow Goose hugged her father. Captain Grant took his place at the sled, and cracked his whip once. The sled began to move. The huskies snapped the reins taut, straining against the inertia of the sled. Slowly, it began to slide across the field, toward a blank, wind-whipped horizon.

Some of the Adventurers were puffing, but none were falling back. Max was easily able to keep pace with the sled, staying abreast of Snow Goose. He asked, "What's next?"

She smiled enigmatically. "We're off for Seelumkadchluk, where the sky meets the sea. Daddy did a number for us, opened the path."

He peered out across the snow. It was as desolate as a salt flat, and not much more inviting. "I don't see anything special."

"You will."

"Okay. Then what? I still don't quite understand what we're supposed to do."

The wind was a faint, consistent howl around them. Hippogryph and Charlene Dula crunched through the snow to walk next to her.

"Daddy told you most of what I know. Somebody whacked Sedna out, and we have to undo it."

"Whacked her out?" Orson puffed as he quick-walked up next to them. "You talk funny for an Eskimo."

"Did you expect grunts and clicks? I have a master's in Cultural Anthro from Alaska State U, Nome." She cracked the whip again, humanely high above the backs of the trotting huskies. "That was before all of this began."

Orson seemed a little embarrassed, but Max jumped into the gap. "Cultural Anthro. I'd think you'd be somebody's class project. I'd love to read your thesis."

"It does make you kind of split-brained to grow up hearing all about the spirits and the Raven, and then go off to school. When they talked about Eskimo lore in the books they might as well be talking about the Great Pumpkin. I'm not sure where I really stood. I mean, I'd seen some stuff that would weird anyone out, but the books explained everything away, made it all sound so reasonable...

"Anyway, when everything came apart it was time to choose sides, and quick. Daddy thinks that I'm the best choice to help you guys survive." She paused, reflecting. "Rephrase: I'm the only choice. You've kind of run out of options, you know?"

Max was enchanted.

Orson puffed, "I think I know what's wrong with your dad."

"Yeah, he's sick," Snow Goose said thoughtfully. "And poor Ahk-lut, he went completely wacko. Some of the first generation, the Raven's children, they look like that. Something wrong with the way they were made, maybe."

"No!" Huff. "Max, I remembered something. Her dad said that talisman"—puff—"was a satellite that fell on Canada in the eighties?"

"Okay... why?"

"If it's the one I'm thinking about"—puff—"it had a nuclear plant aboard. If Martin and Akh-lut—"

"—are both suffering from radiation poisoning. Damn good, Orson!"

"Maybe that's where... magic comes from."

Snow Goose considered. "A powerful talisman is one that has traveled a long way. When I was just a cub, I saw a Swiss army knife that had been carried from Quebec, swapped over and over. Guy traded it for a bear fur and six cases of beer. Long nights. Plenty of time to party."

"Heh," Orson puffed. "That skyfall talisman... went round and round the Earth... hundreds of times." Puff; huff. "So we find the Lady Sedna. What do we do then? Or is that a secret?"

"We have to comb her hair."

"That doesn't sound very difficult."

"Well, Sedna is a very choosy lady. It has to be done just right."

"Great." Orson called back along the line. "Hey! Is there a beautician in the house?"

Max turned to look, and that sweeping glance revealed something he hadn't noticed before: the vista, which had stretched out endlessly only minutes before, was all beginning to change. He said, "The sun looks a little bit brighter. I don't get it. Why would the sun be brighter now?"

The sky had cleared too. The snow had subsided to flurries. Max was sweating in his fur parka, and there were no buttons. "Looks like the snow's letting up."

Orson said, "So we comb Sedna's hair. Then what?"

Snow Goose examined Orson with amusement. "You know, you'll probably be a lot happier if you think a little bit less about what happens later, and check out what's happening now. This isn't exactly safe, and if you don't stay on top of it you're going to end up the world's pinkest Popsicle."

The dogs trotted heartily onward, crunching the snow underneath the treads. A faint cawing sound grew swiftly louder. Max whipped his head up as a flock of geese arced across the sky, barely a stone's throw away. He quickly counted a dozen birds, and there might have been more.

"*Branta canadensis*," Snow Goose smiled sadly. "Tuutangayak. My Canadian namesake. I used to love them. Almost extinct, now. My brother..." She paused, swallowed. "Ahk-lut taught me all about the animals. That was a long time ago."

Orson saw an opening, and went for it. "He's about thirty years older than you?"

"Just about. Daddy's had three wives... that he'll cop to."

The birds swept south and disappeared into a bank of clouds. Snow Goose followed them with a wistful gaze.

It was remarkably easy to get into the spirit of it, to play to the hidden cameras. Max laid a sympathetic hand on her shoulder. "We'll fix things, don't worry."

"Worry for yourself—it's your world on the chopping block."

The pilot cracked the whip, picking up the pace slightly. Behind him, the refugees had begun to huff.

The snowshoes crunched step after step, rasping as the snow became thinner underfoot. Max stared at his feet, and then at Snow Goose in astonishment. "Dirt! I saw dirt! I was starting to think I'd never see dirt again!"

"Check behind your ears," Orson hissed.

The dog sled dragged across the brown patches, slowed by friction. As the snow began to recede, Snow Goose reached down, flipped the sled blades up, and replaced them with wheels. The cart wheels bumped against what he could now see was a rude path that they had followed under the snow.

The first small plants were twisting their way up through the permafrost, cracking their way through delicate rivulets of ice. Max plucked one up, rubbed a tiny leaf between two fingers, and chewed it as he walked along. The sun was warmer and brighter now, and he reveled in it. He had taken that golden disk for granted, as most people did, and as it blazed anew an indefinable depression lifted from his spirits.

He dropped back until he was shoulder to shoulder with Eviane. Her eyes were slitted, and she was watching everything around her like a nervous tiger. Something in her gaze resurrected unanswered questions. "Do you know anything about all of this that you're not telling? Picked up on a clue or something? You're so quiet that I can't help but think that you've got a little hint for old Max."

Her answering smile was quizzical. "Clue? I'm just trying to survive, like the rest of us."

"I still get the feeling that I should stick with you. Does that make any sense?"

She moved a half-step away.

"You don't mind, do you?"

"Ah . . . no."

"Great."

He started to—

Something writhed against his back, as if a sizable snake had slipped down his shirt.

His shoulders arched, and he bellowed. He reached back, clawing for the alien thing attaching itself to his shoulder blades, hooked claws reaching for his heart, fangs gnashing for his spine . . .

Something hard and cool moved in his grip. He pulled it around in front, ready for the worst horror imaginable. Ready for anything but what he saw.

"My rifle?" It wiggled in his hands, moving as if it had become a living thing. He held it out from himself, watching with awed fascination. The rifle was barely recognizable and still stretching, narrowing, taking on a new configuration under his very hands.

The barrel elongated, sharpened. The front sight flattened and the bore closed, flattened into a triangular shape. The framework butt had closed into a tube.

The Remington had become a long, barbed harpoon.

Max suddenly noticed the growing sounds of dismay behind him. The entire group was chattering excitedly, watching each other's rifles change into spears and clubs.

Hippogryph's rifle was now an older gun, a flintlock! A brightly glowing object appeared on the ground in front of him. Hippogryph scooped it up, delighted. "Looks like a magical powder horn!"

In almost as magical a transformation, the group which had been somewhat subdued and quiet was suddenly in the air, whooping their approval.

"Do you believe in maaa-gic?" Kevin sang, and his skinny body pranced and twirled like a crazed scarecrow. Trianna caught one of his hands and swung him around once. When his feet brushed the ground she set him afoot and composed herself in improbable dignity.

Kevin's ears were red, and he stared at her even after she turned away. *Hmmm?* To Max it looked like ... well, young lust, at least.

Suddenly Max noticed Eviane's expression and the Remington that she still held in her hands. Eviane's weapon remained a rifle. For the moment before her face went quite neutral, she'd looked ... grief-stricken? Bereaved?

Several rifles remained unchanged. Why? The spirits must be preparing some, but not all, for situations where spears or clubs would be needed instead.

Shoot a seal with a rifle and it slips back into the water. A tethered harpoon might be more appropriate.

Then again ... would some unnamed ghastly rather face a primitive spear than a rifle? If so, then their fighting efficiency had just been cut almost in half ...

That thought having crossed his mind, Max sobered up and kept his eyes open.

They kept moving. The National Guardsman was watching, running back and forth along the line, almost like a Rottweiler on extreme alert. His rifle had transformed, and he looked so absurd carrying a war club at port arms that it was all Max could do to keep from laughing out loud.

Maybe because of the increased warmth, or perhaps because of the pace of their trek, Max was beginning to feel out of breath. He would have been embarrassed to ask for a halt ... and in all his life he had never needed to. He simply waited.

"Snow Goose!" Orson gasped, very predictably. "Anyone! For God's sake ... take a break!"

Snow Goose ignored him for a while, her eyes on the horizon. Finally, she said, "Daddy said there's a frozen lake up ahead. Warm as it is this side of Seelumkadchluk, it might not be frozen anymore, but that just makes it better for us."

The snow was receding, and Max could see hills now, and splotches of brown and grass-green spreading. An arctic hare, its blotches of pale brown conspicuous against this new backdrop, poked its head at them curiously. Its ears twitched, and it sprinted across the hill.

Fatigue was a dull, leaden throbbing now, balanced by a growing awareness of hunger. He hadn't really realized how starved he was. At the end of this trek there would be a break, with fresh water and food. He scanned the sled as it slid along, its wheels furrowing the icy ground. What was in those packages? Tinned meat? Tinned cake?

Hmmm. Army rations had been a joke since Hannibal, but Max loved the pound cake in army surplus survival kits. He hoped that there was an envelope of that in there. Was it likely, in this crowd?

Thin broth, a lettuce leaf, six spaghetti noodles with no sauce. Bet on it. They'd told him the Fat Ripper didn't exactly starve the weight off. Run it off, that they might do. But no beer...

"No cake," he murmured.

"And," Trianna said, in tune with the flow of his thoughts, "no lasagna or steak Diane or noodles Romanoff, and as for the crepes Suzette, forget it."

"My very thoughts."

Her laugh was musical. Without projecting it, this woman had more sexual amperage than the other three combined. She was holding it leashed: Max was getting no direct signals.

"Playing menus in my head is an old game," she sighed. "It's more fun than thinking about how tired I am."

She was too pretty not to give it a try. "Do you play any other games?"

She gave him a playful chuck with her elbow and dropped further back in line.

Birds called somewhere, although the horizon was still clear ...no, wait—there, at the edge of the sky he saw a few dark shapes, coming closer until for a glorious few seconds the entire sky was filled with birds, a gigantic flock that divided the sky with wing and call. The clouds were more golden and a wider gray, moving slowly across the sky. The sun was burning higher and brighter, hotter, almost as bright as a normal sun.

Nice. He was falling into Dream Park reality. It was becoming easy to distract himself with the teeming sky, the chunky poncho-wearing Adventurers, and rifles twisted into bizarre variants of spears and clubs...it was easy to slip into the dream, and believe that they were on their way to a great adventure. And ignore Orson's whimpering. Would a real Adventure be this tiring?

Worse! Dream Park went easy on the Fat Rippers.

The path twisted up the low rise of a hill. His ankle turned on the gravel. He slipped and almost fell, but caught his balance and straightened up again with Eviane's hand on his elbow. He looked at her and she looked away quickly, but the moment of contact was blistering.

There: another distraction from hunger. Amazing. He walked a little behind her and wondered when they were going to get a break. A nice, hour-long break, and a chance to sit with Eviane and schmooze.

He liked her, without knowing exactly why. Mystery woman? Nothing like curling up with a good mystery...

At the top of the hillock they looked down on a shallow valley and a lake. The air was so warm now that some of the Gamers were taking off their jackets. Red Bear seemed overjoyed that the sled was pulling itself now, and ran arfing toward the distant lake.

The Gamers broke into a run. The lake swelled up in their sight surrounded by reeds and tall grass. Before they went too many more steps, Grant stopped them. "Wait! Something's wrong here."

Orson wasn't the only one who groaned. But Kevin ran up puffing to the front of the sled, freckled face burning with curiosity. "Something like what?" His nose twitched as he scanned the lake ahead. He puffed out his chest, and glanced sideways at Trianna.

"I can feel something wrong. I don't know how."

Snow Goose knelt down, took a closer look at the ground. "Something scary big has moved through here, and recently."

The group gathered at the lip of the hill, gazing down as the wind blew thinly around them. Yeah, the ground had a roiled look, but wouldn't melting and refreezing frost do that? Snow Goose chewed on her lip, then shook her head. The waters of the lake reflected the sun, choppy wind-blown swells rolling up to lap at the shallows and the reeds.

"Oh, nuts," Grant said finally. "Maybe I'm just being paranoid."

The surface of the lake erupted, and fifteen tons of madness intruded on their world.

It burst up, spouting, whistling like a blue and white nuke missile. It hung in the air an impossible moment, a thousand gallons of water raining from its back. With a roar that shook the earth, it slammed back into the lake.

Max's mind worked at Mach speed, trying to correlate. *This is a joke. This is a freakin' joke! You don't find orcas in lakes, f'chrissakes!*

Water splashed away from the immense blue and white mass.

The killer whale lunged again, but forward. The thud shook the earth. The whale had beached itself.

With motions reminiscent of a legless, armless man crawling toward a hated enemy, the whale pulled itself out of the water and humped up onto dry land. Wait: there were arms! A gnarled pair of tree-trunk-sized human arms projected from the body of the beast. Fingers as thick as thighs gouged furrows in the ground as it lifted its head and bellowed in rage.

"Jesus Christ!" Grant screamed, and tumbled off his sled as it slid down almost into the orca's mouth. The sled dogs howled their terror. They tried to run in different directions. The reins held them in place.

The creature was on Red Bear and Otter in a moment, grinning and deadly, its rows of lethal teeth gleaming.

The refugees were scattered across the slope as the beast finished making puppy chow out of the huskies. Eviane had her gun up and firing faster than anyone else. Blood and water sprayed from the beast's hide. Shucking his paralysis, Grant yelled: "Dammit! Fire at will!"

He dropped to one knee and began placing careful shots into the whale as it made a bloody mess of the last of the pilot's huskies.

It noticed him.

It came straight at the pilot with dreadful, unanticipated speed, humping across the ground on its stubby, grotesquely muscled human arms. Captain Grant stood his ground. Those who still had rifles began to fire, and more red splotches opened up on the whale's flank. It twitched but didn't slow.

Hippogryph was running toward it, zigzagging. His flintlock would only have one bullet.

Then the whale had reached the pilot, thirty times his size with a mouthful of razors. Grant shrieked as the teeth closed on him, ripped him into pieces, and swallowed him in an eternity that couldn't have lasted more than six seconds.

The guns were useless. Snow Goose pulled at Max's arm. "Harpoon! Use your harpoon!"

He had almost forgotten that he held it. If rifles didn't work, why would a harpoon?

Because it's magic, you idiot. He hefted the twisted spear and tried to find a balance. What had he ever done that could prepare him for this? Pitch softball? Throw darts maybe?

The beast's next action ended his hesitancy. It reared about,

managed somehow to give the impression of turning a neck that
wasn't there, and heaved itself directly at him.

Max let fly as the creature came within single-lunge distance.
The spear impacted in the dome of its head.

Instead of charging, the creature screamed in palpable agony.
It flinched back. The other refugees howled their encouragement
and let fly with their weapons. Spears and war clubs sailed true,
and barbed the monster's hide until it ran with blood. As it turned
broadside Hippogryph fired point-blank. The beast shuddered and
howled its misery, spraying black fluid from its spout-hole.

It fled for the safety of its lake. It rolled once in an attempt to
rake the spears from its body. Weapons came free, clattering to
the ground covered in whale blood. The spears and spiked clubs,
baptized in combat, glowed with power. They sparkled green and
red, colors arcing from weapon to weapon like tame auroras.

The land whale smashed back into the water. A huge wave
expanded outward. When it subsided the creature was gone. Red
boiled to the surface, and dissipated, and left the water clear.

Quietly at first, they walked dazedly over the site of the combat and gathered up the weapons. Max found his harpoon in the
rubble, and hoisted it. It seemed different somehow. It tingled to
the touch, and the white glow crawled down the length of the
spear and onto his arm. The tingling grew more intense.

Bowles was the first to scream in triumph, lifting his war club
to the sky. His voice was drowned in a dozen others.

"We did it!" Orson cried. He brandished a glowing spear:
longer than Max's harpoon, with a smaller, flatter head.

"I don't get it," Snow Goose said.

Orson looked around, irritated. Snow Goose was a guide: she
was supposed to get it. "Now what?"

"That was a land whale. We should be dead now. All we had
were Daddy's talismans, and they were the leftovers, the weakest
of the lot. Why aren't we . . ." She paused, puzzling darkly.

Orson grinned. "We've got our own talismans. When you said
that a good talisman gets its magic from—wup!"

They were dancing, falling. The land shuddered and roared.
Max was on his hands and knees, but he saw the earth split and a
shaggy, writhing wormlike shape rise questing into the light not
twelve feet away.

Snow Goose's face paled. She murmured, "Now, just a
damn—" then changed her mind and screamed, "Kogukhpuk!"

Max stalked it, spear held ready. The snake wasn't big; no

more than three meters were showing. Pythons came larger than that.

Then the worm-shape trumpeted with pachydermic fury. The ground roared and crumbled above a great shaggy skull. The creature heaved the ground up and away with such ease that it seemed capable of shouldering the very heavens aside. Tiny eyes glared. The rest of it climbed free of the earth, twelve feet tall and twenty feet long, shaggy brownish fur almost draping the ground, worn and cracked tusks curling up and around like the bow of a sousaphone.

"A mammoth! A goddamned mammoth! But—" was all that the Guardsman had time to say, and then it was on him and—

—and past. It shuddered as if in agony, twitching and throwing its head back and forth. Trumpeting, it ignored the Guardsman and went straight for Eviane.

She was firing steadily. At the last instant she turned to run. The beast reared up and landed on her with both front feet. She disappeared in a thundering avalanche of dust, and was just gone.

For two or three seconds the mammoth stood like a stop-motion model, and shimmied. Max could almost hear gears hum . . . but Max was in motion, running to get past the great shield of its head, then screaming as he hurled his harpoon into its side, behind the short ribs, aimed at the heart.

The spear went through it, sailed out the other side, and clattered audibly to the ground.

The mammoth flickered back and forth as if incapable of making up its mind. Other Adventurers were attacking. Bowles whacked effortlessly through its leg with a war club . . . and suddenly it was in motion again. It flailed at Bowles with its trunk, then, with blood streaming from a dozen wounds, it crumpled to the ground and lay sagging like a half-empty rag doll.

Max looked at Snow Goose, and her face was drop-jawed silly. The Guardsman looked the same.

What in the hell?

The mammoth sagged further. It was dissolving. Within a minute it had become dust and bones, then nothing but dust. The torn ground around it healed, until there was no trace that something singular had happened.

And where Eviane had stood, there was no blood, no clothing, nothing but flattened earth. As if she had never existed at all.

"Oh, shit rocks," Snow Goose said, blanching. "She's dead."

"What?"

"She's dead. I..." Snow Goose looked up, bewildered, at twenty-six pairs of bewildered eyes. She said, "The burrowing mammoth has claimed her for his own. T-tonight we mourn." The formal words sounded utterly alien in her mouth. She seemed uncertain of her next word or move. "I...I guess we can camp here. We ran it off. We should be safe now..."

With equal uncertainty, the others shucked their packs. Max distinctly heard the Guardsman mutter, "Well, if that don't beat all—" before their eyes met. The Guardsman was an Actor... wasn't he? But the consternation in his face was real.

As for Max, it was as if the fates, or Dream Park, had promised him Eviane and then reneged.

He prepared to make camp. What else could he do? But something had happened, even if he couldn't figure out precisely what. Was it an accident, or a glitch in the programming, or more goddamn clues?

For once, the guides seemed more shaken than the Gamers!

Chapter Ten

I'VE HAD DATES LIKE YOU

Pins of fire leavened the darkness. That one, much brighter than the rest, had to be the sun. There was little else to catch the eye . . . but here was a tiny twinkling point; there, another; there, a tumbling snowball marked with black fissures. Alex Griffin's video wall was open to the realm of the protocomets.

Weird skirling music floated in and out, low in the background. A tiny voice spoke of billions of iceballs a few kilometers in diameter, spaced as far apart as Earth and sun, growing sparser yet as the sun dwindled aft. Compared to the inner solar system, the Oort Cloud was nearly as empty as interstellar space.

The view zoomed in on a world banded in black and dull reds, nested in a wide ring: Nemesis, a giant planet in a wide eccentric orbit, whose mass periodically hurled flurries of comets into the inner solar system. Nemesis was impure fiction. There was reason to think there might be a Nemesis, a world too distant to have been found by probes or telescopes.

The Oort Cloud presentation must have been infinitely more impressive in Gaming A this morning. Even so, the illusion was so deep and complete that Alex felt as if he and Millicent were sitting sideways above a pit. It surely had Millicent's attention. Her hands moved like independent entities, bringing lobster to her mouth while comets buzzed her in the video wall.

He enjoyed watching her like that, in profile. He saw African and Spanish and English in her features, a recipe that brewed an almost irresistible meld of earthiness and intelligence. She was just what he needed to salve the day's frustrations. But even if the doctor had prescribed her, the nurse still had to agree to the treatment . . .

Words from the screen caught his attention. "—probes will be driven by solar sails, powered by tremendous lasers stationed on Earth's moon—"

"That bothered me," he said.

Millicent looked at him. "Why?"

"I eavesdropped on our guests. They weren't saying anything, but I saw their faces. Some of the Arabs and Brazilians, they don't care about the comets *or* Mars. They want those terrawatt lasers. If a terror-monger could get control of one of those, he could fry Tehran or São Paulo before Earth could launch a ship."

"Not your department," Millicent said. "Anyway, I can't picture a terror-monger with enough schooling to run one."

"Don't kid yourself. A lot of them are sending their kids off to college. MIT. Cambridge. Intelligence and fanaticism live in two overlapping worlds. Life isn't a sliding scale, where you have single-minded fanatics on one end, and intelligent people on the other. Some of us can be very single-minded about things which are purely emotional..."

She said, "We've been moving asteroids for thirty years, and no one's heaved one at us yet."

"No. Thirty years, right? Sixteen asteroids, and three more on their way with Falling Angel crews? That's not many. One asteroid strike can ruin your whole day."

"Brrr. You're rather grim tonight, aren't you?"

Definitely the wrong mood. He reached across the table to squeeze her wrist; which took some care, because she was holding a forkful of scalloped potatoes. "Sorry. All work and no play makes Jack et cetera."

Millicent smiled. "No play at all? That's my Alex."

"If I don't invite the occasional young, beautiful account executive to my humble abode, I'd never find surcease of sorrow." He put on his sincerest expression. "One of the burdens of power is that Communications can beep me twenty-five hours a day. One of the advantages of a loyal staff is that they've promised me the night off, if it's humanly possible."

She sipped at her wine, peering at him over the edge of the glass. Her eyes were alight with mischief. "We can hope, can't we?"

Does that mean yes? He interpreted it as a good strong "maybe" and decided to back off, soft-pedal, and make another approach in a minute or two.

Millicent sensed the mood change, flowed with it. She cracked open a lobster claw with sudden force. "How's Marty doing?"

"He's keeping up. He looks like the point man in a Zimbabwe

expedition. They've got him carrying a flintlock, for Christ's sake."

"Oh, Alex... sometimes it's so easy for me to get lost in the accounts and the computers that... I guess I just miss Security. A lot more craziness."

"Yeah... but you have a lot more talent than we could hold back. I'm glad you made it out."

She sighed. "And Marty's still playing games."

"That's Marty."

"Well. I'm glad you recommended me."

"It would have been criminal not to." He found himself feeling slightly warmish. She lowered her eyes, and began pushing potatoes around the plate, doodling her fork with great intensity. Which smile was that blossoming...?

"Ah, Alex..."

BRRRRRNG!

"I'd hoped," he said, "they'd keep that thing off until eight tomorrow."

Millicent's smile broadened. "No rest for the wicked."

"I've been on duty for twenty hours straight. Millicent, I'm plagued with these things called 'griffins,' nasty little nocturnal animals that only come out at night. They usually"—BRRRNNGG!—"manage to wake up just about the time that my mating cycle is running riot. I remember sex. Why, back in naught-six—" BRRRRNG!

"Alex, the beeper."

"Aye aye. Griffin. Telephone." The comets vanished, replaced by the smooth round face of Dwight Welles. Twenty-four-year-old Dwight Welles was senior computer tech for all of Dream Park, a man whose four-poster at Cowles Modular saw him far less than his cot at Research and Development.

"What's up, Dwight?"

"Griff, we got a problem here."

More Arab madness? "Tell me."

"Alex, somebody's messed with my program for the Fimbulwinter Game. I know I got all of the bugs out of it—"

"Hold it hold it hold it. Tell me what happened first."

"Somebody got killed out of the Game."

Drown me! "What? How—" Suddenly he felt very foolish. "Sorry. Killed out. Right. My heart will return to normal presently." He thought for a minute. "I thought none of the Gamers got killed out of Fat Rippers."

"Not for the first two days. Definite glitch."

"A glitch. Hmmm. It wasn't Charlene Dula, was it? Or Marty?"

"No."

Then it wasn't really a Security matter. "So? Don't you leave room for random—"

"Random events? *Sure* we leave room for random events, but you don't understand. It wasn't 'one of those freak things.' It wasn't an accident. A monster came up out of sequence. We call it a 'burrowing mammoth.' According to legend, they die on contact with air. This one lived long enough to target and kill a Gamer. It shouldn't have been possible. The thing hunted her. I want to know who's been tampering with my friggin' program."

The other line was beeping now, and Millicent was suddenly all business. "Alex, should I . . . ?"

"No, no, wait . . ." Dwight Welles's voice muted as the second line flashed to life. The screen divided into two, and on the other side was Dr. Vail. He seemed tight, tired, agitated.

"Mr. Griffin, something unusual has happened here."

"I'm on it. Somebody has gotten killed out of the Game."

"Hah! If that was all. The problem is that the Gamer who was killed out is coming apart! "

"I'd be a little pissed myself."

Vail shook his head. "Watch."

The screen split again. The new entry was a chunky redheaded woman. Her gaze was all daggers as she studied first Vail, and then a slender Japanese nurse. "I don't know why or how you did this, but I know this is a trick," she said. Griffin recoiled from the raw hatred in her voice. "Tell Ahk-lut he'll get nothing from me, do you understand? Nothing! You have warmth here, and food. People are starving by the millions, and it's your doing."

Ahk-lut?

"Miss Rivers." Vail's recorded tones were carefully soothing. "The Fimbulwinter Game is just that, a Game. There was an accident, and you were killed out. Now, we are prepared to re-fund—"

Her face twisted with anger, and for a moment, Griffin heard martial music in the air. He looked for insanity, but saw only righteous wrath. In that moment she was beautiful, a Valkyrie, a leopard protecting her young. "You call the death of civilization a 'Game'? You call the slaughter of millions an 'accident'? You wait. My people will come for me. They'll come!" She paused, and her next words were delivered with lethal calm. "Unless I get you first."

The recorded image froze, and then the real-time Vail returned.

Alex was on his feet. "I'll be right down there." He clicked that part of the screen off. "Dwight. Are you there?"

"I'm here."

"I'm coming right in. No, wait. First, pipe the records in on the office com line. I want to see what happened to this Rivers. Then I'll come."

He looked at Millicent. "Damn, I'm so sorry about dinner—"

"I've eaten it, Griff."

"Oh. Yeah. You want to go home, or come with?"

"Can I come with? Sounds like old times."

"Glad to have you. Got a bad feeling about this."

He beeped for a shuttle, and one was waiting at the rail by the time his side door hissed shut. The hatch lifted, and he and Millicent scooted in. The pressure of her thigh against his was more comforting than stimulating. His mind was already on the job ahead.

Cowles Modular Community, dwindling behind the shuttle, looked to Alex like a spreading clump of young mushrooms. Irregular, eccentric, but very organic. The people who worked for Dream Park had a lot of respect for the environment, for the way things fit together, for elegance. Something about this action, the way Michelle Rivers had been yanked unceremoniously from the Game, was jarringly inelegant.

By the time that the Modular Community had faded into the distance, Millicent had collected her thoughts.

"Ah . . . if it's not a glitch, and Welles seems certain that it's not a glitch, then . . . what is it?"

"A glitch. People who say that they have all the bugs usually haven't turned over enough rocks. What do you think?"

"I think you sound like a man trying to convince himself."

The shuttle sank into the labyrinth beneath the largest entertainment complex in the world. And kept sinking, three stories deep. There, hidden beneath the surface, were the concrete, steel, and plastic guts of the Park. No one mind knew all of the thousands of turnings, the hundreds of miles of tunnels. Here were the transportation systems, sewage systems, food networks, walkways, slideways; the routes for cars, trucks, transports, the monorails; the conduits that kept the water and electricity flowing, the people moving. Here were millions of feet of superconducting wire, steel pipe, PVC tubing, and fiber optic cable. As they slid along in the shuttle, passing through the center of the labyrinth, endless connecting corridors stretching off in all directions like Krell tunnels, Dream Park felt more myth than reality. Who was to say that there weren't trolls in those tunnels, demons in those depths? Perhaps the real illusion of Dream Park was the pretense of technology.

The shuttle eased to a stop. They hopped out and took three steps to the elevator. The sealed tube rose swiftly to the seventh floor of the security building.

His office was a storm-struck anthill. Cary McGivvon met him at the door with a stack of printouts, their initial security file on Michelle Rivers. The flat photo showed intensely red hair around a pale, heavily freckled face, very plump, with high cheekbones under the padding. The girl was trying to look angry, or competent, or dangerous. She was none of those, really. To Griffin's eye she seemed depressingly young and plain.

"Wasn't she with Ambassador Arbenz's niece? Christ—no wonder we've got so little on her."

Cary sniffed. "Charlene Dula sneaked her buddy in on a diplomatic pass. We didn't match her 'Michelle Rivers' name with anything in our files, computer just assumed she was a first-timer."

"Great," Alex said. "But everyone in the Game went through Psych. Why the hell didn't they catch this looney tune?" She was *short*. One look would tell anyone: this was no old friend from the low-gravity places. This was someone the Ambassador's niece had met on Earth, maybe a terrorist's plant, and they'd want to examine her brain.

"No answers yet." Cary seemed almost defensive. "It just happened, Griff."

"Sorry, Cary. Honest. She got through *me* somehow too. That damned diplomatic override." He slammed his hand down on the desk hard enough to scatter papers. "Why the hell didn't we catch her?"

"She has a real Social Security number. She was clean. She'd worked as a clerical assistant in Montana, spent some time in a hospital in Utah, applied for credit with NipponAmericard." She cleared her throat uncomfortably. "It's starting to look like some of her previous history might have been...falsified." Cary brightened. "We matched her fingerprints, though."

"Fingerprints?" Millicent asked. You always try fingerprints, just because it's easy, but it's not supposed to work. "Does she have a police record?"

"No, she has no record at all, but she's been here before. We had trouble with her under the name 'Michelle Sturgeon.'"

Alex's ears perked up. "What kind of trouble?"

"Damned if I know. It's in a sealed file. Haven't been able to find the access code."

"Who sealed it?"

"Harmony."

"Did you get in touch with him?"

"He hasn't answered his beep, Griff."

"Play it for me again. The death scene."

Cary punched her console and the wall disappeared. Griffin saw the mammoth rise from the earth, the attack, heard the screaming, felt his own adrenaline pump. He saw the flicker as the monster stalked and killed the redhead.

"Hate to meet that glitch in the dark," Dr. Vail said, just behind him.

Vail was sipping at a cup of coffee. The aroma was heavenly. Alex took odd satisfaction that Vail didn't look quite so damned hearty at eleven at night. "Glad you made it, Doc. Yeah, I don't believe it either."

"It's worse," Cary said glumly. "We have an Actor stranded in the game. What's going on in there?"

"Stranded . . . right. The monster did stalk her, it's obvious. Was it supposed to stalk somebody else? Because—"

"Yes, Yarnall, the National Guardsman, later tonight. Now he's in there with no script. Mr. Griffin, he's a recovering alcoholic. He's in there as an Actor, but it was supposed to be therapy too. This Game, we're watching the Actors as well as the Gamers."

Vail said, "Maybe we can work on a player's head better if he thinks he knows the script. It's worth a try, and we're trying it this run."

"What are the other Gamers doing? I mean, right now."

"Eating," Vail said. "In an ordinary Game this would be their down time, their rest and meal time. Because this is a Fat Ripper, we're using this to program. The Game is still live, it's just a different phase."

"Show me."

The Gamers were all sitting around eating, and it was a queer spectacle indeed, reminiscent of nothing if not the banquet sequence at the end of *Through the Looking-Glass*. The food on their plates was . . . alive. It was smiling at them, occasionally talking back to them. Some Gamers seemed to have adjusted; others had pushed their plates aside, appetite vanished.

The computer was coding and recognizing the players so that their names and ID numbers appeared below their images.

Yarnall was quiet. He seemed to be uneasy, restless, and Griffin could understand why. He should have been home by now. On the other hand, salary-wise he was probably on Golden Time.

Marty and Charlene Dula were sharing a flat-topped rock for a table. They seemed companionable enough, but didn't have much to say to each other.

A hefty guy named Max Sands looked uncomfortable too. He kept casting eyes at one of the Dream Park temporary Actors: Gwen Ryder Norliss, an Actress in the Game. She was garbed as an Eskimo, and she was sitting next to a warrior with the same last name . . . a husband. Sands would be suffering from thwarted lust. Griffin could sympathize.

He keyed in the audio.

Orson Sands: "The thing is, we're carrying gear from Falling Angel. The frames in some of our backpacks, the medicines, this"—he hefted a spool of thin line—"that Eviane was carrying: it's all magical. It's all been run around the world enough times to make the Cabal sick with envy."

Gwen Ryder: "That's wonderful, but don't underestimate the Cabal."

Kevin Titus was the skinniest one out there. Alex winced at the sharpness of cheekbones under tightly stretched skin. Bone-thin fingers leafed through a somewhat dog-eared folder: "Did you see this? My dossier has changed. It read different this morning."

Someone said, "You're crazy." But there was a brief flurry of files, and yelps of amusement as the Gamers discovered that the print in every file had miraculously changed.

Kevin brayed victoriously. "Switched! Mine talks about Pewitu, taboos. I can't kill a seal until it's on the land." He pulled a hand-held computer from an inner pocket, started one-finger typing on it. "Sounds easy enough," he said distractedly. "What about you, Trianna?"

There was a lot of energy in that glance. Trianna didn't seem to notice. "My friendly-ghost assistant is named Kaspar. Clerk from Oregon, white, died in Nome in 1910. Shot. I mustn't eat eggs, but I can eat the birds after they hatch. Yucko! If we follow these taboos, do you think we can win?"

She was looking at Johnny Welsh, but Kevin answered. "Why not? We kicked their butts first time we saw 'em. We'll do it again." He tucked his computer away.

Max: "But did Eviane break a taboo or something? I don't understand why it went after her like that."

As he talked, Max cut into what looked like a swordfish steak, and it squealed on his plate. A face formed in the grain of the steak, and said, "Will you please pay attention to me? Try not to talk so much while you're eating? Do you have any idea how irritating it is to be eaten by somebody who doesn't pay any attention to you?"

Johnny Welsh cocked an eyebrow at Max's plate. "I've had dates like you."

Trianna hit him in the side of the head with a balled napkin.

Max glared at his swordfish. "Now listen. We had a fight. You lost."

"That's no excuse for rudeness. I died to keep you alive, and one day you will die to feed my ancestors. Think about it, mister."

Alice, pudding! Pudding, Alice! Remove the Pudding!

The campfire conversation began to chill.

Vail chuckled maliciously. "A perfect example. It is unconscious and emotional ingestion of food, drugs, alcohol, whatever —for other than conscious motivations, that gets people most deeply in trouble. The more respectful attention you pay to your body and the things you put in it, the less likely you are to abuse it."

"That's really interesting, but not what I need." Alex wished Vail would stop waving his coffee around. The smell was driving him nuts. Then again, Dream Park's mad psychiatrist might be ghoulish enough to do it deliberately, studying Griffin's conditioned responses.

Alex gritted his teeth and punched in Marty's "silent" code, knowing that a steady vibratory trill would alert the security man.

Hippogryph waited a few seconds and then got up and moved away from the others. He walked toward where a line of scrubby bushes shaped a crescent moon; but he turned aside before he reached it. The curve of the hill hid him when he took out his communications kit.

"Marty. What happened out there with this Eviane woman?"

"She was stomped by a ghastly. Griff, we just lost somebody. It's no big thing."

"Marty, you don't get it. No one is supposed to be killed out of a Fat Ripper!"

Beat. "What?"

"This isn't a Game for points. You read the material. This is a Game to teach people lessons. Why should she get killed out? She didn't make a mistake. Later on you'll have opportunities to get killed out if you make a mistake, but not now. What point would there be?"

"I . . . all right, I see the logic. I suppose this is a secret?"

"You bet. We don't want everybody knowing we have a problem."

Marty must have heard the impatience in his voice. "I'm slow catching up, boss. They ran me half to death."

In truth, Marty looked exhausted. It would not do to forget that others besides Alex Griffin might be having problems. "How are you, Marty? Are you going to get through this?"

"We warriors will carry out our duty, O Griffin. Besides, the worst part must be over. Have you been watching, Griff?"

He hadn't, but Marty would surely expect him to. "A little."

"That scene in the sauna, the smokehouse? Most of us are overweight, Griff, and we all look like it with our clothes off, and I looked just like them. I felt so . . . fat."

"Any sign of trouble? Aside from terminal embarrassment, I mean . . . ?"

"No. Nobody's trying to off Ambassador Arbenz's niece, far as I can tell. Griff, it's hard to tell what's funny in this environment. I should have been told that we can't be killed out."

"I wasn't told till this morning. I might have told you, and then you'd have been too relaxed. You'll *be* too relaxed, unless you watch yourself."

"So how did it happen to Eviane?"

"The one thing that I do know is that Eviane—her real name is Michelle Sturgeon—was in Dream Park before, and her file has been sealed."

"Well, who sealed it?"

"Harmony. I'm going to have to take it up with him. I don't know what's going on."

"Maybe Harmony kicked her out of the Game."

"I don't think so. He wouldn't have interfered without talking to me. Even so it's awfully queer . . . and clumsy."

"Clumsy. So, what are you going to do with her?"

Griffin looked at the picture of Michelle Sturgeon, smiling and happy in the file, contrasted it with the pudgier, angrier woman who had challenged Vail and his nurse: *"Unless I get you first . . ."*

"I'd . . . better talk to Harmony," he said finally. "I guess it's time I did just exactly that."

Chapter Eleven

HIGH FINANCE

For twenty-seven minutes Harmony had ignored his personal pager. Cary McGivvon looked at Alex expectantly, her fingers floating above the red button on her keyboard. "Should I try the priority override?"

"No... even Harmony has a personal life. I tell you what." He moved around behind her, hands resting lightly on her shoulders. "Give me a movement scan. Tell me the last time his personal code passed one of the checkpoints. Let's be sure he's still inside the Park."

She ran the scan. There was a brief flicker of schematics, and the outline of the entire structure of Dream Park appeared in the wall. A sixteen-hundred-acre rotating pie studded with towers and arcs, the skeletal outlines of roller coasters and dropshafts, the single long loop of the Gravity Whip, the facades of thousands of rides, exhibits, "experiences," shops, stages, mini-hotels, restaurants, tram and train stations, security and information kiosks, and more street vendors than anyone could count. Code colors red, blue, green, and finally executive silver flashed. Thirty-seven hundred and twelve personal checkpoints flashed negative.

"His beeper is still in his office, Griff. He's inside the grid."

Alex liked this less by the moment. "Well... why in the world wouldn't he answer the page...?"

An unpleasant suspicion niggled at the back of his mind. "Get his medivac channel. Get a complete scan."

Millicent jumped. "Chief... ah, Griff, that's personal space."

Cary nodded. "I don't have clearance for that."

Alex fished a flat clear-plastic card out of his wallet. "I do. Override it."

"All right." She slipped Alex's card into a narrow slot on her console, and waited a moment as the wall began to fill with alphanumerics. "Well . . . pulse rate is ninety-eight . . . it's erratic, blood pressure high, skin temperature low. He's very agitated, Griff. Something's wrong."

Cary had discreetly omitted mention of Harmony's alcohol level. It was sky-high.

Alex drummed thick fingers on the desk. "All right, don't go to priority override. I want to keep this personal until I find out what's going on around here."

Millicent raised an eyebrow. "I think I'd better stay here."

"I think you're right."

Harmony's office was in the Dark Tower, the tallest building in the communications and research complex. Thadeus had been booted up there eight years ago, when Alex was brought in, after a short stint at Cowles Seattle and a longer service in military intelligence.

Considering Harmony's importance, one might have expected his office door to be larger, the vestibule more ostentatious. It could easily have been the entrance to a secretarial pool.

The scan system showed that Harmony was still in his private quarters, just off his office. Clearly, he didn't want to be disturbed. Just as clearly, there was no way Alex could honor his wish. All Dream Park executives and personnel above Class 3 were on duty twenty-four hours a day excluding specific vacation time. Get above Class 2 and even that was no protection.

Harmony had accepted the whole bill when he accepted promotion. Not that he was given a choice. In Cowles, as in most major corporations, it was Up or Out.

Harmony still didn't answer the buzzer. Alex didn't want to make a stink with the central computer, so he used his priority override card, passed it through the electric scan, answered the vocal scan's impertinent questions, and waited as the door decided whether or not to slide open for him. It slid.

It was terribly hot in the office. The wall furnace had been turned up to near max.

Harmony was in one of his overstuffed chairs, sitting with his hands wrapped around a glass. His blunt features were heavy and slack. "Alex," he said, his normally mellifluous tones slurred. The slurring blurred the line between amusement and irritation. "Are you going to stand there, or are you going to come in and pour yourself a drink?"

"Well . . . I'm still on duty."

"You're not on duty. Nobody's on duty. Goddamit."

"I am."

"Well, get off duty."

"I need to talk to you."

Harmony raised his voice until it shook the room. "I'm not talking to anyone who's on goddamned duty. You want to talk to me, get off your fucking duty."

Alex moved to the compact wet bar and mixed himself a scotch and soda; weak, but not quite weak enough to be a token.

He sat down opposite Harmony and waited, watching as the gas flames painted shifting patterns across the vast expanse of his friend's face. For all the heat, Harmony's eyes were cold black pits. The telephone rang, and rang. Harmony didn't answer it.

"They won't even let you forget." His voice was unspeakably tired. "They rub your nose in shit, you eat it for them, and they won't even let you brush your teeth." Harmony looked at him and said, "Alex, you've had good times and bad times. I know you didn't like sending that McWhirter kid to prison."

"Well, I've been able to do some things for him there. Anyone who can break through my security system is someone I want on my side. Hell, he's turned Chino into a career college. When he gets out next year he's got a job waiting for him. I still work with him sometimes."

"Yeah. That's okay. I had to do worse than that. I had to turn my back on murder. I knew who the son of a bitch was, and in the end I had to turn around and smile at him."

"Smile at him?"

The corners of Harmony's mouth tugged up, hard. Alex supposed that the result had to be called a smile, but in the firelight it looked like something peeled off a jack-o-lantern. "That's the worst thing in the whole world." His next drink emptied the glass. He turned it upside down, shook it. "The whole mess started about two years before you came, Alex, in '46 or so. We'd had problems around here, some real problems at Dream Park. We'd been so damned successful that we'd had psycho-sclerosis: hardening of the attitudes. Our creative arteries were blocked with administrative fat. Hell! We had it made. Everybody loved Dream Park. We were so damned good, and what was bad was we knew it.

"So we made some bad mistakes. A couple of ninety-million-dollar movies bombed. We tried to push through that Dream Park coproduction deal in the Mediterranean. Remember that synthetic island? Hell, we lost a quarter billion dollars in three years.

"We couldn't even get the idiots out of here, because half of them were related to Old Man Cowles. Well, to say we were cash poor would be like calling Australia 'an island in the Pacific.'"

"I see," Alex said, not seeing at all.

Alex watched Harmony study his glass and decide that he really, really didn't want another just now. "This was all happening at the same time that an interesting new theory was evolving in the Surgeon General's psychological services office. It really started with the development of the Show Scan system back in the 1970s, the system that old Doug Trumbull created. Superfast film projection, enough frames flashing per second that your brain can't tell what's real and what isn't. The big problem was, not only were the images as real as real, but they were also bigger than life."

"A 'hot' medium," Griffin offered, struggling to remember an ancient college lecture. "Twentieth-century television was a 'cool' medium, because the images were smaller than you."

"Bingo. When Cowles Industries introduced Interactive Holography, 'hot' went 'supernova.' They called it 'Reality Distortion.' The papers called it 'Dream Park Syndrome.' Confusion, nervous exhaustion, memory disorders, the whole lot. Too many people don't realize that Dream Park techs can make it look even realer than they do. We're afraid to. Afraid of overloading people. Two thousand years of civilization does not undo a million years of genetics. Rumor has it that the original Haunted Mansion at Old Disneyland was so realistic that people were fainting and vomiting."

"Story probably grew in the telling."

"Maybe." Harmony took a pull at his drink. "The upshot of all of this is that there was a slight but unnerving downward stock market trend for Cowles Industries. As the price dropped, somebody out there was buying it up. Now, at the same time, Cowles management was being raided by corporate headhunters."

"Hitting us hard?"

"Made Jivaros look like altar boys."

"Kind of odd that all of this was happening at the same time."

Harmony smiled sarcastically. "Yes, isn't it? It was not, in the immortal words of Bartholomew Cubbins, 'something that had just happened to happen and was not very likely to happen again.' It was a massively well financed, utterly ruthless takeover bid. Wasn't even that hard to figure out who. Our Saudi Arabian friend."

"Fekesh? Kareem Fekesh?"

"The very one. Funded by oil, backed by the same radical assholes who tried to blow up a space shuttle forty years ago, he's built an empire like few in the twenty-first century. He thrives on destabilization—of people, organizations, countries. Hell, he doesn't give a shit about OPEC, or Allah, or anything.

"Well, once we knew what was at stake, we were able to kind of circle the wagons, act with a little common sense and foresight. Then it happened—the one thing we'd always been afraid of. It was in the first run of the Fimbulwinter Game." He paused, noting Alex's take. "Oh, yes, the same game that's playing right now in Gaming B, drastically altered, of course. A real gun got in there. People got shot."

"Oh, shit. How badly?"

"Two down. One badly injured but recovered. One got nailed square in the hooter, dead before he hit the ground."

Alex drained his glass and headed back to the bar. He was going to need some help with this one.

"We moved the Gamers out and sealed the area. Game ended. The woman who actually pulled the trigger was shattered emotionally. Arrangements were made with her father." He rubbed his thumb and forefinger together, indicating *money*. "He was a real winner—didn't give a damn about her, thought she was from Venus anyway. 'All that sci fi drove her nuts.' We threw in some mumbo-jumbo about Dream Park Syndrome, coughed up a generous annuity, and he never peeped." Harmony's face was so dark Alex could barely read it. "We sent her to Brigham Young. They're the best. I wanted to keep track of her, but the doctors didn't want us meddling. I prayed she'd come out of it. She was so frail... Alex, for years I've watched the faces come in and out of this place, and I've seen the portfolios on the Century Club— the people who have been here more than a hundred times. She was just a poor lost thing, Alex."

Harmony stood, throwing out his arms for emphasis. "This was realer than real, Alex, bigger than life. It was her refuge from a world that had no room for magic, a family that didn't care. We let her down. Then we buried her."

For a long time Harmony was silent, and Alex thought he was finished, but then he began to speak again. "We never found out how the gun got in."

Alex said, "It was an inside job, wasn't it?"

"It had to be. Everything was perfect. Someone knew exactly how to get through the holes."

"I hate to think about that."

"We cleaned up Security afterward. *More* complacency. There shouldn't have been holes. Still, no outsider could have done it." Harmony stood next to the fire, the flames and shadows laving his body with a shifting mask of black and red. "I've had eight goddamned years to sit here and think about it. Every time I deal with someone who worked here in '48, I think about it. Why do you think I had you brought in from up north in '49? Why do you think I went right over good people, damned good people like Bobbick, and promoted you? Why? Because I didn't know who to trust. Do you know how that makes me feel? I sit here, and I eat with these people, and I play with them, their children... I've watched some of their kids grow up. I know most of them love what we're building here, that they believe in what Arthur Cowles dreamed all those years ago... and one of them is a killer.

"One of those wonderful wackos at R&D. One of the Gaming staff... what would you bribe 'em with, for Christ's sake? What could you give 'em that they haven't already got? But somebody did. Somebody got to 'em. Somebody gave 'em something we couldn't give.

"And so, I work here because I love it. But all the time I work here, all the time I do, I look at the faces, Alex, I look at the faces and I wonder, 'Which one? Which one?'"

Alex let Harmony wind down, waited for the great body to relax before he spoke again. "So what happened, Thadeus?"

"Oh, the whole thing was hushed up. The kid who died, Calvin Izumi, was out of R&D. He was only there because he had the right facial characteristics for the Game. Lucky Calvin. Calvin, his brother Tom, and his mother were all rabid for Dream Park. They had their lives, their money, everything wrapped up here. Drowned if they were going to let some goddamned terrorists get away with this. They helped us hush it up.

"We bought off the coroner, Alex. I hope you don't want me to pretty it up. We greased palms. We made it look like a hunting accident, we covered up murder. We had to. It'd have knocked our stock through the floor. There were about twelve of us who knew everything that had happened. Twelve of us with blood on our hands. Four have retired. I don't know how they handle it. We don't talk much anymore."

"And you think Fekesh?"

"Fekesh. I know it in my guts, and can't prove a thing. When the Barsoom Project came along they told me to just forget the whole thing, you know, close my eyes and think of England. And like a good little monkey I did."

Griffin waited to see if Harmony was going to add anything else. The only sound in the room was the slow crackle of the fireplace. Then he threw his ace onto the table, and watched his friend carefully. "Was this woman's name Michelle Sturgeon?"

Harmony turned snake-quick. His gunmetal eyes were level and cold. "How did you know that?"

"She's back, Thadeus." Griffin smiled. "Do you believe in Providence? She's come back to Dream Park, and at the same time as the man who destroyed her. What are the odds of that? We've been making miracles for everyone else for so long, maybe we're in line for a little one ourselves."

Harmony leaned forward. His eyes were intense. His thick fingers, templed against each other, trembled. "She's come back?"

"And Fekesh knows it. Somebody kicked her out of our replay of the Fimbulwinter Game. Almost destroyed her mind."

Griffin had seen piranha with more kindly, inviting smiles. "Lovely timing, don't you think? The bastard who originally seeded that rifle into the Game must be fudging his shorts. Poor girl's mind must be like a scrambled egg, but maybe she still knows something."

"Well, or somebody's afraid she knows something."

"You know, we won, but we lost. Fekesh lost, but he won. Missed his takeover bid by four votes. But the bastard bought his stock low, and made his profit when Cowles won the design bid for the Transcontinental Subway. Didn't lose a dime."

"How can you be so sure about Fekesh?"

"When you follow the money back through all the filters and all the fronts, after it changed hands through all the brokers, it went right back in his lap."

Alex rolled his glass in his hands. You could follow the money, and that would tell you the truth, all right. But it was nothing that could be proved in court. Even if Fekesh had been a U.S. citizen. Even if there had been a reported crime. Shit, what a tangle.

Harmony was looking more peaceful. His shoulders were more relaxed and his voice less strained. *Damn well should be. He's dumped it all onto you, boyo.*

"I grew up in the corporate world. We bent a lot of rules, sometimes broke rules, but it was a structured world. The world worked because of structure. And you know, sometimes in the back of my head, I always hoped you'd fix it, Alex. I brought you in from the outside. You grew up in a different tradition, where the world was a little more real. I was hoping that you could trace this all down. Help me make sense of it. Maybe I'm asking for too much, Alex. Maybe it's all been dead for too long. But I've got to hope."

Alex thought for a long time. He sat, watching the fire. He thought about all of the people, all of the time, all of the factors.

There would be few leads to follow. Nothing to prove. But... if there wasn't something, why would the unknown traitor have tipped his hand by trying to kill Michelle Sturgeon out of the Game? That didn't make any sense, either. There had to be something.

And if there was... it still had to be found. Maybe if The Griffin stirred things up a little?

"All right, Thadeus. I know my move."

"Good! What?"

"I don't know what else to do. It's not fair to anyone involved. But it might work. It might work small, or it might work big. The girl is the key. Eviane. This Michelle Sturgeon. Somebody wanted her out of the Game? Hah! I'll put her back in."

Harmony sat heavily. His eyes glittered in the firelight. "You can't do that. She's emotionally unstable. It's against the rules."

Alex grinned mirthlessly. "That's where you're wrong. That's where our traitors made a big mistake. There aren't any rules, Thadeus. There aren't any rules at all."

Chapter Twelve

BREAKFAST EGGS

Warm in the foil/foam sandwich of her sleeping bag, Gwen rolled onto her side and pressed herself back against Ollie. Her sigh of satisfaction, quite appropriately, sounded much like an old-fashioned kettle venting steam. Exhausted, surrounded by berserk Gamers and mad Actors, she and Ollie had managed to attain a little madness of their own. Sly, very sly he had been . . . wiggling up behind her "for warmth." Heh-heh. Then came the stealthy linking of the bags, and much suppressed giggling and jouncing about while the Gamers around them slept. Or pretended to sleep. Frankly, my dears, she didn't give a damn.

The air was warm, the dome above them covered with fluffy Dream Park clouds. She snuck a peek at her watch: eight o'clock. Unfortunate. Not enough time to get in a quicky with Ollie. Fair enough. It was the long slowies she liked best, anyway.

There was a crackling sound behind her. Gwen craned her head and saw Trianna standing just beyond the circle of heat-reflective cocoons, dressed in some kind of pink leotard, going through a slow, dancelike stretch routine. With surprising grace for so bulky a woman, Trianna torqued and twisted her body a joint at a time, working out the morning kinks. Behind her stretched a jagged, misty, whitecapped stand of iron-gray mountains, the object of the day's exercise.

A low crinkling sound from behind caught her attention. Francis Hebert, dark face soft with fascination, was watching Trianna. She *was* lovely, Gwen conceded. There was a woman of tremendous sensuality hiding in that lumpy body. Every twist and turn was a scream to be touched. Kevin and Hebert were both interested.

What did Trianna want? Hebert had much the better body—

"Arrrgh!" The voice was right behind her. She rolled over and got up on her elbows, amused as Johnny Welsh fought toward consciousness. "Mother," he moaned, "what has become of your little boy?"

The crackle of his foam and foil sleeping envelope was enough to rouse Robin Bowles, who sat up suddenly, not yet completely awake. Bowles looked around with eyes that seemed still focused on the last dream. His gray beard was ragged, his hair mussed, and he wore a ridiculous pair of red and black flannel pajamas. For all of that, he carried himself with immense dignity.

Bowles's wandering eyes fell on Welsh, and the flickering smile which had raised feminine pulses for three decades curled his lips. "Well, Jonathan. Are you determined to subject us to another litany of woe?"

Welsh smiled sheepishly. "Oh, don't pay any attention to me . . ."

"You may rely upon it."

"I know I need this. I saw the tapes from my last concert. Those close-ups were the worst. I had more chins than the Taiwan telephone directory."

"Jeez." Max Sands hoisted himself up on an elbow. "It's too early for this shit." All around the campsite, the Gamers were stirring to life.

Gwen reached down into her sleeping bag, found the torn remnants of her body stocking (Ollie, you beast!), and slipped it on. Jumpsuit on top of that, and then she reached around until she found her costume, pulled it down inside the bag, and began to dress.

She felt pretty good about the Fimbulwinter Game so far. The group had started pulling as a unit by the end of the first day, and judging by her mildly urgent hunger, the Dream Park magicians had been up to their standard tricks in the night. Usually she wanted crescent rolls, oatmeal with cream and sugar, eggs, sausage, and biscuits for breakfast. For some reason, all she wanted right now was fresh fruit.

And . . . she wanted answers, and didn't have them. The National Guardsman was a few feet away. He had slept in a makeshift bag formed out of two emergency thermal blankets. He was sitting cross-legged, glaring out at the world. His name was Yarnall, and the problem was that he had no Game personality at all. Like the pilot and copilot and stewardess, his part was over; he was to have been killed out.

Trailing his sleeping bag like a snake half out of its skin, Yarnall wiggled over to the center of the campsite. Breakfast had magically appeared during the night.

"Small mercies," he muttered. He was in his late thirties, a light-skinned black man with a good-humored face that made it difficult to take his grumbling seriously. "I can't believe this."

"Screw-up still gets to ya, huh?" Kevin Titus stood and stretched, the bones of his ribcage like barrel bands under his skin. He was startlingly thin and pale. "Just relax and enjoy it. What'cha makin' now? Time and a half?"

"Double time."

"So what's your beef?"

"I'm tired. I thought I was going to sleep in a bed last night. I want a scotch and water. If I can't have that, leave out the water. Worst of all, I ain't got no script."

"Join the crowd," Kevin said, yawning. "When they fix the screw-up, the first thing they'll try to do is kill you out. The longer you can keep 'em from doing that, the more money you make."

Yarnall thought about that for a minute. "By . . . by the Implementors! If they give me a direct order to throw myself in front of a spear I suppose I'll have to do it . . ." He raised his voice until it was almost a shout. "Of course, since it wasn't my fault, maybe the Gods will give me a fighting chance to stay in the Game."

He waited and stared up at the sky, and then shrugged. "Good thought, though."

The clouds above them shimmered and twisted themselves into a fleecy Cheshire cat grin. A thunderous reverberation rolled across the space of Gaming B:

"Are you . . . a gambling man, Mr. Yarnall?"

"Bet your ass. Who speaks?"

"Subdeity Welles. Kindly restrain your language. There are cherubim listening. As you must know, I have a discretionary budget. I would be willing to bet you, say . . . triple time against zip that I can kill you out before the end of the day, without bending any rules. What do you say?"

Yarnall realized that he suddenly had an audience. Gwen was fascinated—you could hear the gears churning in his head. "No cheating?"

"Gods don't need to cheat. We know what fools you mortals be."

"If I lose?"

"You forfeit yesterday's salary."

Yarnall looked around him. All of the Gamers were awake now, gazing up at that ethereal grin, waiting for the National Guardsman's answer. He slapped his leg. "All right, Welles, you son of a bitch! You're on!"

The cloud-smile transmuted into a ten-foot hand and snaked down from the heavens. It hovered just above Yarnall, and then the Actor reached up and shook it. The Gamers broke into cheers as the hand dissolved, and Yarnall looked around sheepishly.

Johnny Welsh was in stitches, tears rolling down his face. He slapped Yarnall on the back. "Let's see 'em top that in Vegas!"

Ollie's arms came around Gwen from behind, gave her a little squeeze good morning. "Let's get going," he whispered.

"All right!" she called. "Forty-five minutes to Game time. Men's showers in the gully, women's in that stand of trees. Breakfast is on the table. Hurry up, people! We have a big day today."

Yarnall still stood silently, staring up at the dissipating clouds. Gwen was overwhelmed with admiration: Welles had taken a bad situation and turned it into a day at the circus.

Belatedly, she wondered if she could have gotten the same deal.

They had been on the march for an hour, and now Max Sands could make out more detail on the mountains ahead. He and his brother Orson walked abreast, and to Max's satisfaction, Orson was humming softly.

Kevin Titus had been looking at him oddly since breakfast, as if trying to place that face and body. Oh, well . . .

He could understand that feeling. He had been staring at Robin Bowles, memories of countless B-movies flooding through his mind. He found it vastly amusing that before Bowles got his first major roles he had played low-budget quickies. If memory served him right, before the two Oscars had come a Golden Turkey award for his portrayal of Abdul Alhazred in the musical comedy version of *The Fungi From Yuggoth*.

Yarnall carried his rifle/club at port arms, scanning in every direction for trouble. He expected something to drop from the sky, pop out of the ground, materialize from thin air . . . So far, nothing had happened. Too soon, Max thought. Welles would wait and wear him down.

Up in the mountains were the nests of the Tin-mi-uk-puks, or Thunderbirds, fabulous creatures which Snow Goose said could take them closer to Sedna . . . if they had enough magic to command the creatures. Snow Goose wasn't sure. If not, they might just as well paint themselves with mustard, lie down, and be lunch.

Minus Eviane, there were nine Gamers and three Actors. It should have been ten and two by now, and even *that* felt a little sparse. How could they run so expensive a Game with so few

players? Certainly not on the fees Max had been charged—
though steep, they couldn't pay for all of this. The Actors out-
numbered the Gamers!

Snow Goose had explained it to him just after breakfast.
"Dream Park has most of the bugs out of the program now.
They're going to monitor our progress. If everything goes as
planned, home marketing follows. They'll sell a cassette, see? A
tougher Game. Your average player would have to run it a dozen
times before he gets all the way through. They figure that much
interactive role playing in a Total Environment room can affect a
major behavior shift. Sixty-three percent of Americans have TEs
available to them. Could be a major sideline."

The slopes had begun to get steeper, and his legs ached a little.
Max looked back down the mountain, and was surprised: they had
climbed close to a thousand feet. The campsite was far below them.
Looking down he could see the lake, and the floor of a gentle valley
that swept away to a snow-crested horizon. It was difficult to
believe that anything ugly could be hiding in this world. Around
them the mountains stretched endlessly, and although the going was
increasingly steep, he found that he enjoyed the effort. The breath
came harshly in his throat. He was sweating. He liked the sharp heat
of exertion. The air was very clean, bracing, cold enough to make
him feel totally awake and alive.

Beside him, brother Orson was having a harder time of it,
sweating and gasping but gritting his teeth and gamely humming
a tune. Max listened long enough to pick it up, and then started
humming along.

Trianna was right behind him. Her breathing, though labored,
was as evenly paced as his. "What's that song?"

"Ah...I'm not sure. Ask Orson."

"Orson?" She called out.

"Yes, ma'am?"

"What are you humming?"

Orson grimaced. "'The Ballad of Eskimo Nell.'"

"Can you sing it for me?"

Orson started to blush. "It...I...well, the truth is that I
don't know the words. Do you, Max?"

"Never learned 'em," he said, rolling his eyes soulfully. "I
was deprived as a child."

"Oh," she said, dejected.

Orson breathed a sigh of relief when a squeaking voice cried
out, "I know it! I know it!"

"I might have known, Kevin. Now keep it to yourself, would you?"

Trianna turned and grabbed Kevin's arm. "Oh, come on. Singing always makes a hike more fun. Give us a verse."

"Maybe the little shit's too winded to sing," Orson hissed hopefully.

No such luck. Kevin's eyes glowed at Trianna's contact. "Where are you? Let's see. *'So Dead-Eye Dick and Mexican Pete* . . . Dah de dah de dah . . ." He inhaled deeply, trying to remember. " *'And as they blazed their randy way no man their path withstood. And many a bride, her husband's pride, knew pregnant widowhood.'* De dah de dah . . ."

"That's enough, Kevin," Orson commanded.

"No, I'm trying to get to the good stuff."

"Kevin, I will pitch you off this mountain."

Max looked down, and damned if it didn't look like they were halfway up Everest. The campside lake was barely visible. Clouds veiled most of the valley, diffusing the morning sun into a weak yellow splotch.

"*Now Dead-Eye Dick, he bangs 'em quick—he cast the first aside,*

"*And made a dart at the second tart, when the swing doors opened wide.*

"*Then entered into that hall of sin, into that harlot's hell,*

"*Walked a lusty maid who was unafraid, and her name was Eskimo Nell* . . ."

Orson's ears were getting red. "Kevin. Kevin, me boyo. Don't do this. I'll make it worth your while."

"What'ja have in mind?"

"My next dessert."

Max choked. "Is that all it takes? Hey—anybody ever heard 'Kafoozalem'? *'Hi-ho Kafoozalem, harlot of Jerusalem. Prostitute of ill-repute and daughter of a Rabbi—'* "

Orson's scream echoed up and down the mountain.

They heard the sound before they saw anything. The group was far above the clouds now, and the mountain trail was little more than ribbon-wide. Robin Bowles actually lost his footing once. He should have fallen but bounced back onto the ledge, propelled by he knew not what. A hidden net? Author control? They were in the midst of clouds, barely able to see more than a few feet. Nets would make sense.

The first sound they heard was a tittering, scraping sound, followed by a dull *crack*.

Snow Goose crept up to the front of the line, to where the trail dead-ended against a ridge of rocks. She stealthily climbed up, and peered over. Within moments she returned, shuddering. "I . . . I've never seen anything like it."

Orson's embarrassment evaporated in a flare of curiosity. "Max? Let's take a look." He hefted his mutated spear as if he meant business. Maybe he did. He and Francis Hebert were the first to the top of the ridge: Hebert moved like an Indian scout. Max puffed as he climbed the last few feet, and then gaped at what he saw.

In a saucer-shaped stone depression thirty feet across lay a nest, a nest for birds the size of rocs. The parents were gone, and there had been six eggs in the nest. Two of the eggs had been shattered, the chicks within dragged out and brutally hacked apart.

Attackers were at work on a third egg. They might have been barrels covered with black hair . . . or obscenely fat, four-limbed spiders. Their fingernails were immense and crusted with filth, and grew out of the fingers like knives stuck on the ends of sausages. They chortled as a third Thunderbird chick, a wet, yellow-feathered infant the size of a plump turkey, struggled sluggishly for life. They tore it to pieces with their fingernails and consumed it raw. Each of the six monstrosities was larger than a man.

Orson ducked back beneath the ridge of rock. His breathing was asthmatically harsh.

"Do you know what that is?" Hebert's little eyes were wide with excitement.

"*Yes*, I know what that is!" Orson said. "The book calls them mountain trolls. Flesh-eaters, man. We don't want to mess with them. I don't remember anything about how to survive an encounter."

Hebert checked the action on his rifle, one of the few that hadn't been converted. "Bull. We can't let them kill the Thunderbird chicks. This is our chance to look good to the birds!"

Johnny Welsh and Hippogryph had joined them. Without peering up over the edge of the basin, everyone seemed to know exactly what would have to be.

"All right," Hebert said. "Are we together on this?"

Snow Goose gulped. Yarnall gave the sky a dirty look. "No cheating," he muttered.

"Then—let's DO IT!"

Hippogryph and Hebert began firing. Hebert's Remington was unimpaired by magic, but Hippogryph had to pause to add powder and shot with every blast from the flintlock.

The trolls screamed, their misshapen barrel bodies shuddering with the shock. A monster's flat, hideous face dissolved to a smear of red light. It fell back twitching.

But the others charged, howling their rage.

With gibbonlike agility they scampered over the rocks, mouths dripping with Thunderchick blood and yolk, impossibly long arms sweeping out like scythes.

Fear froze him for a moment. Then Max broke free, ducked under the sweeping black arms, and thrust upward with his harpoon. The creature swatted the spear aside, and grabbed him by the arm. Not a hologram! Its other hand almost lovingly displayed the foot-long nails, traced them lightly across his neck, and then hissed and drew back—

Yarnall! The Guardsman smashed into it with his war club. The troll squealed and released Max. Max hit the ground, heart triphammering.

All around him were scuffles, and screaming, and the sound of rocks sliding beneath climbing, running feet.

His hands searched until he found the harpoon. He grabbed it in the middle and turned as the troll advanced on Yarnall. Screaming, he raised the spear. It plunged deep into the furred back and—

(For just a moment, he wondered if he had seen correctly. In other circumstances he would have sworn he saw the head of the spear retract, and the flesh around the "wound" actually close in to grasp the haft. Ah, well . . .)

—the troll gasped in pain, blood flowing from its mouth. It turned and ran. Max wrenched his spear from its back as it plunged over the side of the cliff and disappeared into the clouds below.

Max and Yarnall slapped hands, then whooped and searched for fresh meat.

There, Trianna stood her ground, firing into an advancing hulk. Although its blood drizzled onto the rocky ground, still it plodded another step forward, and another.

Johnny Welsh and Max got there at the same time. Max, unable to contain his exuberance, performed "Mr. Mountain's Avalanche." He sprang into the air, knees flexing to chest, feet hammering out, slowing down at the last minute so that his partner wouldn't be hurt—

Oops.

The monster slammed into the ground, and Max heard it say "Ow, goddamn!" as it tried to crawl away.

Johnny Welsh was staring at him. "Well, I'll be. Mr. Mountain! I watched you wrestle last month against Skinhead Slade!"

Max groaned. "Not so loud. I'll tell you about it later. Let's finish this up."

"Pleasure!"

Nearby, a troll was being clubbed and speared into a glowing mess. The knifelike projections of its nails scratched blindly at the rock. The other trolls were either dead or in retreat. The Adventurers screamed challenge at them, and whooped with bloodthirsty joy.

"We beat 'em!"

"Yeah!"

"We sure as hell did it!" Orson bellowed at the top of his lungs.

Snow Goose was examining the eggs. Where once there had been six, now there were three, and one of those had a cracked shell. She looked worried.

"What's wrong?" Yarnall asked, wiping a smear of troll blood off his club.

"I'm . . . not sure we should be up here right now . . ."

Before anyone could ask why, the sky rang with a scream of primal despair. Above them, two titanic winged creatures circled in the sky. They were like eagles, only with silver fringes to their golden feathers. The sun caught their highlights, ignited them gloriously, transforming the Thunderbirds into flaming avengers. They circled twice, cawing, then plunged straight down at the Gamers, hooked talons spread and gleaming.

Chapter Thirteen

AEROBICS

The male Tin-mi-uk-puk carried a caribou in its outsize claws. As it caught sight of the carnage it screamed and released the carcass. Gamers froze as it dropped toward them. That mass was carrying enough kinetic energy to kill Rambo XII.

The caribou brushed the edge of the nest and dropped into the mist amid a shower of leafy debris, lost before it crashed against the side of the mountain.

Max was frozen as the male approached and swooped down. As close as he came, it was the female who actually landed first. She stalked directly to her babies as her mate circled overhead.

She nudged one of the broken shells, her eyes and body language almost unendurably grief-stricken. One of the turkey-sized, feathered corpses was still partially intact. She nudged it, pushed her great beak against its lifeless mass, before giving up and inspecting the other shells.

The male landed. The birds weren't as big as houses, but certainly twice the size of dray horses, the size of small elephants. The smaller of them easily sported a twenty-foot wingspan. Their bodies were golden-eagle bodies tinged with silver. For birds, they were extraordinarily muscular. Each clawed footstep, each ripple of a wing conveyed a sense of majesty, authority, *power*.

The male studied each of them in turn.

"Nobody panic," Snow Goose commanded. "We might just survive this." She turned her head. "Mr. Welsh. Give me your charm. And no jokes."

Johnny stared, then shut his mouth. He fumbled in his pack, extracted a small carved bird figure. Max caught only a glimpse of it as it passed from hand to hand, but it seemed exquisitely rendered in some dark, smooth stone.

The female approached the male and rubbed her great head against his, and they cooed together. He silently inspected the nest and intact eggs, then returned to nudge at the bodies of the slain monsters. He looked up at the Gamers with a clear question in those huge, black, intelligent eyes.

Snow Goose stepped forward, charm in upraised hand. "Hail to you, great warriors of the wind. We saved your children from the mountain trolls. In return, we ask a favor."

Max was aghast. The two enormous creatures looked at Snow Goose as if she were insane. Their babies lay at their feet—their feet were wet with yolk and blood—and this impertinent tidbit was asking for favors? Max gripped his harpoon and readied for some fancy footwork.

"Take us to the top of the world," Snow Goose demanded. "Only with your help can we enter Sedna's realm, and set right that which has gone awry. Will you help us?"

The Gamers drew back as the two birds came nearer, and then nearer still, until either could have lunged forward and caught a plump, screaming human in its softly gleaming talons.

Max shivered as the male inspected him. It cocked its head sideways and stared at Max with one huge, hypnotically deep black eye. Gazing into its depth was dizzying, but Max dared not back down. He was spinning, spinning, and prayed not to fall.

Without knowing why, Max stretched out one trembling hand. The Thunderbird watched his hand suspiciously, then jerked its head out of reach.

"What'd I do?"

"Watch your hands, smartass," Orson hissed. "Thunderbirds are not pets! In Inuit mythology they're usually the villains. Whatever Snow Goose did, I hope it's strong enough."

The male threw his head back, and the golden feathers around his neck ruffled. His scream reverberated to the heavens, rang up and down the mountain range like a thunderclap.

For a moment, the Adventurers were frozen in their tracks. Then from far away there came an answering scream of recognition.

Johnny Welsh coughed nervously. "I think someone just rejected a collect call—"

On the edge of the horizon, looming up now, came a quartet of winged figures, identical to the first two, but even larger.

The newcomers were older, the gold in their feathers more tarnished by time and the elements. They carried curious leather appliances in their claws, fitted with dangling straps and buckles.

"We've got the grandparents, I think," Orson said nervously.

They circled, then came in for a landing. While the younger couple kept an eye on the Gamers, the older Thunderbirds examined the evidence. They found a spear still lodged in a blood-spattered troll corpse, bit and wrenched it out with the toss of a great plumed head.

One of the Thunderbirds carried it over and respectfully laid it before Snow Goose. The others folded their wings and sat in front of the Gamers, heads bowed.

"Well, I'll be dipped . . ."

"Hurry," Snow Goose said, handing the charm back to Johnny. "We have five birds. One will stay to watch over the eggs. Break into groups of two or three. Fix the saddles and mount up."

Docilely, the great beasts presented themselves as Max approached and nervously threw a saddle across the back of the nearest Thunderbird.

Hologram? Must be, and yet they expect us to . . .

The saddle landed on something solid. Max reached forward, and touched feathers. He struggled with his surprise, and then subdued it. *Stop trying to figure out when they make the switch!*

Hebert and Trianna were the handiest with the leather saddles, were fastest following Snow Goose's directions as she helped them buckle and strap the contraptions into place.

"Guess they've had riders before, eh?" Hebert puffed.

Snow Goose smiled enigmatically. "So the legends say. I assume you mean the birds?"

Max and Orson nodded to each other, then split up. Orson went with Charlene and Hippogryph, while Max got into line in front of Trianna and Francis Hebert.

He tugged at the saddle, anchored just ahead of the giant wings. As much as the idea scared him, they were really very secure. He climbed up onto the waiting back and strapped himself in.

Trianna slid up behind, wrapped her arms around his waist. Her breath warmed his cheek, had that sweet-and-sour excited tang that is irritating from a man, but a turn-on from a woman. And Trianna was a lot of woman. His belly muscles flexed within her arms, *feel the hardness*, without consulting his forebrain. His lower body tingled with localized, increased circulation.

Ah, well. His heart yearned for Eviane, but the rest of him seemed more pragmatic.

Hebert climbed on behind Trianna—and the three of them, he

estimated, added up to a hefty tonnage. He hoped the Thunderbirds were as strong as they looked.

The last Gamer had boarded his mount. Snow Goose checked all of the buckles with sober, expert care, then climbed aboard the lead male. It ruffled its feathers and ran at the edge of the bluff. Without a moment's hesitation, it dove over and disappeared into the clouds.

Max barely had time to say "What?" when his own mount turned stiffly toward the cliff. It took five running steps that reminded him of something out of a Disney film on ostriches, and dove off.

He screamed, and swore to himself that he would scream all of the way down. His stomach contracted as if trying to squeeze his intestines out of his nostrils. When he opened his eyes his Thunderbird was plunging straight for the bottom—

(And he remembered, briefly, a quote from twentieth-century stunt man Evel Knievel: "I've gotten to where I can say the Lord's Prayer in ten seconds.")

"OurFatherwhoartin—"

The bird leveled up and began to climb. And climb. Up and up, and when he looked back he saw the other Thunderbirds and their passengers behind and below him, sleek black wings beating against a dwindling backdrop of mountains. The wind burned his eyes, and they began to water.

The clouds drifted past. Within a few moments the plateau was a memory. He turned around and faced Trianna, who although strapped onto the saddle still gripped his waist with eyes closed.

"We're all right," he said. When that produced no visible result, he nudged her again. "Go ahead. Open your eyes."

"I'm afraid of heights."

He looked down. Distantly, a blue carpet of sparkling sea glimmered through the clouds. Not the place for an acrophobe. "Better keep 'em shut, then."

Behind her, Francis Hebert was gazing down at the view, eyes as wide as a child's in Santa's toy shop.

The view was somewhere beyond wonderful. After a few minutes, the birds curved around and began to head toward a range of mountains so distant that they registered only as wrinkles on a far horizon.

This was the life! The air beating against his face was pleasantly cool. The strong, steady stroke of the Thunderbird's wings was a heartbeat rhythm, as soothing as it was exhilarating.

He began to lose track of time, pleasantly mesmerized by the frozen vistas below. Endless stretches of glacial ice and snow-locked rivers passed. From time to time his mount would bank gently and then level out again, but on the whole the trip was hypnotically placid.

Hebert was the first to spot trouble. Max heard the man's shout and followed his pointing finger, detected a flock of tiny black dots approaching from the eastern horizon.

"They've got wings," Hebert bellowed, leaning far out around Trianna's shoulder. "More big birds. Does it look to you like they're coming right at us?"

"Could be," Max said.

"I wish we could ask Snow Goose."

Max wished he could ask Orson. The other Thunderbirds were lumbering along with slow, steady wing strokes, but they were too far away for a good shout. Again he scanned the horizon. The other flying creatures were disquietingly close.

More Thunderbirds? He doubted it. The line of wing and tail on these great golden eagles was a marvel of nature. The new figures were somehow . . . misshapen.

Hebert was checking his rifle. "Hope this'll be more use than last time. Trianna, dammit—open your eyes!"

"I can't! I'm scared!"

Max swore under his breath. "Well then, give me your rifle!" He reached back to try to tug it out of her hands, but she hung on like an alligator. "Shit!"

"No!"

He looked back again. The creatures were only a kilometer away, and now he could distinguish them more clearly. They seemed a melding of bird and beast. He could make out a gigantic, misshapen wolf's head grafted onto the body of an enormous falcon. They weren't as large as the Thunderbirds, but there were nine, make that ten of them.

Before he could say or think anything else, the creatures swooped to the attack.

He had a brief glimpse of wolf snout and falcon claw as his mount suddenly folded its wings and dove toward the earth. He gripped a handful of feathers for dear life, and squeezed his eyes shut.

Sun, earth, cloud, and white-speckled mountains merged dizzyingly. His stomach, and the fluid contents therein, sloshed every way but out and up. His Thunderbird swooped and dove, careened like a berserk roller coaster, striving to evade the two monstrous Wolfalcons which had set upon it.

Suddenly, and with a speed that left his spine somewhere back at the last loop, the Thunderbird doubled back on its own trail and caught one of the unholy hybrids. The beast screamed, but its scream was the scream of a wolf, and it was the wolf head which turned and set its teeth into the Thunderbird's neck.

Feathers and skin came away as the Thunderbird shook its tormentor loose, and then savaged it to pieces. Max peeked around his mount's shoulder, saw the Wolfalcon fight back, then go limp and offer no resistance. Its ravaged body plummeted toward the ground.

The second Wolfalcon swooped close. With the whoosh of wings Trianna Stith-Wood finally opened her eyes, and her gun almost flew into her hands. Hysterically she pumped bullets into the creature's face.

That face exploded with crimson and it flopped away, vanishing into a cloud.

The Thunderbird wheeled around and dove back toward its family.

The eight remaining Wolfalcons fought demonically. One went straight for the Guardsman. He ducked and swung his war club futilely, then laughed hysterically when a second, dive-bombing, was snatched from the air by the vengeful claws of Max's bird.

"Hey, Welles!" he yelled, hands cupped to mouth. "Missed me! Nyahh nyahh!"

Their mounts took terrible damage, and the aerobatics continued in dizzying flurries. Max was no longer sure which way was up. At last the final two Wolfalcons screamed in frustration. The cries were not those of beasts, but of men—men rendered inhuman by bloodlust and hate.

One of the two remaining enemy swooped close before it withdrew from the fray. There in its chest Max saw the face of a human being embedded among the feathers. It was the face of a man who lived to hate, fed on hate, felt no other human emotion. It was quite mad, the eyes alight with sufficient loathing to fry Max's marrow.

Then both were gone.

Chapter Fourteen

THE AFTERLIFE

The girl on the couch was drowsy. Her head hung from an unsteady neck, and her eyes were defocused. The tranquilizing tabs Vail had placed on the skin over Michelle Sturgeon's carotid artery had done their work.

The tiny holding room in medical central was adequate for a situation like this, but not particularly comfortable.

Vail stared at a computer screen. He cleared it, summoned up a new batch of data, cleared it again.

Griffin rapped the desk impatiently. "Well?"

"We could get sued for our lungs and kidneys."

"To hell with that," he growled. "Listen. For eight years her father took our money, and tucked this woman into that hospital in Salt Lake City. Then he demanded the rest of the money in a lump sum. We gave it to him. He blew it, and tucked her into a state home in Saint Paul. When Minnesota went through a recession last year, they let her go. That's when she started using the name 'Rivers.' She's still, pardon the expression, a loon."

"I don't understand those esoteric medical terms, Alex."

"I'm hardly a doctor."

"Precisely."

"Dr. Vail." Alex's voice was deceptively mild. "Let's cooperate with each other, shall we? We both made mistakes. It could be argued that yours was larger—unless you'd like me to believe a sealed file kept you from reading her Rorschach blots."

To Alex's immense satisfaction, Vail stammered for a beat before composing himself. "We—ah, utilize a more complex battery of tests than that, I assure you. But Michelle Sturgeon is a classic schizophrenic, and she took the test as her Eviane personality. There were, ah, no pathological symptoms."

Vail's voice wavered. Griffin almost felt sorry for him, but bored in relentlessly. "Oh, I'm sure she's as right as rain. Now,

Doctor, why do you think she came back here? Don't you think she had a reason? She thinks Dream Park is the medicine she needs. I think she's right."

"I'm not sure you understand the significance—"

"Don't be patronizing," Alex said. "I'm not in your league, but I minored in psychology. You tell me if I'm remembering straight."

Vail narrowed his eyes cautiously. "All right. Shoot."

"We're talking selective amnesia and a multiple-personality disorder, brought on by a strong tendency toward dissociation, and a high hypnotic responsiveness."

The doctor sat up straight. "That's—actually quite perceptive. Go on, Alex."

"Now bear with me. When Michelle Sturgeon shot three players in a Game, she subjected herself to massive guilt."

"In essence, yes..."

"Michelle Sturgeon sees herself as a murderess, even though she was innocent. Eviane, on the other hand, is a heroine who only fought to protect her cause. Michelle is a rabid mouse, Eviane a lioness. She needs to become Eviane to live with herself."

"You have about half of it," Vail said, almost reluctantly. "The question is, what is she doing back here? She intends to relive that shattering moment. Do you have any idea how dangerous it would be to put her back into the Game?"

"Dangerous to her? She's already pretty screwed up, wouldn't you say? Could it get worse? Dangerous to us? Hell, we can put a security shield around her. We already have Marty in the Game. It won't happen a second time. I can guarantee that."

He leaned very close, and consciously flexed the muscles in his chest. A big man's trick: Alex was perfectly willing to use subliminal physical intimidation if it would get him what he wanted. "And Vail, this is what it boils down to. We don't know whether or not she can identify the killer, but the killer can't be sure either. That's good enough for me."

Vail thought about it for a long moment. "If you put it like that..."

"I do."

"Then it seems there is very little to lose, and much to gain."

"Don't get cute—I know we're risking what's left of her sanity. I think Eviane and Michelle would both agree with me, and approve of the cause."

Vail tapped his fingers. He touched a few more buttons on his computer, then crooned to it softly.

"All right. I think that I may have an answer. When I was in medical school, we performed a rather interesting experiment. If modified, it may suggest a solution. The key to it is her susceptibility to hypnosis." He looked at Griffin, face showing the traces of surprise. "By the way—how did you figure that? It's not in her dossier."

"She's a Dream Park junkie," Griffin said. "This whole place is an altered state of consciousness." Alex paused. "You mentioned her father. What about her mother?"

"Dead. And I think you guessed it—her mother's maiden name was Eviane Rivers."

Michelle Sturgeon floated in a tank of water a few degrees cooler than skin temperature. Hundreds of pounds of Epsom salts were dissolved in the water. She was as buoyant as a balloon. There was no light. There was no sound. 100 mg of synthetic tranquilizer/hypnotic had left her without the urge to do anything but lie here and relax.

Without light, without sound, without a reference of physical sensation, her mind drifted in its cocoon of warmth, and her recent troubled sensations died away.

Who was she? Eviane? Yes. Eviane. Strong. Powerful.

Who else? Some part of her was far, far away, alone and miserable. As she should be. Michelle was bad. Had done something terrible. Eviane didn't want to think about that part.

Wait, now. There were lights in the darkness!

They sparkled, and moved in rhythm across her line of sight. They were differing colors, jewel-like. She liked them.

There was sound. A heartbeat sound, one that she felt in the water, in her body, in her chest. She was getting . . . not sleepy. She was beyond sleepy somehow, but still awake. Her body was sleepy, her mind alert . . . at least, part of her mind.

It was confusing. Everything seemed to be happening so slowly. So much had happened in the past hours. It seemed like a dream.

Everything was slowing, slowing . . .

Eviane fought to hold on, but felt herself swirling down and down into the void, into an infinitely deep black hole rimmed with red, following the steady pulse of the light, the rhythmic beat of the sound, the gentle lapping of the warm water. Down and down and down and dark.

Out of the dark came light. She was in a place she knew, a beach, a place from her past.

The surf rolled in, and she sat in the warm sand, watching passively. She was warmed and comforted by the touch of the sun, and utterly content.

A man came out of the surf, dripping water and foam, smiling at her. He was a tall man with light red hair. His smile made her feel warm.

He reached out his hands to her. They were large and broad. Had she seen him before? Could she trust him? She wasn't sure, but she liked him.

Where was Mommy? Michelle looked for her mother, Eviane, the stern one, the protecting one, and didn't see her. Her hand stole nervously into the hand of the stranger, and he held it warmly.

They smiled at each other for a time, shared the sun and the warm, hissing surf. "Michelle," he said, "you're a very good girl. I've heard that from everyone. You're a wonderful girl."

Michelle liked hearing that. Her heart opened to the stranger.

"Can you remember all of the times you knew that you were good, had done something good, were told that you were good?"

She nodded her head.

"Good. Remember those times." He paused, and a deep wave of warmth and positive feelings swept her. He nodded. "That's right. Now. Do you know that sometimes good people can be tricked into doing bad things?"

The beach suddenly wavered. The water crashing against the sand became icy, and something rose thrashing from the foam.

"Look at *me*!" he commanded. "Look at me."

She did as he said, breathing steadily, slowly. The thing in the surf began to dissolve.

"Good. Good."

She liked the feel of his arms around her, and pressed close. Their heartbeats seemed to merge.

"Sometimes, good people can be tricked into doing bad things, by bad people. They try to hurt little girls. And then the little girls need their mommies. They need Eviane. And Eviane is here to help you whenever you need her. But right now I need to talk to Michelle."

She trembled, and clung to him, and examined his words. He

held her without judging. His arms were strong, and his voice soft. And he promised that Mommy could come back.

Frightened, but relaxing into trust, she pulled back and gazed into his face.

"Yes," she said. "I know."

"Will Michelle help me?"

"Yes, Michelle will help you."

"Good. Thank you." The big man with the rough face smiled and touched her nose softly. "I want you to tell Eviane that she is going back to her friends. Magic will take her back. Her friends need her. They will find her in the land of the dead, and then everything will be as it was. She will remember nothing once her friends find her."

Michelle nodded, without comprehending.

"But listen," he added, urgently. "All the time that Eviane is with her friends, fighting and helping them, Michelle will hide behind her mommy and watch. Michelle will learn. And when Michelle learns what she came here to learn, she will find a way to let us know. In her own way, in her own time. But she will let us know. Will you help us?"

"Mommy doesn't have to go away?"

"No," and the big man's arms were warm around her. "Mommy doesn't have to go away." He stopped, and added, "But neither does Michelle."

Griffin watched as a heavy-lidded Michelle Sturgeon was led from the executive Total Environment room. He wiped his brow with a moist, shaking hand. He hadn't realized what a drain it would be playing out that role.

Vail opened the door and peered at Griffin with amusement.

"That was rather well done, Alex. Maybe you went into the wrong career?"

"I just figured that Dream Park has something that none of the doctors have."

"What was that?"

"We have what she wants: a shot at the son of a bitch who screwed her up. I'd say we can ride that rascal all the way home."

A video window opened in the wall, and Alex watched Michelle Sturgeon enter the frame. Numbly, without protest or eagerness, Michelle slipped back into the isolation tank for additional work.

"Say another two hours prep and she should be ready. Alex, have you looked into the Game? Do you know what a *tornrait* is?"

"A ghost. A helpful ghost. Why?"

"We're going to give Michelle—excuse me, we can give *Eviane* an excuse for remembering the future." Vail glanced at his watch. "You know, I could be making more money in private practice, Alex, but goddamn, where would I find cases like this?"

"Write it up," Alex sighed. He sniffed at his collar. The Epsom salts were still moist upon it. Mixed in it was another fragrance. The scent of a delicate young woman, cruelly used; and something else, something feral.

Chapter Fifteen

HOLY SMOKE

Max's Thunderbird was wounded. Its left wing fluttered
weakly against the driving wind. The great eagle strove to pace
itself: two strong beats, and then a rest. Gain altitude, and then
pause into a gentle downward glide.

They flew through a clear layer between two cloud decks. The
upper haze layer let the sun through as a brighter disk. It was
thirty degrees above the horizon of the lower cloud deck, though
the time must have been about noon.

They flew above a knobby white landscape, so dense that Max
could see no trace of an earth below. Suddenly, and for the first
time, he felt the primal fear of falling, that cling-to-Mommy,
hairless-ape-in-the-treetops fear. His Thunderbird's beak was
open, and he could hear the ragged whistling of its breath even
above the wind.

Trianna put her lips to his ear and whispered, "Look," and
pointed down.

Curiously, as his air sickness increased, hers had begun to
fade. A mile below them there was a break in the clouds. They
could find outlines of a mountain range, vast and foreboding, all
jagged peaks sheathed in impenetrable ice.

The Thunderbird began to glide down, making its slow and
gentle descent. A mist of blood streamed from the wounded right
wing.

The Thunderbird was fighting for its life, for their lives. Max
felt gratitude and admiration for the creatures, repaying their debt
in so heroic a fashion. The only problem was that he could see no
place to land. The mountain was all cliffs, all bare rock faces at
varying angles.

There might be ledges, landing places, somewhere below; but
diving blind through the clouds would be suicide. What would
the wounded bird do?

Half-hidden by mist was a tiny ledge, too narrow, narrower than the bird's spread wings.

Max's chest ached with the tortured wheeze of its breathing. He felt its triumph of will as gilded wings spread wide. It swooped toward the ledge. The wings half-folded—he felt the drop in the pit of his stomach—and the bird's feet slammed into rock. Three hopping steps brought it to a halt.

It looked back at them. In its eyes shone a mixture of pride, and anger, and gratitude. Max swung himself over and landed heavily on rock. "Off! Get off, Trianna. Let the beast rest!" He helped her descend. She was heavy . . . and he saw her surprise at the strength in his arms.

Francis Hebert descended without help and at once began trying to stretch his back out.

The other birds came down behind them, landing with half-folded wings on the same narrow, fog-shrouded ledge. Stiffly the Gamers unstrapped themselves from their mounts and tumbled to the ground.

Max's toes curled hard against the ground, and his knees half-buckled, then became firm again. His stomach felt a little shaky, and he called an old trick into play: find a spot on the horizon, gaze at it until the dizziness passes . . .

He chose the distant, pale disk of the sun, yellow-white and wan in the mist. He had to squint a little . . . but this world's sun, crippled by magic, was such that his eye could meet it squarely.

Even on this side of the magical barrier, Seelumkadchluk, there was something visibly wrong with Sol's disk. A shadow, perhaps an enormous sunspot: an alien shape that didn't quite belong . . . The clouds thinned for a moment, but Max held his gaze against the increased glare.

What in the world?

His eyes were squeezed tight against tears. "Does anyone have a pair of binoculars?"

Kevin Titus dismounted just behind Snow Goose. He reached into his backpack. He pulled out a leather case. He extracted a pair of binoculars with molded plastic handgrips, and gave them to Max a bit reluctantly. "Be careful with 'em."

"Actually, I was planning to heave 'em off the . . ." Max aimed and focused, squinting hard. Even through the clouds, it was too damned bright, but . . . "I will be dipped in shit." There, in the center of a pale wavering disk, was the shadowed form of a great black bird. The shadow's beaked profile turned...looked at him?

He handed the binoculars to his brother Orson. "What do you make of that?"

Orson focused the glasses. Presently he said, "I'd say we know where the Cabal is hiding the Raven, wouldn't you?"

There was a general ripple of excitement as news of the discovery spread down the line, then Max handed the binoculars back. He felt pretty damned good. They had just solved a major piece of the puzzle.

Snow Goose was gazing into the sun. "I can't believe it. How could the Cabal get enough power to do something like this?"

"What would it take?" Robin Bowles asked. He walked with an exaggerated, bow-legged gait. The ride must have left him sore.

"The Raven created the world! I can't even imagine that much power. I just don't know..."

"The satellite?" Orson asked hopefully.

"Right, sure. The satellite. And they caught the Raven while he was in human form." She sounded doubtful but afraid. "We've got to find Sedna."

The five Thunderbirds preened, and ministered to each other, and inspected their wounds. From time to time one would glance up at the frail humans who had set them an impossible task. The birds seemed so beautiful, so terrible, but there was a fragility beneath the strength. Try as he might, he couldn't get the image of those shattered eggshells out of his mind.

Human and Thunderbird owed each other much. Max felt fumble-tongued, but he knew he should speak.

They let him approach, watching him from the depths of those emotionless, void-black eyes. Max stood close enough to touch, but didn't. Dammit, he didn't know when Dream Park switched from hologram to mechanical, and he didn't want to spoil the illusion now. For him, at this moment, these creatures were as real as his companions.

"Thank you, great ones."

A low, buzzing voice reverberated through his body. *"We have repaid our debt. When next we meet, beware!"*

Then the great eagles, one at a time, spread their wings and veered away. The Gamers stood silently in the snow, watching until the Thunderbirds vanished into the clouds.

Snow Goose spoke. "Legend says that the entrance is here in

the mountains. I don't know exactly where." A gust of wind blew her straight black hair into her face, and she paused to wipe the strand aside. "We're going to form a circle, and have a prayer smoke." She motioned them down against the mountain wall, under a slight overhang where they had a little protection from the weather. When they were all seated in a circle, she produced a leather pouch from her backpack. She undid the thong tie with fingers and teeth, and shook a hand-rolled cigarette out.

"Tobacco?" Max was shocked. "I haven't seen tobacco since Milan."

"Nicotine can save your life," Snow Goose said piously. She lit it, inhaled deeply, and then exhaled in a thin stream that was so white it seemed to glow. "To my brothers in the north," she said. "Brothers of the mind, children of the wind. Guide us, help us. Help us find the doorway to the nether kingdom, to the land of the dead, to the realm of the All-Mother."

She blew a second puff directly into the whistling wind. The smoke should have vanished instantly, but it didn't. It merely drifted, as if on the faintest of breezes. "The south. Brothers of the heart. Help me feel my way. Let your water nurture us, and help us in our quest!" Another breath. "Brothers of the east, you who are of spirit, beings of fire and light. Open the path. Show us the way!"

With a final puff, she saluted the West. "Brothers of the west! Children of the Earth! Holders of physical form, guardians of the body, protect us in our quest."

The smoke: it had not dissipated into the wind, although the wind continued to build. Four tendrils of smoke were drifting haphazardly, ignoring the wind.

Snow Goose was sliding into a trance. "Ohhh . . . they are near. The dead, the endless legions of dead, are near. Show us! Great . . . great evil! There is great evil . . . !"

Four tendrils of smoke turned and twisted in the wind, but would not go where the wind went. Instead they were beginning to move all in the same direction, turning like four blind snakes who have caught a scent. They drifted toward the mountain wall. One by one they brushed against the gray rock, and again, and, gradually, were gone, scattered by the wind or absorbed by the rock.

The mountain began to shudder.

"Jesus! What's going on?" Orson yelled.

The snow above them began to tremble. Snow Goose, stirring

from her trance, suddenly screamed, "Up against the wall!"

Kevin muttered, "—motherfuckers!" But he was moving, rolling, like the other Gamers.

Snow Goose's warning barely came in time. The slight rumbling that had alarmed Orson abruptly became a thunderous, malevolent roar, and their entire world turned white as countless tons of snow and displaced rock crashed past them.

They huddled together, tight against the wall. Somebody down at the other end screamed, and Max didn't blame him a bit. He felt sick to his stomach, genuine gut-fear hammering at his desperate attempt to remember that it was only a Game. He closed his eyes tightly, and waited.

After an endless time the ground stopped shaking, and Max opened his eyes again.

And could see nothing. His reaching hand met a solid layer of snow.

Francis Hebert triggered a flashlight. The luminescence lit them an eerie yellow in their tomb of ice. The overhang was all that had saved them.

For a long time, no one spoke. There was the sound of their constricted breathing, and the low, bass rumble of a distant tremor. Then even that died away.

Snow Goose broke the silence. "I guess the Gods were listening," she said calmly, and lit another cigarette.

She exhaled in a long, long stream... in fact, she didn't stop exhaling, even after a solid thirty seconds of feathery breath. The smoke formed a glowing cocoon around her. It lit the interior of their makeshift snow cave so brightly that Hebert switched off his flashlight.

Without another word she turned, and walked directly at the wall of snow. It melted before her, the water flowing and fusing into the crystal ice walls of a snow tunnel.

She almost floated as she walked, yesterday's college-girl persona completely submerged. She seemed to be a different person entirely, one not wholly of this world. All they could do was follow her. Max looked to Orson for advice or comment, and Orson shook his head.

The snow tunnel twisted and wound, angling steeply into the very heart of the mountain. Max stretched out a hand to touch the walls. They were hard and cold, although the air in the tunnel was pleasant.

Ahead of them walked the glowing Snow Goose, carrying

herself as might a great lady, a princess, the mistress of all dark secrets. She had stopped puffing on the cigarette, but a steady stream of vapor poured from her mouth, her nose—Jesus! Her eyes and ears, continually re-forming that glowing cocoon that melted snow and rock ahead of her, building a way for the rest of them.

She stopped, canting her head as if to hear phantom music. Snow Goose shuffled a few more steps, then halted again.

At the low end of the audible, Max heard the rumble, and felt it in his bones. Sudden claustrophobia raged at him. Were they going to be trapped underground? Were they . . . ?

No. The screaming had a personality. It was the roar of something alive, something huge.

They were approaching the gates of Hell. Didn't he expect the Inuit equivalent of Cerberus?

Orson gripped his spear. "Snow Goose. Can I have one of those cigarettes?"

She nodded, and a twitch at the corners of her lips told Max that his brother, as usual, had been dead on the money. There was a swift babble of requests as the rest of them followed suit, and then swift multiple fires as the sacred cylinders were lit all around.

Max braced himself for the worst, and sucked smoke. He was surprised. For unfiltered, hand-rolled cigarettes, these were mild, almost like smoking air. But luminous smoke poured from his mouth and nose as he exhaled, and his harpoon began to glow.

Ahead of him, Snow Goose stopped, exhaling smoke against an unyielding wall.

Hebert joined her, blew hard against it, then slapped at it with the pink palm of his hand. "What's the matter?"

"The ice's been protected against magic." She said it in one of those matter-of-fact voices that made you ashamed to have asked such a stupid question.

"How do we get through it?"

"We can't stop here. The way to Sedna lies beyond the underworld." Snow Goose frowned. "Where magic fails, perhaps muscle . . . ?"

The face of the ice sheet measured eight feet across. Behind it, something flickered dimly, a vague, sluggish movement. Max had the impression of something monstrously tall that moved with unnatural vitality. It seemed to be balancing on one leg.

Then the shadow was gone, and the skin on the back of his neck ceased to creep.

"*Karate Kid*," Kevin said. "Part Seventeen."

"Exactly," Snow Goose said softly. "Let's put our backs to it."

Max set his cheek against the ice. Orson and Trianna joined him; both flinched from the cold. "Go," said Orson, and they heaved. The ice might have moved a tenth of an inch.

Charlene moved between Orson and Max. *Heave.* Nothing.

She and Orson shared a ragged smile. "What's a nice boy like you doing in a place like this?" she gasped.

"My brother said, 'Let's go for a walk.'"

"Heave," Max said, and they heaved. The ice wall might have shifted, or not. "Rest. Let it settle. Heave!"

Kevin consulted his pocket computer, then politely moved Charlene and Orson aside. "I've got soot!" he chirped. "And Max has an owl claw. That makes us the strongest ones here!" He leaned against the ice and strained mightily.

There was no more conversation, just the sound of fevered breathing in a confined space, as the largest and smallest of the Gamers bent their backs against eight feet of ice.

With a long brittle note, the first fissure appeared in the wall. As it deepened, a vast network of tiny cracks turned the entire sheet milky.

Max stepped back. He heaved for breath and said, "Hulk smash!" and ran at the wall.

The thud must have been audible in Gaming A. There was a moment in which nothing happened, and then the entire barrier shattered, almost in slow motion. Max lurched through a couple of steps, skidding on shards, before he could stop.

Kevin flexed his arm and made a tiny biceps, face positively luminous.

The air was gray with a dense mist that flowed like an angry ocean, churned in the cavernous opening like cold smoke. Every sound they made, every footstep or whisper, reverberated like a sneeze in a tomb. The mist chilled Max to the bone. It was a sticky cold. The furs and thermal-reflective lining of his jacket seemed helpless against it.

His mind rioted, trying to make sensible shapes out of that roiling fog. It formed and re-formed itself into grotesque illusions, shadows cast by impossible shapes: a suggestion of tremendous jaws, a sudden glimpse of a hundred pairs of eyes, the bones of a hand brushing across his face. As the other Adventurers pushed through behind him, he felt their unease as an extension of his own.

"Welcome to Hell," he said quietly, helping Trianna past a stack of ice chips. She looked pained.

Without any stated intention, the group formed a circle, standing close enough to touch shoulders. One could not see the size of it, but the moving rivers of fog, the echoes, all told of a cavern as big as the world.

Max felt the urge to scream, to do something to fill the horrid emptiness around him. He felt utterly cowed.

"It must be your decision to go ahead," Snow Goose said. "I don't know how much protection I can offer you."

Yarnall peered out into the mist. Somewhere on the other side of that shifting veil, a vibration sounded. It might have been something natural—the sound of the earth shifting, perhaps, or the cry of an animal. If it was an animal, it was a maddened one, and the hair on Max's arms stood up and tingled. "We've gotta go," the National Guardsman said. "Listen. There's something out there. We can't go back—the sun is dying, and so will we. We can't stay where we are. The Cabal will just send something to get us."

Frankish Oliver's club raised in agreement. "Let's meet it head-on."

Snow Goose nodded approvingly. "We will sing songs for the spirits of those who die."

"Unless we all buy it," Orson reminded her.

"A rainbow of light and happiness, you are."

Chapter Sixteen

THE PAIJA

The fog swallowed them. Snow Goose seemed sure of her directions. There was rarely a choice. They followed ridges and smooth rock, the path of least resistance. Where the path forked, Max glimpsed smoke drifting from Snow Goose's mouth.

Now they were crossing a land bridge so high up that the floor vanished into the mist, and only giant stalagmites rising up like mountains through the clouds told them there was any floor at all. They trooped single file, and Max found himself behind Charlene. She was limping. A glimpse of her profile showed excitement and anticipation and a certain sadness.

"Charlene?"

She half-turned with that oddly angular grace: she reminded him of a praying mantis. She was breathing too hard, trying to disguise it behind a game smile.

"Do you miss your friend? Eviane?"

Charlene sighed. As tall as she was, she was losing inches, drooping. Gravity was pulling her down. Brother Orson hung back to listen to the conversation.

"We're friends, but . . . we'd barely met," she said wistfully.

"How's that?" Orson asked.

"We met on the Gaming channels. For maybe a year we've been playing everything we could get into, and she kept telling me about Dream Park. I'd heard of it. She said that I had to come. Tell the truth, I wasn't all that hot on it. I thought one of the Cook Islands, or maybe Greece. But I wanted to meet Eviane." She paused. "I don't have that many friends. So I came, and before I could blink, Eviane was killed."

"Doesn't seem fair, does it? How's your leg?"

She smiled ruefully. "I thought I was hiding that. I can walk it out."

Orson noticeably straightened up. "If you need help carrying anything, let me know."

Her long face softened and her eyes shone gratefully.

The bridge narrowed up ahead, and now walking single file became more critical.

Max knew he shouldn't look down, but his eyes wouldn't obey. Down there in the frozen, crawling wastes, something lived, something watched. He knew it. Maybe not alive. Maybe dead and damned . . .

From up ahead came a repetition of the roaring, piercing bass note. Quake! The entire cave shook with it. Max dropped to his belly, set his cheek against the stone of the natural bridge, and waited. He saw Johnny Welsh lose his balance, drop to his hands and knees, and roll toward the edge anyway.

Trianna caught him with one arm, helped him, shaking, to his feet. "I'm always falling for blondes," he said.

The mist thickened and thinned in pulses. The tremors had not quite died. Yarnall, taking an unsteady lead, kept peeking back over his shoulder as if the bunch of them might rabbit at any moment. The bridge now measured barely two feet across. Beneath gaped infinity.

If you focused your eyes carefully into the depths, the mists occasionally parted, and the cavern stretched away into endless night. It seemed to Max that he could see stars down there, but it might have been the reflection of strange light on ice crystals. He shivered.

Step by careful step, they crossed that bridge. Those two feet of path began to feel like a tightrope. Snow Goose stopped them. "Wait. Stop now, and find your breathing."

"What?" Bowles said cautiously.

"Your breathing." She placed her hands about an inch below her navel. "Breathe down to here, to the center of your body. You will find the balance you will need."

"I don't know what you're talking about," Orson complained. "Center of my body?"

"Ignore the flesh," she insisted. "Feel your way to the center. Steady your breathing and visualize, or you will not survive."

"What I visualize," Orson whimpered, "is getting chucked off this bridge, and controlling my breathing all the way to the bottom."

The wind keened, sighed mockingly. Despite his uneasy balance, and the strangeness, and the fear he felt here on the edge of infinity, Max searched within himself, struggled to see something beneath the layers of clothing, the muscle,

(the fat)

the organs and tissues,

(the fat)

and down to the bones themselves, saw himself as a skeleton, standing on a two-foot bridge over the very pit of Hell, that damned wind whistling hollow through his bones.

When he found that place, curiously, he felt warmer, more relaxed. When he opened his eyes, there was less fear.

Her next words touched his ears as from across a gulf. "Now keep your breathing constant and smooth, and follow me."

Max chose his steps with care. Once he stumbled, wavered, lost his balance, but his toe found purchase where there should have been only air.

(He reached his toe out again to test the "air" beyond the strip of bridge. He found solidity, but it was invisible. He decided not to trust it . . . but he felt better.)

The path began to widen. The group had just heaved a collective sigh of relief when—

Another terrible scream of rage.

Close, and from no discernible direction.

Yarnall moved more quickly, trying to get them onto the widened path. It was almost six feet across here, and they began to walk in twos, Yarnall and Kevin in the front, war clubs facing off against the unknown. Kevin clutched at the bag around his neck, as if milking it for strength.

Behind him were Orson and Snow Goose, and behind them Max and Charlene.

The mist congealed and cleared again and showed him unreality, illusion. Max tried to blink it away:

It stood twenty feet tall. He would have called it a woman, because of the pendulous breasts only partially concealed by an eight-foot cascade of flowing black hair. But the face was a demon's face, wild and inhuman, with brown teeth like chisels and eyes that closed to slits. With each breath, the entire wrinkled face expanded and contracted. Her arms, muscular and wide-spread, were tipped with evil hooked nails longer than the head of Max's spear.

That wasn't the worst. Not by a bunch. The creature had only one leg, and that leg came from, well, from the genitalia.

"What do you call someone with no arms and no legs, with a

wooden stick up his backside?" Johnny asked quietly.

That thick, obscene leg flexed, and the creature stretched down. Hooked nails curled around a misted stalagmite. A quick convulsion of python muscles, and the great chunk of rock snapped off in its hand, a ten-foot limestone club that coruscated in the darkness like a wet fuse.

Snow Goose backed them up. "Paija!" she said urgently. "We've gotta go back to where the path is too narrow for her to follow, and get ready."

"No argument here," Max heard Yarnall mutter.

They backed up along the path. The Paija hissed venomously at them, Cerberus at the gates of Hades.

"Your amulets!" she cried.

Where did I put that? Max rooted around in his bag until he found his gift from Martin the Arctic Fox, an owl's claw petrified almost into a knot. Snow Goose took it. She took Kevin's leather pouch and poured a thin stream of black powder into the palm of her hand. Her round face crinkled happily. "Strength! Soot is stronger than fire."

"I should be carrying Ajax cleanser," Johnny Welsh said. "Stronger than soot."

Trianna rubbed his shoulder. "Your bird worked when we needed it, Johnny."

He abandoned his scowl and gave her a quick hug.

Each Adventurer made his contribution in turn, and the little pile grew. The woman-demon grew tired of waiting. She hopped a step closer along the stone bridge. The bridge groaned in distress.

"Hurry!" Snow Goose bit her lip, thinking quickly. "You spoke of the fiber in your backpacks. You said it had power, perhaps more power than the amulets. Quickly, take them off, stack them in a pile."

Yarnall, Hebert, and Ollie shucked their backpacks and complied. They kept worried eyes on the she-thing and flapped their arms for balance, but moved as quickly as possible.

"The suspense is killing me," Kevin said to Johnny as they shucked backpacks. "What do you call someone with no arms and no legs, with a wooden stick up the backside?"

"Pop."

"Groan."

Hippogryph added his backpack to the pile.

"What *is* that creature?" Bowles asked.

"Good question," Max said ruminatively. "Looks like something out of 'Saucer Sluts Meet Hercules.'"

Bowles looked pained. "Please. I was a child. When I signed the contracts they called it 'Space Maidens on Olympus.'"

"Sorry about that."

"Shh," Snow Goose said urgently. "It's called a Paija. It's a demon, but the Cabal must have brought it here to guard the entrance. This isn't good."

Max whispered, "Why *would* it be?"

"Heh. Yes. But they must have more power than Daddy thought. Hurry."

She took a leather thong from around her neck, pulled a tiny goose-doll out of her cleavage. She looked around at the others. "Ahh . . . Johnny, we don't want to deplete your charm. Let's see. Oliver. Frankish Oliver." Ollie stepped forward, and she opened the bundle that he wore around his neck, and sighed with relief. "Good. You also have a winged Inua. We can lead." She hunkered down. "Now, the rest of you. All of you have spirit selves. All of you have both flesh and a spirit form. The fleshly form is not strong enough. But perhaps our spirit forms could prevail. If we can trick it, then its magic, its life force, will be ours to command."

She took her totem, and Oliver's, a hawk carved from some hard black substance. "I need string, and I need something that was part of a satellite," she said.

Charlene handed her a pair of gloves. "Put these on."

"No, it's for—"

"Put them on, Snow Goose."

The Inuit maiden shrugged with her eyebrows and pulled the thin gloves over her hands. Delicately, Charlene handed her a spool of thread. "Falling Angel cable. The gloves are made of it too. You don't want to touch the cable with anything but the gloves."

She nodded. She wrapped the two totems together with the thread, then looped the spool into the bundle as well. "We need a song," she said. "A sacred song."

"We don't know any," Max protested.

"No—one of yours will do. Weren't you singing one earlier that spoke of our land? We must pull our worlds closer together."

Orson groaned. "Kevin?"

Smiling and buck-toothed, Kevin strode forward. "Let me see . . ."

Orson covered his ears as Kevin elaborated on his previous theme, picking up the adventures of Eskimo Nell, Dead-Eye Dick, and Mexican Pete in the midst of the most grueling contest in the annals of song.

Snow Goose was all business, chanting happily over her little bundle. The group chimed along with Kevin as the Ballad of Eskimo Nell progressed to its glorious climax.

"Now!" Snow Goose said. Her eyes rolled up, her lips moved, *Dah dee dah dee dah diddity dee*— "Inua of my Ancestors! We fight to keep your rite. Inua of my Ancestors, be at our side this night. O Children of the freezing air, come live within me now. Air spirits come, and join in war to shatter Ahk-lut's dream, ally with us against an evil folk who would blaspheme. Set us free of heavy flesh, set us free from our illusions, set us FREE!"

The air was humming. The bridge beneath their feet vibrated like a plucked guitar string. Max could feel it in his teeth, in his fillings. (Dammit, that hurt! The feeling was like the little chill he'd had on the airplane—what seemed a lifetime ago, but now deeper and stronger, and ouch!)

Snow Goose joined hands with Frankish Oliver. He seemed nervous at first, trying to twist his hand out of her grip, but she held on as the vibration grew stronger and stronger. At last the sound was recognizable as human voices, stripped of euphonics and amplified staggeringly. It was a chant, a ritual chant that was all undertones, a sound like a row of giant gongs ringing beneath three feet of oil.

Snow Goose's outline was the first to change, followed swiftly by Frankish Oliver's. They became like fluid metal, running together, peeling apart, and the light expanded until it surrounded the other Gamers as well, bathing them all in a silvery, gloriously fluxing incandescence.

At first Max saw only a blurred glow. It moved, shifted, and he understood: something intangible was pulling itself free from Max. A moment later he could see its shape.

It was himself, in a way. Once, after a debilitating stretch of fever, he had lost enough weight in his face to see the cheekbones that shaped it, and he recognized them now. But that perfect, idyllic shape turned and gave him a nod, smiling as if they shared some great secret. Max couldn't hear the undertone chanting anymore—it was more like he was a part of it, his body one of the notes. He turned to the other Gamers, and was astonished. From each of them flowed an ectomorphic form, more beautiful than anything they could have aspired to in life. The forms rose above them, hovered there, then joined hands in a circle.

Max stared, trying to absorb what he was seeing. The cave, once the very heart of darkness, glowed with a light which was not of man, or of man's doing. It was a holy light, a miniature aurora borealis, a light which flowed from within the floating, flaming figures.

The floating "spirit" of Snow Goose rotated slowly in the air, her face a calm oval. "Now," she said, "we go."

The spirit forms ranged ahead. Max felt his spear humming with power, and clutched it tightly. It felt warm. The stone bridge they traversed was as narrow, and as frighteningly high over an unfathomable pit, as it had been before; but there was something else. Something new had entered the equation.

It was a sense of *possibilities*.

The Paija stood waiting for them. It was gigantic, bestially beautiful, profane beyond his imaginings, balancing on that single obscene leg like something spawned in a Tijuana freak show.

Its single leg was more like the trunk of an elephant. Boneless. Flexible. It weaved from side to side like some kind of top-heavy cobra, beckoning them onward to death.

For a moment the tableau was complete, and still. Max faded back a little, watching the others, saw Frankish Oliver gripping his war club as if it connected him to the spirit image floating above his head.

The Paija sniffed at the air, her thick, bovine nose wrinkling as if scenting something distasteful.

She gripped her stalagmite club and screamed defiantly and smashed it down on the bridge. The span of rock danced savagely. Dust and rock rained from the invisible ceiling. Kevin fell to his knees and had to be helped up by Bowles. For a moment a twist of genuine fear crossed that freckled face. Then bravado won out, and he was strong and brave once again.

The Paija opened its mouth, *her* mouth, and grinned. Max had never seen so many broken edges in one place. It looked like a junkyard for dental cutlery. The teeth were set in at odd angles, rows and rows of them, like shark's teeth.

The Paija attacked.

"Onward!" Snow Goose yelled, and like the fools they were, they charged.

And above them, so moved their ethereal doubles. With every

step they took, the floating figures above them seemed to gain power. They shone more brightly. The Paija ceased her raving, examined them suspiciously, seemed to reconsider—

Max saw Trianna's spirit fly at the enormous creature like a fairy on speed, moving with such grace and agility that the breath froze in his throat. Quite simply, she was beautiful. The Paija swung at her with its improvised club, and she backpedaled, doing a kind of breast stroke in the air.

Max snuck a peek at the flesh-and-blood Trianna, who was transfixed, her lips slightly parted, eyes gleaming with excitement.

The Paija couldn't seem to touch her. Now the other spirit forms flew in, and when they linked together, that aurora effect was magnified. A fluxing electric rainbow blossomed, and touched the Paija.

The creature screeched in pain and indignation that these tiny creatures would dare to harm it. Far from being slowed, it charged, swinging the club. The stalagmite smashed down just short of Snow Goose, who scrambled back and then caught her balance again. "Don't run! Don't run! It will feed on your fear!"

The Paija glared at them, the forest of black hair shadowing her face. Grunting, it took another step.

The ethereal figures fluttered above it, weaving in and out like a flock of glowing hummingbirds. The Paija swiped at them with the club, handling it like a flyswatter, and only the unnatural agility of the spirit forms kept them from—

Oops. The Paija made contact with Orson's image, just a glancing blow, but Max's brother said, "Ooof!" and rubbed at his shoulder, where a red glowing mark began to grow.

The Paija was beginning to catch the rhythm now. Charlene's image caught a nasty wallop, and Charlene cried, "Wha'?" A red stain began to grow on one leg, glowing in the dark like some kind of phosphorescent fungus. The spirit creatures began to fade.

"Join hands!" Snow Goose grabbed Hebert and Hippogryph, panting as if with physical exertion.

Max reached out for Yarnall's wrist. Yarnall joined with Kevin. The twelve Adventurers formed a semicircle facing the beast.

The creature snarled, sensing victory. The club smashed again on the bridge. The Paija dropped the entire force of its being into the blow. An eight-foot section of rock gave way, splintering and crumbling with a roar like the end of worlds. Max stutter-stepped, struggling for balance.

Snow Goose remained erect, but her face was no longer so strong and determined. She stared down into the gulf before them, the chunks of rock spinning in crazy slow motion into infinity, and she was no longer sure.

The Paija grinned at them and leapt over the gap. Her suction-cup foot gripped the bridge, leaving a moist ring where it landed. She hopped forward.

Max saw Snow Goose crumbling, and he forced himself to his feet. Dammit, he had to do something, and he had to do it now. Tag-team!

In a pro wrestling match the audience would see you screaming obscenities, but they couldn't hear. It didn't matter what you said. Max stood as tall as he could and he screamed up at the Paija. "Monsterrr! We challenge you! We're gonna rip your lips off and make you kiss your own backside!"

Not particularly inspired, but it got her attention. She smiled a smile that said, *me and you, numbnuts* in a universal language. He hefted his spear and pointed it, waiting for magic.

Nothing.

I'm dead, he thought.

But the ethereal double was more substantial now, brighter: he could no longer see through it. It was true! The Paija fed on their fear, and their doubles fed on their courage. He put on his best drill sergeant's voice. "Get up, you slackers! Face this thing off!"

The Paija growled at them, as if undecided, and then Max saw his double launch its spirit spear directly between the Paija's eyes. The monster screamed, reared back, and clasped its wound. The club rose up, and thundered down again directly at Max.

Here goes nothing. Max gritted his teeth and kept the spear upraised. The club landed to the side, deflected by his spear thrust.

The monster was horribly confused now, and in pain. The other Adventurers joined him, joined hands, screamed in concert. They backed the Paija up a short hop, and when they gestured aggressively, their doubles attacked.

It was playing possum. It sprang back to life, and caught Hippogryph's double a good lick. Hippogryph yelped and grabbed his shoulder, which began to glow red. Charlene's double, trying to swoop in close for a shot at its eyes, caught a grazing blow and went spiraling off to the side, almost slamming into a stalagmite before it could catch itself. Charlene's entire right side went red.

But slowly, surely, the Paija was driven back. They cheered, and they screamed, and Max said, "What the hell!" and hurled his spear. It caught the creature in the throat. The Paija staggered backward a hop, teetered for balance, and fell from the bridge. Howling, it tumbled blindly into the blackness.

They all moved to the edge to see it fall, watch it die. Max's double landed in front of him, beautiful, lean, and muscular glowing in that darkness within the earth, and it smiled.

Hell. He was a hero!

Chapter Seventeen

BUTTERFLIES

Slightly blue-faced, Gwen exhaled with relief. For a few seconds, the wail of the wind and the Paija's receding death-howl were the only sounds. Then the Gamers behind her were leaping and screeching and clapping each other on the back.

Gwen watched Hippogryph with some amusement. Hippogryph screeched and Hippogryph leapt; but his face didn't turn toward the sky in triumph; his eyes remained at the level; his big bouncing body formed an unobtrusive barrier between the others and Charlene. Just as well. Her legs looked a little unsteady.

The darkness helped . . . but Gwen could never quite believe that the holograms would mask her and Ollie well enough to produce the illusion of flight. But everything had gone perfectly. Now the Gamers crowded at the lip of the precipice, watching the Paija's image fall to its death. She saw their faces; every damned one of them had been moved by the sight of his spirit image. They stood straighter, walked prouder.

Gwen knew the gimmicks hidden in the Game, and still she felt the effect. She took the time to square herself, then dove headfirst into her "Snow Goose" routine again.

"All right, team! Way to go!"

"That was great!" Orson was vibrating where he stood, his considerable mass jiggling and wiggling with delight. "I feel ready for anything!"

"That's what's next," Charlene surmised. She was panting as much from excitement as exertion. Gwen heard a low beeping tone in her ear, and she glanced over at Ollie.

His left hand was covering his ear, as he listened to medical reports from Central Processing. With his right hand he signaled her: a finger pointing to the ground, followed by a horizontal palm: *slow down.*

It might be that Charlene's vital functions, picked up and

broadcast through mesh underwear, had alerted Central Processing. Maybe it was the heavier Sands brother. For all Orson's jolly sarcasm, Ollie thought he looked ripe for a nice, juicy cardiac incident...

So Gwen's eyes unfocused, and her hand closed powerfully on Orson's wrist as he was about to speak. "I hear them," she said, "whispering," rolling her eyes, "the Gods. They—" She waited for their attentive silence, then squeezed her eyes shut and made a happy pout. "They are most pleased. They say that they will bring us gifts!"

Through the darkness at the cave's unimaginably distant roof there shone a shaft of golden light. It pierced the black and danced palely on the far side of the gap. The beam was broken up by a fluttering motion, something like fat snowflakes...but every "flake" was a living thing, reflecting and adding to the light.

Trianna said it first. "Butterflies!"

Exactly right. White butterflies. They drifted this way and that, creasing the light, reflecting it, questing into the darkness for a moment, then returning to coruscate and sparkle anew.

They landed in a cone, prancing and fluttering in heaps, and covered the ground as if huddling together for warmth against the winter. They crawled over each other in a churning Brownian movement. Any trace of individual identity was submerged in an amoeboid tangle.

Gwen watched the Gamers' eyes, squeezed Ollie's hand in acknowledgment and thanks for his signal.

Then the butterflies took to the air again, leaving behind them—

A huge platter heaped with apples and grapes and pears. There was a small mountain of crackers and breads, four wide-mouthed jugs, and some miscellaneous cans.

"Lunch!" Johnny Welsh said reverently. "My stomach was about to sue me for desertion. Wait a minute—"

The Paija had shattered the stone bridge. They looked at lunch across an eight-foot gap. Kevin asked, "How do we get to it?"

Orson said, "Why don't we just twist you into a rope bridge and walk across?"

"Ha-ha," said Johnny Welsh. "Humor makes me hungry."

"Listen to me," Gwen said. "The stone bridge is destroyed, but in conquering the Paija, we have all gained great power. You must now have pure intention in order to use it. You must truly desire the food."

They were looking at Gwen warily: *crazy and dangerous.* "Believe me, honey," Hebert promised. "That food and I are going to share a deep, spiritual communion."

"Do you remember the lessons you learned from the food last night?"

Sheepishly, Trianna raised her hand. "We need to treat the food like a living thing."

"Is that different from the way you usually treat it?"

She hunched her shoulders. "I remember the lectures, dear. I love food, but it's like building blocks to me. I can make pretty, tasty things out of it—"

The pile of food rustled, and a bunch of grapes turned into butterflies and flew away. Gwen said, "Watch it! The food here is very sensitive."

"I pay honor to the Inua of the food!" Kevin said. Perfect.

"I'd be surprised if he eats at all," Orson growled.

"Did you say something, Mr. Sands?" Gwen made her voice deceptively sweet.

"Well . . ." Puzzles. Orson had to solve puzzles. "I pledge that if this food will, will serve me . . ." He paused to hunt for the right words.

"Then we will serve the food," Johnny Welsh said solemnly. Hippogryph, blind-sided, burst into helpless laughter.

But Orson had his lines worked out. "I will pay honor to it, and attention to what I eat, and only take into my body what I need for nourishment."

Gwen's eyebrows went up. "Can't argue with that."

Max leaned over to Bowles and stage-whispered, "Did you pack your hip boots?"

A shaft of light shone down from the heavens, directly upon Orson.

"Step forward, Orson. If that was the truth, I think it's meal-time."

"I meant it—" Another bunch of grapes started turning white, and Orson shrieked. "All right! All right! Give me a minute, will you! Damn." He was the picture of frustration. He glared menacingly at Gwen. "How'd you know?"

"The Great Spirits. Or maybe a lucky guess. You have that kind of face."

"Don't I know it. All right." He forced his shoulders to relax, and then shrugged. "I haven't done it until now. I was just testing. But I will try, for this meal at least. I promise."

The butterflies fluttered back into the light, settled, and transformed back into grapes.

"If you told the truth," Gwen said, "step out. The Great Spirit will support you."

"You want me to step out on air?"

"No." She said piously, "On faith. Heh-heh."

Orson peered out over the precipice. His lips made a wet, unhappy sound. He took a step, feeling out over the gap with his toe, the rest of his balance safely held in reserve.

His foot was balancing on nothing. He breathed a sigh of relief, and took another step. Then Orson Sands was by God doing magic, walking on air like Gene Kelly. All he needed was Jerry Mouse dancing alongside.

He stopped in the middle of the gap and looked down past his feet, down into the depths where the Paija had vanished, and then back at them with a smile that showed every tooth. When he crossed to the other side he salaamed deeply, damn near kissed the ground, then did a little jig-step which took him over to the food.

Orson prodded a grape with one heavy finger. The sun came up behind his eyes. "It's real!"

He plopped down and grabbed handfuls, a pear in one hand and a bunch of purple grapes in the other—

Then he set the pear down and began eating grapes one at a time.

Gwen beamed. "Next?"

One at a time they went through the ritual. The "Great Spirits" seemed to know when they were lying and when they weren't. Gwen savored their bewilderment.

Now that they had enough of a break to realize how long it had been since breakfast, hunger was a raging fire. The butterflies returned every time a lie was told, and Gwen called them on it.

Trianna swore she would honor her food, but she was lying. Gwen knew it, Trianna knew it, and most importantly, the technicians back in Gaming Central knew. They knew from reading body signs from the mesh underwear: blood pressure, skin temperature, galvanic skin response, heartbeat and respiration rates.

Tears streamed down Trianna's lovely face. Her shoulder-length blond hair seemed flat and lifeless. "What do you want from me? I love food. How can you say I don't? How do you think I got this heavy if I didn't?"

"Do you love it," Gwen asked soberly, "or do you use it? You hide in your body, Trianna."

Trianna was so upset that she was actually bawling now. "What do you want me to say? I—I . . . shit!"

Kevin took her shoulders. "Just slow down and notice your food."

Her eyes raked him; they should have raised welts. "And you? You damn skeleton, when did you ever notice food? You look like nobody ever told you about that part."

Those words had hurt: Kevin blinked his hollow eyes against the pain. "I'm here too," he said quietly. "We're pretty much the same, Trianna. Both of us need to be okay with not being perfect. I'm tired of being scared." He smiled tentatively. "Aren't you?"

Trianna swallowed hard. Gwen felt sympathy but bit it back. Trianna ate sedately enough around the group, but it was increasingly easy to picture her at home, alone in her apartment. A mindless Oreo cookie zombie, shoveling food into her mouth as if that gorgeous face and that lumpy body lived in different zip codes. Deli of the living dead.

Trianna said: "I swear I'll try. I want to tell the truth about it." Her voice was a little girl's, barely a squeak. "I want to." This time Gwen didn't get a warning beep in her ear. Trianna tottered across the bridge and sat, snuffling quietly, and picked at her lunch.

Kevin watched her, licked his lips, and ran a thin hand across the parchment of his face. On the far side of that gap was health, self-respect. Salvation.

What war was it he fought? He spoke of perfection. What was his unattainable ideal, that he compensated by being perfect at self-denial? What was so spin-dizzy in his life that he made up for it by controlling every crumb he ate, would take perverse pride in his conquest of the physical hungers?

His anguish was almost too painful to watch.

"What do you want from me?" he asked finally.

Ollie's voice was kind. "Just the truth, Kevin."

"If I eat too much I'll have to throw up." He said it as if the admission had cost him skin.

Kevin was afraid, literally afraid to cross that gap to where the others sat eating, bathed in golden light.

Slowly, Trianna came to her feet. Tears still slicked her face. She held her arms out to Kevin, and Gwen could almost see lines of strange magnetism connecting the two of them. As if they were bizarre mirror-images of each other. The fat lady and the skeleton boy, prides of the side-show.

No one said a word. There was no sound, and then Kevin made a soft, wet, desperate sound, and stumbled across the gap, dancing on air, into Trianna's comforting arms.

One by one they went through it. Gwen was relieved to note that nobody tried to test the boundaries. It might have been interesting to try keeping Max Sands from charging across that bridge. He could carry her and Ollie without much of a second thought. Carry, or dump them over the side.

But at last they were all seated, eating, actually enjoying the meal Dream Park had set for them. The pears were crisp and flavorful, and the cheddar cheese was so sharp it almost singed her tongue. Gwen herself loved pears. It was easy to respect a good pear, because a bad pear was *so* bad.

Johnny Welsh was drinking coffee from a paper cup thoughtfully provided by the Gods, and chewing on a makeshift cheese sandwich. He looked as if he had died and gone to heaven. Everyone ate more slowly than they had at breakfast. Maybe the excellence of the food and drink had something to do with that. Something, but not all.

Johnny belched contentedly. "Java blend," he said. "Last coffee I had was on the tube out from Denver." He made a face.

Hippogryph was willing. "That bad?"

"Let's put it this way. I had the concierge send it out to a lab. Got a call back saying 'Congratulations, your moose is pregnant.'"

Hippogryph sprayed a mouthful of grape juice, narrowly missing Kevin, who lunged out of the way. "Jeeze—will you watch your timing?" Kevin said plaintively.

Johnny smiled wickedly. "Sorry about that."

Orson popped open one of the cans, drank, and made a face at Snow Goose. "You brought me all the way to Hell for *sugar-free 7-Up?*"

They sat in a circle on a stone bridge over the pit of infinity. Max looked a little distant, wistful, that massive, muscular body sagging somewhat in repose. Gwen wondered what he was thinking. There was no way for Dream Park magic to give her that piece of information.

Yet.

They were on the move again, and the trail began to lead gently downward. The air was chilling, and the wind plucked at Max's face and hair more fiercely.

Part of it was his imagination. The howl of the wind had increased more than its velocity. The temperature had only dropped a few degrees.

The path grew narrower and narrower, and then the walls were well within reach, rock glazed with ice. The wind was a hollow, reedlike whistle in their ears. Moods recently elevated by a fine meal went edgy. They gripped their weapons tightly and walked single file.

At first, the cries might have been mistaken for a trick of the wind. Then Max heard them for what they were—the endless moaning and shrieking of the Eskimo damned.

So far there was nothing to see. Light had diminished to a murky dusk.

Then a glowing aurora illuminated the scene, and Max felt the pit of his stomach tighten.

Naked men and women stumbled blindly through deep snow. One man staggered across jagged rocks with a caribou lashed across his shoulders. His feet were torn and bleeding. Blood trailed down his back from a gash along the caribou's ribs. The caribou kicked and wriggled in nightmarish slow-motion.

Snow Goose stiffened, then ran jerkily to a spot where a stone wall caused the path to branch. An Eskimo was lashed to the wall with leather thongs. Butterflies fluttered around his head, and he snapped at them with his teeth. He caught one and ate it. Other Eskimos were bound identically. Their movements were sluggish and awkward as they lunged uselessly against their fetters.

"Wood Owl!" Snow Goose cried.

He looked up at her dully. "Who . . . ? Who is there?" Then she stepped closer, and his eyes focused. His lips curved, making a small sad smile. "Snow Goose. It is you. How did you die?"

"No, Wood Owl. I come with friends. We fight to destroy the Cabal."

He nodded. A butterfly fluttered too close to his mouth. He snapped it out of the air, and chewed thoughtfully. "Could use a little salt."

"What's it like being dead?" Hebert asked.

"Not bad, really," Wood Owl answered after a moment's consideration. "Like waiting for a tax refund, only slower." He looked at Snow Goose regretfully. "I would not have made you a good mate, but I loved you."

"You died for me. So you were a lousy hunter. I turned vegetarian at ASU. No problem."

"When you see your father again? Tell him I've seen cousin Gray Otter. We can stop wondering about why Gray Otter's wife cut his throat and drowned herself. Seems he was sharing furs with Weeping Walrus when he was supposed to be fishing."

"Soap operas in Hell," Bowles mused. "The mind boggles."

"Death will not release you," Wood Owl agreed.

Snow Goose smiled bravely, and they continued on. Max kept looking back at Wood Owl, lashed to his stone and snapping at the cluster of butterflies around his face, until they rounded the corner of the wall.

Hell was a small place, evidently. The next group of damned they encountered were all half-naked women. Blue lines and dots made patterns on their faces. They cried, holding their hands out to the travelers, and begging in a language that he couldn't understand.

"What was their sin?" Max asked Snow Goose.

"They have bad tattoos."

Orson's jaw dropped, and he looked at the Eskimo dead with new interest. Studying their tattoos, of course. Max said, "That's pretty minor. What kind of Gods are these?"

"Petty, like all Gods. On the other hand, there's no penalty at all for masturbation."

"I'm changing religion," Kevin said positively. "Obviously, I have strong Eskimo blood and never knew it."

The women were all black-haired and sullen, except for a woman in her thirties, with flaming red hair, who hung numbly in her bonds. Her green eyes were partially unfocused. Slowly, she lifted her head. "Who . . . ?"

Max cried, "Eviane!"

Her confusion lasted only a moment; recognition following swiftly. "My comrades," Eviane said. Tears streaked her face. "I knew you would come for me. Even Hell couldn't keep us apart."

Chapter Eighteen

RESEARCH AND DEVELOPMENT

Transit time from Security to Research and Development, on the far side of the park, was about forty-five seconds when Alex could catch the right routing.

There was the gentle bump as his shuttle capsule hit the bottom of the vertical tube, a moment's hesitation as the gyros rotated the capsule, and then a *shush* as he accelerated, like a bullet fired beneath the thriving metropolis that was Dream Park.

For some of the trip, the clear walls of the shuttle revealed nothing save an occasional flash of light.

The maintenance shops were along this route. The Chief of Maintenance liked the transit tubes through her sector to be clear, so that she could see the shuttles streaking past.

Six years ago, a study had given Maintenance the greatest efficiency level of any department in Dream Park. This was considered puzzling. Someone noted that instead of the green or blue worn by maintenance personnel in the other companies, the Dream Park crew wore white, more like a doctor's gown than the uniform of one who keeps pipes and wires humming.

Sandy Khresla, a chunky little woman with a Ph.D. in environmental engineering, was the pipe-smoking head of the division. When someone asked her why she chose such untraditional garb, she smiled as if she had been watching her clock and her calendar, wondering when the big brains would get around to asking that question.

"We service the veins and arteries of Dream Park," she said around a mouthful of sweet, quasi-contraband Turkish smoke. "You guys are the brains or the arms, and transportation is the legs. But we're the heart. Without us, everything dies."

Alex Griffin remembered that story as Sandy's offices flashed by. Three white uniforms huddled in conversation. A pair of eyes flicked in his direction, then indifferently away.

He thought of all the people who took their jobs so damned seriously, toiling for seventeen and twenty hours a day, who often had to be pried away from their desks and terminals. They believed in the dream. How would they feel if they knew? What if they knew of his mission?

The capsule *shushed* to a halt in the basement of R&D, quieted for a moment as it was switched to a rail, and then began to rise. The shuttles sat up to four people, and were completely modular, capable of hooking onto either the vertical or diagonal tracks that could take them anywhere in the Park.

An insanely complex machine. There were problems with such complexity, of course. The more complex a machine is, the more vulnerable it is to sabotage or simple breakdown. Obviously Fekesh had implanted a cancer somewhere in the organism that was Dream Park. Alex hoped it had not yet metastasized.

The shuttle door clicked open. Alex stretched his legs and pushed himself out.

He was standing on his head in the middle of a desert. Date palms hung by their roots below the horizon. A slow-moving line of camels walked upside down in the distance.

Alex stopped, checking his sense of balance. He didn't *think* he'd fallen over. So he took a few cautious steps in that direction, to see if the perspective would shift.

It didn't. He looked down at his feet. He was standing on a cloud. Arms stretched up to their maximum buried his hands in intangible sand.

"Hello? Is anyone here?"

No answer, but he thought that he heard a cough. The sun was beating up with unnatural ferocity, but there was no heat. It felt more like the air conditioning was turned up to full, possibly as a minor side effect of turning the entire region upside down. Dream Park had finally figured out a way to make the Sahara livable. How much would Fekesh pay for that?

"Hello? This is Alex Griffin from Security."

"Oh, shit," someone said from behind a shimmering dune. The entire illusion flickered, then died.

He was standing right side up in the hall, surrounded by gleaming Formica floors and fluorescent ceilings and all of the usual floating video boards and packed trophy cases. The only unusual thing was the holo projection device out in the middle of the hallway, inverted and poking halfway out of a door.

Curious, Alex approached cautiously. "Ah—hello? What exactly are you doing?"

The young man wiggling from under the machine was brown-eyed and innocent, with long wavy brown hair and an engaging thin-lipped smile. He looked more like a fullback than a lab tech, and was dressed in a pair of blue denim overalls. He spread his hands in supplication. "I don't know who the hell built this thing," he said, "but the only way you can reach the main processor is from the bottom. The function keys are on the top. I'm having a wonderful time."

The device was a standard holo projection unit, an older model, vaguely reminiscent of an old planetarium projector.

"Can I help you with something?" the young man asked.

"I'm looking for Dr. Izumi."

"Oh, yeah—" He twisted over from his uncomfortable position and pointed down the hall. "Third door to the left. Think he's in Bioworks today."

"Thanks."

As Alex walked away, man and machine vanished again into the desert, and the young man said "Eureka!" a second before the entire machine shorted out. A colorful stream of adjectives and gerunds followed Alex down the hall.

The second door to the left was standing open. In the midst of a lab filled with monitors, cameras, and floodlights, a human skeleton sat calmly on a folding canvas chair. It turned and looked at Alex, and said, "Yes, can I help you?"

Alex managed a rather lopsided smile, searching for the human being operating the armature. "Ah . . . yes. I'm looking for Dr. Izumi."

The skeleton clicked its teeth in a bizarre rictus that might have been a smile. How would you know if a skeleton was smiling? It was the lip articulation that made most of a "smile" happen.

It stood up and stalked across the room like something out of a nightmare. It held out a bony hand.

All right, he'd go along with the joke, and as soon as the hand went through his, he would declare the joke over and force Izumi to get down to business.

His fingers closed on warm flesh—and then dissolved. The

flesh of his hand ended at the wrist, and two sets of finger bones intertwined.

He gritted his teeth.

The skeleton laughed heartily. "That was priceless," it said. "Just the expression on your face. Excuse me."

It turned its head. Alex expected to hear a creak of tortured bone, but what he got instead was that bemused, cultured voice saying, "Izumi. Save program two-eight-internal and mute."

The air shimmered, and Tom Izumi appeared. He was of medium height, with straight black hair and an incongruously small mouth. For an embarrassing moment, he reminded Griffin of a villain from an old Dick Tracy comic strip, the kind whose physical features mirrored and indicated their criminal tendencies.

"What in the hell was that?" Griffin asked.

"A real-time holographic medical analysis simulator. Utilizes ultrasound projectors built into the walls."

"Don't you need lasers to make a hologram?"

"Heavens no. Any form of energy that can be carried by waves: sound, light, microwaves, or X-rays."

"Whatever happened to 'turn your head and cough'?"

"There's a ton of diagnostic devices in here. I've been scanned up and down and sideways. We just create a three-dimensional model and project it onto the patient."

"What kind of... ah, depth? I guess 'depth' is the word I'm looking for."

"Oh, we can adjust it to any level. Izumi, circulation." His skin disappeared. Alex looked into a coursing network of veins and arteries, with the contracting fist-sized muscle of Izumi's heart pulsing queasily in stage center. The room behind the missing flesh shimmered as if he was seeing it through a heat mirage.

"Could you disappear entirely?"

"Here, in the room? Sure. Could I play invisible man out in the street? Nobody's miniaturized the equipment that far, but I suppose it's possible. The problem would be in reproducing every conceivable angle, so that anyone looking from any direction would see what he expects to see. A little adjustment for focus, maybe..." He became thoughtful. "Come back next month."

"Great." A security chief's worst nightmare, available next month from the gentle lunatics at Research and Development. "Mind turning that off? It's giving me a headache."

"Sure." Izumi smiled toothily, and appeared, fully clothed.

"You're Alex Griffin," he said. "Tomisuburo Izumi."

Alex shook the man's hand again. It was soft, like a baby's. There was something curiously childlike about the man. He had that soft round cheekiness, without the angularity which normally intrudes during adolescence. There was no trace of a beard, and the black hair was undisciplined. The eyes didn't fit in that face. Dark and deep-set, they were fiercely intelligent. "What can I do for you?"

"I don't feel comfortable in a room with so many scans hooked up to it. Is there somewhere we can talk privately?"

Izumi thought for a moment. "There's the party room. Come on." Izumi carefully locked the door behind them and escorted him down the hall.

"Party room?" Alex asked.

"Yes. Our rotation doesn't come up until two in the morning. Australia and Canada will keep things going most of the day."

"What's the record?"

"Nonstop holo party, thirteen months. With the feeds we've got right now, there's no reason to assume that it will ever stop. We're at eight months and cruising."

They stopped in front of a small green door with the legend: "Environmental stress workshop. Please sign in." Alex stifled a laugh as Izumi thumbed the door open, and they entered.

The room buzzed with activity. People laughed, drank, ate from a buffet table. A couple in the far corner were dancing a rumba. Some of the guests looked a little tired. They raised their glasses as Izumi closed the door, and a male voice said, "Tommy y'old slacker! G'day, ey? Good to see you. Who's the straight?"

"This is Alex Griffin, Chief of Security here. Griffin, meet Robin Schultz."

He was short and a bit pudgy, with a magnificent sandy beard. He tilted a bit as he stood up. "Welcome to the party, mate. Shake hands if I could, but you know how it is."

Alex was overwhelmed with curiosity. "Where are you sending from?"

"University of Melbourne, old love. Plasma physics. We've had to shuffle the party around from one lab to the other this week. It's been hysteric."

"Why?"

"Rules. Officially, no one's supposed to know. Unofficially, it's the biggest open secret on campus, and they queue up waiting for us to drop a line." He glanced at his watch. "Well, we only have to host for the next twelve hours. Then Canada takes over. Be glad too. Three days ago, I was the only person here for two whole hours. Lonely, of course, but hey! The party must go on!"

"Listen, Robin," Izumi said, "I need a quiet conversation with Mr. Griffin, and this is the best place here, so we're going to drop off line for a while."

"All right, Tommy. Later, hey?"

The room disappeared. They were in a small studio, maybe a third the size of the ballroom, and Alex swallowed his amazement.

Dammit, he wasn't going to get goggle-eyed again. He just wasn't going to do it.

Izumi said, "So. What can I do for you?"

"Are you sure we're secure here?"

"Very."

Izumi gestured to a couch, and Alex tested it with the tip of his toe before sitting. "I want to talk to you about your brother Calvin."

Tom Izumi stopped breathing for a moment, and his eyes closed. A network of little muscles clenched and relaxed under his eyes. When the mini-rebellion was over, he opened them again and examined Griffin.

"You were not even at Dream Park when Calvin died, Mr. Griffin. What is it that you wish?"

"I need to know more about the circumstances of his death. All of the files are sealed, or erased. The county coroner's office had a terrible accident about eight years ago. Impounded some kind of electromagnet as evidence, and ended up erasing data files. Your brother's included."

"That is most unfortunate."

They paused as someone walked down the hall outside. Izumi reached over and bolted the door.

"What can you tell me about the death?"

Izumi leaned back against the wall, holding a private debate with himself. Then he began to speak. "It was in April. April of '48, I believe. Calvin was working on the combat rifle range we had set up for the California State Sheriffs' Association. He took one of the rifles outside the park for additional testing up in the mountains. One of two shells had been a hangfire. While he was changing targets it detonated, and he was struck in the head. Killed instantly. A hunter found him." He paused, and Alex saw calculations flashing behind those penetrating eyes. "That's really all there is to say. What is it that you're looking for?"

"The truth. I know that Calvin died here, in Dream Park. I know that there was an accident in a Game involving live ammunition. I know that it was no accident. I know about the cover-up."

Tom Izumi was silent. Slowly he rose. "I'm afraid that I have to get back to my work. I'm sure you can understand."

"I can understand your wish to protect Dream Park. I can appreciate your loyalty. You're thinking this is what Calvin would have wanted. But what you have to understand is that there is a chance, just a chance that if you help me, we can nail the people involved. We can do it without airing Dream Park's laundry in public."

Izumi sat back down again. "I don't understand. How?"

"Something new has been added. The Fimbulwinter Game is running again—"

"I know that."

"The girl's back too. She's in the Game under a pseudonym."

Izumi mulled it. "What of it?"

"Persons unknown got her killed out. I've put her back in. And that's it, Tom, that's all I've got. I don't understand enough of what happened yet. Tell me. Help me. Somebody's frightened. If I can get enough information, maybe I can find a pressure point."

"And if you can't?"

"Then we'll be no worse off than we are now. I won't do anything to jeopardize Dream Park, or your family. And at least we'll know that we tried."

Izumi seemed to weigh his words, then he shrugged. "Tried . . . okay. Calvin was a little heavyset, and he liked acting. They asked him to be an Eskimo in one of the Games over in Gaming A. He'd done it a couple of times, I think. Certainly no one expected any trouble. Then we got the call—there had been a terrible accident."

"Who called you?"

"Medical staff. One of the doctors."

"All right, go on."

"My mother and I were working on one of the displays in a trade show set-up, and we hurried to the dispensary. It had been cleared out. Dr. . . . Vails. No, Vail. That was his name, Vail."

"Chief of Psychiatric Services?"

"No, not then, he was just one of the psychs. And Harmony

was there, and two others. A half-dozen security people knew the truth, and three medical personnel. They were all sworn to secrecy. When they showed us the body, we had to make our own choice."

"Just like that?"

"No, it wasn't just like that. Mother fell apart. We had to sedate her. But when she was calm, we realized that justice could not be served. If we tried to find the murderer publicly, the whole thing would come out, and the killers would get the disruption they were seeking. So we covered it up, and we all helped, Mr. Griffin." He paused. "It killed her, you know. She only lasted another year."

In some corner of his mind Alex tallied up another life, gone for nothing. "How did you manage it?"

"Calvin and I were about the same height. The head of Prosthetics joined the conspiracy. She made me up to look like Calvin. Mother started crying again when she saw how good the job was. Really unbelievable. And then I went to a couple of conferences as Calvin, let myself be seen, and then took that rifle out into the mountains."

Alex visualized the pieces thus far presented, letting them fall into place, in proper perspective. "You said you couldn't try to find the murderer publicly. What about privately?"

Tom Izumi smiled mirthlessly. "We went over every possibility, Mr. Griffin, and we came up with only two ways that rifle could have gotten into the Game."

"I'd like to know. I want to see."

Izumi paused, and nodded, and said, "All right, come with me."

Griffin wondered briefly how his subconscious had known that they would end up in Maintenance. Why else would he have had such a strong reaction to passing that window?

Sandy Khresla spent a lot of time outdoors. The sun had put streams of red in her straight black hair and turned her skin nut-brown. She was a demon softball pitcher; he'd watched her. She had the muscle to put speed on that heavy ball. Most women develop soft, smooth muscle contours; but a few, like Sandy Khresla, grow hard and defined. He'd lay long odds she pumped iron.

The blue smoke of an aromatic pipe tobacco hovered around her. Alex missed her leathery smile. She looked dangerous without it. She had never looked at him like this: like an enemy.

He said, "So you know about all of this too?"

Sandy's voice was surprisingly deep. "When they started poking around, Griff, there was only one place to go. We're the only people who have complete knowledge of every entrance and exit, how everything moves. I was just a junior supervisor then, but Calvin and I were tight. When his brother came to me and told me the truth, they knew they could trust me."

Alex nodded. He felt like a Johnny-come-lately around these old-timers. "So what conclusions did you come to?"

"We have to go back to an earlier set of detail maps. A lot of additions were made six years ago, and new security put in."

She called maps up on the computer, until a scale map of Dream Park rotated on the table in front of them. The image flashed and expanded, flashed and expanded, until they were looking at the dome of Gaming B, tangential to Gaming A but sharing no walls or surface connections.

"If I remember right, the Game was this winter thing. Eskimos. Sun going out. We had every refrigerator unit pumping at once."

"Fimbulwinter."

"Whatever. Okay, at the end of the Game the Gamers have lost almost everything, but there are still some weapons left behind after an airplane crash. These are handed out to the Gamers who need them so they can fight this last big battle. Are you with me so far?"

"No problem."

"Now, all of the rifles are coded and numbered. The rifle that killed was indistinguishable from a Dream Park rifle. It hadn't been modified. Somebody smuggled it in at the last minute, and handed it to that poor little mouse—"

"Michelle Sturgeon."

"Yeah, that was it. Kid never had a chance. She had the highest score of anyone in the Game, you know that? They may have picked her for that."

Alex examined the checkpoints. The Dream Park armory was an ultra-high security area, and all weapons were checked, rechecked, and the complete breakdown recorded on videochip for reference. Some of the weapons were replicas, and could never fire. Many were fantasy weapons dreamed up by R&D. But a few were antiques, or army surplus, and needed safety modification.

Tom Izumi traced his finger along the underground connecting tunnels. "This rifle entered the Game here, at a service duct, or here, at the players' entrance. This corridor, where the equipment is brought up, is very secure."

"But . . . ?"

"But. One of our Eskimos disappeared after the Game. Poof, gone. Laid a false trail and was out of the country, as far as we can determine."

"Pictures?"

"Yes," Izumi said. "I can have them to your office this afternoon."

"One of the Actors smuggled in a rifle, switched it, and carted the modified rifle away?"

"It seems the simplest explanation," Sandy said.

Alex thought, and thought, and finally sighed. "I need more information. I think there must be a simple answer. Get me the data on the Actor. What was his name?"

"Called himself Toby Lee Harlow Jr. All of the files were lifted, but I got them out of the system, and kept them." Once again, Griffin was treated to that utterly merciless smile.

"Just in case."

Chapter Nineteen

OLD FRIENDS

Millicent Summers's office was tucked away beneath the Blue Lagoon swimming spa. A wall-wide window piped in a view of clear blue water. Healthy young and firm old bodies smashed through the rippling mirror-surface and drove swarms of bubbles under as they plunged.

Millicent's head snapped around, and she sprang out of her chair delightedly. "Alex! I was hoping you'd come by."

"Couldn't stay away," he said. He didn't need a mirror to know that his smile wasn't very convincing. "Besides," he said with more bitterness than he had intended, "I don't know who I can trust."

She was taken aback, opened her mouth and closed it without speaking. Millicent spun without touching him, and raised her voice. "Are you there, Jackie?"

"Yes, Miss Summers."

"Hold all my calls for the next hour."

"Yes, ma'am."

Millicent led Alex by the hand over to her desk, and sat with him. "Why don't you tell me about it?"

"I don't have enough yet, but . . ." He reached over to her key pad. "Mind?"

"What's mine is yours."

He typed his security code in, and made a few quick routing instructions. When he looked up, he saw that she was seriously concerned.

"Alex, you don't usually ignore an innuendo."

"Millie, I can't trust anyone who was here ten years ago. You came in seven years ago, so that's why we're talking."

"And here I thought it was my lucid personality."

"I need that too."

"So talk." The smile was gone. Millicent knew him too well

to expect pleasantries, or anything pleasant at all.

He took a deep breath. "All right. Ten years ago, Cowles Industries was in trouble."

"Financial trouble. I know, I've got it in my files."

"There was going to be a hostile takeover, but enough stockholders held on out of loyalty to make it difficult. And then somebody, no one's sure who, but his initials are Kareem Fekesh, set up an accident that would help to scare off some of our supporters. Enough to tip the scales."

"Kareem Fekesh ... I'll look him up. What kind of an accident?"

"Murder. A man named Calvin Izumi was killed during the playing of the Fimbulwinter Game. The woman who killed him is a Michelle Sturgeon. She popped back up in the park two days ago."

Millicent sat down hard, her face tight. "Oh. That Michelle Sturgeon." She searched his face for clues. "All right, Griff. What can I do?"

"Help me sort through this. This first part isn't pleasant at all, and maybe only Harmony has had the nerve to look at it."

"What's that?"

"It was no outside job. The current theory among the bereaved is that someone came in as an Actor, switched rifles, and carried the dummy away somehow."

"You don't buy that."

"Not for a hot second. *Ah.*"

Millicent's wall screen beeped, and a picture took form. It showed a man in Eskimo makeup, pouchy cheeks, epicanthic folds, and long, glossy black Mongol hair. The next picture was of the same man out of makeup. The two pictures matched only vaguely.

"Have they run this through FBI? How long ago did this all happen?"

"Maybe ten years. And the FBI wouldn't have looked too carefully. We never let them know just how serious it was."

Millicent's puzzlement was obvious and easy to understand. Griffin took a few minutes to explain the facts of life. When he was done, she exhaled harshly. "Wait. I'm going to need some coffee for this. You?"

"No, thanks. My ulcer already has all the acid it needs. Anyway, my bet is that that picture isn't of our man. Anyone who could tamper with the Game data banks to reprogram a hologram can certainly change a few pictures. And the person who can do both of those things is no short-time employee. Even if he was, his intimate knowledge of Dream Park security and operations means that he had a collaborator."

"So what do you think happened?"

"Not that difficult. Our traitor entered himself pseudonymously into the Gaming Actor roster. Donned makeup. On the day of the Game, guards ferried rifles from the armory to Gaming B. Our traitor got several of them to be distributed. He disassembled one and restored it to firing condition. For a practiced expert, maybe two minutes of work, but he had to be carrying the tools and parts he needed. He passed the rifle to Michelle Sturgeon, and got out of there . . . let himself be killed out, I'd guess. The stolen parts were dumped in a scrap-metal recycler." Alex sighed. "That's really all there is to it, Mil. I wish there were more."

"Sure there's more. Did he replace another Actor? Or was there just one extra Eskimo in the Game, made up out of whole cloth?"

"One extra. Numbers changed throughout the program."

She mulled it. "So what can I do for you?"

"First, I want to know which Dream Park employees at the time had large registered blocks of stock in the company. It's thin, but a natural way to pay off the traitor. Second, I want you to put a trace on the level of interest Mr. Kareem Fekesh had in the Park at the time. That will be hard. I'm sure that he covered his trail."

"I . . . don't know whether I can get that information, Alex."

"Not alone. I'm going to get you help."

"Help?"

"You'll see."

Sunlight was beginning to dwindle by the time Millicent teased the first precious pieces of data out of the computer banks. The list of stockholders in Cowles Industries circa 2048 was immense—there had been a profit-sharing plan in place far earlier than that, and many employees funneled their funds back into the Park. Only about twenty current employees had had over two hundred shares. Harmony's name was there, and so was Dr. Vail. The other names were just names.

"Does this give you what you need?"

Alex scanned the list, nodding slowly. He glanced at his

watch. "And my helper should be available any moment now."

"Are you deliberately trying to be mysterious?"

"No more than usual—ah!"

A beep on Millicent's desk told him that the new call had been routed through. It hadn't taken long.

One section of her screen cleared, and a young man appeared. He had reddish hair and a thin face. His eyes looked tired but still very alive. His lips were curled sardonically. "Griffin. How go things in La-La Land?"

"Not so good, Tony. How's Chino?"

"Another eight months and I'm out. Till then, I sleep on my back. I don't suppose—" He finally seemed to see Millicent. "'Scuse me. Have we met?"

"I don't think so . . ."

"Tony. Tony McWhirter. Few years back The Griffin was responsible for sponsoring me into this boy's club."

She nodded. "Right."

"Curiously enough, once I was here, he did just about everything he could to make it as comfortable as possible. Almost as if he had a bad conscience about the whole thing."

"Why would Griff have that?" Millicent was not a good liar. She should have shown surprise.

"The very question. I've asked myself that one many times, and come to no useful conclusion. At any rate, I doubt that this is a social call. What's the job, O Griffin?"

"Tony, I got you a work dispensation to get you points with the parole board and to keep you current on computers until we can get you out. If you're smart enough to break our security system, I want you on our side."

"La-de-dah, S.S.D.D. Same shit, different day. Come on, what's the pitch? You need something, don't you?"

"I surely do. I need you to investigate a man named Kareem Fekesh. Offices in the DuPont building, downtown Los Angeles. Find out everything you can about his involvement with Dream Park, Cowles Industries, as far back as you have to go. A lot of it will be hidden."

"Do I get to violate his civil rights?"

"He's not a citizen."

Tony's sardonic manner dropped away. He studied Griffin's screen image with wonder and a little fear. "That doesn't make it ethical. Anyway, it'll take more computer time than they give me here."

"Yes. Millicent will make one of the banks here available to you. Set up the program and let it run overnight if you have to. I need you to break security on his accounts, stockbrokers, banks, anything else."

"Illegal too."

"You're a criminal, aren't you?"

"Such a mouth. What's in it for me? More time if I'm caught?"

"Tony, everything I've done for you was *gratis*, because I know you never wanted that guard to die. You do this for me, and you will have paid back everything. If you work it through the lines here at Dream Park, your legal risk is minimized."

McWhirter stared at the ceiling. "I don't know. I've only got eight months till parole. Maybe I'll just coast."

Millicent laughed.

Both men looked at her. She said, "Griff, he'd do it for the phone calls."

Emotions chased each other across McWhirter's face. Ultimately he said, "Millicent, wasn't it? I'd like to meet you."

"Meet? Sure, in eight months. Don't count on anything till the second date."

"No, just meet. You're something. Griffin, she's just barely wrong. I get lonely. It's enough to drive me crazy. You have to meet these people. They never heard of role-playing games. They compete for who can remember the bloodiest scene in a slasher movie. They fight over what TV channel to watch! But this is dangerous. Isn't it? I won't die to get phone calls from The Griffin."

The calls were that important to him? Alex found that unnerving. He said, "All right, Tony. This is the most I can say. If you can definitely prove that Fekesh was behind a takeover bid about ten years ago, or that his present involvement in the Park is malign, I'll pull every string I've got, and we'll get you out of there. You'll have a job here waiting for you. Prove it *in court*, Tony."

McWhirter thought. "In court. And he's not a citizen. It's a poor bet, Griffin."

"And?"

"I have a holding account on BIX. Dump your data in there, along with my password and account number into Cowles. Unlimited access?"

"Don't try to screw me, Tony. You play this straight, and your life will turn out fine. Try to take advantage, play with files you shouldn't, and you won't see sunlight until the next Ice Age."

"Aye aye, Cap'n." Tony signed off.

"Whew," Millicent said. "That's a hell of a day's work."

"I'm not through yet. Get me Kareem Fekesh."

Millicent routed the request through the switchboard, and from there a probe hunted for his whereabouts and finally located him in one of the theme hotels. The beeper sounded over and over, then a face of Middle Eastern extraction appeared on the screen.

"Yes, may I help you?"

"I need to talk to Mr. Fekesh." Alex suddenly recognized him. It was Razul, from the War-Bots scenario.

Razul clearly didn't recognize Griffin as anything but some random American. There might have been a gleam of satisfaction under those heavy eyebrows, or it might have been Alex's imagination. "I'm sorry, but he is not available just now."

"This is Alex Griffin, head of Dream Park Security."

The man thought for a moment, and then the screen went blank. Alex drummed his fingers for a full minute, and then the screen came on again.

Fekesh was the picture, the very soul of elegance, and Alex had the distinct impression that he would have felt underdressed in a tuxedo.

"Yes, Mr. Griffin." He spoke like a man on his way to catch a tube.

"I was wondering if I might speak to you for a few minutes. Person to person."

"On what subject?"

"Shall we say . . . unresolved matters of business."

"And how long have these matters remained unresolved?"

"Eight years."

He smiled blandly. "Then I'm afraid they can remain so a while longer. I am a very busy man, Mr. Griffin. In fact, I am due in San Diego in half an hour. Please call my secretary. Perhaps I can find you five minutes next month."

He inclined his head politely and the screen cleared.

Griffin spoke sadly to the blank screen. "I assume you realize: this means war."

"Tough cookie," Millicent said.

"Even tough cookies crumble. I just hope Tony can come up with the leverage."

Chapter Twenty

SIN CITY

A butterfly formed out of the thin fog and fluttered near her mouth. It was a delicate yellow thing, wings tinged with black, and it came too close. She snapped at it, didn't feel her teeth touch anything, but tasted a sweet, mellow tang like sugared toast.

Eviane sighed. It was butterflies today, butterflies tomorrow, butterflies until the end of time. She was trapped in this drifting darkness, surrounded by strangers and silence. She had resigned herself to that fate.

Then clumsy footfalls and raucous voices broke the silence, and she knew that her living comrades had come for her.

Now, this was curious: she felt no surprise. She didn't even turn her head. She only waited with the placid patience of the dead . . . until the moment she heard Max Sands's wonderful, vibrant voice. A moment later he was beaming at her like a full moon, his huge round face shining with astonished pleasure at the sight of her.

Eviane's heart leapt as if she lived.

She noticed Snow Goose cupping her ear, frowning. "Eviane," the Eskimo Princess said, "we were . . ." She stopped, and conferred with Frankish Oliver for a moment. "Yes," she said. Frankish Oliver went away for a few seconds. He came back holding a vicious-looking modern rifle.

"This led us to you, because you held it close to your body." Snow Goose paused, then shook her head violently. "Eviane, I'm not used to this. You're dead. Any of my professors would freak."

"I don't understand," Eviane said, and she didn't. But by her own unreasoning fear of the rifle, she sensed its power.

"It was with you at your death. It has great power, and its link to you was strong. If you wish, we could use it to bring you with us from the underworld."

"Bring me back to life?" Eviane asked, as though somehow she already knew the answer.

Snow Goose was embarrassed. "No, dear. I'm sorry. As a shade, one of the dead, a *tornrait*. You would serve me the way a *tornrait* serves an *angakok*. You would gather information that human senses can't reach. You could be of great help to us, if you would."

There wasn't a moment's hesitation. "I will come." She took the rifle.

The Inuit women around her nodded their approval. Eviane stood and joined the line of heroes. A butterfly drifted too close. Reflexively, Eviane snapped it out of the air. Again, the sugary taste. Also, and curiously, her teeth met no resistance, and she felt nothing go down her throat as she swallowed.

Max was ready to whip worlds. He walked beside Eviane, and could barely restrain himself from grabbing and hugging her.

"Well," he said, trying to begin a conversation. "What's it feel like to die?"

The smile froze on his face. Unmistakably, she was searching herself for an answer. "Well," she said after a long pause, "it's sort of like gym class, only quicker."

He took five more steps before he turned and stared at her. Her face was perfectly serious. Her eyes met his. It couldn't have been a joke. Eviane never joked. And yet. And yet . . .

The path wound among flat boulders of sedimentary rock, more and more of them, until they faced a wall of boulders rising into the gloom of the underworld cavern. The troupe of Adventurers trickled to a halt.

Eviane looked terrified. Max asked nervously, "Something wrong?"

"I remember . . ." Eviane began, and then her voice trailed off.

Charlene and Hippogryph loomed close. "You remember what?" Charlene asked.

"I'm not sure. It was back when I was alive."

Hippogryph looked concerned. Charlene said, "Eviane, dear, if you've got anything to say that might save a life, please—"

"To give information is the task of a *tornrait*," Snow Goose said flatly.

Eviane did her best. "Falling. Slowly. Shapes around me, big massive shadows. Like a dream. Like being dead. But I wasn't afraid of going splat. I was afraid of being crushed."

"Anything else?"

She shook her head.

Snow Goose walked out to where the path disappeared into the boulders. The rocks were flat-sided slabs eight to twelve feet long by half that wide, a bit too uniform for credibility. Thirty or forty feet up, the darkness swallowed them.

She gestured to the rest. "Come on—" Bubbles burst from her mouth and streamed upward. Max gaped, and she grinned at him. Bubbles?

A fish swam past his head. More of an eel, really, some kind of curvy, twisty thing that wiggled fluidly. Its tail almost flicked his nose.

"Son of a bitch," he said. Bubbles obscured his vision for a moment.

Snow Goose gestured to them again, impatiently. "Come on. We're going to have to climb."

Max didn't look down. He could guess how many of the other Gamers were still at the bottom, staring up, thinking how impossible it all was. The rocks were not that badly tilted. It was like climbing a crude stairway, if each stair was a meter higher than the previous one. Hippogryph was climbing backward, pulling Charlene upward by her wrists; they both seemed to be enjoying themselves.

It got harder as Max got higher...but he couldn't catch Eviane. She climbed steadily, unstoppable, panting through gritted teeth, pushing forward and upward toward what terrified her.

And now he saw that the wave of boulders spilled against a vertical rock wall. The wall rose seamless into darkness. It might have been a thousand miles high, the core of a hollow Earth.

"We have to breach the wall," Snow Goose said. "Everyone needs to push. Come on."

Swell. But Max could see what Eviane was doing: choosing a big, nearly flat boulder for her perch; setting her feet, hands flat against the monolithic wall. The boulders were not big enough for two. He chose one next to hers.

Charlene and Hippogryph took Eviane's other side. Like Max, they tried to imitate Eviane. Strange, wasn't it, that she always seemed to know just what to do? So she was just a bit quicker than anyone else. Was he the only one who noticed?

Kevin was giving it his all, but he had climbed no higher than Orson, who was sweating and glaring up at his brother. Trianna and Johnny Welsh had reached the top. Welsh said, "Hulk smash?"

Snow Goose grinned and nodded. Welsh chose a boulder and set his feet. "Push?"

"Push. All at once."

"One, two, three, heave!"

They heaved. Max pushed with everything he had. He could sense the mass of his companions: if they had anything going for them at all, it was mass! But the mass of the stone wall felt infinite. And yet... there was a gritty, crunchy sound against his ear. They'd done something.

Orson and Kevin reached the top, paused a moment to suck air, then joined the effort. Push *harder*—

Snow Goose dropped back, gasping. "All right, take a rest. And then—"

The rest of Snow Goose's sentence was lost in a growing rumble. The rocks began to shimmy.

Eviane's eyes flew open. "Oh my gosh! This is about to—"

All at once and nothing first, the wall disintegrated. The pile of boulders spilled outward. Screams sounded muffled; bubbles streamed from their mouths; and the party was falling through dark water in a cloud of shattered rock.

The entire cavern had dissolved, crumbled. Max was on a falling boulder... for that matter, everyone was on a falling boulder. They sank in a murky cloud of detritus, but they sank faster. Smaller boulders, rocks, pebbles, grit, all rose out of sight and left the view clear. Each Adventurer, astride his own individual boulder, sank sleekly into depths that graded from dark to utter black.

Max felt his ears pop. He laughed. That was too realistic! He hooted, and waved his arms to brother Orson, whose rock was spinning in a slow, lazy circle.

(He could breathe! He had only just noticed that. He was breathing underwater. Unself-consciously he rubbed the side of his neck, looking for gills. Nope, nothing there...)

Although they had to be far below the surface of the ocean, and the water was murky, shafts of light pierced the darkness like silver pillars. The travelers sank down into the depths on a gentle diagonal, slipping through dark and light, past the finny denizens of the deep.

A school of ugly blind fish cozied past him. Showing more good mammalian sense than their cold blood should have allowed, they waited for Trianna. They made kissing motions at her, following almost close enough to touch.

Vaguely through the murk, the bottom was taking shape. Max could almost... he could make out the titanic outline of a woman in repose, though the head was wrong: lumpy, misshapen.

A flutter of panic: the Paija? Nahhh. Too big.

It was a woman, and she was huge. Three hundred feet high if an inch. Bigger. *Sedna*.

The surrounding murk made anything but a vague impression difficult, but it seemed to him that she sat in an attitude of sorrow. Her arms and knees hid her face. She might have been carved of alabaster or of mud; it was just not possible to make out detail. Her shoulders were gently rounded, slumped.

Although she was a giantess, a goddess, Sedna, the mother of life, Max felt the burden which hung heavy upon her. He wanted to hold her, shelter her, protect her.

Well, damn—that was why he'd come, wasn't it?

A wayward current was floating them down toward the gigantic head. He'd been right: Sedna's head was misshapen. A pale brownish mass capped the back and left side of her skull and was spreading down her neck. It had an angular look, less like fungus than like a growth of crystals. White, veinlike threads intersected everywhere, like... roads?

Orson screamed, "Max! They've built a goddamn city in her hair!"

Charlene called, "We're going past!"

The current was sweeping the falling boulders past that growth. *Good.* Landing in a parasite city would have given them no time to think, to plan; but the current was dropping them toward flowing black locks.

This close, Sedna's hair looked like tangled cables. Max began to feel like a wind-caught flea. Their impossible little rock-chariots sifted like sand grains into Sedna's scalp. Max squeezed his eyes shut and braced himself for a bump.

There was none, only a gentle settling sensation.

The boulder seemed to have landed on solid ground, but damned if he would just assume that. Max got down on hands and knees, and backed off the boulder, feeling with his toes until solidity pushed against the metatarsals.

He stood ankle-deep in a mass of cables... of hairs. He

reached down and hefted one: a quarter-inch thick, soft to the touch, running back out of sight. The hair was relatively sparse, thank God, or the Adventurers would have been choked immediately upon arrival.

He checked that the others had arrived safely. There was no need to wonder: each and every boulder had dropped without mishap onto the glorious head of Sedna. Max had an absurd urge to plant a flag. Was this how Neil Armstrong had felt?

His peripheral vision caught something on a strand of hair. Something crawled away, disappearing as he watched, something bigger than his hand.

It gave him the creeps.

Hebert was the first to comment. "I see some kind of big bugs around here. I don't know what to call them."

Johnny Welsh volunteered, "Water bugs, maybe."

The rest of them began to look around, peering in the mesh of cables for "water bugs," but found nothing.

Snow Goose called them to attention. "All right. I think we can safely assume that we made it here in one piece. Which way do we go?"

"Aren't you the one who knows that?"

She laughed. "Please. I've just about run out of magic. Why don't one of you take control of that point?"

Robin Bowles looked very serious. Just as serious, in fact, as he had been when passing sentence on the psycho-killer in *Judge Knott*. A little more puzzled, perhaps. "I think I heard something from over in that direction," he said finally. "Let's take a look."

The hair was piled into thick rows. It was (he hated to admit) slightly greasy to Max's touch. "You'd think that a Goddess could wash her hair twice a week, wouldn't you?"

Orson shot him a dirty look. Trianna said, "She can't comb her hair. That much I remember. No fingers."

Something crunched under his feet, and he heard a high-pitched squealing noise. Peering carefully through the forest of follicles, he saw three more "water bugs."

They gave him the creeps. Smaller than a dog pack, but far too big for bugs. *Yerch.*

Before he had any clue as to what was happening, a net of webbing had settled over him. Before he could respond to it effectively, a second flew over from the opposite direction, and he was entangled. Then his feet were gone from under him, and if the hair hadn't been so spongy and resilient, he might have had a nasty fall. As it was, it was a lot like falling into a stack of fresh-cut grass. Embarrassing, but not at all uncomfortable.

Dream Park wants no lawsuits.

Behind him, Bowles shouted something that Shakespeare never wrote, and grabbed at hair with one hand while trying to keep his balance with the other. It didn't matter: he went down anyway. All of the Adventurers were going down. Kevin dodged and ran, and there were multiple *sputt* sounds before they managed to catch him and drag him down.

Max tumbled and rolled as unseen forces pulled him along. At the lowest threshold of hearing, he could hear tiny, squeaky voices singing:

Hi ho, hi ho, it's off to work we go—

Bump. Bump. A hair as thick as a pencil flapped across his face. Sedna's hair flagged out above him in the drifting currents like a bed of kelp.

They came to rest in a broad bare area, a bald spot in the middle of Sedna's scalp.

Max tugged at the net. Strong. Was it strong enough to stop him if he gave it everything he had . . . ?

Probably.

He wiggled over until he was on his other side. Brother Orson lay about four feet away, one eye visible through the black stalks.

"Looks like we're cooked," Orson said, resigned.

"Such a Pollyanna, he is." Max hoisted himself to one knee, then tumbled over.

The hair began to tremble, and only then did he really focus his eyes on it. Multicolored bumps moved along the strands. They were seven and eight inches long by half that wide. They moved and crawled, and when he rolled over in his net to look at them, they squealed and ran away.

Finally one turned and looked at him, cocked its head sideways, and hissed. It was a cross between a human being and an insect of some kind. The head was disproportionately large. Its face was a Punch-and-Judy caricature, medieval in its exaggeration. Even on a face that tiny, the projection of evil glee was unmistakable.

It grinned at him and skittered away; but another faced him, a bug with the body of a walrus turned inside out. And below that one was a lascivious woman-creature. It whistled at him—tiny, very high-pitched—and wriggled its two-inch-wide derriere suggestively.

Just what did you have in mind, honey?

Kevin choked back a face full of laughter. "What is all of this?"

"It's the sins of mankind. I think I've seen vanity, and wasteful killing, and loose sexual practice."

"Jesus," Hebert hissed. By wriggling around in the net, Max could just make out his dark face. "I think you're right. I've got murder, I think, and maybe theft."

"All right, then. We know where we are, but what do we do?"

There wasn't long to wait. The sins were busy around them . . . busy, busy, busy . . . and from the roots of Sedna's hair rose a city. They watched it form one shell at a time, built by carapaced creatures that flowed from every follicle. It was an array too vast and differentiated to even begin to categorize.

There was every sin that he could recognize: sloth and gluttony and greed and murder, and actions mimed but beyond his understanding. The creatures reached Sedna's bald spot, and there they shed their shells and wriggled forth like glistening varicolored slugs. The shells built up and up in a heap. It grew like a coral reef. Hundreds upon thousands of individual beings contributed one bit at a time. A bizarre castlescape rose up and up while the sluglike occupants mingled in obscene pools or piles in front of the structure.

The castle ringed them, twice as tall as a human being, with walls several feet thick.

How many sins? How many ten-inch sins did it take to make a structure of that size? He searched his mind, the confusion drowning out the equations before he could come up with an answer . . . but the net was relaxing. He could move.

Max shucked the net smoothly, the way he would wiggle out of a full nelson. Sedna's scalp was resilient, bouncy. Max crawled on hands and knees, found Eviane and helped her out of her net. This time she didn't fight him, and her fingers stayed, warm on his wrist, for a lingering second.

Cityscape stretched around and above them, a megalopolis for rats. Sins were still swarming forth like denuded rats, writhing and fluxing in vile pools, in a moat of living tissue. The corners of Sin City were four parabolic arches, and the flat wall beneath each arch was bulging, sculpting itself . . .

Until four human figures faced them, standing in the corners of the miniature city like dark brothers of the four cardinal directions. The shells that shaped them were still occupied. Crawling sins even shaped a suggestion of faces; but the features moved restlessly, semi-independently.

European, African, Asian, Eskimo. The nightmare figures examined the Adventurers, reaching out of the architecture to poke and then drawing back as if the prospect of touching a human being was distasteful. They retreated back into their directional corners, and sighed heavily.

The European figure spoke, and Max could see a hundred mouths moving. Its voice was a buzzing composite. "We have..." It wanted "s" sounds where there were none. The sibilance was disturbingly reptilian. It adjusted slightly. "Yesss. We have waited for you, long, long time. And now you are here. Yesss." It turned to its brothers, lifted its arms jubilantly, and screamed: "Let the trial begin!"

Chapter Twenty-One

TEMPTATIONS

Dwight Welles watched, waiting, his fingers splayed over the keyboard like a concert pianist's, bare feet gently touching the pedals.

He watched the four screens. Occasionally his eyes flicked to the holo stage where the entire Judgment scene was displayed in miniature.

Truth be told, he preferred the two-dee screen—it flattened and simplified the images, and thereby sped his responses. This was vital. Even though he had time-delays built into the program, he needed every split second to focus the massive power of Dream Park's computer banks on the job at hand.

In play, and at his best, Dream Park's chief computer wizard was a blur of motion, fingers and feet moving so swiftly that they dazzled the eye. But unlike a concert virtuoso, Welles was engaged in a piano duel in which the theme alone had been preselected. Melody, tempo, harmonies, and phrasing were all variable. It was the ultimate challenge, and only a Game as complex as Fimbulwinter could have lured Welles from his dry theorizing for three days of extemporaneous madness.

He felt drunk with power. Even the Lopezes would have flinched from running the next scene.

He flexed his fingers, wiped moisture on the pale T-shirt which read *Nice computers don't go down.*

Hell. Sex couldn't even come close.

Four composite creatures stood at the four corners of the clearing. Max Sands found it easy to guess which figures represented what.

One, positioned to what he assumed was the north, had stereotypical Eskimo features. The figure was short and pudgy and nut-brown.

The shape to his right was Oriental, colored comic-book yellow, like a jaundice victim.

Further around the clockface, to the south, stood an ebony figure made of crawling black shells. And to the west, as white as a sheet, was the figure representing European man.

The Sins of Mankind.

"You came to destroy us," the Eskimo-shape said, grinning like a happy-face button. "But we knew of your coming, and have captured you. Now we decide your fates."

Kevin Titus spoke up. "You mean your buddies the Cabal?"

"They are not our friends. They seek to use us."

Eviane surged against her bonds, then relaxed, watching the creatures with eyes that were cold and hard. "The Cabal will free Sedna when they choose, and then inherit the world."

"Their power will destroy them. They will be corrupted by their own sins." The Eskimo inspected each of them as it spoke. Its eyes were hard to meet. Its grin was wide and white; its teeth were miniature bald heads.

The Eskimo spoke in a chorus of tiny voices, thousands upon thousands of them, each chanting in the same rhythm. "Let me tell you," it said. Its voice buzzed maddeningly. "Since the time of the Great Raven, the world has been in balance. The Raven creates, Sedna sustains. The shamans and witches, those who functioned in the realms between worlds, helped to keep the balance.

"But the Sins of Mankind always weighed heavily on Sedna. When the Eskimos break taboos and forget the laws of their fathers, then we break free—"

"Sort of like zits," Max whispered.

The Eskimo smiled vastly. "In the year 1920 a man named Robert J. Flaherty came to us, came to the people of the ice, and he made a movie, *Nanook of the North*. And when it was released in 1922, the entire structure of the world was thrown out of balance."

Hebert squinted, confused. "Why?"

"Because the white world, the outside world, became a part of the community under Sedna's protection. Every culture has its Gods and deities, and some are powerful, and some are powerless. Sedna is powerful, as she must be to protect her children, who live in the most rugged region of the world."

In his peripheral vision Max watched the other three composites. They were almost immobile. From time to time they nodded, or the shells that made their expressions shifted slightly.

There seemed little chance of starting an argument among them. They were too close. They were four lobes of a single brain, Max guessed, and the sins were its cells . . .

Orson spoke. "Why wouldn't Sedna's discovery by the outside world give her greater strength?"

"Because there is nothing in your culture which adds to the spiritual strength of the Inuit people. In truth, we owe you much," the Eskimo said. "It is through you that we, the sins of man, came into our true power. Ever have we been a secondary force, mere symbols of your misdeeds. Verbs a-crawl on Sedna's scalp! Now we thrive as never before. Now we may cripple your world."

Kevin was the first to speak. "If we've done you so much good, why don't you turn us loose to do more?"

"Because we can use you," the black/south/Africa shape said. "We, your sins, can use you against the Cabal. If Man and Cabal can both be neutralized, then we may rule. Ever we have been both effect and cause. We are the corruptors and the product of corruption. The beginning and the end, alpha and omega. We wish to take our true position as masters of the universe."

"Then what's stopping you?" Orson said testily. "Why can't you just take what you want?"

"You must welcome us into your lives," white/west/Europe said solicitously. "Actions performed by coercion are not sins. We know that among you are hearts eager to touch and be touched by our ultimate pleasures. You will come to us voluntarily."

Orson wasn't buying it. "If you can't make us do it, if you have to have our cooperation, then you aren't the ultimate forces that you imagine. There's gotta be law and order, even in a Game . . . even here. Who are you afraid of?"

Max glowed. Come on, little brother!

"None—"

"Bullshit!" Eviane said suddenly. Everyone turned to hear her. "If we created you, then we have power. You're joined in a big dance with us. What is in our hearts determines our fates. Isn't that right?"

The Oriental snarled at her. Its neck stretched out toward her, shells taking new alignments, until it resembled a cobra standing in a basket. The yellow/east/Asia composite glared down into her face. Eviane didn't flinch. It drew close, and then pulled back, hissing.

"You! You are not alive! You are dead!"

"Yes."

"You should not be with these."

Sins hissed in chorus, and flowed into new patterns. Something that might have been fear showed on the Eskimo. Its eyes were tiny, twisted faces that licked their lipless mouths mirthlessly.

Orson's voice raised above the hubbub. "Yes! We have enough power among us to bring back one of our dead. I guess you don't like that a whole lot."

The Eskimo said, "It really doesn't matter. It only means that you would be even more highly prized as slaves."

The European spoke. "We will hold you for trial. More of you will join this one in death. But the one of you who revels in your sins, in the sins of your people, who will pledge to help us against the Cabal, him we will reward beyond all dreams. We are the sins of the flesh and the spirit. We are the embodiment, the purified form of acts so irresistible that since time immemorial folk have risked imprisonment, shunning, torture, and damnation for their sake. We know what is in your heart, and what is in your dreams. Pleasures beyond imagining can be yours."

The figures flowed and changed again.

The sins joined, formed friezes and weird topiary. These images were far from G-rated. There were shimmering, coupling human bodies with vaguely recognizable...

Max blushed. *That* figure looked remarkably like Max, and in its arms was a *zaftig*, voluptuous female figure with flowing blond hair...

Trianna was blushing, too.

Other sins had formed themselves into bodybuilders, shining race cars, scale-model mansions of phantasmal opulence...

Welles was thoroughly enjoying himself. Much of this cycle was prerecorded, images of wealth, health, sexuality taken from the Gamers' psychological evaluation files.

That gave him time to notice individual peculiarities among the Gamers, filing that information away for later reference. For instance: Eviane's line about "you're joined in a big dance with us. What is in our hearts determines our fates" was a direct steal from a line of dialogue later in the Game. She had played Fimbulwinter before!

Did that relate to Griffin's insistence on her re-inclusion in the Game? Griffin must be playing one strange game...

On one computer screen, blood pressure and skin temperature readings from the mesh underwear were displayed, and yes indeedy, his little show was having an effect.

A few subliminals thrown in for flavoring. Touching a toggle clarified the images until they were tantalizing beyond endurance.

Johnny Welsh was being tempted with a soufflé which begged to be eaten.

A glowing encyclopedia volume several feet across hovered before Orson Sands and Kevin Titus. When it opened, the pictures within expanded into three dimensions, with full sound and motion. Here the Battle of Waterloo fought itself; Saturn's rings formed, thickened, separated, changed with the shifting positions of minuscule moons; a line of dinosaurs mutated across a quarter of a billion years, until the page was full of birds. The pages flipped seemingly at random, each with the same depth and range, each bursting with a kaleidoscope of images and information. Poor Kevin was nearly salivating.

General's stars whispered seductively to Francis Hebert.

And in front of Max Sands paraded the hypermuscular body, golden lamé cape and mask of a wrestling hero... faceless within the mask. Would he notice?

In the home version of the Game, players would have the option of answering a copious questionnaire before beginning. Via phone lines, the home computer would access Dream Park's vast library of images. Dream Park would supply the precise visuals, and the home processor would take it from there. It had to be optional, of course. A mandatory questionnaire would scare some players off, perhaps those who needed the Game most.

Fantasy on parade. How wild it could get was anyone's guess, and odds were that within six months a copycat company, one of the hundreds of peripheral merchandisers who nipped around Cowles's heels, would offer a triple-X-rated version of the Game. It wasn't hard to figure the come-on: with computer-reconstructed images of any movie star in history, and the customer, locked in erotic gymnastics. Hook *that* up to an ultrasound lean-tissue analyzer as a reward system, combine it with the "feelie" system R&D was playing with...

Welles jerked his mind back on track. It was too damned easy to get lost playing what-if games, and there was work to do.

"This," the image of Africa said, "this and more can we give you. And it is only the beginning."

"Wait," Robin Bowles said, shaking his head. "You're talking about the death of mankind. If mankind dies, our sins die with us."

"Yesss..." the Eskimo nodded. "We are hoping to recruit you. Powerful, virile. Breeders. You will stay here with us, eating, reveling in pleasure, a nonstop orgy, mounting each other, breeding sins for all eternity! Our two worlds will truly coexist, as they were meant to from the beginning of time."

All four voices joined together, and spoke thunderously. "Let the trial begin!"

The walls flowed. The cityscape closed in. Abruptly the walls had become solid, and waist-high barriers had risen before each of the composite figures. White-shelled sins spilled across their heads to form periwigs.

Sin City had become a courtroom. Their four judges surrounded them at the four cardinal directions.

"Hear ye, hear ye," the Eskimo image began. Between the shells that formed the walls, individual sins popped up, made rude faces, and disappeared. Little eight-inch abominations stood on each other's backs and shoulders, cheered and hissed and laughed, and wriggled their glistening bare behinds at the Gamers. "This Court is now in session."

Robin Bowles said, but not as if he believed it, "I insist on the right to legal counsel."

The white judge leaned over, grinning. "Ah, yes. And if you cannot afford one, one will be appointed for you. Let me see—"

Out of the reeking pool of sin, a ghastly caricature of the figure of blind Justice rose up grinning at them, clattering her teetering scales.

"To hell with that," Max shouted. "I vote that Robin Bowles represent us!"

Bowles turned, a little shocked. "Are you sure?"

Welles was just as startled. Granted that Bowles was prepped to handle the defense. So were Ollie and Gwen, with prompting from Welles, of course. Welles had expected to have to push a little, argue a little. But the Adventurers seemed to have made their decision, and in Bowles's favor.

Welles hit the Stall button, and a prerecorded loop played, buying him five seconds to think.

"Whoa!" Hippogryph yelped. Max glanced over, and saw a troop of six sins dragging a roast beef across the courtroom floor, tumbling and fumbling like circus clowns with their load. They were almost to the far side of the room when three sin-sheriffs, complete with badges and riding sea horses, scampered in pursuit.

The entire tableau took about five seconds. Then Kevin remembered himself. "You do want the job, don't you, Mr. Bowles? I saw you in *The Judge Crater Story.*"

"You and six other people," Bowles said ruefully.

"But you can handle it!"

Snow Goose cried, "All in favor!"

A thunderous chorus of ayes filled the air.

"Opposed?"

Not a single nay.

"The ayes have it."

The black judge looked at them impatiently. "We are here today to try mankind, represented by these sorry assholes, for its sins. In the court we use the Code Napoleon. Your guilt is presumed until you can prove yourselves...ah...what's that word?"

A skeletal bailiff goose-stepped over to them, its joints and bones constructed of tittering sins standing on one another's grotesque shoulders. It stage-whispered, "Innocent!"

"Why, yes. That is the word I was looking for." He harumphed, cleared his throat, and spat out a sin. It landed at Charlene's feet. It wore a black robber's mask across its face and a three-digit number across its chest. Chittering, it ran up to her and dug under her trouser cuff. She squeaked and pulled away. The sin hugged a big gold coin to its chest, smiled evilly, and sprinted for cover.

Robin Bowles sighed, and then spoke in a voice like rolling thunder. "We are willing to go on trial, but only if we know that we will be tried fairly. If this is a mockery of a trial where you can bend law and logic to fit your own dictates, then we might as well be silent, and keep our dignity while you do with us as you will."

Orson hissed at Bowles, who bent over, listening and whispering.

The Oriental hadn't waited. "We will play fair with you. There is no need. Lying is a sin, but sins do not lie."

Robin Bowles straightened his back, and smiled unpleasantly. "You had better not. My colleague has reminded me of something."

Max's little brother stood, cracking his knuckles with glee. "All right. The Raven and Sedna are out of operation. But Sedna has a mate. And Eviane is a *tornrait*—"

Kevin hastily consulted his pocket computer. "Torngarsoak! Lord of the land animals!"

"Thaaat's the one. Eviane gives us a direct connection to the spirit world. Torngarsoak is out there, listening and watching. If we are guilty, then he will punish mankind for harming his sweetheart. If we're innocent—" He smiled charmingly. "Then Torngarsoak will be upset with *you*."

He turned, bowed sweepingly from the waist to the wild applause of the Gamers. Charlene Dula seemed beside herself with enthusiasm.

"Thank you, colleague Orson."

"It was nothing, colleague Robin."

Bowles spoke in his most professorial tones. "All right," he said. "That having been said, I move for a dismissal of all charges."

"On what grounds?"

"On the grounds that we, representing the Western world, were ignorant of Eskimo law, and therefore must be held blameless."

The four judges conferred for a moment, then shook their heads. "No. Your motion is disallowed for two reasons. First, even if we discounted sins which are exclusive to the Eskimo world, there are enough overlapping sins—murder, for instance —to condemn you."

"And the second?"

"Ignorance of the law is no excuse. This is well known in your Western law."

Robin nodded his head, and paced back and forth. Suddenly he stopped. "What are the sins of which we stand accused?"

"Murder. Abortion of children in times of plenty. Men who have no hunting skills. Women who disgrace their communities by dressing poorly. Destruction of the family units."

"I submit to you," Bowles said, "that these sins have been with mankind since time immemorial, and that the universe was created in balance despite them. There has been no increase in sin—it merely looks that way because of the increase in communications."

The four man-shapes laughed in a thousand voices. "We have heard that argument before. 'If you hadn't caught me, it wouldn't be a crime.' And it is disallowed."

"But you must admit," Bowles continued, "that more than the human race is on trial here. What must also be weighed is whether *you* have overstepped the bounds of your power. If you are wrong, and there has been no vast upsurge of sin, then you yourselves have acted to throw the universe out of balance. Torngarsoak's vengeance would be terrible. The question is . . . have you sinned?"

Robin asked it in powerfully insinuating tones. The judges recoiled for a moment, then answered: "We cannot sin. We *are* sin!"

Breathing harshly, Bowles mopped his forehead. Sweating underwater?

"I propose," Bowles continued, "that we simplify the issues. Choose the one sin of which we are most demonstrably guilty, and let us defend ourselves against that. Choose the one—we can only be hung once as a species, as a culture. If modern man is so wicked, has fallen so far from the path, then choose one."

Max was thunderstruck. Bowles projected more power, more sheer emotional force than the screen had ever conveyed. To be this close to a master actor at the height of his craft was awe-inspiring.

"Murder," the white/Europe judge suggested.

"I think not," Bowles replied. "We punish our murderers. They often repent. The Gods have always granted the right of repentance, and loved a people who police their own. The Gods made man, flaws and all. They have also made it possible for men to repent."

"Abortion."

Bowles thought. "Your concept of abortion—"

"—includes yours," the Eskimo finished.

Trianna Stith-Wood was on her feet. Bowles noticed and deferred to her in body language. She didn't notice at all; she was already talking.

"In times of hardship, Eskimo babies were sometimes left in

the snow, given back to the elements. There are places where a baby doesn't even get a name until it can name itself! I don't say that's a good idea. We don't like it—we never have. The fact that some people have abortions just because they're"—she paused for a moment, and her voice went a little tight—"too lazy to get implants is, is bad. We don't like it any better than you do. But you can't make abortions illegal—you'd just drive poor women to back-alley clinics, while their rich cousins go to nice clean family doctors. That's murder too. At least the children who are born are really wanted. Don't condemn us because the Gods gave us love, and reproduction, but limited the available food and space."

When she finished her outburst and sat down, she was crying. Hippogryph seemed embarrassed, but Charlene reached forward and held her shoulder.

Welles paused. What had brought *that* on?

A few taps of the finger, and Trianna Stith-Wood's personal file was on the screen. He could only devote a tiny fraction of his attention to it. His quick scan found no reference to abortion, or trauma, or specific incidents which might have triggered it. Not surprising—the dossiers were voluntary, and easy enough to leave discreetly incomplete.

Ah, well, he thought. Not his concern. He might mention it to Vail.

The judges began to confer. They were yards apart, but they buzzed at each other in a torrent of tiny incomprehensible voices. It was all buzzing now, rising in vehemence and falling back, while the judges blurred with internal motion.

The water seemed a little thicker. A few more fish wafted by.

The judged turned back. "We have come to a decision. We believe that it is possible to select a single sin, one unrepented in your culture. We are willing to condemn you for this one sin."

The Eskimo leaned forward, and gave a conspiratorial wink, a thin translucent eyelid covering a tiny screaming head. "I believe that this is called 'plea bargaining' among your people."

Robin Bowles nodded.

"We choose your meat-packing industry."

Orson blinked in confusion. "Excuse me?"

"Every year, billions of animals are raised in captivity in disgraceful, barbaric circumstances, and then shunted down assembly lines—"

The air above the sins wavered, and they were in a meat-packing plant, and the smell of blood and animal fear was in the air. An endless line of steers streamed toward an iron-walled factory building.

A fluid camera movement took them into the slaughterhouse itself.

A castrated bull waited, its head in the killing-slot, a milky foam bubbling from its mouth. A robot arm pivoted, braced an automatic gun against the head of the hapless bovine. There came a brief, explosive hiss, and the cracking sound of a shot. The steer collapsed.

"This is the way that your people slaughter cows—and chickens—"

There was an immediate, accompanying image of an endless conveyer belt of chickens, each hapless fowl in its own metal collar, heading toward the decapitation machine. A nauseating, blood-spurting close-up. The chicken's legs twitched spastically as the conveyer belt rolled on and another bird took its place.

It was a Treblinka, an Auschwitz, an infinite chorus line locked in a mechanized dance of death.

There were images of seafaring boats catching countless millions of tuna, and then those fish dumped through automatic sizing and gutting machines. The sequence culminated in a mountain of fishy refuse, guts and heads stinking in the sun. They could see it, and smell it. To Max's right, Trianna Stith-Wood was turning green.

"To us, this is the ultimate sin. To us and to Sedna, this is abortion, and on a scale almost beyond imagination. Compare this practice with the old ways, the traditional ways," the judges said. Suddenly there was a crisp, calm Alaskan vista. Men tracked caribou across the tundra; furred hunters crouched beside ice holes for the momentary appearance of a walrus, and then the sudden thrust of a spear—

Max could feel the howl of the wind, the adrenaline burn as the Inuit hunted in the manner of his ancestors. Something told him that *yes*, this was the way that these things were supposed to be, the way it should have been done, should always have been done...

They were pitching on a high sea, seized in the black grip of an angry ocean. A boat rode the water, a whalebone framework with a sealskin envelope, carrying four men. They were tough men, hardened to the elements, inured to suffering. They were staking their lives against an unpitying wasteland in hope of bringing home precious food.

They pitched and yawed, and then a flash! Just a momentary flash, and a seal broke the surface. The lead hunter made his cast, and—

A modern supermarket. Bovine, doughy shoppers pushed baskets down gleaming, Muzak-gentled aisles, choosing between packages of prewrapped, precleaned, prekilled meat.

The buzz was almost gone from the voice of their Eskimo judge. "Where is the threat here? Where is the life? You have lost all sense of the unity of man with his world, and of the price which is paid in blood and suffering by one creature to give life to another. And your sin is greater than this," the Eskimo said, his voice rising.

He's really getting into this, Max thought. Good! A demi-god should enjoy his work. Otherwise, what's the point of demi-deity?

The supermarket fogged... and cleared to show a cartoon image. It was Ferdinand the Bull.

Oh yes, Max knew Ferdinand. Everyone in America and sixteen other countries knew Ferdinand, spokesbull for the Lazy Taco string of Mexican restaurants. Famous, infamous, having gone from mouthpiece for a fast-food emporium to a series of B-movie misadventures to an eventual holovision series. Ferdinand, the Lazy Bull who slyly coaxed cows into the clover and other bulls into the bullring or onto the dinner table, was instantly recognizable.

Ferdinand looked out at them and said: "Come on down to Lazy Taco. We serve the best Beeefs in the wooorld." Suddenly he grinned stupidly and his eyes grew huge with mock surprise. "Oh! Beeef! Thass *me*, I theenk!"

Max was humiliated to remember the many times his sides had ached from Ferdinand's routine.

It didn't stop there. The parade of animals, real and cartoon, who had encouraged or begged customers to eat them over the years was long and disturbing. Foghorn Leghorn ("Ah say! This here is some mighty tasty chicken!"). Charlie the Tuna ("Sorry, Charlie").

The parade was endless. Daffy Duck, Clarabelle Cow, Porky

Pig, Chiquita Banana—Orson put his head down into his hands.
"Oh, no. Even the plants. We're screwwwwed."

All were dancing and prancing, shaking their collective rear
ends, happy happy happy to make that consummate sacrifice.
Distracting consumers from the bloody reality of death.

Max felt shamed.

The four Judges of the Apocalypse looked out at them. The
Eskimo figure said, "There can be no defense. You have dis-
honored the Inua of the creatures which give you life. Sin!"

"Sin!" said the black man.

"Sin!" agreed the white and the yellow men.

"It only remains to pronounce sentence—"

"Ah say! Now just a cotton-pickin' minute there, boy!" The
voice was Foghorn Leghorn's, and every head snapped around
... Johnny Welsh had spoken. A moment later he was hypersu-
percilious. "I believe this is my field of expertise—do you mind,
Robin?"

"Not at all." The distinguished actor looked both surprised and
relieved. Bowles sat heavily.

Johnny paused, gathering himself. "You know—I don't think
the issue here is the killing of animals—the more people you
have, the more food you need. Having babies is honored in your
culture—in fact, anything that builds up the community. Am I
right? Couples without children pray for babies. It's expected that
we be fruitful and multiply, right?"

The Eskimo judge nodded sagely.

"All right. The meat-packing industry is just trying to feed our
babies. If we didn't do that, that would be a sin. We want more
of our babies to survive. So we have people who are doctors, and
engineers, and teachers, and cops, and everything else that it
takes for a society to survive. We're like fishermen who stock the
lakes, or the farms, or whatever. And we kill the animals as
humanely as we can. Is there really anything more humane about
dying with a spear through your guts at twenty below? A gut-shot
reindeer—Trianna?"

Trianna had a plump arm up. She said, "The dietary rules in
the Torah demand that kosher meat be slaughtered as humanely as
possible. I'm sure that every culture has rules like that."

Johnny beamed approval. Orson's head was up; his eyes were
unfocused.

The Oriental judge peered down at Trianna. "Not every culture. Japan differs. And where exactly does this line of reasoning lead you?"

Welsh mocked the Oriental's tones. "It leads me to believe the issue is whether we have honored the spirits of the animals. You think that Charlie the Tuna, and Ferdinand the Bull, and Chicken Boy, and Tom Turkey and the rest are insults to their spirit."

The judges nodded vigorously. "And so they are!"

Johnny shook his head; his cheeks jiggled. "No. You missed it. Where we come from, one of the highest forms of compliment is the joke. I know this stuff. I make my living with this stuff. Only after an actor or politician has become great do we bother to make jokes about him. If there is a disaster in our lives, the first thing we try to do is find the light side. That's how we keep things in perspective. It's how we survive."

Johnny was beginning to roll, and Max finally understood where he was going. Out of the corner of his eye, he saw Orson relax.

"When we take a chicken, or a cow, and make a cartoon out of it, we're giving 'em the same treatment we give our dogs and cats. And considering that dog and cat care is a multibillion-dollar industry, you'd better not even suggest we don't love the little fuzzballs. They end up running our homes, eating our food, and breaking our hearts. Oh yeah—we know damned well how much we depend on animals for our survival."

Orson leapt up. "Snow Goose's father showed us implements, utensils that had carved images of animals. Out of proportion, almost grotesque. What we would call 'caricatures.' I submit to you that these advertisements are our offerings to the Inua. They are our way of giving affectionate respect. And more than that, we don't just make one or two little carved-bone items. We send these images out to billions of people. Every day we pay more honor to the Inua of the animals than the Inuit peoples did in a century. We are absolutely in the spirit of the Eskimos, and we say that you have lied, and stolen, and tricked your way into the balance of power. We ask the Gods, whatever they be, to look into our hearts. Every time we say grace, every time we make a joke, every time somebody works overtime to make a little more money so he can spend two hundred bucks on sushi for four, it's a tribute. I call this whole damn thing a mistrial."

The judges seemed frozen. Only their faces were in motion . . . but their features were little lost sins randomly a-crawl. Then the judges began to come apart. One buzzing voice spoke, the voice of west/white/Europe. "No—you are lying . . . we have the right of inheritance! We have that right!"

The ocean above them swirled, the water beginning to boil, and the walls dissolving too. Piece by horrid piece, Sin City was falling apart. The water boiled more swiftly. They clung to the strands of hair, dug in their tiny claws; the current took them away.

Then all was hidden in a wash of bubbles.

It felt like Sedna's scalp was sagging beneath Max. Then the bubbles cleared, and he saw. He was in a bubble and the bubble was rising. The other Gamers were rising around him, each in his own bubble.

Welles sat back and relaxed—the rest of it was programmed. He pushed himself away from the console and yawned, suddenly aware of the massive energy output of the past forty minutes.

He heard a patter of applause and turned to see Dr. Vail's slender, sardonic figure at the door of the control room, a beer in each hand. "Thirsty?"

"Unbelievably." Welles snatched one before Vail could blink, and downed half before coming up for air. "Ahhh. I pay belated honor to the Inua of the beer."

"That was nicely done," Vail said. "And we've almost completed our programming."

Welles made puppy eyes. "Does that mean I can start killing them? Please, sir. Just a few of 'em. For their own good."

He drank in haste, then called up an image from the Tunnels, the subterranean world beneath the Gaming areas. A cluster of uniformed men and women were working hydraulic lifts, switching supports and props under the Gamers so that they could make their ascent.

"I still can't believe how many Gamers don't care how we do it."

Vail sipped his brew, watched the screen, lips curled with gentle humor. "I'll bet you read magic books when you were a kid, and told everybody how the lady turns into a tiger."

"Better. There was an old magician in town. He put on shows in a magic shop, and on Saturday night, he'd get drunk. He'd screw up his timing, and you could see the rabbit peeking out of his coat. I loved it."

"The fact that the old man had lost it?"

Welles took another drink. "Is that wrong? He'd lost it just enough so that I could see how the miracle was done. Maybe some of the other people laughed, but I thought: 'He used to be great. Now he's just good.'"

He drained his beer and tossed it. "Hell. Anybody can be good. It only takes practice. But looking at that old man, for the first time in my life I thought that maybe I could be *great*..." He rubbed his eyes, then looked at Vail with sudden suspicion. "Are you working on my Psych evaluation?"

"Tut-tut," Vail said innocently. "Just curious. Just curious."

Max looked down through the water, and he saw Her.

Sedna. Eskimo, or Inuit, and beautiful. The encrustations around her face were cracking and chipping away, revealing smooth brown flesh beneath.

She was still burdened by her load of sins, but many of them were breaking free, unable to maintain their hold.

Sedna had a chance. The universe was coming back into balance. The Paija beaten, the *angakoks* could cleanse Sedna if the road remained clear...

Above them, far above them, light sparkled and shimmered on the surface of the water.

Chapter Twenty-Two

SKYHOOKS

A rocket rose up the sky . . . up the dome of Gaming A, off to Alex Griffin's left. At first the launch looked normal enough. But stratospheric winds twisted the vapor trail into a bizarre knot of subliminal skywriting, and the oversized Phoenix craft still hadn't tipped over to make orbit. It was roaring straight up. The flame died, but the tiny silver dot kept rising. If something else didn't happen it would presently come roaring straight down.

Alex had come in in the middle of something. Seeking enlightenment, he plucked earphones from a rack.

"Rockets are inefficient. Even fusion rockets, even antimatter rockets are wasteful compared to most of the machines in common use . . . to a zapcar, for instance. A zapcar uses only stored electricity. Its reaction mass is the road beneath the wheels and the planet Earth beneath the road.

"There are ways to send spacecraft into the solar system without burning tremendous masses of onboard fuel. Collectively these devices are called 'skyhooks.' None have been built. Some of them won't work. But we only need one that does . . ."

Ten-person carts were available, but not many were in use. The majority of guests were spaced around the rim of the dome in little clumps, watching, but also pressing the flesh, meeting contacts, making deals.

High on the dome, the rocket was still rising.

Peripheral vision caught something coming from Alex's right. It drifted across the sky toward the rising spacecraft, like a wide-mouthed predator of the deep, long and narrow like an eel, with luminous markings . . . no. He could see stars through it. The crisscrossed lines he had thought were markings were *it*. It was just a net, a net of superconducting wire, shaped by magnetic fields into a bizarre large-mouthed eel drifting on great square fins that must be solar power collectors.

"The Starwhale is no more than an orbiting rail gun, but it will serve our purpose. To put a spacecraft into orbit costs fuel. We'd find it much cheaper merely to fire a craft two hundred miles straight up. At that point—"

The Starwhale ate the spacecraft.

The ship was tiny. It entered the mouth of the net at tremendous speed . . . at five miles per second or better, if the Starwhale was in orbit. The Starwhale was much bigger than Alex had thought, and moving much faster.

The ship slowed and came to a halt before it reached the tail. *"We can catch it, accelerate it to orbit, and leave it there. Or we can continue accelerating the ship—"* It sped back toward the mouth of the beast. *"—up to another five miles per second, to send it to the moon, or Mars, or the asteroids.*

"Of course we must steal kinetic energy from the Starwhale. But if we can catch incoming ships to decelerate them—" A ship entered the Starwhale's tail at meteoric speed, slowed near the mouth, sped back down the long, long torso, left the tail, and began to fall toward Earth. *"—ships carrying cargo from Mars or the asteroids, we can put the kinetic energy back!"*

Most of those in Gaming A were listening to the presentation. Alex Griffin wasn't, and he didn't believe Harmony was. He had come in late and he felt a little lost, but the presentation wasn't his prime motive here.

Alex had avoided Thadeus Harmony for the past half-hour. It was no mean trick. The big man had stalked him purposefully. Alex had declined to answer three phone messages, and ducked out of the back of his office once. It was easy to guess what Thadeus wanted, and Alex wasn't prepared to give it.

"The Beanstalk was the earliest skyhook conceived," the narrator's voice said. *"It would be the most useful, and the most expensive.*

"A satellite orbiting 22,300 miles above the Earth's equator will circle the Earth in the same time it takes the Earth to turn, in twenty-four hours. It remains in orbit above one point on the Earth's equator." A glowing, dotted line painted itself wide around a huge blue and white Earth. *"Suppose we were to put a space station at geosynch . . ."* A classic wheel-shaped space station appeared, with a green-skinned giant atop it. *". . . and let down a line to the Earth's surface."* The giant flung coils of heavy rope downward. Maybe it was vine; the giant was garbed

in leaves. *"It would fall, of course."* The weight of thousands of miles of vine dragged the startled giant off the station and down. He became a streak of meteor flame.

Two more giants popped up on opposite sides of the space station. They hurled lines inward and outward. *"We must extend another line outward for ballast, to keep the center of mass at geosynch..."*

Alex spotted Kareem Fekesh without difficulty. The dark, slender, elegant sheik was the still center of a flow pattern of supplicants from a score of factions seeking a word with him. His man was letting few of them through... that was Razul, recovered nicely from his Battling Robots duel. Fekesh was watching the artificial sky. Neither Razul nor Fekesh appeared to have noticed Alex Griffin.

The green giants' line had mutated, had become one smooth, continuous tether. Capsules ran up and down its length in faintly visible nets of magnetic force, elevator cars running with no cables. *"Of all of these proposed skyhooks, the Beanstalk is the most difficult to build. It must stand the greatest stresses. But the Beanstalk can lift cargo from ground to orbit, and fling them out to the stars, for the cost of the electricity, a few dollars a pound.*

"But that cost is deceptive. The Beanstalk is also the most dangerous of the skyhooks. For if the cable ever snapped—"

🔹 Flame flashed where the cable broke, somewhere above the midpoint. Meteor strike, or only the sudden release of terrible energies? Part of the cable fell toward interplanetary space. The rest... thirty thousand miles of single-crystal iron fiber composite wrapped itself around the Earth's equator, carrying meteoric energy levels. The Earth strangled in a noose of fire.

A hundred voices murmured uneasily. Alex was watching Kareem Fekesh.

Was that a smile? What kind of smile? Alex had seen smiles like that, a faint curl of the lips, before Dream Park personnel plunged into the details of a major problem. A very bright businessman might be envisioning an answer to a potential difficulty...

Or a terror-monger might be watching a new and exotic means to trigger Megadeath. Fekesh turned and whispered to Razul. Razul frowned, considered, nodded—

A large hand fell on Alex's shoulder. "Alex," Harmony said urgently. "I've got to talk to you."

"Shhh. This will be over in a few minutes."

"And you'll arrange to be paged away. *Now*, Alex." Thadeus's eyes were blazing.

Alex nodded and backed up until they were under the shadow of a model mining derrick.

On the dome above them, the Barsoom Project was building a tower. They built it from the ground up, and it was already too high. No material known to man would support it. The tower stood because it was another linear accelerator. Ferrous rings shot upward through the interior at scores of miles per second. The tower's magnetic field pushed down on them as they rose, lifting itself against gravity, slowing the rings to a stop near the tower's crown; pushed down on them as they fell, still lifting itself, accelerating the rings until they reached bottom. There, at scores of miles per second, they looped around in a bitch kitty of a magnetic field and started back up the tower. It was a staggering feat of engineering. Alex ignored it.

"What are you doing?" Harmony asked furtively. "It wasn't until this morning that I realized what I've done. Name of God, man—!"

"Don't worry," Alex said soothingly. "I'm just keeping an eye on things."

"And talking to Izumi and Khresla? And activating Tony McWhirter?"

"What busy little ears we have."

It was all that Harmony could do to keep his voice from cracking. "Alex, I was drunk! I should never have said anything at all!"

"So there you have it." Through the skeletal derrick Alex could see four "skyhooks" on the dome at once: tower, Starwhale, Beanstalk, and a tremendous spinning cable whose endpoints dipped into the Earth's atmosphere. *"Even the cheapest of these projects would be expensive; the others are much worse. Each of these fantasy devices could lift cargo to space at a few dollars a pound. Each would cause awesome destruction if it failed. And each would be far cheaper, easier to build, less massive, and less dangerous if built to serve Mars!"*

Mars replaced Earth. *"Mars rotates in just over twenty-four hours, but is far less massive than Earth. Stressed by only two-fifths of a gravity—"* Sudden close-ups of the Beanstalk and Pinwheel showed each to be considerably shorter and much more slender. The rings being fired up and down the tower moved more slowly; the Starwhale was scores of miles long instead of hundreds of miles.

"Each of these devices can serve Mars for around fifteen percent of their cost at Earth. Their lower energies make each far safer. More to the point, they may loft their goods from the surface of Mars and land supplies for the colonists and materials for the terraforming project; but if they fail—"

They failed all at once. The Beanstalk wrapped Mars in fire. The endpoints of the Pinwheel, which had been dipping low above the surface six times per orbit, now pounded the desert itself until shock waves shattered it. Misdirected rings shredded the tower. A rising spacecraft entered the orbiting rail gun off-center and tore it into a chaff of shredded superconducting wire.

Disasterlight painted Harmony's broad, battered face with crimson highlights. His eyes blazed.

Alex could see the panic there. He asked, "What do you think I'm going to do? Publish a letter in the *Times*? Activate the Dream Park hit squad?" Alex's mind's eye built him an army of three-dimensional cartoon figures dressed as Ninjas. A black-robed Minnie Mouse, a sword-wielding Baby Huey, and Popeye the Sailor covered with Yakuza tattoos, closed in on a whimpering Fekesh . . .

"Alex!" Harmony's voice was rigid with alarm. "Stop smiling like that."

"Sorry. I'm easily distracted."

"Dammit, this is serious. You're likely to stir up more problems than you've ever dreamed of!"

Behind them, with staggering sound and visual effects, Martian colonists were battening hatches and shoveling Marsdust to cover glass walls. Mars was ringed in fire and meteoroids.

Alex pulled back from his friend, deeper into the shadow of the derrick, away from the illumination of the fireclouds. "Thadeus, you hired me because you trust me. Not just to do the day-to-day work, but on the big things. And just maybe you hired me specifically for this."

Harmony wagged his head regretfully. "I was crazy. We're talking about a hundred billion dollars. At least. Alex—"

Something on Alex's face must have given Harmony pause, because suddenly he was speechless.

"Thadeus," Alex said softly. "Did somebody get to you?"

"If they fail, the meteors will pound only a lifeless world. We'll build again. And again, until we get it right. And then we

can build skyhooks for Earth. And then the solar system is ours!"

Spacecraft rose from Earth and Mars, all sizes, all shapes, in ever-denser numbers, flung outward by Beanstalks and Pinwheels. They spread across the solar system . . . but Alex Griffin and Thadeus Harmony saw none of that.

Harmony wiped a broad hand over his vast forehead, checked the palm for sweat. "No, Alex. They're just watching all the time. Sometimes I feel like a goldfish in a bowl. Listen, I'm worried."

"You should be. But, Thadeus, now it's in my lap."

"We backed down before that son of a bitch." Harmony had glimpsed Fekesh. He studied the tall Arab, then abruptly looked away. "We backed down, but we had reason. We don't do that lightly, Alex. He had us."

"You'd almost whipped yourselves before Fekesh ever got there. You told me about it, remember? We're stronger now, Thadeus. And the girl came back. Raw coincidence, the stuff of dreams and parables. If there's a trace of superstition in Kareem Fekesh, he must think the fates have come for him."

Harmony's mouth opened and shut twice without producing sound. Then: "You're dreaming."

"Maybe."

"Will you at least let me know what's going on?"

"Minute by minute."

Harmony gave a long, sighing exhalation. "All right, all right. I'm going to go and make a public face. Just . . . hell. I'll be in touch."

Harmony slouched away, a big, worried bear with an artificial smile plastered across his face, trying to make happy with the guests.

Alex watched him. Harmony wandered across the room shaking a hand here, clasping a shoulder there. Then, as if in response to Alex's somewhat sadistic prayer, found himself facing Kareem Fekesh.

Both froze. Then Fekesh smiled graciously, walked around Harmony, and disappeared into the crowd.

Alex watched Harmony's expression as he turned to watch Fekesh leave. The public smile had cracked open. Beneath it was something incandescent with loathing.

Max popped out of the water. The bubble above him burst, left him standing on a perfectly balanced piece of ice in a choppy

sea. Other Gamers popped to the surface around him. The world
buoyed for a few moments, then righted.

A few yards away, Hippogryph and Charlene bobbed up.
Charlene was leaning on her rotund companion. They weren't
exactly holding hands, but . . .

Brother Orson's eyes were fixed on the couple, and there was,
if not primal fury, at the very least disappointment and discomfiture in his gaze.

Max's chunk of ice drifted to the edge of an ice field, and fit
into the rest of the floe as neatly as a piece of a jigsaw puzzle.

The sky flowed with an endless ribbon of color. The northern
lights? Aurora borealis? It was stunningly bright, seemed near
enough to touch, and he stood on tiptoes, stretching his fingers
up . . .

"What in the world are you doing?" Eviane asked.

"Ah . . . stretches."

She was pulling a lightweight jacket out of her backpack, and
he followed suit. The air carried a bit more chill here. Nothing
but white, nothing but ice in all directions. Wherever they were,
it was in the heart of the arctic. They had no magical reprieve
from the cold.

He looked down at Eviane's feet, startled to realize that she
cast no shadow. Where she walked, her feet left no imprint. It
gave him the creeps.

There were no birds overhead. There were no mountains or
trees to break the endless, bleak plain. The wind howled, and the
chill seemed to penetrate to a level beyond the physical.

The other Gamers donned their jackets. Max noted that Yarnall, the National Guardsman, was still with them. How hard had
the Gods tried to kill him out? Hard to guess . . . but Max expected the Game to get considerably rougher now. He put a hand
on Eviane's shoulder, and then walked over to Snow Goose. A
light wind from the . . . east? blew steadily, carrying an unwelcome load of snow.

"What next?"

"Ceremony," Snow Goose said. "We need shelter from this
wind, so that we can perform a ceremony. There aren't enough of
us who are Eskimo to build a snow shelter, so we'll just have to
use Robin's prefab units."

The Gamers gathered around in a circle to hear her. They
looked tired, but exultant. The wind around them moaned a
dirge, but their mood was unaffected. They were strong. They

were victorious. They were on a goddamned roll.

"We're going to need to construct shelter," she told them. "There's a storm coming in."

Robin Bowles took center stage. "In the bottom of everyone's pack there should be a segment of a shelter unit. Please extract that. Now, there are instructions included, but if you'll just listen to me, you won't need to take the time to read them . . ."

The Adventurers formed a circle, and Max fit in next to Eviane.

Each shelter section was roughly triangular, and included telescoping rods that clicked together into a rigid frame. Additional coiled wire ran through cloth conduits. The whole thing swelled and stiffened admirably, until it looked more like an igloo than anything they had seen since their plane crashed.

The plane crash. How long ago had that been? Forty-eight hours? It seemed worlds away, and so much had changed since then.

Eviane still looked somewhat pale, and perhaps a bit forlorn. He imagined that was appropriate: he thought that if he were officially dead, he would be somewhat forlorn as well. But with strong, busy fingers she helped, in all likelihood as cheerful as any dead person could be.

The igloo grew until it was about twelve feet across and five feet high. The Actor attached a hissing gas cylinder to the tent. Struts swelled with pressure. The tent had become a gelatin mold.

They crawled in, single file.

The temperature outside had begun to drop. In the last few minutes of their task, Max's fingers had grown numb. He was delighted to get inside, where Bowles was already setting up a small conical heater. Temperatures rapidly grew comfortable, if not toasty.

Snow Goose removed the tin can of cigarettes from her pack and sat cross-legged on the ground, waiting for the others to arrive. She was centered and calm, every bit the picture of a woman who strode between two worlds, the Inuit and the white.

Outside, the wind howled ferociously. Max could almost hear the voices of the Cabal: thwarted, angry, vengeful . . .

But in the igloo, there was peace.

Eviane gazed at Snow Goose as if trying to remember something. Studying. Absorbing. Then she seemed to give up.

The Adventurers ringed them 'round. Bowles. Stith-Wood.

Hippogryph. Yarnall. The Sands brothers. Dula. Titus. Frankish Oliver. Welsh. Eviane. Hebert. These were the warriors of the West, and they had to be enough.

Snow Goose spoke. "You know we've won, like, major gold."

There was a round of applause, and a great hearty lot of back-slapping. Snow Goose let it die back down. She said, "We should get a chance to rest pretty soon now."

"I was wondering if anyone was going to remember that part!" Trianna said. "I'm pooped."

There was a general chorus of agreements about that too.

"We need another ceremony first. We must reach my father. The elders who helped us with our last ceremony cannot aid us now, but I have something that they didn't—one of the Dead, whose love for this world brought her back to be with us. She walks between worlds, and in traveling from death to life has gained great power.

"Eviane, you will sit at the center of our circle. You will help us to open a window between worlds."

With evident reluctance, Eviane moved forward and sat next to Snow Goose. Cigarettes were passed around. Max shifted, and then shifted again, trying to get comfortable on the thin padding under his aching buttocks. Nothing helped. Finally he folded his jacket and sat on it.

Again, the cigarette was unfiltered, and a little shorter than those of which he had seen pictures. He didn't personally know anyone with a nicotine prescription, but one could still find a bootlegger here or there smuggling Oaxacan tobacco. Rumor had it that a few outlaw "Smokies" still grew the precious leaf up in Oregon, in patches disguised as marijuana fields.

They lit, and exhaled. Once again the smoke streamed up toward the roof, but this time it congealed above Eviane's head as well as Snow Goose's. A glowing image formed.

Martin the Arctic Fox was kneeling before a foam-plastic crate. They could hear him chanting, and though they could not understand, it was clear what he was doing. For several seconds they watched him negotiating with the Inua of a score of cans of corned beef. Then his head jerked up and his leathery face crinkled in delight.

"Snow Goose! You still live?"

"Yes, Daddy."

"Have you made any progress? How many of the strangers still survive?"

"We've only lost one," Snow Goose said, "and Eviane is still with us as my *tornrait*. Daddy, we have warred with the sins on Sedna's scalp and defeated them, but they must still be combed away."

"You didn't stay to—?"

"No, Daddy, we're warriors, not barbers! Our people may need help to attack the Cabal. Will you take care of Sedna? It's really your job."

"Yes, I must dress her hair while others fight," Martin said glumly. "Carry on, daughter. Well done." He faded.

Snow Goose rubbed her palms together briskly. "Well. That's that."

The tension in the air slackened. Johnny Welsh coughed politely. "I don't want to interrupt the reunion, but my stomach is about to sue me for nonsupport. Do you think we could get some food?"

There was a sharp popping sound, like a vacuum tube imploding. Suddenly, another vision misted the air.

It wasn't of malevolent Cabal members, though. It was a beautiful woman whose long, straight black hair fanned out in an ethereal halo.

Sedna. She smiled on them through full lips. "My children," she said, and each word had, not the bubbling sound he would have expected, but a lush, hushed woman's voice.

"You have freed me from my bondage. You have justified my faith in you. Though you were of another culture, you are joined in a dance with us. Though you unknowingly sinned, you have repented—what is in your hearts will determine your fates.

"The Cabal awaits you. You have freed me, but they have gained great power, and still hold the Raven in thrall. They will be all the more dangerous now that they know you are strong enough to thwart them. You must be careful.

"Somewhere out over the ice is the next challenge, your penultimate test."

Sedna's face wavered, and in its place there appeared a strange vista. It seemed to be a mountainous island. No, not a mountain. What Max had seen as a natural formation was an endless network of slabs of ice set against one another at crazed, impossible angles.

Kevin shook his head in disbelief; but Max was more disturbed by Eviane's gasp of recognition. Her eyes were fixed, staring. He took her hand: it was rigid.

"Here is your challenge," Sedna said. "There will be dangers both physical and psychic. My own energy is taken with healing. I can give you one gift. I can return to life one who has suffered in your service, one who died, and even through death served you.

"Rise, Eviane."

A nimbus of pale light played around Eviane. Her mouth opened in a surprised "O." The other Adventurers stared. Eviane began to shake. Then the light faded, and Eviane stared at her hands in amazement.

Max prodded her with a sturdy forefinger. "Yep. All meat. No filling."

Sedna's full lips smiled warmly. "Rise, living woman. Restored to your compatriots, restored to life, still you have seen beyond the veil of death. The power of foresight is yours, now and forever. Rise, Eviane, restored to hope, to love. Rise."

Chapter Twenty-Three

THE SNOWMAN'S WAR

"Gotcha!"

Max ducked, too late. The snowball hit him in the side of the head, exploding in a burst of fluff.

"Point!" one of the two judges called. The judges were unusual. They looked like snowmen: more the Frosty than the Abominable variety. Complete with carrot noses and black top hats, the two odd creatures had appeared at the beginning of the evening break, and led the Gamers on a whistling march to a mountain concealing a network of ice caves. Inside the cave was a suspiciously warm spring, and a banquet of fresh fruit, vegetables, hot breads, and lean proteins.

After the meal most of the Adventurers had been coaxed back into the bracing cold for a little game.

With the glowing sky above them, the vast expanse of arctic plain surrounding them, and the specter of tomorrow's destruction before them, the Gamers had adopted very much of a "Tomorrow we die" air, and engaged in the greatest snow war of all time.

Johnny Welsh wouldn't play; he didn't like things hitting him in the face. Orson wouldn't play; it just didn't sound like fun. Max no longer found that surprising, but it still bothered him. Those two watched from the sidelines, looking obscenely comfortable.

There were two trenches twenty feet apart, with low parapets of snow. Max, Eviane, and Trianna manned the battlements. Behind them crouched Hebert and Kevin. Together they composed the Reds, a gang of desperados if ever there was one.

They sucked frigid air, dizzy with exhaustion. A few minutes earlier they had repulsed an all-out assault by the Blues.

They had Charlene on defense, and although she had to stop every few minutes to massage her knees, she was actually quite good. She couldn't run anymore, but dogged practice had given her fair control of a snowball, and indecently high speed. Her first attempts were hilarious; her reflexes didn't know which way gravity went.

Kevin threw himself into the game with maniac zeal which was already beginning to flag. He had no reserves at all.

The Blues were headed by Hippogryph. Max had experienced firsthand the full brunt of the man's tactical brilliance—

("The Cabal!" Hippogryph screamed. When Kevin turned his head to look, *pop*.)

—and his courage: hiding behind a shrieking Charlene, approaching under a white flag to strike swiftly and devastatingly. Max decided that he didn't like the man. The only reasonable course was assassination.

"Kevin?"

Kevin was winded, and flushed from where a snowball had brushed the end of his nose, followed a moment later by a dinosaur-killer that exploded on his parka. The skinny computer-warrior wasn't going to be much use much longer.

The situation was grim.

"We have to lure that son of a bitch out," Max said.

"How?" Pant pant. "Got any ideas?" Pant.

"Well, he already used the white flag, so that's no good. What about single combat?"

"What?"

"I remember reading about a form of Eskimo single combat. I could challenge him. If it looked like I was losing, you could bomb him."

"Why do you think he'd go for that? You're bigger than he is."

Max grinned. "Yeah—but I think he's Dream Park Security. If he is, he's well trained. He won't be intimidated by size."

Eviane nodded. "Sounds good." Her face clouded for a moment. "Are you sure we have guards posted? I like playing—"

"We're on break—" Kevin started.

Max shut him down with a wave. *Stay in character.* "I've got Johnny and Orson keeping an eye out for the Cabal. We need the relaxation."

"Yes, yes, I'm sure." Eviane seemed vague.

"So what's got you so worried?"

"I feel blind. I still get glimpses of the future, Max, from back when I was dead. But I don't remember any of *this*."

Trianna and Kevin tried not to roll their eyes too obtrusively.

The two snowmen referees looked somewhat like fluffy white Gumbies. One waddled over to the Red team's walls and intoned, "The score is twenty-four to twenty-four. The rules allow for an extension of the play period, or you can go for sudden death."

Max beamed. "Sudden death!"

"And the preferred mode?"

"*Mano a mano*. Get that lardass Hippogryph off his duff. Quote me."

The snowman's eyes twinkled: an odd sight. "You can be sure of it, sir."

Kevin brushed snow out of his hair, and plopped back against the snowdrift. "Do you really think he'll go for it?"

"I can hope."

"And if he does, do you think you can fuck him up?"

"Kevin, do you *eat* with that mouth?"

Kevin shuffled his feet, embarrassed. "What I meant was, I've never actually seen you fight, but this isn't some choreographed bullshit—"

Max batted an arm at him. Kevin yiped and skipped away.

Eviane drew lines in the snow with her finger, thinking absently. "I've . . . been here before."

"Here? You mean this exact place, reliving this exact day?"

She smiled shyly. "Something like that. It's the place, and I think I was doing the same thing. And it was just as important as everything is today . . ."

"But?"

"But different people were there. No snowmen. And four of us were dead before we ever reached here. We've been lucky."

"I wasn't there?"

Her green eyes flashed at him. Devastating. "No. You weren't."

The snowman plodded back over to him. "The leader of the Blue team has accepted your challenge. We have a traditional Eskimo combat ready for you."

Max peered up over the lip to be sure that no snowballs were arcing merrily toward him, and then climbed up out of the slit.

Opposite him, Hippogryph was discarding his external garb. He peeled down to a thermal shirt. Charlene Dula stood beside him, delighted. *My hero!* She grinned a challenge at Eviane.

Max saw his chance, and took it. "My lady," he said to

Eviane. "I fight for all of us, but would you honor me by allow-
ing me to be your personal champion?"

Eviane stared blankly. "What do you mean?"

"Allow me to carry some little memento into battle with me."

A smile tugged at the corners of her mouth, and finally she
giggled. Actually giggled! and said, "Sure." She took off her belt
and handed it to him. Max wrapped it around his thigh, cinched it
tight, and tucked the tail in. He bowed expansively to her, and
trudged off to do battle.

The two snowmen led the way. They were great clumsy
beasts, the heads sometimes wobbling for balance. One of them
tripped. The head fell off, made a squashing sound as it hit the
ground. He had to feel around for a moment to find it.

The procession marched along—

(It was a moment before Max realized that there were actually
martial strains in the background. Soft, integrated with the wind
until he could persuade himself that it was his imagination; but
no, there it was. Sousa march? Maybe.)

A hundred yards from the snowball battle area was a patch of
ice fifteen feet across. Max looked down into it. He saw a stirring
in the depths. A mermaid floated to the surface and blew a kiss at
him, pressing lips and palms against the surface of the ice. She
was gone before he could react.

"Wasn't she cold, dressed like that?"

"Secrets of the deep," the snowman said solemnly. "And now,
will the two antagonists please take their places on the opposite
sides of the ice rink?"

Max looked back at Eviane, then waved toward the sidelines.

"The object is to cause your opponent to lose his balance,
while keeping your own. If you cause any part of his body except
his foot to touch the ice, he is debited a point. If you lose your
balance at the same time, no point. If you force him out of the
ring, one point. If you both go, no points. The first to gain three
points wins.

"Are there any questions?"

"What is illegal?"

The snowman grinned. "That can be decided by the two of
you. We merely act as referees."

Max and Hippogryph approached each other across the ice.
Max's boots didn't grip the ice at all well. He wondered how
Hippogryph liked it.

Max sized his opponent up. Hippogryph was four inches

shorter, but almost as large across the shoulders. The man was disturbingly light-footed for his girth.

"No punching," Max said.

"Agreed. Or kicking or poking."

"Fine. Or any of that stuff." Max paused. "How do you feel about slapping?"

"Fair enough," Hippogryph said. "But not to the eyes, or face."

Max studied him. Hippogryph had a secret. Dream Park Security training? Something else? Max had a secret too. He turned to the snowmen. "We haven't started yet, have we?"

"Not until you return to the edge of the ring."

"All right." He extended his hand. He didn't trust this guy. "Shake."

Hippogryph's gloved hands clasped his. Strong. Man knew gripping. Judo, maybe? Made sense: that, plus some standard police tactics, would cover any ordinary security situation.

Well, he was sure as hell going to find out in a hurry. He looked up at the sky. The aurora was rippling like a magic banner. Any minute now it might branch into a "Go, team" pennant.

It was warm for an arctic day at the end of the world. Max flexed his knees, felt and heard them crinkle-pop. Out of the corner of his eye he saw Eviane's face, a pale oval partly bleached by snow glare. But he could still make out the expression. If "worshipful" was too strong a word, "admiring" was too weak.

They could sort it out later.

Hippogryph and Max faced off across the ice. Max shuffled forward, trying to keep his center of balance low. One false move and he would end up on the ground with Hippogryph. That wouldn't do. What might do? He didn't have enough traction for a lot of the techniques he knew, and this was just a friendly match...

Hippogryph body-checked him. Max felt strong arms reach up, wrap themselves around his neck, and torque him over. Suddenly he was in the air. He hit the ice hard, Hippogryph atop him. Max was more surprised than hurt, and thrashed for a moment before righting himself.

Hippogryph was grinning at him. "Man-mountain, eh?"

Max squinted up at the smaller man. "Does everybody in the world know that?"

"No point!" a snowman called.

Hippogryph came in low, and Max stiff-armed him. Hippogryph lost his balance, started to go down—grabbed Max's arm as he went, curled his body, and Max was in the air again. Max hit the ice hard, but was up before his opponent.

"Hey! What's going on here?"

"No point!" the snowman said.

Hippogryph was softening him up. These tactics wouldn't win him any direct points, but they would slow Max down.

All right, then. Sauce for the goose . . .

He circled Hippogryph, who lunged, then pulled back, too fast. He lost traction on the ice, waved his arms, and—

Max wagged his finger, and waited. Playing a little possum, are we? He could wait.

On the sidelines, Eviane's eyes were unblinkingly wide as she watched the action. One of Max's hands was hanging out there, a little slow to react. Hippogryph lunged for it, and caught the wrist.

Max caught the catching hand, yanked, torqued sideways, and did a jumping scissors—left leg in front, right leg in the back— and twisted his hips clockwise. Both of them hit the ice, but poor Hippogryph was underneath.

Trianna screamed in sympathy. Next to her, Francis Hebert winced. "Goddamn." Charlene looked first bewildered, then alarmed.

Girl still doesn't understand gravity.

"No point."

Hippogryph got back up, but some of the deviltry was out of his eye, and in its place was a little more respect. "For a clown, you move pretty good."

Max grinned and glowed. He charged right at Hippogryph, and then pulled back as the smaller man dropped to hands and knees.

Max's feet slid on the ice. He lost his balance, and wobbled wildly trying to save it. He couldn't.

"Aw, shit!" he screeched, flopping back against the ice as Hippogryph stood up.

"Point!"

Max looked ruefully back at the crowd, and winced as they groaned.

Hippogryph was at him before he could finish getting up, and scythed his standing leg out from beneath him. "Arrgh!" Max screamed, and slammed into the ice again.

This time he stayed there for a minute, and glared up. Two points. Two points down, just like that. How embarrassing. Well. He was back up to his knees, and Hippogryph circled him.

He wobbled. Favored the left leg, and circled Hippogryph limping. Hippogryph grabbed one of his hands, whipped Max around until Max countergrabbed and stopped himself dead on the ice. The two men were frozen. Then Max inhaled powerfully, reached down between Hippogryph's legs, and hoisted him completely off his feet and into the air, all two hundred and thirty pounds of him.

Then slammed him into the ice.

"Point!"

Hippogryph lay stunned, eyes unfocused, and started to get up. He thought better of it and stayed down. The two mermaids floated up to throw kisses at him through the ice.

Hippogryph stood up. They circled each other, Hippogryph more cautious now. He had learned something that he didn't enjoy. Max slid a step forward, tried to steady himself, balanced on one foot—

And Hippogryph, unable to resist the opportunity, lunged in with a pushing hand.

Max spun, and banged bodies with him. He grabbed and threw, somersaulting in midair—

And landed back first, on top of Hippogryph. He felt the impact, heard the wind driven completely out of his opponent's lungs.

Max carefully picked himself up. He had never touched the ice.

The snowman looked at him with an expression which could only have been incredulity. "Ah . . . point!"

Hippogryph stood. His face darkened poisonously, then cleared. He shook his head with regret. "Nice move," he said. "We could have used you in Mexico City."

Max laughed and extended a hand. Hippogryph snatched at it. Max calmly pulled his back, and watched Hippogryph's feet dance on the ice as he fought desperately to regain balance.

Max leaned forward and pushed Hippogryph's left shoulder with his forefinger. The smaller man's feet flew out from underneath him, and he thundered into the ice.

The applause was even louder.

Max bent and untied the belt from his thigh, and turned back toward Eviane. Her mouth hung open slightly, and she stared at him, those beautiful green eyes as wide as saucers.

"My lady," he said, holding the belt out. "I won this for you, and for you alone. It is to your pleasure, and in your name have I battled."

He handed it to her, and she was still staring up at him, dazed. "And?"

"And..." She was standing very close to him. Very. "And I claim my reward," he said, and bent to kiss her. Her lips brushed his. Her eyes, so clear and bright, clouded. With no warning at all, she turned and ran.

The others laughed as she disappeared. But Max had seen something in that moment, a glimpse of a different person. He wasn't sure who or what it was he had seen, but it was nothing to laugh at or about.

Leaving the others behind, he ran out after her.

Max stood in a gentle snowfall, peering through the white for the woman who had fled the recent battleground.

"Eviane!" He called her name, heard his voice echoed by the low whine of the wind, reflected from far mountains. There were more mountains visible now, dotting what had earlier seemed an endless plain.

They were just barely visible in the drifting snow, despite the crispness of the air and the comparative clarity.

"Ow!" A lightly packed snowball hit him in the side of the head, causing more surprise than dismay. He whipped around.

She smiled at him, then ran. Prototypical woman-reaction, and he loved it.

The storm swallowed them both.

She ran, not quite fast enough to stay ahead of him. At the end of those short, sturdy legs, her feet kicked up brief blizzards of Dream Park snow, tossed them back at him. The sound of her giggle was intoxicating.

She winded, he didn't. Max caught her by the wrist and she laughed, grabbed his wrist, and turned her back into him, clumsily trying to throw him over her shoulder. Failing, she broke away again, finally plopping down into the snow beneath a small overhang on the outer wall of the ice cave.

He sat next to her. The ridge overlooked a frozen sea. It didn't stretch out indefinitely, though. Fog clouded it up at the far end, an endlessly breaking wave of fog that rolled and hovered and seemed to want to stay just exactly where it was.

Eviane was breathing hard. One thing about being Mr. Mountain: for all of his bulk, he was actually in decent condition.

"I didn't know you were such a fighter," Eviane said.

"Yeah, well, neither did I."

She smiled shyly.

"Does that make a big difference?" he asked hesitantly.

"Always," she said. She stared at that bank of fog as if it concealed answers to every important question. "Oh, girls say that they want strong sensitive men. When we can't find both, we settle for strong."

Some part of him resented that. "Evolution in action?"

She nodded. "Sure. Deep down inside, we all know that something like this could happen. That the civilization we'd spent so much time and money building up could all come toppling down. And if it did, what would get us through is strength."

"Not just physical strength, though." He was trying to get into her mind-set.

He expected this to be more entertaining than easy. She was too deep into the Game. He believed she was nice-crazy, harmless crazy. Maybe just lost in the fantasy a little more than most. Somehow the fight with Hippogryph had changed him in her eyes. Her admiration turned him on. Hell, he'd always wanted to be someone's knight in shining armor.

Out on the horizon, distant winds shaped the fog, picked it up, and curled it like a gray, storm-tossed ocean. Eviane shuddered, and leaned almost imperceptibly closer.

"I'm afraid." Her whisper was so soft it could almost have been a trick of the wind.

"Are you?"

He felt, rather than saw, her answering nod. "I don't know what we're going to face tomorrow. I know it's important. I know that everyone is counting on me." She paused, fumbling for correct phrasing. "Michelle is counting on me."

"Michelle?"

No answer, just: "I'm afraid."

Crazier than he'd realized? Yet it felt good to have her lean against him, and even better to slip his arm around her shoulder. At first he thought she would let it remain there, but she stood. "I think we should be heading back," she said, as if there was something, spoken or unspoken, that had ruined the moment for both of them.

Max got to his feet. It was not love, but lack of love, that caused madness... and Max could not have told where he got that notion. In his mind other notions were equally powerful. *Love cannot be forced.* And *We're all in this to find help.*

"I think I know what you mean, about being afraid," he said. "I always get the jitters just before I go out to fight, even though it's only scripted."

She looked at him uncomprehendingly.

"You haven't figured it out?"

"Figured what out?" They had begun walking slowly back to the ice cave. The ground had a snow-cone feel to it, crunching under every step.

"I'm Mr. Mountain. For the past four years I've been a professional wrestler."

"Is that good?"

Bless you, child. "I don't know. It's honest farce, I guess. I guess there are maybe seven people who still believe it's real. Even the grannies are in on the joke. We honestly work hard, and do the best show that we can. I guess it's as good as I let it be."

"So you make a living fake-fighting?"

"Yup. Three or four nights a week. It was fun at first, but lately..."

She stopped, leaning against the outer, crystalline wall of the cave. He could hear the others inside, hooting and calling to each other as they played games. "And now you're tired of playing a role? Tired of playing that game?"

"Yeah," he said. "I don't want to be the clown anymore. I want to be the hero. I want the crowds to cheer me, not laugh at me. I just want..." He groped for the words. "Respect."

"How does it feel?"

"That's what I can't handle. Every time I go out there in those goddamned purple tights, I feel like I've betrayed myself."

"You want to be a hero." Her eyes shone at him. "You are a hero. I saw what you did in there. I saw the way you faced those monsters. I've never seen anything more heroic than that. How can you say you're not a hero?"

But it's not real! How crazy...?

It's as real as you let it be.

He closed his eyes, and let her words sink in. He was a hero. Underneath all of the flab, beneath the memories of jeering crowds... "So I don't have to be all muscle?"

"Silly." She slapped his hand lightly, held it to her cheek. Then she dropped it. Their eyes locked. The contact became entirely too intense. Max saw something, someone else behind those eyes. "Who are you?" he whispered.

She broke the gaze and turned away. "Eviane."

"Who is Michelle?"

"Michelle?" Her expression became vague again, questioning. "Michelle is . . . someone who needs me. Someone I let down."

Max touched her cheek. It was warm, and firm. The tip of his finger painted a little heart there with melted snow.

It was just the two of them in the little overhang. Max saw some of the others (was that Trianna?) running and playing, absorbed in their break time, running out sore muscles, sharing their fantasies.

And here he was, with this fragile, powerful girl. She burned with such energy and seemed so terribly weary. She pushed her cheek against his hand, and made a sound in her throat very like a muffled sob. He took her chin in his other hand, and tilted it up, until their faces were only a bare inch apart, just a fraction, just a breath of frosty air separating them. They were sharing the same breath of air now, and then her eyelashes, moist with melted snow and eyes shiny with repressed tears, closed slowly. She tilted her face forward.

Kissing her was like kissing an artless child.

Their eyes met, and then hers lowered. "I'm sorry. I'm really . . . please forgive me."

"For what? There's nothing to forgive." He could feel her contracting into herself like a hermit crab. It disturbed him.

"I'm so ashamed. If you knew me. If you really knew me." She looked up at him, trembling. She kept trying to be strong. To be Eviane. Untouchable, unflappable. A woman who could stare down monsters and fight demons from Thunderbird-back.

He tried to smooth her hair. "We're all here to heal," he said, as softly as he could.

"It's so hard. I feel so guilty."

"I heard something once that helped me through a lot of bad times. It was written by a man named Neal Birt. He said, 'The only way we can be perfect is to be perfectly willing.' You're willing, Eviane, or you wouldn't be here. If you let Michelle down, or if Michelle let you down, you have to be willing to forgive each other, and get on with life. Things don't always turn out the way you want them to."

"Just like that?" Her voice was wondering. "You can forgive yourself just that easily?"

"Hahaha! No. Sorry. But I sure love it when someone holds me and reminds me that it can be that easy."

"And how often is that?"

"Not often enough," he admitted.

Not nearly often enough.

She looked up at him. "Max," she said shyly. "Could we... try that kiss again?"

"Hey, it was fine the first time—"

"Oh, well, then."

"Anything worth doing is worth overdoing."

She must have missed the lessons on banter. She only kissed him. But this time there was both child and woman in her kiss, and her arms tightened around him...

Outside in Dream Park's winter wonderland, the light was fading, but here, in their ice cave, amid small, tremulous gaspings and the rustle of unneeded, unwelcome clothing, a special kind of light was coming up.

And it was just exactly as warm as they needed it to be.

Chapter Twenty-Four

OVERVIEW

Outside the snow might have been howling, but inside the ice cave it was comfortably warm, warmed even more by the unexpected circumstance of a warm-water spring. The cave was half the size of a football field, with vaulted ceilings that sparkled with meter-long icicles.

Yarnall was doing laps in the spring. Charlene had never really noticed, but his lean dark body was actually quite nice, probably the best among the Adventurers. At Falling Angel only first-comers carried muscle like that. If Yarnall hadn't been so intense and serious, she might have been interested.

A flash of pain shattered her train of thought.

"Did that hurt?" Oliver let a little air pressure out of the pneumatic bandage on her knee.

"I'll be all right." She gritted her teeth. Her knees ached, but there was no swelling, and no grinding, and she was damned if she was going to let a little pain get between her and what she hoped was going to be a memorable evening.

Trianna Stith-Wood and Johnny Welsh dove in tandem. Water splashed high and far. They bobbled up laughing and spitting warm water, playful as seal pups. "Race you!" Trianna yelled, splashing a palmful of water into Johnny's face.

"What's the wager?" he said mischievously.

"What do you want?" she asked. Their eyes locked for a moment, and then he pushed off and thrashed across the pool.

> *"I am a follower of Cthulhu*
> *And I lead a mad horde*
> *Searching everywhere for our vanished*
> *Overlord . . .*
> *But though we need him more than want him,*
> *Still we'll have him for all time*

When his city of Rl'yeh
Ascends from the sliiimmme!"

Snow Goose—Gwen—was leading the other Gamers in a series of rousing, bawdy songs. Orson Sands's voice was surprisingly high and sweet, though it broke occasionally. She sighed. Orson might have been interesting, but the Hippogryph wasn't letting anyone close.

He was her personal bloodhound, and a dear boy. She wished he would be less protective, or else make a move on her himself. There was something about this Dream Park that got her hormones running.

The environments within Falling Angel were designed for survival and for work. One could lose oneself in the thousand little necessities of life, software and momentum and radiation shielding and recycling of toilet paper, and forget that human beings need more than air, water, and food to be whole.

Then again, Charlene Dula was Ambassador Arbenz's niece. She was damned rich, and that kept a lot of the men at bay. And there was her height...

What it boiled down to was a set of teen-aged nerves in a twenty-five-year-old body.

"There. I think that's all we need." Ollie slapped the side of her knee gently.

"And aside from the knee, how am I doing?"

"Everything is fine, hon." Ollie cocked his head at her. "My professional opinion is that with plenty of sleep, and the help of your calcium supplements, we'd have your muscular and skeletal system up to Earth normal in about two months. But you're handling the stress just fine. Now—go and have fun."

"Doctor's orders?" Married, he was. Just testing—

"Doctor's orders."

She pushed herself up and tested the knee carefully, walked over to the campfire by the side of the spring.

There had been plenty of driftwood available for a fire, much to nobody's surprise. In Dream Park, the Gods provided. The Adventurers circled the bonfire, clapping, drinking fruit juice, and finishing their dinners. Two paid special attention to her approach: Hippogryph/Marty, and Snow Goose/Gwen.

Gwen's face lit up. She asked, "Is Ollie all finished with you?"

"So he says."

"Good. Kevin?"

Kevin had been keeping an eye on the spring, watching Trianna and Johnny cavorting. Those two climbed out of the water now. They dried each other primly, but shared the same towel. Johnny wound it into a rope and snapped the tip at Trianna's bottom. She squealed and ran jiggling to the firelight.

Gwen said, "Kevin?"

"Oh . . . yeah?"

"Have you got the verses?"

He was a little sad, but forced some jollity into his thin voice. "Sure. You go ahead."

Gwen kissed Kevin on the cheek, and ran off to join Ollie. Kevin swung into the next verse:

> *"You see I met this crazy Arab,*
> *And he showed me his book.*
> > *I thought it couldn't hurt me just to take one*
> > *little look.*
> *But though I couldn't read the language.*
> *It did something to my mind.*
> > *Now I'm searching for something*
> > *I'd rather not fiiind!"*

Charlene kneed Hippogryph in the shoulder. He made a contented grunting sound and scooted aside to make room for her. He had been trying to sing, but the poor darling couldn't carry a tune if it had handles. He was trying hard to be a Gamer, but just wasn't quite fitting in.

"How's the knee?"

"Nice," she said, and extended her leg, flexing it a couple of times. "Feel?"

Hippogryph probed it gingerly with a forefinger. A little light went on in his eye as he carried the probe down to the meat of her thigh.

She flexed unobtrusively, she hoped. She had worked long and hard to put firmness there. Too many of the women of Falling Angel never put in their full time on the treadmills and climbing racks. They had rubbery, gelatinous thighs in spite of countless posted cautionary notices and the imposition of penalty points.

There was even a fashion movement to suggest that it was more attractive, sexier somehow, to be flabby. Ridiculous. Charlene screwed up her courage, and asked: "You like?"

Hippogryph tried to slap his professional mask back down. "Lady..."

She reached over and touched her forefinger to his lips. "I'll tell you what. You take a walk with me, tell me all about it?"

"I don't know about this." His face was darkly humorous. He was attracted to her, no questioning that. But duty was calling.

"Of course, if you don't want to, I'll just stroll outside by myself. Maybe I can find a nice terrorist to keep me company."

Marty levered himself up. "Truly, whither thou walkest I must walk too."

So she walked him over to a quieter corner of the cave. Her bedroll was already out, and a plate of fruit was nearby, just in case. As a girl she had been a Moon Scout. Charlene believed in being prepared.

Marty squinted. "I'm being seduced, yes?" He sat down, and offered his arm for support. "Oh, well!" A thick black-furred arm as solid as an angle iron.

They sat together in the shadows. Marty put his arm around her ribcage, and sighed. "I wonder if I can be fired for this."

"Bushwah. You're supposed to be a bodyguard. So, guard my body!" His wide neck was in the crook of her elbow; her fingers played in the thick fur of his chest. She leaned her cheek against his scalp. His hair still smelled a little of good clean sweat from his match with Max. She giggled.

"What now?"

"Oh, I was just thinking about watching you throw Max around. He's a lot bigger than you. You really did well."

"Yeah," he growled, "but they're the ones off celebrating."

She nibbled at his ear. "Oh, we're allowed to celebrate too. Call it a moral victory." Another, softer laugh. "Besides, Eviane deserves it. She's been taking this whole thing so seriously. Then getting killed out, then brought back, and she's so *perfect*, she never falls out of character! You'd think it was for real points."

"Or real money with a piece of the gross. Eviane's a strange one."

"Oh, she's nice. I like her." Charlene paused. "Listen— you're in Security. You must have seen her files. What do you know about her? Or is that classified?"

He laughed. "Not much to tell. She's not an Actress, if that's what you're thinking. And Eviane isn't her real name. But I didn't pay much attention to the Gamer files before I jumped into the Game. Never saw her before."

"What *is* her real name?"

He chucked her under the chin. "Now, that *is* classified."

"Aw, pleeease."

"Nope."

She rolled him over on his back, and started looking for places to tickle. "Pretty please with moondust on top . . . ?"

"Help!" He was laughing uncontrollably now. "Dammit, stop taking my mind off work—" Her hands started moving slower, more surely, and Marty stopped laughing, suddenly relaxed. "Oh, bloody hell," he said, and rolled her over.

"Careful, lover," she said, eyes alight. "You'll break something."

"The only thing I'm breaking is training," he said, and pulled her to him. He murmured into her breath, into lips just touching his, "My self-control is legendary."

"Good."

"Half history, half myth. You feel solid enough. Are you fragile?"

Blood was rushing in Charlene's ears when they broke the kiss. Very distantly, she could hear the Gamers singing:

> *"We will have a mighty orgy*
> *In the honor of Astarte*
> *It will be one helluva party*
> *And it's good enough for me!*
> *Give me that old-time religion*
> *Give me that old-time religion*
> *Give me that old-time religion*
> *It's good enough for me!"*

Yes indeed! she thought contentedly. Yes indeed it was.

Everything that happened in the Game came to Dr. Vail. Everything, whether it was supposed to or not. Questions of morality or privacy meant little to Vail. Efficiency was everything, and it was efficient for him to know everything that went on. When. Where. What.

Who.

Dr. Vail's jaw hung loose as he watched the monitors. Jagged green-on-green lines shaping hillscapes. Columns of numbers, color-coded. Max Sands and Michelle Sturgeon in a pile of clothing. Yarnall moving smoothly through the warm water. Trianna and Welsh testing a self-inflating mattress to destruction. Bowles in a circle of conversation, breaking off suddenly to bellow a chorus.

Vail looked stupid; he looked stunned. A camera watching him would have shown no more . . . but Vail's mind was racing, correlating.

He had just learned something very strange.

But what was he to do with it? He would have to tell Griffin *something*.

Chapter Twenty-Five

MADELEINE

Down the corridor, down the long, dark hall framed with steel bars and steel doors, punctuated with steel windows peering out onto a steel courtyard, Tony McWhirter heard screams.

Likely it was a wirehead in need of his juice. It probably wasn't a beating. It probably wasn't a rape.

Not tonight. Not again.

For the ten millionth time, Tony cursed his stupidity, cursed the day that an olive-skinned woman tempted him with an unusual proposition.

One bad, stupid decision could twist a life completely out of true.

It had started out as a lark . . . as a hack, a theft of information, a bit of industrial espionage committed in a deeper reality . . . like Dream Park's Games.

And Tony McWhirter, would-be soldier of fortune, was sent to Chino Men's Prison to pay his debt to society.

The words and symbols on the computer screen blurred out. He stopped, rested his head against the keyboard, tried to find a little breathing space.

Two more years. God in heaven. Two more years of this place if he didn't make parole.

At first he had been able to con himself into looking at it as another great adventure, filled with sinister secrets and a certain noble romanticism.

Then Acacia stopped writing.

Because of Alex Griffin!

Tony rubbed his wrists. They were numb, often felt cold. The doctors said that it was in his mind, that there had been no nerve damage—no *permanent* nerve damage caused by the jagged chunk of glass and the frantic midnight attempt to take his own life. The cold was just an externalization of the emotional void within him.

Hang on! Two more years. Maybe less, if you can get this, he reminded himself. *Hell, you're Tony McWhirter, boy genius, soldier of fortune, hacker supreme. You can get through any defense system in the world. Alex Griffin knows that. That's why he comes to you with the tough problems. That's why he's done things to make Chino tolerable.*

Tony forced himself to concentrate. These moments were so sweet. Normally he had access to a computer only three hours a day, and even then he was denied access to outside lines. He could program, and run programs, but they weren't going to give him a chance to tie into the Bank of New Caledonia and transfer a zillion or so into his legal defense fund.

Right now, his only goal was to penetrate the defensive shields of a man or corporate entity named Kareem Fekesh.

The routing was standard. Dream Park had an executive line, which automatically allowed it to talk to the computers of other companies on a more intimate basis. It was like knowing the address of your intended victim, and having enough grease to get past the guards at the front gate. You still had to have the chutzpah to get through the guard at the front door, con your way up to the bedroom, find the combination safe, and crack it.

But he was in the front gate!

Dream Park's computer called one of Fekesh's subsidiaries. There were over two hundred. In spite of his general misery, McWhirter had to whistle. This man was loaded.

Oil, gold, entertainment, and transportation were the very least of it.

Entertainment...

A tiny light went on in the back of his mind. Tony McWhirter had a private obsession, and part of his mind traced back over it even as he was probing the defenses of an autoteller system that served a merchant bank. He was tinkering, teasing the system, trying to understand its protocols and methods.

And while he did, he thought back.

Over the years, every time Griffin opened Dream Park's communications systems to him, Tony had taken a little of his time, not enough so that anyone could notice, to investigate the structure of Dream Park and Cowles Industries. He knew just about everything that there was to know about Alex Griffin.

Tony even knew how many times Acacia had visited him at Cowles Modular Community. He knew that they had gone skiiing together twice in Aspen. He didn't want to know any more than that; he forced himself to be satisfied knowing that they had last communicated by phone, eighteen months ago.

This was only self-flagellation. Other probes were more practical.

Seven years ago. A dark-skinned woman named "Madeleine" offered him twenty thousand dollars for a special job.

During trial proceedings, Dream Park's artists had asked for a complete description of Madeleine, to be made into a computer-built Identifax portrait. Tony had given them everything he could remember. They had searched; he had checked; they had found no trace of the mystery woman.

Later he had fished the composite out of Dream Park's memory banks. Every time he penetrated the security system of a company having anything at all to do with chemicals or entertainment, he entered their personnel files and looked for Madeleine. No luck. Over seven hundred major companies and subsidiary lines had given him nothing at all.

Still, he looked.

The automatic program had wormed its way through the exterior defensive shields. More involved ones would be coming up. Tony bore down for an hour, testing "doors," looking for a way into Fekesh's system.

He found it in their accounting department. He couldn't transfer funds, not at this level of sophistication, but he could look into files which had been set aside for a tax audit. There he found a coded key which got him up to the next tier.

He ran around the edge of the tier, and then found a bridge to enter the core system. He was in. Just looking, but in.

And while he was in . . .

He began to co-process the personnel files, looking for Madeleine.

Oh, yes, Fekesh was into everything, and everything was into Fekesh. There were no direct financial ties to what Griffin was looking for, but beyond a shadow of a doubt, Fekesh had invested heavily in Cowles Industries eight years before . . .

Tony wondered about something and took another look, this time at the current investment portfolio.

Interesting. There were tens of millions of dollars invested in entertainment, and *none* of it was headed for Cowles! He insti-

gated a side search program, looking for corporate shells . . . and
something snagged in his peripheral vision, a little red flag in the
lower left corner of the screen.

For a moment he didn't realize what it meant. He hadn't seen
it in this context in over seven hundred attempts. Now, cautiously, he opened the flag and studied what came through.

The name "Madeleine" wasn't mentioned. The face which
matched Dream Park's Identifax belonged to a woman named
Collia Aziz. She had accompanied Kareem Fekesh to a company
picnic, and was described as "attractive."

The man who had written that line could never have been
close enough to touch her, or smell her perfume, or watch her
moving lips and changing posture and the signals they sent,
across a room or the width of an oil mattress . . . Tony clamped
down hard, shutting out the memories. That way lay madness.

Collia or Madeleine or Eleanor Roosevelt she could call herself, but Tony McWhirter would never forget. She'd cost him
Acacia, she'd cost him seven years of life and counting, and *it
was her*.

And wasn't it interesting that the woman who had destroyed
his life had connections to a company Griffin was interested in
right now.

The other processing job finished itself. Routed through a
half-dozen corporate shells and off-shore accounts, over this past
year Fekesh had put together an investment company which had
bought 128,000 "sell" orders of Cowles Industries.

Now, why would Fekesh be expecting the price to drop?

Tony sat back, feeling muscles relax throughout his body. His
success had the taste of new threats. Fekesh was planning something. He'd tried to destroy Dream Park once; maybe twice. This
time, would he succeed?

Why was Tony McWhirter feeling protective of Dream Park?
Fekesh's machinations had put him in Chino. Thwarting Fekesh
would be appropriate.

And hey, he'd done it, he'd found his ticket out! Griffin was
going to shit bricks.

Chapter Twenty-Six

THE BEANSTALK BRUNCH

Alex Griffin snapped awake, totally alert and sweating. He had to have been dreaming . . . those were the only times when he awoke wondering, confused, eyes focused and staring, lips pursed to whistle for the ceiling light, then pausing.

He had to have been dreaming, but he couldn't remember the dream. Since childhood, Alex had had trouble remembering his dreams. It rarely deviled him. Alex supposed he was one of those rare and fortunate people for whom reality was enough.

But when he woke up slimed with sweat, gelatinous night-images sliding away like corpses sinking in oily water, then he knew that he was lying to himself. Of course he dreamed. He'd never stopped. He just didn't really want to know what was down there in the depths.

He lay there for a few moments, breathing shallowly, then rolled out of bed. He felt around for his slippers and slipped them on. He turned the clock to face him.

One-thirty. In five hours he would be expected to be up and about, attending to the business of the day. He might as well get to it now.

Alex lifted his body out of bed. He felt heavy, and didn't quite understand why—he was in perfect physical condition. Disconcerting. A diet, maybe?

How about the Fat Ripper Special?

There was something intrinsically absurd in that idea, but he didn't laugh. He was too tired. One part of his mind kept digging for that last elusive dream-image, and it kept wiggling away from him.

Musing, he headed for the shower. If there was really something important lurking in his subconscious, it would eventually come out and say "Hi."

● ● ●

The midnight streets of Dream Park were deserted facades once again, but in Alex Griffin's mind, they were full.

He nodded occasionally to a roving security or maintenance man. Ordinarily, he loved walking these streets. At moments like this it seemed that the Park existed for him alone.

Oh, there were the times that the Park, or a section of it, was closed to all but employees and their families. At those times the entertainers put on their very best performances. It was rawer and bawdier. Outsiders had paid hefty bribes to get into those parties. That back-stage feel was Dream Park at its best: celebration for its own sake, and an opportunity for them all to take a breath and relax, and see what they had accomplished, and smile to each other.

We are the magicians! they could say, did say at those times. *We bring the dream to life, and we're the only ones who can. And around the world, people put hours and sweat into jobs that often have little meaning to them, saving up to come to Dream Park, to buy the most perfectly packaged Dreams in the world . . .*

And now Alex wandered along Glory Road by dead of night. (The Starship Trooper Game, always a big hit, was being refurbished again. There was often damage in that one. The adrenaline really started rushing when the bug-eyed monsters came charging at you.)

Tonight, there were no couples from Kansas and Calcutta, tow-headed or olive-skinned children tagging along in a state of shock. The deserted streets offered his imagination a panoply of clowns and capering performers. There was so much here, so many exhibits, that he rarely roamed the streets without discovering something new and precious. He smiled fleetingly up as the faintly glowing shape of the Sta-Puft Marshmallow Man™ swaggered past.

Tonight he had no real sense of wonder. Tonight he searched the faces of the employees, looked at the buildings, remembered the illusions, contemplated his tomorrow.

Because something was happening in Dream Park. It was going on right under his nose, in the middle of the Barsoom Project, in the middle of the Fimbulwinter Game. It deviled him, because instinct, or some subrational thought system, had identified a world of true problems, potentials for hideous disruption, and they wouldn't let him sleep.

Or was his nightmare only a memory of failed skyhooks smashing across Mars and Earth?

For a time, Alex Griffin had looked upon this magical place as a job, cushier and more interesting than most other jobs, to be sure. But the South Seas Treasure Game had taught him things about himself, and his ability to slip into fantasy, that he never would have believed. He had learned something about Dream Park that he never could have learned from the outside looking in.

At the next board meeting Alex had formally proposed that every employee be required to attend a Game as a condition for promotion.

Alex Griffin's lesson had come late and hit hard. In the South Seas Treasure Game, reality had intruded lethally upon fantasy. There were zombies and monsters and wizards and thieves, a hidden murderer, and a wonderful, magical interlude with a beautiful girl named Acacia; and all of his conceptions of Dream Park were jarred to the core.

He'd been voted down. But how else would his people learn the true nature of the Park? How easily could cynicism grow if one saw only the nuts and bolts, and rarely experienced the final product? How could you empathize with the customer unless you saw what the customer saw? Unless, at least once, you felt what he felt?

If you truly understood, then when you saw customers staggering around the Park in a general state of emotional overload, you could help them, or at the very least comfort them with a silent *Yes, I know.* And that made all the difference.

How would the public feel if they knew about the men in black who manipulated the puppets? The stage assistants who spirited the lady out of the box and put the tiger in? And other, darker, uglier magics. They shouldn't know, didn't want to know, and it was his job . . . their job . . . to protect the illusion. That was why it was necessary to understand, to experience that illusion deeply and intimately.

The streets were deserted now. Only a few of the neon, plastic, or holographic signs were functioning. A few forlorn sweeper 'bots cruised the streets, and one of them cruised at him, then paused, humming at his feet. It beeped apologetically, and continued on its industrious way.

Alex Griffin understood how it felt.

Ambassador Arbenz had been surprised but polite and responsive to Alex's request for a midmorning interview. "I haven't

time for a private breakfast, but I'll take my morning constitu-
tional on my way to the Beanstalk conference."

So Alex tubed over to the Hotel Gulliver to meet the Ambassador at nine o'clock.

Hotel Gulliver was always a wild experience. The furniture
was constructed as if by miniature hands for the pleasure of
giants (in the Lilliput wing) or roughly hewn as if by giant hands
for brownies (in the Brobdingnag wing). The desk clerks were
helpful elf-sized figures who happily balanced atop one another
in their eagerness to sign you into the books. Elevators were
hauled up and down the elevator wells by giants who paced outside the windows, pulling enormous cables.

Ambassador Arbenz was in the Brobdingnag wing.

Alex took the outside elevator. Through the glass wall he
could see a titanic man with a receding hairline pulling him upward by a thick hemp rope. The giant panted; he perspired. There
was a conspicuous knot in the rope where it must have broken.

Beyond the great bald head Alex could see the Laputa tower
floating unsupported. He couldn't see his favorite, the tower of
the Houyhnhnm, with its statues of Saint Francis and Saint Ed.

"Mr. Griffin," the Ambassador said. He strode across the
room, and clasped Alex's hand firmly. Richard Arbenz wore a
well-cut purple walking suit that flattered his ectomorphic profile. His hair was gray; he might be the oldest of the Falling
Angel crowd; but he seemed perfectly comfortable in Earth's
gravity. Griffin guessed that Arbenz worked long and hard to
keep his muscles, bones, and ligaments strong.

"I have a very full schedule today, please forgive me if we can
only talk on the move. These are crucial times in the negotia-
tions."

"What I came for won't take much time," Alex assured him.

In the kitchenette the smell of fresh-brewed coffee was becoming obtrusive. "Coffee?" Arbenz asked. "The President of
Colombia sends it personally. An appreciation for a hydroelectric
project Falling Angel helped to plan and execute."

Alex found he was edging backward with that wonderful scent
in his nose and a memory of battery acid in his belly. "Sorry, no.
Ulcer." *May Castro's ghost raise revolution in Colombia!*

"Oh. Pity." Arbenz finished his own cup in one smooth gulp.
"Well, then, let's proceed."

The Ambassador led Alex out and to the nearest elevator. He
set a swift pace. Their elevator was lowered by the same perspir-

ing bald giant. The city beyond him seemed composed of blocks the size of houses. Despite the size of the inhabitants (and the rather disquieting realization that the floor *thrummed* slightly each time one of them took a step) the view was really rather enchanting.

"Very well," Arbenz said, looking down on the top of Alex's head. "What is it that I can do for you?"

"Well . . ." Alex still felt a bit uncomfortable. Arbenz was seven inches taller than he, even though Earth's gravity had stooped him by an inch or two. "There was an incident in one of our Games. It's the Game your niece is in."

Arbenz became very alert indeed. "An incident?"

The elevator thudded down, the door opened as if jarred, and Arbenz strode through the lobby at a brisk walking pace. At least, for Arbenz it was walking. Alex would have felt ridiculous breaking into a jog, but as he tried to match the Ambassador's long-legged stride, for the first time in his life he understood why race-walking was an Olympic sport. The gray hair must be premature. No old man raised in low gravity could outrun Alex Griffin!

It took him a minute to make his pace both efficient and comfortable. That gave him his breath back. He said, "It could mean nothing. It's one of *those*. A hologram monster attacked the wrong person, and the computer killed her out of the Game." Alex spread his hands. "No real problem. No explanation either."

Arbenz's long face creased with concern. "Was it Charlene?"

Alex gulped air, felt the first flush of perspiration under his collar. Arbenz looked perfectly comfortable. "No, it was her friend Eviane."

Arbenz passed through the VIP gate and headed for the Tower of Night, a slender silver projection glistening in the morning light . . . Alex blinked. He'd passed the Tower yesterday evening; it had been tall. This morning it went up forever! What he knew to be the Tower's roof continued without a break, tapering to a silver line, stretching into the blue zenith.

Three years ago he'd seen the plans. For two years Alex had been looking at the restaurant itself. He'd eaten here; he'd loved the way the elevator took him into the sky . . . and still he hadn't known it for what it was. Now he remembered the Barsoom Project's discussion of bridges to the planets. The Tower of Night had been a Beanstalk all along.

By now Dream Park's special guests were used to the sight of the Ambassador, and barely noticed his passing. All things considered, he was one of Dream Park's less startling sights. Even on the reduced schedule demanded by the Barsoom Project, there were still enough KaleidoKlowns, dancing 'Toons, and multispecies street vendors to steal the thunder from a mere six-foot-five Lunarian.

"A strange girl," Arbenz said finally. With savage satisfaction Alex noted that Arbenz had finally broken into a sweat. "I met her only briefly. Apparently she and Charlene are quite close. No one was hurt?"

"No one. What I want is to go back over the threats that were made against you."

Arbenz hadn't looked tired until Griffin said that. "The usual. They consider the Barsoom Project an abomination, the desecration of the heavens. Even the name 'Falling Angel' has been considered demonic. It is an absurd pseudo-fundamental Moslem view of the world. People are being exploited for personal gain."

They had reached the Tower of Night. They entered the elevator. As the door closed, Dream Park vanished.

Outside the clear-plastic windows was burnt-umber sand and a pink sky shading to black. Dead, waterless, almost windless; a dust storm receded toward the too-close horizon.

"You said personal gain. Who stands to gain by scaring you off? Or killing you?"

"Considering the number of contracts that are at stake, I'd consider that question unanswerable. And I *surely* don't understand why an *imaginary* monster should have attacked my *niece*, and *missed!*"

Alex nodded reluctantly. He didn't either.

The elevator rose rapidly. The tiny Martian spaceport town dropped away at fantastic speed, and even without the accompanying sense of acceleration, his stomach flopped and gurgled. He gulped as Mons Olympus rose over the horizon with thin clouds streaming from its shallow flank at two levels, then shrank to become a bump on a shrinking sphere.

If Charlene Dula had been killed out, where would she go? Someplace unprotected?

If the terrorist had missed Charlene, he must be a fool. But ... fool enough to think that Marty would stay in the Game with Charlene out?

"Mr. Ambassador, has your niece ever been named directly in one of these threats?"

"No. But indirectly, yes, and a kidnap attempt was made on Mitch De Camp's boy."

"De Camp's the President of Falling Angel."

"Correct."

Alex closed his eyes, reviewing the information. When he opened them again, Mars was a beach ball held at arm's length, and the Beanstalk span stretched below them like a tightrope across the Abyss. "All right. Is there anything else you can tell me?"

"Not really," Arbenz said. The elevator came to a halt. "And now I must ask you to excuse me. There are appointments waiting."

The inner door opened. Beyond was conversation and sanity, the smell of food, and the feel of solid ground.

"Thank you for your time," Alex said, and shook the long broad hand that Arbenz extended to him. "Ah . . . I think I'll come in for a moment. I need to check on some things."

"By all means."

The door hissed shut behind them.

Chapter Twenty-Seven

THE ISLAND

Eviane shielded her eyes, guarding them from a killing glare. Far away, across a vast blue-white sheet of ice, their destiny waited. Now it seemed like nothing so much as an empty plain, but she knew: in her heart she knew.

Her pack was heavy against her shoulders, but her heart was light: for the first time in many months...

Years?

Ever...?

Inwardly, she shuddered. Why didn't her memory reveal other friends, other lovers? It was all a mist. Perhaps she had taken a blow on the head.

(*No, that's not it*, a voice whispered. And the voice was disturbingly familiar. She could almost, but not quite, remember the name that went with the voice. Almost. It wasn't the first time that the voice had spoken to her, but the sound of it was growing more and more welcome, like an old friend...)

Max adjusted the strap on his pack, and looked down at her, one massive arm resting on her shoulder. It was a comforting weight, and she took unutterable comfort from his nearness.

Last night... last night. The panic had been there, as if he really were her first lover. She had been prepared to hide it, as she would hide her fear before a battle, but it hadn't been like that at all.

He had been so gentle with her that her panic had fluttered and receded as his hands, those large, clumsy-looking, powerful, gentle hands, somehow did their magic. His hands were so strong. She thought that he could mold rocks the way children use modeling clay. But last night he had treated her with such consuming tenderness that she had finally dug fingernails into his neck, bitten his shoulder, hissed and whimpered until he had treated her like a woman, not an overgrown child.

And panic turned into something else, something that was desperate for human contact, something that used him and welcomed his use of her. What started out as a cry of loneliness became a scream of triumph. Both of them, together, howled against the wind, and laughed, and laughed, and touched.

She grinned, thinking how it must have sounded on the other side of the rock. At least nobody had come to the rescue.

Afterward they just held each other and whispered in the darkness of the ice cave. No talking about the past. No talking about the future, when the Cabal had been defeated (Max had said: "When the Game is over." Men. Even in the direst of circumstances, they somehow still believed life was all a big game). Just the kind of talk that two strangers make, when the roar of their glands has momentarily subsided, and the flesh is cooling, and the wonderful, terrifyingly intimate afterglow is erasing the barriers between them. In those times lovers talk, speak quickly, say anything to keep that space open as long as possible, knowing that too soon it will iris closed.

Or, in other times, times that she dimly remembered, during those same moments partners sometimes turned away, lit cigarettes, rose to fetch drinks, visited the bathroom. Succored every bodily need except intimacy. Fought like demons to keep the moment from becoming too intimate, as if intimacy was the most terrifying thing in the world.

And, Eviane reflected, perhaps it was.

There were gentle clouds on the horizon. The twelve other Adventurers stood assessing the coming challenge, measuring each other for strength and weakness. Charlene and her escort Hippogryph were only a few steps away. Soon, Eviane thought, she and Max—

(She liked the sound of that. Eviane and Max. Just like a real couple. Just like a normal, healthy. . .

(Eviane and Max. Why didn't that sound quite right? As if there was someone else in the loop. Did she have a rival? She looked around herself in the group. No, there was no one else her man was interested in. She *knew.*)

Charlene Dula broke the spell. She angled over to Eviane. Her slender face was still a little slack with sleep. A light breakfast hadn't dispelled the dreams completely. She stood four inches taller than any of the others, and was starting to carry the extra height and weight more comfortably. Whatever aches and pains she had started with, her body was making the necessary adjustments.

"All in all, I'd say that you have had an excellent night." Charlene cocked an inquisitive eye, perhaps hoping for details.

Eviane hugged Max's arm. Max looked up at the clouds and whistled tunelessly.

Snow Goose slide-stepped across the icy ground. Like the rest of them, she had fastened a pad of Velcro-like hooking blades to her shoes. They increased the traction wonderfully. She came close to Eviane. "All right," she said. "Which way do we go?"

Eviane closed her eyes. In the darkness, shimmering like a heat mirage, was the city. The ruins. She raised a hand and pointed toward the horizon. Snow Goose touched her arm lightly, correcting it a few degrees.

"The spirits say that if we head north, we'll reach our goal."

Kevin shrugged his bony shoulders. The air was chilly, but not quite unpleasant.

The Adventurers formed a line and began to move out, the blades on their shoe bottoms grating against the ice, keeping them stable.

Hippogryph sidled up next to Max. "Good bout yesterday, Mr. Mountain."

Max smiled. "Yeah, I guess it was." He looked at his former opponent. "You were really trying, weren't you?"

"Nobody takes falls like that for fun. I should have brought a goddamn parachute."

Max's grin broadened, and a little tune came into his whistle. His bear paw of a hand slid over Hippogryph's. "Thanks," he said. "That means a lot."

There were no signs of life. It was as though they had gone beyond the pale. Nothing but the incessantly howling winds. No birds, no plants. Just the slow crawl of the blue-pink fantasia arcing endlessly overhead.

Eviane began to feel a certain heaviness in her guts, a sourness. She looked back over her shoulder. Already the mountains were far behind them. In this strange and magical land, time and distance didn't seem to have the same significance they did in the outside world. More of the Cabal's doing, she would imagine.

"Are you afraid?" she asked Max.

He wore a three-day stubble of beard and frankly, she liked it. Without it there was a certain babyishness to him; he seemed soft and vulnerable. With the dark beard, he seemed dangerous. For that matter, so did Orson.

"Of course." Max's eyes were hooded, serious, but his voice was merry. "Only a fool wouldn't be afraid."

Ah, her man. He didn't fool her for a moment. He was the bravest, handsomest—

Once again she caught a sidewise glance at those flashing eyes, peering ahead into the danger as if there was nothing in the world that could stop him. At that moment she was sure that he was right.

And she was happy that he was hers.

And Michelle, still hiding behind stern, strong Eviane, giggled like a happy child.

They had been walking for an hour before the ice began to vibrate.

It was a gentle sensation at first, and she marked it down to loose shoes, or the slipping of her ice grips on her soles, or the sound of the marchers around her. But terror was already rising along Eviane's spine.

A few seconds later she heard it thrumming more powerfully, rhythmically, a deep ringing like a man striking a gong. She felt it more than heard it, as if she were an ant crawling along the edge of the gong, and now the terror was yammering in her frontal lobes.

"Hey—" Robin Bowles was the first of the others to comment on it.

And there it was again. This time the entire field shook. The memory of the burrowing mammoth flashed through her mind and body and held her paralyzed and mute.

Max grabbed her shoulder and yanked her back. All of the others stepped back away from the locus of vibration. The waves shivered through their feet, up their legs, rattling their brains, shaking them as if with titanic hammer blows.

"Back!" Yarnall screamed. "For God's sake, get back!"

And the ice began to split.

The fissure line was tiny, a delicate hairline that suddenly tore apart and became something hideous. Jagged sheets of ancient frozen water cracked and jutted like a miniature mountain range. Eviane rose clumsily to her feet and scrambled backward. She grabbed Max's hand, but lost it as he rose up five feet on an angled ice cliff. She yelped and slid down on her backside, thumping into an abutment of ice.

The environmental craziness began to spread.

The sky crackled. The aurora borealis was temporarily obscured in a swirl of storm clouds and blinding sheets of lightning. The roar of the storm, the thunder melded with the sound of the ice just a few hundred yards away as the entire shelf split. A dark and mazelike form loomed up from beneath it.

It must have been two or three kilometers across. The cry of the shattering, groaning ice was a terrible thing, rising above the wind, above the clash of lightning, filling earth and sky with a bone-jarring cacophony. The birth of a mountain range might have been like that. It overwhelmed the senses, eye and ear and sense of touch all overloaded to the point that the Adventurers couldn't run, couldn't hide, could do nothing but watch, mouths agape with shock.

The mist and the hail grew thick enough to turn day to twilight. The hissing of a dark ocean somewhere deep beneath the ice roared as if regurgitating the last drop of caustic from a poisoned system.

What burst into the air was impossible, and the Adventurers sprawled on the ruined ice floe gazed at it in amazement and horror.

It was a maze of sorts, like a windowless alien city carved out of some black stone. The angles of it actually hurt Eviane's head to examine.

Max's arms snaked around her from the side as she pressed palms against her temples. "Sweetheart," he asked in alarm, "are you all right?"

She couldn't speak her answer, could only press tightly into his comforting warmth.

The city's skyline was jagged with crystal spires too thin to support themselves, that should have vibrated and shattered in the wind, and spans between towers that twisted like facets of a gem, viewed through the center of that perfect stone: the angles were there, the angles could be perceived, but not understood. They didn't make any sense.

Max and Orson helped each other down from one of the higher shelves; and looked at it in astonishment. "Like something out of an Escher painting," Max muttered.

Orson, for once, just shook his head, then looked around for the skinny redhead. "Kevin? What have we got here?"

Kevin sighed. "Mythologically, I haven't the foggiest fuck of a notion. Effects-wise, I think it's a modified three-dimensional holographic binary decomposition of a Mandelbrot set."

"Kevin?" Orson said.

"Yeah?"

"Get a life, would you?"

The other Adventurers had collected around them by now, gazing up at the impossible reality. "What is this?" Yarnall whispered. "Anybody read about anything like this in Eskimo lore?"

There was no direct answer, but Kevin looked at the vast crystal forest of buildings and shook his head slowly. "Damned if it doesn't remind me of something, but I can't remember what."

"Eskimos . . ." Orson said. "But does it specifically have to be Eskimo mythology, or could it include mythology about Eskimos?"

Trianna pulled her collar tighter. "Why? What's the difference?"

"I remember something from Lovecraft about a tribe of degenerate Eskimos who worshiped . . . worshiped . . . I'm sorry. It just won't come."

Cautiously, they began to move forward.

The ground, although uneven, had better traction here. The maze was only about three hundred meters away. The avenues between the blocks were slick with ocean damp, freezing dry, a glare of ice forming over everything even as they watched.

Frankish Oliver was the first to step onto the new ground. He tested it with one foot, then looked back at them, and nodded his head in a sickly approval. "Let's do it," he said, thumping his war club against the ground. He might have been trying to convince himself that the street wouldn't collapse under him.

Max leaned close to Eviane. "This is weird," he whispered. "Long time ago I saw a movie. Made in about 1910. Silent, black and white, flatfilm. Name of *Nosferatu*. None of the angles looked right. Everything looked wrong. This is like that, only worse."

"Worse?"

He rubbed at his eyes. "Yeah. Not only can't these angles work to hold buildings up, they shouldn't even be angles."

"That doesn't make sense."

"Neither does what I'm seeing."

Snow Goose shushed them and pushed them back into the shadows. "Look!"

Something came shambling by. Mercifully, it passed at a distance: an enormous black shape, an impossible cross between an ape and a spider, with long, hairy arms and the gait of a man who has had his limbs broken repeatedly and set at weird angles... and then can still move, with a strange and fluid coordination that set Eviane's hindbrain aflame with panic.

From past or future, she *remembered* this thing. With a dull, heavy certainty, she knew that some of her friends were going to die. The world began to darken, and the breath came hard in her throat. For a moment she lost it completely, and didn't know where she was until Max was suddenly shaking her shoulders.

"Eviane? Are you—"

Charlene and Hippogryph and the others were looking at her with alarm.

"I'm all right."

Snow Goose and Oliver examined her carefully, comforting her. Oliver consulted some sort of a monitoring device strapped to his wrist. Strange, she had never seen it before. He peered fixedly into her eyes. "Were you...ah, having visions?"

"Maybe. That monster. It's called...an Amartoq, isn't it?"

Oliver gave Snow Goose a sidelong glance, said something that Eviane couldn't hear. "Yes," Snow Goose said. "I was just about to tell you that."

"And if you get scratched by its nails, you die?"

Snow Goose nodded.

Eviane reached out for Robin Bowles and hugged him, gripped at his arm with pitiful strength. "Don't! Don't go in there! You'll be murdered. Worse."

He pulled back. "What...?"

And she turned back to Snow Goose. "And you. You're going to be killed by *things*. Things with no heads."

Snow Goose took a moment to collect herself, and then spoke calmly. "Eviane. We have to go forward. There are things to do, things to learn. If we have to face monsters, then that's the biz." She smiled wistfully. "I don't want to be here. I'd rather be back in the dorm eating pizza. But we have an ace. We have you, and you can see things. And you'll tell us what you see, won't you."

It wasn't a question.

Eviane nodded, numbly. She turned her head into Max's arms, and sobbed.

Chapter Twenty-Eight

SECOND THOUGHTS

By now, Max was totally confused.

The woman he held in his arms wasn't the warrior, or even the passionate creature it had been his pleasure to discover last night. It was someone new, almost a different personality, motivated now by a balance of knowledge and blind fear.

The bizarrely twisted spires of the Cabal's stronghold rose around them, ice sculptures that were a twisted wonderland of disturbing angles and facets.

Hippogryph bent over them, concern in his round, flat face. "Is there anything I can do?"

Max sighed. "I think she's going to be all right. I think we've just got a certain amount of exhaustion here. It's been a hard couple of days."

"Just another few hours..." Hippogryph said, but he must have been wondering if she could hold together that long.

Charlene Dula slid in next to them, and her long, long arms went around Eviane's trembling shoulders. "Why don't you go on for a while, and let us girls have some privacy?"

"You've got it."

Max crept around the side of the ice wall, and looked down at the shambling Amartoq. It paced as if keeping guard.

"Can't we just go around it?" he whispered to Snow Goose.

"I doubt it's alone. This is the stronghold of the Cabal. It's mobile. They must keep it moving around the Arctic Circle—"

Johnny Welsh was suddenly behind them, his voice, for once, completely serious. "What for? Ah—they're racking up traveling points! The further something magical travels..."

"That must be it."

Hebert hefted his rifle. "We've got all of this wonderful Falling Angels gear. Aren't we powerful enough to just take them?"

Snow Goose shook her head. "We have powerful artifacts—

more powerful than theirs. But they have the knowledge. If we go blundering in there, they could take our talismans from us and become twice the threat."

"What can we do?"

Snow Goose slid down and sat on the ice. Her eyes scanned the misted horizon. "One last ceremony. One final spell. We must work the magic of our talismans, and call for their strength."

Max drew his collar up tighter around his ears. "Goddamn it's cold!"

"Yes," Snow Goose said. "Ahk-lut may have misjudged. We don't have much time."

She gathered them around in a circle. "We have been through much together. We have slain beasts and overcome fears, have walked through the land of the dead. We have much more power now than we did at the beginning of our trek. But our task now is the greatest of all. I've got to tell you that Eviane is probably right—not all of us will survive. But we had to try. This is our time."

Each Adventurer nodded or murmured assent, not exactly sure of what to think or expect, but willing to go along.

"We must pray—if Sedna has grown healthy enough, she may be able to help us."

"Help us what?" Johnny Welsh asked.

"Although you have totems, and magical objects, you are still too European. We must complete your transformation."

Again they sat in the sacred circle, this time buffeted by the wind. For a third time they smoked the sacred cigarettes.

Max wondered what the old tobacco companies would have made of this, back when you could display tobacco ads on a hundred million TV sets and never face a misdemeanor rap. What an advertising campaign! *Smoke Camels! The cigarette that saved the world! Warning: The Surgeon General is known to be a member of the Cabal.*

Once again the smoke rose up, ignoring the wind and the driving snow. The smoke puffs shaped a beautiful Eskimo woman without fingers. Sedna. Her hair was still unkempt, but there was more life to her now, and she smiled to them.

He "heard" the words, but not through his ears. There was a general buzzing all over his body. The very wind seemed to be modulated by the sound, so that the gusts of snow seemed almost to be talking.

"My children," she said, and Max felt all gushy-warm at the sound of the words. "I know that you need me, and I am ready to give you what help I can.

"Look! Look to the sea! My creatures gladly give their lives that this evil may come to an end."

Once again, the ice beneath their feet began to vibrate; but this was no quake. There was a drumbeat music to it, a rhythm that reminded Max of the music in the qasgiq. A rift formed in the ice not fifteen meters from where they stood.

A black ocean swelled beneath that shattered ice, an ocean tossed by strange powers, an ocean that rolled and screamed, its spray dissolving before the driving wind.

And out of the ocean crawled . . . a seal, but no ordinary seal. Its eyes were huge and black, and they were fixed on Orson. It humped across the land to him, shuddered and died as he reached to touch it. Its body deflated, muscle and bones dissolving like a melting ice sculpture.

Orson, frozen with his hand outstretched, completed the motion and picked up a flaccid sealskin.

Snow Goose said, "Put it on."

Orson lifted the spotted brown skin and wrapped it around his shoulders. Immediately, his expression changed. "Ooo! It's . . . it's so *warm* . . ."

As the seal's transformation ran to completion, the sea began giving them more gifts. Max heard another splash to his right, and a gigantic walrus crashed up onto the land. It rolled onto its side and began to melt away. A killer whale thrashed painfully out of that black and restless ocean, humped across ten meters of ice, and died. While the Gamers shuffled toward the great, gross corpse the wind flensed the flesh, then etched away some of the bones, until only six naked, gleaming ribs protruded from the spine.

The ribs were pointed, grooved . . . spearlike.

Max touched one of them, ran his hands along the smooth, polished length. The other Adventurers gathered around, reached out and grabbed ribs, pulled and torqued until, one at a time, the ribs detached from the spine.

Clubs. Spears. Each rib was carved, covered in runes. Max examined the side of the rib he had chosen. Pictoglyphs carved by no human hand—

(There he was, popping out of reality again. He sighed, and resigned himself to ride the illusion out to the end of the Game. If

they put him away afterward and gave charge of his finances to
Orson, well, he was riding with Eviane.)

—depicting the marriage of earth and sky, hardy men and
women battling the elements, the denizens of the sea sacrificing
themselves that frail humans might live.

Trianna had reached the whale too late to get a spear, and was
kicking at the spine in irritation. Max handed her his and examined the walrus.

Already the beast was half etched away. Its intact eyes
gleamed at him blackly. Also intact was an enormous, obtrusive
erection. *Must be mating season*, Max thought.

Eviane was beside him, and her eyes flashed from the walrus
to Max and back again. Max began to blush.

"*Usik*," she said flatly.

"What? Here in front of everyone?"

"The genital bone. It's magic . . ." Her voice was far away.

The walrus was gone by now; only the one bone remained
lying on the ground. He hefted it. A war club! And a magical
one. He wondered if the Eskimos had ascribed any noncomba-
tive, more intimate powers to one who wielded such a mighty
tool . . .

"No. Don't take it." Eviane pulled at his arm. The first note of
a belly laugh emerged like a dog's bark; Max throttled the rest.
She didn't notice. "If you do, you'll die."

"What?"

"I . . . saw someone . . ." Her eyes were getting that unfocused
look again.

"Dear, it's war."

She stared up at him. Her red hair flagged in the wind. Ice
frosted the collar of her coat. She looked absurdly like the arche-
typical little match girl. She shuddered. "I don't want to lose
you," she whispered. "I've lost too much." She leaned forward
into his arms.

What in the hell do you say?

There was a pause. All weapons were checked. There were
rifles and a few rounds of ammunition. Hippogryph still carried
his flintlock. The rest of the tools—knives, clubs, spears—were
all traditional. These were checked and made ready.

Yarnall raised his hand. "If none of you mind, I'll take the
lead." He shrugged. "I've been on borrowed time here anyway. If
anyone gets killed, let it be me."

"I don't know—"

"Listen." Yarnall was grinning broadly through two days of stubble. His eyes squinted against the driving snow. "I got through the full day! I beat the Implementor! The only thing that I ask from you is that when you nail those bastards, do it good. Do it solid."

Robin Bowles nodded soberly, black beard, black hair caked with ice until he looked like a mountain man. "All right."

In a thin line they entered the maze of ancient ice.

Yarnall held up a hand to bring them to a halt. Frankish Oliver came up tight behind him, and they conferred. Max couldn't hear. Then Yarnall turned.

"Let's break into teams. I want one force to cross this open space, while the other team circles around to approach from the other side. A pincers. What do you think?"

Johnny Welsh raised his hand. "Listen, everybody. I'd like a chance to lead. I'm just a funny fat man, but if we're coming down to the line . . . I'd like to be some use. There may not be another chance. If you need a decoy, what the hell—I've always been an odd duck."

Kevin, a rifle in one hand and a spear in the other, raised a skinny arm. The skin from the deflated corpse of a sea lion made him look a little less like a walking skeleton. "Me too. First group."

"Any other volunteers?" There were, and the group split into halves. Max moved forward to join the first group. Eviane hung back, pulled at his hand imploringly.

There was work to do, Max thought, squeezing Eviane's small hand. Dangerous work, but they were heroes all.

Heroes all.

Chapter Twenty-Nine

THE MAZE

Max's breath sounded rough in his throat. He was too aware of his hurts. Muscles hurt everywhere . . . as if he'd been in a match, a rough match against an inept and overpowered opponent, a match that had lasted for days.

He was worried about Eviane. Getting into a part—that he could understand. It came to him now that *he had never seen her leave it.*

How were the others doing?

Kevin was doing fine. The kid had seemed all sticks and parchment a few days before. Now he was whalebone and rawhide. The wind blew snow into his thin face, fluttered the furred edges of his parka, and he barely seemed to notice. Kevin had taken the lead in their column.

The two groups of Adventurers moved in a modified pincer movement through the tumbled blocks of the city. The oddly angled blocks rose twenty stories tall. At first Max had thought that they were composed of ice. Now he saw that they were stone, ancient blocks of stone sheathed in ice, carved with hieroglyphs unlike anything he had ever seen.

Kevin clutched his war club and sidled up to the edge of an abutment, poking the club out and waving it gently as if trying to draw sniper fire. Nothing.

He looked back at them, sugarcube teeth showing in a wide smile. He was nervous, but trying not to show it.

Just a Game, right?

Right.

They peered out across the space separating them from the central citadel.

Most of the chunks of wreckage seemed to have been abandoned ages before. He guessed that the ice on the blocks was as layered as a cross-cut redwood. Lights showed in a central complex of buildings. Somebody lived there, or something. The presence of life in the midst of this black desolation was no comfort at all.

Behind him, Eviane was wheezing. She was a little better than she had been a half-hour before, no longer paralyzed with fear, but she was still baggage.

There was movement in the ruins.

The thing that shambled through the ruins was man-shaped, but had no head. It was huge. It reminded Max of one of the Goons in an old Popeye cartoon. It stumbled through the ruins making odd sniffing sounds, poking in the shadows. It wasn't exactly alert, but it was tenacious, consistent. It kept moving constantly.

But without a head—?

There was another movement in the plaza. A door on the far side opened, and a line of human beings trudged out. They were naked. They walked as if they were asleep.

Robin Bowles asked Kevin for his binoculars. He focused them through the snow on the line of slow marchers.

He grunted in surprise.

"What is it?" Kevin asked.

Bowles dropped back down into the snow beside him. "It looks like Mik-luk. He worked for me at the trading post."

"Why is he walking naked in this cold?"

"Magic?" Bowles rubbed snow out of his beard. "Maybe the Cabal has some kind of spell on him. If they do, and I can get him to recognize me, it could be the break we're looking for."

The six of them thought for a minute. Yarnall looked doubtful. "On the other hand, it could get you very killed."

"If I don't go down there and try to save him, I'm betraying our friendship." He hefted his whale rib. "I have this. Sedna wouldn't have given 'em to us if they wouldn't do the job."

"Then we all go," Yarnall said.

Eviane would meet nobody's eyes. She shuddered.

Bowles shook his head. "No. No need to risk everyone. The rest of the team is moving around from the other side. Someone has to be here to tell them what happened, just in case."

"Well, then, what about two of us?" Max asked. "Me and Yarnall."

Bowles considered it for a moment, then nodded. "All right."

Yarnall turned to Ollie. "Trade you." He exchanged his war club for Ollie's rifle. He hefted it lovingly, sighted along the barrel. "That will give us one modern weapon and two traditional ones. That's a decent spread."

Eviane clung to Max's arm. "Max—"

"Have you had another premonition?" He was only half-kidding.

She closed her eyes, and he saw her eyes moving under the closed lids, searching for visions. "No. No, but it comes and goes, Max. I don't know—"

If she could play for the hidden cameras, so could he. "Listen, Eviane," he said. Damn, he could almost hear the music swelling in the background. "A man's gotta do what a man's—"

His miserable attempt at humor was wasted on her. Her eyes overflowed with genuine tears, and she pulled herself against his chest and sobbed. He looked beyond her to brother Orson, who shrugged.

Max pushed her out to arm's length. "Now hear this. You knew that all of us might die on this trip. We all understood that. I'm just playing out the hand as dealt."

She nodded dully.

Max shucked his pack. He peeked over the wall.

The wind had died down a bit. The line of naked brown bodies was still trudging along, overseen by the one headless creature. Its long arms lashed at them, urged them one at a time into a low stone-slab building on the far side of the clearing. From that building, flush against the jagged rise of cliff, there issued forth irregular, horrifying screams.

The line moved forward again. Mik-luk was third in line at the door.

Carefully, cautiously, Yarnall, Robin Bowles, and Max moved out from their hiding places, covering each other as best they could.

(How exactly do you "cover" someone with a walrus prick? The *usik* wasn't a ray gun! Max's rising sense of the absurd would drown him if he wasn't careful.)

Max ran a modified zig-zag pattern through the ruins. He stopped, heaving for breath. Max turned and ran his fingers over one of the blocks. Hard, cold, carved. The layers of ice prevented his fingers from actually touching the carving. He saw glyphs and pictographs portraying strangely shaped creatures, some of which looked like the result of an obscene, and surely fatal, mating of human and pachyderm.

They were oddly hypnotic. He wanted to spend more time

studying them, but a whisper from across the path pulled him back to his mission.

Yarnall motioned with his war club. Bowles had moved on ahead, maneuvering to a piece of masonry within ten yards of the line of naked Eskimos.

Max was twenty yards away. From here the men and women appeared listless; they stood as if in a deep trance or drugged state. Their hair fluttered in the wind, and they stared straight ahead toward the low opening.

He could see a little into the room now. There was no door, just an arch formed by stone slabs that seemed almost haphazardly thrown about, by earthquake or tidal wave or long ages under water. Certainly, no living force could move blocks so massive . . . ?

Deep within the recesses of the alcove, lights flickered and shapes moved. When the wind ceased howling for even a few moments, he heard screams that turned his stomach.

Bowles was right. No one could leave a friend to such ministrations, regardless of the risk.

They were heroes!

He checked both sides and joined Yarnall. Yarnall slapped him on the shoulder and, crouching, ran up to join Bowles.

Bowles was flattened out against the wall . . . heh. Well, the stout actor was certainly trying to flatten himself. Watching, waiting. He showed Max a sickly smile. Max read fear and hope and a touch of genuine heroism in that smile. Bowles motioned Yarnall over to the other side of the divide. Both took aim at the headless thing—

And it turned to face them. Max almost screamed.

It was brownish, with skin that folded over and over itself like an old overcoat, cracked and blistered, moving like sheaths of heavy leather. It had no head, but it had a face. The face was set into its belly. It was heavy and bovine, leaden-jowled, with bright little eyes the shape and size of almonds.

It was utterly evil, almost an abstraction of malevolence. Slits for eyes, and a mouth that looked like the teeth within it had chewed their way to the surface, leaving the lips raw and tattered, the incisors sharp and encrusted with red and brown filth.

It was the face of a Yeti, and it snarled at them, and opened its mouth for a scream—

Bowles threw his spear. It missed and clattered on the far side. Yarnall began firing.

The first two shots seemed to have no effect at all. But the third drove the beast to its knees. The fourth knocked its bowed legs from beneath it. It flopped back onto its massive, gnarled shoulders.

Bowles motioned them back, and dashed out, and pulled one of the naked men out of the line. The others stood cowed, afraid to move, or too numb from cold...

Or something.

But the instant that Bowles grabbed Mik-luk, the Eskimo grabbed him back. His mouth opened hugely. In less than a second it had expanded to the size of a kitchen oven. He screamed like a dying wind.

Bowles's scream was quite a lot louder as he tried to tear himself loose. Max started out from his hiding place, and saw shadows emerging from the depths of those odd, disquieting angles.

Bowles screamed, "Get back! Get back! He's already—"

That was all that he had time to say before the others were on him, all of the naked, frozen men. Bowles went down, their nails and teeth savaging him.

A second Amartoq stepped out in front of Yarnall. The Guardsman was too close to get his rifle up. The torn, lipless mouth set in its stomach-face snarled, and it wrenched the rifle from his hands and bent it into a "U" shape. Yarnall was frozen for a moment, and only Bowles's screams roused him from his shock.

From Bowles they heard a last inarticulate cry as the light within the alcove brightened, and Robin Bowles was dragged inside.

Yarnall scrambled back, tripped and fell. Max looked at the Guardsman's face. The fear there was not an act. The sight of the beast advancing on him was as intimidating as anything that Max could imagine, though by now his imagination had turned wild and crazy.

But Max was in motion, moving forward, swinging the *usik*. He brought it down with a thump, squarely between the monstrous shoulders.

He felt the thump. It startled him. The beast grunted with pain. Other shapes, other forms emerged from the shadows, hissing curses. He swung the club backhand across the thing's face, and howled victory as he saw the damage.

It screamed again, covered its maimed face, and staggered

back. Max scooped up Yarnall, shoulder under armpit. "Come on, we've got to get Bowles."

"No! No, Max!" Yarnall had found his feet. "He was right. We need a unified plan. Otherwise we're just going to get picked apart."

From shadows all around them, the misshapen figures clawed their way out, grunting and slobbering, reaching for them with long black nails. Yarnall picked up his twisted rifle. "Mothers are strong!"

Max and Yarnall helped each other stumble back a few feet before they were cut off. Three of the creatures lumbered toward them, the eyes in the misplaced faces alight with blood fever.

Yarnall and Max stood back to back. Max jabbed at the nearest. It tested their defensive perimeter with a looping paw stroke—

Max swung, felt no contact, but saw a paw flash red. The creature sniffed at the wounded arm, and slowed; but the others charged.

A claw got past his guard. Although he felt only a buzzing sensation in his shoulder, a bright red splotch appeared. He cursed, and began to swing his *usik* left-handed.

But the creatures, for all their size and strength, were clumsier than he, and at a disadvantage: none of them used weapons. Time and again Yarnall and Max bloodied them, and Max's *usik* struck one of them a thundering blow, crushing it to the ground. The Amartoqs' torn, lipless mouths snarled at him, and Max snarled back.

There came a swirl of motion, and now the creatures were caught between two groups of screaming, blood-maddened Gamers.

Johnny Welsh had abandoned his rifle for the moment. His whale-rib sword rose and fell in a glittering arc. An Amartoq howled as its hologram chest was cloven to the teeth.

Max's peripheral vision found Charlene Dula as a seven-foot elvish beauty, with long thin arms and long slender legs and pale skin, and a lantern jaw making her look like nothing so much as Elric of Melniboné. Her ivory sword flashed and struck. She moved in and out on those improbably long legs, sore knees forgotten in the heat of the moment. She was glorious, swirling in her skins, a primal woman from some lost tribe of albino NBA superstars.

And then the rest of his comrades arrived. Max howled, flashing his war club, noting the red slashes that appeared on the bodies of the enemy as he struck.

Out of the corner of his eye, he saw Yarnall take another hit from a monster's claw, and—

A shocking buzz surrounded him, made his whole body tingle. He hadn't been paying attention, and a stroke from a five-clawed hand had almost disemboweled him.

He staggered back, and looked at his midsection in disbelief. The spreading red stain wasn't exactly realistic, but it was damned disturbing. He lifted his club—

And got a warning shock.

He backed up. This wasn't fair! It wasn't supposed to be like this. He was about to die! The monster was coming closer and closer, its lidless eyes staring, its mouth drooling blood as broken teeth chewed at its own lips.

Max backed into a wall, and he lifted his one good arm in defense or in supplication—

And suddenly Orson was there.

Two-Ton Orson Sands ran thudding to the rescue on the point of the "B" team as they rushed from the shadows, tumbling pell-mell into the jaws of battle. Orson interposed himself 'twixt brother Max and the monster, and thrust his whale-rib spear with a speed that Max would never have suspected. The monster looked down at its guts in amazement, and crumpled.

Max started to jump back into the fray. An electrical buzz in his underwear told him that Dream Park had other ideas. So Max lay where he was, covered his face with his arm, and moaned helplessly. Paralyzed, he watched Orson the Barbarian carry the day.

Orson carried it fine. The fighting snarl on his lips would have done credit to a blood-maddened jungle cat. Orson parried the deadly paws, slashed and mashed, sliced and diced, and generally made a red ruin out of the Amartoqs as they shambled in to attack the helpless Maxwell.

What a man.

Through and occasionally around Orson's trunklike legs, Max glimpsed snatches of the rest of the battle.

There was Trianna capering with her spear, moving with the grace and poise of a dancer.

Hippogryph used a harpoon more adroitly than brother Orson, and was giving the monsters the old what-fer at a frightening rate. Max admired his erstwhile antagonist's form and style.

(Uh-uh . . . brother Orson missed the slash of one claw, and got a glowing red band across the ankle. The monster paid for it dearly, sagging to the ground, pierced to the core.)

Oh, what a lovely fight it was. The claret flowed, war cries arced to the heavens, and in general, a mighty fine time was had by all.

Max searched the battlefield for Eviane, and finally spied her hiding behind a piece of bizarre, convoluted statuary. She was sighting her rifle and carefully placing shot after shot down into the battleground, to devastating effect. One Amartoq fell to the ground, shot in the gut and forehead by a single bullet.

Quite possibly, Max mused, an all-time first.

He only glimpsed Eviane for a few instants at a time. Her face was a small, pale oval screwed up in concentration. She punctured another beast. It staggered to the ground, long black paws scratching its back; moaned and thrashed, then was still.

Kevin Titus was a tiny red-haired whirlwind in the midst of the madness, swinging a war club almost as big as himself. He was a now-you-see-him, now-you-don't dervish of motion. As long as he kept moving, nothing was able to touch him. But then he reeled and fell against a skewed block of black ice, face to the wall, panting like a dying man—

And an Amartoq clubbed him down from behind. The arm passed through Kevin. He looked down at himself, suddenly saw all of the blinking black and red light. He said something which, though inaudible, was doubtless vile enough to blister paint. He followed it by saying, "Now wait just a second—OW!" Kevin grabbed at his buttocks, moved by the hand of the Almighty.

Then he bowed to the inevitable, bowed further, and toppled to the ice, dead. He glowed black and red in the snow, sprawled as if boneless, chest still heaving.

So. The kid gloves were off. The rules had changed, and now death was a very real possibility. They had lost two. Max looked down at himself, at the huge red stain across his midsection. Three?

The last monster fell. The Gamers leaned on their weapons, panting and gasping for breath . . . really heaving this time. Orson had dropped his weapon. He stood with hands braced on knees, giving himself over solely to panting. Kevin was on his back on the ice, eyes open to the sky, dead, breathing more easily now. Robin Bowles was . . . gone.

This engagement had been more intense, had continued longer

than any of the others. Red-faced and sweating in the snow, they stared at one another, counting. Only ten of them were left.

Snow Goose came out of hiding. Her eyes flicked to each of her companions, studying them: their breathing, their color. At last she stood over Kevin. He looked up at her. "Isn't there anything you can do . . . ?"

She turned away sorrowfully. "In this damned place, even the dead still speak. We must perform ceremony, or else this one will be awakened to life against us."

"Ah—ceremony?" Kevin asked blankly.

"Oliver," Snow Goose said solemnly, "we need your war club."

"Now just a second—Ow!" Kevin was shocked back into silence.

Oliver appeared beside her, implement of destruction in hand. "All right. What is it that you need?"

"The head must be crushed, the arms and legs severed, or he will walk against us."

"Wait just a cotton-picking—Ow! Will you stop—Ow!"

Snow Goose's expression was mournful. "Truly, it is easier on the recently slain if they accept their new station gracefully."

Kevin gritted his teeth and lay still. Max wasn't watching Kevin. He was watching Oliver, who had stealthily made an adjustment on his war club. He had palmed one of the blades. An illusion now projected from the back of the war club, nasty and axelike.

"I don't think the rest of you want to watch—" Snow Goose said. They gawked.

"Now wait just a—Ahhh!" Kevin said, mighty uncooperative for a corpse, as Oliver's war club rose and fell, and the blade clove one of Kevin's thin legs. The entire leg went black. Kevin stared at it. "Jesus Christ! Snow Goose? Ahh!"

The war club rose and fell again, and again, and now Kevin was armless and legless, basically a trunk murder victim still conscious enough to complain about it. He looked up at them, and sighed in resignation. "Ain't life a bitch?"

The war club fell again. His head went black. Kevin muttered inaudible curses.

Snow Goose examined Max carefully. "You can be saved, but we must make ceremony for you."

"Not like that, I hope to God."

Despite herself, a grin touched her face. "No, I think we have something a little more peaceful for you."

He tried to sit up. "Well, then, I—" A sharp shock made him lie back down again. "Let's get on with it."

She touched his chest with her fingertips. "No, I don't think that you should try to get up and around, the strain could be fatal." She turned to the others. "Stretchers! We need to move this man to a safe place!"

Several of the Adventurers dug into their backpacks, pulled out flexible shelter sections, and joined them into a makeshift stretcher.

It took five of them to carry him, and they didn't have breath to complain. Trianna was the only woman, and she seemed as strong as Hebert. "I didn't know cooking built that kind of muscle," Max whispered.

She just gritted her teeth and kept going, *bumpity bump*.

The procession ended in a tumbled pile of slabs and blocks. It might conceivably have been a temple once, but not for any Inuit or other shamanic civilization that *he* could imagine.

The inside was covered with those oddly ominous symbols. Again, he had the feeling that the glyphs portrayed something important. The images were fascinating, but until they got some torches set up, it was too dark to see anything.

Snow Goose shucked her backpack and came to stand over him, hemming and hawing. "Well, Daddy said there'd be days like this."

"Like what?"

"I'm going to have to perform a healing ceremony on you."

"Have you done it before?"

"Only on a dog."

"Well, that's something."

"The dog died."

"On the other hand, modern miracle drugs—"

"Will avail you nothing—"

"Falling Angels stuff! *Magic!*"

"You have been injured by a headless one, an Amartoq. Without spiritual treatment you will die." She turned and examined each Gamer in turn. "Any of you who have been wounded by the Amartoqs, come forward."

Orson, Charlene, and Johnny Welsh stepped forward.

"You three, lie on the ground next to Max."

"Not my idea of a dream date, but—" Johnny grumbled, but lay down.

Snow Goose rummaged in her pack, and after a few moments, pulled out a flat, twisted pear-shaped mask tufted with caribou hair. The mouth featured a rather surreal gap-toothed smile. One eye was closed almost to a slit. The nose seemed less a nose than a continuation of the deep eye-sockets. It was carved of some dark wood.

Snow Goose slipped the mask on. "Now the rest of you step back."

She mumbled under her breath, and began to chant, hopping and dancing around in a great circle. Their lanterns threw odd shadows on the wall as Snow Goose moved slowly around the injured Gamers.

As she danced, she seemed to become another person, left behind the trappings of the twenty-first century. She took on a more primitive aspect, hearkening to an earlier, crueler time in human history.

Max, being very near death, rolled his eyes and strove to look the part. He wondered how many people would see the final tape, and vaguely, he wondered how much money it would make. Perhaps his agent should have looked at that release form before he signed it.

Ah, well. Money be damned, dying or not, he was a trooper. The show must go on.

He moaned, he thrashed. His body twitched in time to each of Snow Goose's capers. The other Gamers got into the spirit of it: moaning, twitching, leaping. Damned if Orson didn't begin to foam at the lips, and heaved with sympathetic convulsions. Orson had watched Max perform often enough . . .

They squatted in the shadows of that tumbled space, and chanted, and grunted, and slammed their spears and clubs and rifle butts against the ground in primal rhythm.

Snow Goose was lost in her dance . . . the thrum of slamming feet and the strike of the weapons, the voices rising in crude harmony . . . the torches and the leaping shadows, the writhing bodies of the wounded . . .

It was all incredibly hypnotic. He felt his body pulsing with it, rising and falling with it, as if it called to something in him that not only had forgotten that this was a Game, but that he was a twenty-first-century man.

A part that didn't care whether the capering of the witch doctor or shaman was fraud or fact, magic or science. A part that lost itself in the arhythmic movements, the animal postures taken on for brief moments, then abandoned.

Snow Goose's dark hair was plastered against her head with sweat. Snow Goose came close to him. The leering mouth of her mask was momentarily shocking and disturbing, and he felt his entire body tingle—

Another shock through the underwear? This one was more like a trill of sensation, the same kind of quasi-musical note that he had first experienced on the plane. It was exhilarating, and frightening too.

Snow Goose screamed, shaking a bone at him, then screamed again. He arched his body in response, and opened his mouth wide, shrieking with all his strength.

Gee, that felt good.

The red stain began to fade.

Snow Goose screamed, the cacophony growing louder, and the other Gamers, stomping their feet to the rhythm, chanted.

"Uttoe-seek," Snow Goose said, bouncing on one leg repeatedly. *"Aypok, pinayoke, sutomok,* Aiiyeee!"

And she turned to the others, and nodded, encouraging them to chant along with her. *"Uttoe-seek, aypok, pinayoke, sutomok,* Hiyeee!"

Over and over, until they caught the rhythm. Max realized that she was counting up to four, over and over again.

And she hopped, first on one foot, and then the other. She bent over them, and shook her bone at them. His body tingled, and the red spot grew smaller.

"Uttoe-seek!"

And Charlene's body arched, and she screamed and sobbed—

"Aypok!" and Orson thrashed. His hand, reflexively, reached out and found Charlene's, and they clasped fingers.

"Pinayoke!" and there was an answering chant from the six chanting Adventurers. They slammed their weapons and their feet against the ground.

"Sutomok, Aiyeee!"

Snow Goose's body arched, and in her furs she seemed not even human, but suddenly and spectacularly—

Her form momentarily shifted. He saw it, saw the flicker of change. She was flowing, changing, the furs transformed for an instant into white feathers. Her neck was long and elegant, and when she stretched out her arms, she seemed almost to hover, her feet not touching the ground. He felt that trilling again. The torches flickered, and the shadows on the wall took on lives of their own, became the shadows of animals. In that moment the Gamers saw their animal totems in shadow form or sharp relief. Here was a seal, there a walrus, there a great eagle, dark wings stretching and folding, and there, and there—

And Snow Goose, human again, collapsed onto the ground, foaming, convulsing, hips and shoulders slamming against the ground again and again as if electric shocks were coursing through her.

And then she was still.

For a moment there was no sound.

Max rolled over slowly, examining each round, sweat-streaked face in turn.

Were these really the same people who had been pulled into a Game in an airline terminal a few days before? They looked so different, huddled here in the darkness, protected from the shadows by the flickering of oily torches, faces smudged with smoke and oiled with sweat, eyes that had seen death and destruction, the end of one world and the opening of another.

Snow Goose rose to her feet. She was panting, heaving. "Damn," she said. "I never believed . . ." Max looked at himself. The red was faded, almost gone, and as he watched, it winked out.

"Rise," Snow Goose said. "You are healed."

Chapter Thirty

THE CABAL

As Max sat up groggily, Eviane threw her arms around him and squeezed until she could hardly breathe.

It didn't matter that the others laughed. Their little party of ten was almost alone in the world. The survivors would inevitably pair off for mating. She was staking out her territory now, and any woman who trifled with Max was going to be sorrier than she could believe.

Orson and Charlene roused muzzily, and shared a brief, intense hug. Hippogryph's face darkened. Evidently he didn't like that much.

She didn't blame him. She'd seen the way Hippogryph stayed next to Charlene, a subtle but effective barrier between the Moon Maid and the rest since the beginning. He seemed to consider anyone, including Eviane, a potential threat to her. Frankly, she hoped that Orson was slipping into what Hippogryph had considered exclusive territory. Serve him right.

Her man stood, once again strong and firm. It was good to know that Eskimo white magic was as powerful as the dark variety. There were not only evil forces, but forces of light and warmth in this strange new world. It was comforting...

"Hey! Look here!" Hebert cried excitedly. In a corner of the cave, hitherto unnoticed, were what seemed to be a pile of rags and a small stack of boxes.

A quick and feverish inspection revealed the grim truth: the rags were what remained of an Eskimo expedition. Under the rags were human bones, gnawed and broken.

"Jesus Christ," Orson said. "They must have made a last stand here, been attacked by some of these creatures."

Max looked at the boxes. They were marked *flare grenades*. "I'd think we could make use of these..."

"And these!" Hebert said. There was a cache of survival choc-

olate in one of the boxes. Hebert grabbed a handful, peeled
wrappers with his teeth, and began to chow down.

"Ah...maybe you'd better go easy on those," Trianna said
nervously.

"Hey. *You* wait for a bowl of fruit to show up."

Orson began to inspect the wall carvings. "You know," he said,
"there's something about these drawings that bugs the hell out of
me. I'm not totally sure what it is...Maybe it isn't anything
important, but I think that I've seen them somewhere before."

Charlene stood next to him, six inches taller. "These don't
look like Eskimos."

"No, not a whole lot. These other things don't look like any
beasties we've seen so far."

The creatures were vaguely star-shaped or octopus-headed.
One image set the creature next to what might have been...a
brontosaurus?

The creature stood a head higher.

Eviane felt awful pressure behind her eyes, and fought against
the darkness. There was an image of an enormous door opening.
Something lurked behind it, something unspeakably large and
horribly alien.

"Are you all right, hon?" Max said.

She leaned back into him, let him wrap his arms around her. For
a moment she lost herself, had the sensation of floating above her
own head, watching as she was cuddled safe in the strong arms of a
man who cared for her. Some tense, knotted part of her began to
relax.

After all, it's just a Game...

Her head nodded to her. Just a Game...

Thank you, Michelle.

"There's that Michelle again," Max said. "Who is this lady?"

"Who? I..." She thought for a moment, then disentangled
herself from his arms. "I didn't realize I was talking. I'm sorry."
She touched her lips to his, and went over to talk with Charlene.

The moon woman rolled her shoulders, and twisted the
slender bone-sword around and around in her grip, experimenting
with different positions. "Hi," she said without looking around.

Hippogryph was bristling. Eviane laughed inwardly. What
kind of name was Hippogryph, anyway? "We might not get another chance to talk," she said to Charlene.

"I know that we're close to the end," Charlene said. "We

haven't spent much time together. You look like you've been enjoying yourself, though."

"Charlene, can I ask you something?"

"Sure, anything."

"I know that we knew each other, knew each other somehow before this all happened. But I'm not sure how. I just don't know."

Now Charlene turned around. "Boy, you really get into it, don't you?"

Eviane tried to smile, but the strain was too much. "Please. I know that it sounds strange. Humor me. Maybe I took a little bump back there in the fight. A little amnesia?"

Charlene was ready to laugh again. "You know, I don't know whether to take you seriously or not, Eviane. You've gotten so deeply into the Game."

Eviane raised a hand. "The Game. I keep hearing everyone talking about the Game. I . . . need to know what you mean by that."

"I mean—the whole Fimbulwinter Game," Charlene said, mystified. "All of this, you know. Monsters. Eskimos. Fighting. Talking swordfish steaks and butterfly-eating ghosts." Charlene was looking worried now. "It's a commercial product. Or you could say we're dreaming somebody else's dream."

"Somebody else's dream." Something in Eviane's mind relaxed for a moment. For just that moment, everything seemed clear: it was all a Game, and Charlene was her friend, and they were all in a place called Dream . . .

Dream Park?

The mists closed in again, but this time they left her feeling unaccountably calm and centered. She stood, brushed herself off in a businesslike fashion, and said, "Well, shall we get on with it?"

"Sure," Charlene said. She tried to keep her face sober, but another grin broke out. "You know, you've really made my vacation."

Impulsively, Eviane bent over and gave her friend Charlene a quick, affectionate peck on the cheek. It felt right.

The shadows of the tilted slabs offered shelter from prying, inhuman eyes, but not enough to make Max comfortable.

They had lost two! That realization hit him hard. They had been living in a fool's paradise. Death waited around every corner . . .

The island fortress had the appearance of a city partially destroyed by an earthquake. Great slabs of rubble lay toppled everywhere. He had the disturbing impression that a gigantic, insane child had striven to build a city, and then, tired of its accomplishment, had destroyed it in a fit of pique.

And there were ... things moving in the rubble. Things that had no analog in the world that he knew, creatures grotesque beyond his imaginings. Creatures on the hunt.

He didn't have to be told what they were hunting for.

Johnny Welsh crawled up through the shadow to crouch next to Max. They were in an enclave formed by the shadow of two slabs joined together in a steeple shape. From their perch they could look down on the Cabal's meeting place.

The cave was ringed with broken statuary. Once again, the statues seemed not of Inuit derivation. They portrayed strange, alien shapes, hideous shapes, and Max felt a little ill just examining them from a distance.

But there was worse going on down there. Although the line of shambling Eskimo zombies had disappeared, a ceremony continued in full swing. They could hear it, and through the dark, heavily veined chanting, they could hear a familiar voice screaming in agony.

"That's Robin," Johnny said. "They've got him, and I don't know what the hell they're doing with him, but we've got to stop them."

Just ahead of Max, Yarnall agreed. "All right. Now listen—I think we can work our way around above the place they've taken Robin." He pointed. "See that stream of smoke? I think there's a vent hole there. We can spy."

"Let's be careful," Max said. "That terrain looks rough. Last thing in the world we need is a twisted ankle."

The three of them crawled backward along the narrow tunnel until they'd reached the other Adventurers. "All right," Yarnall said. He scanned each anxious face in turn. "We have to mount a rescue operation for Robin. We've got to work our way to the other side of the clearing. I need volunteers."

Charlene raised her hand, and then Hippogryph, and Max. Eviane's shot up an instant later.

"All right. Here's the plan—"

"Ah—just a second, Yarnall," Hebert interjected. "Who died and made you king?"

"If you've got a plan, now would be a terrific time to share it." Yarnall was smiling indulgently. "Otherwise, I would suggest that we proceed."

Hebert reluctantly agreed.

Yarnall was warming to his task. "All right. Two groups. Volunteer group, how are you at climbing?"

Charlene was most enthusiastic. "I can do that. I've been feeling stronger every day."

"All right, then. Both groups will work their way around, one at a time. Each group watch for the other. Cover in teams. When we reach the far side, that's when we need the most care. Then we send the volunteer team in . . ."

He began to draw a diagram on the ground.

I've been here before, I've . . .

Eviane stumbled, but darling Max caught her hand and pulled her to safety.

The jumble of tumbled slabs was disturbing in a way that she found difficult to express. At other times during their adventure she had experienced *déjà vu*. Here, she had the feeling that some of the angles weren't angles at all, that they were illusory pockets. When she stared at them, it was like staring at one of those damned optical illusions where the angle went from obtuse to acute as your depth of focus changed.

She waited in the shadow, waited for Yarnall to give her the signal to cross. The space was so vast, the hieroglyphics so disturbingly unearthly that she felt like a bug dashing across an alien cereal box.

She ran as fast as she could, heart pounding in her chest. Hippogryph caught her hand and pulled her up to the level of the next slab. Their eyes met for a long, tense moment, and then he crinkled in a smile. "Come on—too late for that—you're spoken for."

From somewhere deep inside she summoned a laugh, but it was in no way genuine. Her hand found a grip, and she pulled herself up. The last few feet of horizontal slab had been somewhat spongy. Damned lucky, in case anyone fell—

She looked down at the slab. From where she was, the hieroglyphics took on a new appearance, like viewing the abstract rock drawings in the Andes that old von Daniken had used to "prove" that the ancients had set out welcome mats for vacationing aliens.

From up here, the hieroglyphics seemed to fit together. She could see that the images were in series. As she climbed higher from slab to slab, she could see more of them. In this whole area, the crumbled wall which seemed to stretch a thousand yards and more, the hieroglyphics resembled nothing so much as a comic strip, an illustrated story. As Max helped her to the top slab, she lay down on her stomach and read the story stretched out below.

"Do you see what I . . . ?"

"Yeah," he said. "But I don't quite understand what it means."

Trianna was climbing below her. She stopped too, and brushed a few strands of blond hair out of her face to examine the pictures below.

"Come on," Max hissed. "Time to read the comics later."

Eviane crawled across a pitted stone surface to the other side, where, finally, they could look down on the stronghold of the Cabal.

The sound of chanting and screaming had grown more pervasive, and Robin Bowles's voice more distinct.

Eviane clutched her hands to her head. Visions of horror crushed in on her, devouring her desperately needed confidence.

When she thought about the plain of hieroglyphics below, she could see the pieces, the shadows and outlines, but she also saw a hideous shape, a form that was only hinted at in the drawings; and this was no drawing. In her mind she saw it: titanic, octopus-headed, making sounds that it would be blasphemy to translate into any human tongue.

"Are you all right?" Trianna asked. Eviane opened her eyes, stared into her companion's face. Was this woman going to die? She had had visions about some of the others, and one of them had already come true.

They were trying to rescue Robin Bowles, but with every fiber of her being, Eviane knew that it was already too late.

But was Trianna, specifically, already one of the dead? Eviane stared into the face, trying not to listen to the wind, to remember the creature around her, to resolve her riddle named Michelle, and discover—

Was Trianna going to die?

"Why are you looking at me like that?" the girl asked.

Eviane lied. "I just realized that this is almost over, and we never really sat down and talked. I don't know you at all."

Trianna smiled. "We'll have time after it's all over."

"I hope so," Eviane said. "I really hope so."

The Adventurers looked down over the rocky decline that separated them from the stronghold of the Cabal. A wisp of pale smoke drifted up from a round ventilation hole, marking the spot.

"I think I see a path," Francis Hebert said. "See there?"

Max shielded his eyes. "Dammit, I can't tell whether that's

concave or convex. This place is crazier than chopsticks for a snake."

"I'll go first," Francis said.

Hebert slipped the first couple of feet, adjusted himself, and found purchase. Eviane noted the bone-breaking distance that he would fall if the next slip were as bad as the first. She held her breath.

Ollie and Orson followed him down the side of the cliff at intervals. Ollie had jury-rigged a bandoleer from his belt, and strung a string of flare grenades from shoulder to hip. They clanked when he moved.

Hebert winced at one of the clanks. He glared back at Ollie and, just for a moment, forgot to watch where he was stepping.

Eviane saw what was going to happen a good three seconds before she managed to scream.

One of the shadows *fluxed*. It concealed an angle which had seemed convex until Hebert's foot moved across it. Then it was no angle at all; it was a black gap, and Hebert's foot was in it, and Hebert was still descending. Then it was too late.

Hebert scrambled for purchase, eyes mad. Ollie tried to get down to him, but it was to no avail.

Hebert didn't cry out. Even at the moment of death he kept control, knowing that the sound of a scream would betray them all.

And then he was gone.

"Mistake," Max said nervously. "He made a mistake."

Orson looked back over his shoulder. "Test the ground. Test the ground at every step."

"Too late for Hebert," Eviane muttered.

Ollie tested the ground where Hebert had fallen through. There *was* no ground there, just the illusion of solidity, and a shadow that seemed too dark to be entirely natural.

Cautiously, Ollie moved around it.

Three!

They had lost three in as many hours. It made them nervous. They slid down the side of the defile, testing those odd, hallucinogenic angles one after another, staying in the shadows, ever closer to the place of Robin Bowles's torture and imprisonment.

They reached the smoke hole without incident. And paused, as the music fluxed, and Robin Bowles screamed again.

The stone throbbed beneath Eviane's feet. She could hear the chanting, and she could feel the moans of agony. What were they doing to Bowles? She remembered those sounds—*déjà vu*—but she had no image of what was going on. Just the deep, terrible dread.

She bumped into Yarnall's foot, and swallowed an "oops." He touched a finger to his lips, then scooted sideways so that she could move in next to him.

There was a spot where the stone slabs parted to make room for a rising column of smoke. From time to time the pulse of smoke ceased, and then Yarnall shielded his eyes and looked down into the hole.

He pulled his head away, struggling against a retching cough. "I can't see a thing," he whispered as another soul-tearing scream vibrated the stones.

Charlene reached into her backpack, extracting a pair of snow goggles. She whispered, "Here, try these."

Eviane adjusted the strap, and snugged the glasses down over her eyes. She touched Yarnall's shoulder to move him out of the way, and peered down.

For a few seconds, she couldn't see anything. Then the smoke began to shift.

Every few seconds she turned her head away from the hole to pull in a breath of fresh air, and then looked back down. Slowly, slowly, she began to place the objects and events in the ancient temple below.

The room functioned as a qasgiq of sorts, perhaps even the one seen in their earlier vision.

There was a circle of men and women around a central fire, and there was something else.

Stretched out on a lateral framework, writhing in torment, was—the corpse of Robin Bowles.

Oh, he was dead, all right, Eviane knew that much. A low fire cast hellish orange shadows on the walls, illuminated the proceedings to show her more than she wanted to see.

Robin Bowles's corpse was stretched spread-eagled on the rack, and his internal organs very carefully removed. A cavernous hole gaped in the middle of his body. One of the men sitting in the circle stood, and reached into the corpse. He wrenched free a handful of glistening red, and cast it onto the fire.

Eviane gagged. The wind changed, and she accidentally inhaled a rancid whiff of sickeningly sweet smoke.

The man spoke. "Interloper!" he said. "You who came to break our power. Your soul is ours now, and I command you to tell us everything."

Robin twisted on the rack as if he was still alive, the bonds cutting into his already red and raw wrists.

"Told you. Told you."

"No!" the Cabalist thundered.

"Everything. Everything."

Eviane pulled her head away from the hole, breathed a few gulps of clean air, and then hazarded another peek. She recognized the man this time. It was Ahk-lut, the son of Martin the Arctic Fox. His dark, scarred face was twisted and gaunt.

Now that she thought of it—

All of them looked sick.

Her tendency was to mark that down to the unspeakable evil of their practices. But now, looking at the twelve members of the Cabal, she saw that one and all seemed spent, sickly, and diseased, as if each had paid some ungodly price for the necromantic gifts and powers they coveted.

The leader reached into Robin's body and chanted something so low that she couldn't hear it and then he *twisted...*

Robin screamed. She hoped never to hear another such scream. She slid back against the rock slab, panting. Yarnall pulled her goggles away from her, and donned them, hanging over the smoke stack to hear what was going on.

"Aiiiee!..." Robin sounded like a soul dragged over the coals. "All right. All right. All right."

The leader's voice was smarmy with self-satisfaction. "Good. Speak. What could have given you enough power to overcome our barriers?"

"We... my companions carried magic of our own."

"Magic? Greater than the sky-metal?" There was a general hush of anticipation, and Eviane heard herself saying:

No! Robin! Wherever your soul is, don't let them force you—

"Aiiie!"

She didn't need to see to know what had been done. Yarnall crawled back next to her, choking. "Good Lord! Did you see what they were—"

Charlene took the goggles away from Yarnall and looked for herself. For about three seconds. "They play rough," she said.

Bowles shrieked madly, "Falling Angel wire! Woven into our backpacks and tents! Round and round it goes, and where it stops—"

Yarnall blanched. "Let's get the hell out of here. Robin just spilled his g— I mean he's told them everything. They're going to be looking for us."

"For us?" Charlene asked. Her lantern jaw worked furiously on a nonexistent stick of gum.

"If they can get the Falling Angel wire, they'll have more power than ever before. We may have made a mistake, bringing it to them."

The three of them cautiously climbed back up the mountainside, testing the shadows as they went. Eviane felt sickened, but utterly determined. They worked their way back to where seven Gamers waited for them in a pocket of shadows.

Johnny Welsh and Snow Goose spoke simultaneously. "What did you see?"

Yarnall informed them, in graphic terms, of the Cabal's dread necromancy. "Can we turn him off somehow?"

"Robin is beyond any help I can offer." Snow Goose looked sickened.

Orson and Max squatted together. "What's our play?"

Orson leaned back against one of the stone slabs. "Well...I would say that Yarnall is right. We're in for a bad time. Look at it this way. We've freed Sedna, and she's growing healthier by the moment, I'd guess. The Cabal must be desperate. They need that wire. They also know we're here, so I would expect things to hot up."

Frankish Oliver crouched next to them, looking slightly Pancho Villaesque in his bandoleer. "What are our options?"

"We've come too far to back out. And if we run, we have nowhere to run to—as long as The Cabal is safe, the whole world is in danger."

"So what do you think?" Snow Goose asked.

"Well—the satellite, the sky-metal. It's here somewhere. They worship it. It's been the source of much of their power. It *has* to be here."

"We can't take it with us—you can see what it did to them. Damned thing is radioactive."

They were downcast, looking at each other as if hoping that one of their faces might hold an answer.

Snow Goose spoke quietly. "I hate to suggest it, because it is a totem of such power. But if it cannot be used safely—"

"I'd say not," Yarnall reiterated. "Look how sick the Cabal are. Nothing but magic is holding those bastards together."

She nodded. "Then it must be found, and destroyed."

"Destroyed," Charlene said. "How?"

"That's a good question. Daddy never said anything about this."

"Maybe we could get it out of their reach," Charlene offered. "Bury it under a glacier, or in the sea, or maybe give it to one of those land whales."

"I think one of them *is* a land whale," Orson said.

"Blow it up," Yarnall said. "Oliver's got those flare grenades—"

Johnny Welsh shook his head. "Not enough, I'd think."

Orson had been staring into the wall. "Listen, people," he said, voice dreamy. "These magical objects are like storage batteries—the further they travel, the more magic they hold, right?"

"Yeah . . ." Johnny Welsh's mobile face was twisted with concentration, as he strove to second-guess Orson.

Orson rubbed his hands together, warming to his theme. "What if the 'storage battery' metaphor holds true in more ways than one? Couldn't we rig some kind of forced discharge? I mean, or short-circuit them . . ."

"Got it," Max said. "Snow Goose, if we gathered all of the Falling Angel wire into one place, all of the backpacks and tents, dumped them on the satellite wreckage, do you think you could cook up a spell that would drain it?"

Snow Goose thought for a moment. "Wait," she said. "I need to meditate about this."

She closed her eyes, and pressed her hands against her ears, chanting softly.

Eviane felt the excitement. It was a terrific idea. Executed properly, it could destroy the power that the Cabal had used to bind the Raven, throwing the whole situation into a new ball game.

Done wrong, of course, it could kill them all. She could not foresee the result . . . and that was the best part. What she could foresee from the choices she knew, was blood and ice and universal death.

She could hear all of the breathing in the confined space as if it was her own. Finally Snow Goose opened her eyes. "All right," she said. "We can do it."

They would have hooted or hollered or something, but the nasties that haunted the island would have heard them, and come for lunch. So they just formed a circle and hugged each other, and began to lay their plans.

Chapter Thirty-One

CHALLENGE

The multitowered rise of San Diego's EnCom Plaza was a billion-dollar paean to the ego and accomplishments of one man:

Kareem Fekesh.

Alex Griffin shielded his eyes as he emerged from the tube station. Although only an eighteen-minute ride from Dream Park (including tube transfer) the tubes had been relatively quiet, and dark. Alex had closed his eyes, trying to keep the tension at a dull roar.

Understandable, considering what was sitting in his lap, and what he had to attempt.

The sidewalks buzzed with activity, and in the midst of it he felt slightly uncomfortable.

How long had it been since he ventured outside the environs of Cowles Industries? With all of the resorts, shopping malls, entertainment complexes, and health services, he actually hadn't needed to leave the corporate environment for...

Over a year?

Astonishing, now that he actually thought of it. Closer to two years, maybe.

The executive jets, the tubes, the vacations in Aspen and fishing in Bermuda... All of these things had been owned, controlled, designed by Cowles Industries, if not outright owned and maintained for the use of the executive staff. A totally self-contained world.

Alex was suddenly, painfully aware of how vulnerable he felt.

There was no nod of recognition from the hundreds and thousands of people passing him on the street. The street sounds were foreign to him—there were still internal-combustion engines in San Diego, albeit small, efficient ones. He could smell it in the air.

It was new, and in a way exciting. He ran up the dozen steps to the Glass Tower, the tallest and most prominent building in EnCom Plaza, rising above the others like a giant standing on stilts.

He ran up those steps, a tall, redheaded man, lean in his three-piece suit, extremely fit, and alert. Perhaps the nervousness didn't show. Perhaps.

The guard at the front door stopped him—him!—and asked his business.

The guard was portly, with dark skin that didn't seem to be any protection from the sun. His skin was peeling badly on the tip of his nose, and on his neck. Alex handed him the coded card Fekesh's secretary had sent via courier.

Oh, very well, Mr. Griffin. If you insist that your business is that important, and that personal, I suppose Mr. Fekesh could squeeze you in for five minutes tomorrow.

Mighty white of her.

Arriving in EnCom Plaza now, Griffin could begin to believe that the man was actually as busy as that.

The guard grudgingly took the card and entered it in a computer slot, read the results. He had a more respectful look when he returned to the door. Not much, but an improvement.

"One moment, sir."

Alex stepped back as a door hummed open for him, and stepped into a shielded pocket between two three-inch-thick slabs of plastiglass.

He felt an initial humming, and then nothing for several seconds, although the skin on his forearms tingled.

Probably just nerves. Right.

The inner door slid open.

Alex watched everything. The guard clipped a card on his pocket, and said "Penthouse" unnecessarily, pointing toward an elevator.

Alex had seen the plans for the building—there were six elevators visible, and two hidden: Executive and Freight.

The door hissed shut behind him.

He didn't find it easy to violate the ageless ritual of watching the numbers change on the digital display. It took effort to observe his surroundings. Typical elevator cubicle. Five feet deep, four wide. Seven feet high. Moved soundlessly. The walls seemed made out of burnished copper, but were smoother to the touch; they felt like some kind of plastic. Had the elevator started moving yet?

The door opened soundlessly.

Griffin found himself in a suite of luxury offices. The entire floor seemed to be walled in glass, partitioned off with wood. It made for an interesting mixture, somehow elemental: earth and sky mingled together.

A beautiful brunette at the front desk rose and extended her hand in greeting. "Mr. Griffin, of course. Mr. Fekesh is expecting you."

I'll just bet he is. "Thank you. May I go in?"

"In a moment. May I get you something?" The ritual question. *Coffee.* "Club soda, if you have it."

She laughed musically. "In twenty-six flavors."

"Lemon, then."

"I'll just be a moment."

Alex sat, aware of his own nervousness, aware that he was probably being watched. The sweet lull of the music—what was that? Something by Mozart? He wasn't up on his classical music, and for some reason that added to his discomfiture.

There were a dozen people working at various desks, in various stages of activity. But the real work was undoubtedly going on behind the various closed doors. They simply hummed with hidden power.

The receptionist returned clucking to herself as if she were keeper of the world's best private joke. She handed him a foamplastic cup. "And Mr. Fekesh will see you in a moment. Please."

She motioned him to an office door down the hall. He smiled his thanks, took a sip. It was at the perfect edge of coldness, brisk and refreshing. He had always liked the way lemon tasted in fizzing drinks. Cleansing somehow.

The office door was open, and he walked in. The office was a little smaller than he would have expected, and perhaps a touch less opulent. There was a whisper of air, and a faint canned smell to it. He consciously noted something that had only been peripherally registered: the pneumatic hiss of the doors as they shut. Fekesh had a self-contained air supply, doubtless computer-controlled. No hydrocarbons or nitrogenous compounds for Fekesh's aristocratic lungs.

The entire office was walled in glass. From Fekesh's perch atop the world he could see the entire sprawl. Griffin looked out.

The damage from the Great Quake had gobbled a bit of shoreline, but something like that couldn't stop developers, not when they were talking about the most expensive land in the world. So beach fronts had been reclaimed from the tide, at enormous costs passed right along to the consumers. Tidal breaks, stilts, condos with sub-sea-level apartments, and every stunt possible to human ingenuity had been employed to steal back a few extra meters from the sea.

Eventually the sea would have them back again. For now, the men and women who built her, who had stolen those precious cubic meters, could enjoy the illusion of a conquest worth the battle.

Until the next time. He would hate to be in one of those sublevel apartments, bedroom window looking out on the kelp beds, come the next quake.

The office door opened, and Kareem Fekesh walked in.

Alex was a little taller, and a little broader than Fekesh, and needed every cubic centimeter. The man was impressive.

It wasn't just the clothes, although they made Alex feel impoverished. Or the grooming. A man with a personal barber on twenty-four-hour call could *look* as good as Fekesh. No problem. No, it was little things in the carriage. He moved like a totally healthy animal. His smile was broad and warm, his teeth an orthodontial dream. His eyes were bright, bright black, and were laughing even when the rest of the face was at rest.

Fekesh rolled into the room, sat at his desk, and smiled out at Alex. "Please," he said. "Won't you have a seat. I'm sorry that it has been so difficult for me to arrange this meeting, but there are, as always, a thousand things to do."

"I understand," Alex said, trying to create rapport.

Fekesh smiled a smile that said *I doubt that*, folded his hands, and said, "And so. What is it that I can do for you, Mr. Griffin?"

"I'm going to be presumptuous and assume that you know what I am," Alex began.

"Not presumptuous at all. We have dealt before. If not directly, then over the video. I make it my business to know all I can about the people with whom I work."

"This is going to be a difficult meeting, and I hope to simplify it a little."

"Please, by all means."

Alex cleared his throat. "As I believe you know, approximately eight years ago, there was an attempted takeover of Cowles Industries."

Fekesh's expression never changed. "And?"

"Although nothing can be proven, it is believed that you had a major stake in that takeover bid."

"Mr. Griffin. Such things are hardly the concern of the Security Chief of Dream Park."

"Mmm. But by an interesting coincidence, a terrible accident occurred at the same time. One which, if it had become public knowledge, would have driven down the price of Cowles stock, making a takeover all the more feasible."

"Well, then, let us rejoice that the information never did become public."

"Have you any interest in clarifying your role in all of this?"

Fekesh drummed his fingers on the table in front of him. "Mr. Griffin. I am a busy man. I was under the impression that you had matters of urgency to discuss, not issues dead a decade ago."

"And I do," Alex said. He opened his briefcase and extracted two folders. He pushed them across the desk to Fekesh. "I know that you have been a principal player in the Barsoom Project, so what I am about to say may sound a bit strange."

"Yes." Fekesh opened one of the folders, and glanced through the information, expression noncommittal.

"I spoke of a terrible accident at Dream Park some eight years ago. A woman who was an unwitting accomplice to the sabotage—we might as well call it that—"

Fekesh's eyebrows lifted a quarter-inch in question.

"—recently returned to the Park to attempt to play out the same game that she was injured in. Someone tried to get her out of the Game."

"Someone?"

"Someone. It suggests that whoever was responsible for the first occurrence is still present at Dream Park. This suggests the possibility that something is scheduled to happen. Something big."

"Involving the Barsoom Project?"

"As you see in the folders, we know that someone has taken a major position on Cowles Industries again. There are indications that twenty-six percent of your liquid funds are tied up in assets unknown. You are known to be intimately involved with the Barsoom Project."

"I'm afraid that I don't know where all of this is going."

"Where is it going? If anything unusual happens, I want you to know that we're going to be right on top of you."

Fekesh came as close as a human being could to yawning

without actually opening his mouth and doing so.

"Mr. Griffin. I wonder how your superiors would feel if they knew that you had threatened me in such a manner?"

Alex's lips twitched. *Harmony would have a calf.* "It wasn't exactly a threat."

"Nonsense. Don't insult my intelligence as you have my integrity." He browsed through the folders. "You have quite a bit of information here on my financial activities. I wonder how you got it."

Griffin smiled thinly. "We have our sources."

"Indeed you do. And some of your sources have obviously reached into our computer files. We have security of our own, Mr. Griffin, and I daresay more efficient security than that of Dream Park." He smiled with those astonishingly white teeth. "Present company excluded, of course. Tell me, Mr. Griffin. Have you ever thought about changing companies? We have excellent benefits for men who honestly know their jobs and loyalties."

"I do. In both categories." He didn't say anything more, just smiled.

"Well. We'll leave it open, all right? But this other matter..." He looked at the files again. "We can no more tolerate security leaks than you, Mr. Griffin. I'm afraid that we will have to do something about this. Computer theft requires—how would you say? A terminal solution."

Griffin's back straightened. "I don't think—"

"Indeed you don't. And you obviously didn't before you started this. Mr. Griffin, the records say that at one time you were in military intelligence. For the last eight years you have been living in Fantasyland. Apparently you have forgotten how the real world works. Very well. I shall have to remind you." He looked at his watch. "Ah. My time is up. If you would excuse me?" He stood. "Until another time, perhaps?"

Griffin stood uncertainly. He tried to find a conversational riposte, but cleverness eluded him.

That wasn't what this was all about, anyway. So he left.

Chapter Thirty-Two

DREAMS 'R' US

It was big, and mean, and sounded hungry.

The thing shambled past their cave, hairy and brownish-white, sniffing in their direction.

Snow Goose held the spool of Falling Angel wire like a crucifix. In her hands it glowed like tame lightning. Her eyes were tightly closed.

The beast at the entrance sniffed. She whispered "Winigo" under her breath, more a prayer than a comment. Finally it turned and left.

"What in the hell was that?" Johnny asked.

Orson snorted. "Looked like an Abominable Snowman."

"We call them 'Winigos.' They eat people. I should have been able to make us totally invisible to it."

"It went away," Trianna said reasonably.

"It came too close." Her round, pretty face was troubled. "I think that it wasn't just a Winigo."

"What do you think it was?"

"I think that the Cabal is taking over the minds of their beasts: seeing through their eyes, hearing through their ears."

"Oh, shit."

"Now, just a minute here. If they're out looking for us, they can't be protecting their sanctum properly, now can they?"

Yarnall thought it over. "I'll buy that. Look: we need some distractions. Say a couple of flares on the far ridges? While we're doing that, a couple of us can slip into that ruined building, temple, whatever. We'll have to work fast—take on the Cabal, destroy the satellite."

Snow Goose looked doubtful. "Never work . . . mmm. Unless we split their attention?"

Max was warming to it now. "Right—I'll buy that. Now listen. Who was it that got the sealskin?"

Charlene raised a nervous hand. "Me."

"White seal against the snow. Hard to see, right? Maybe hard to sense, too?"

Snow Goose was hiding a grin. "It sounds plausible. What are you thinking?"

"We split into three teams. Two of the teams provide distraction, while the third sneaks into the temple, spearheaded by Charlene under the camouflage of the sealskin. Do you really think your plan can work, Orson?"

"Don't see why not," he said.

"The Gods have looked upon the play with favor," Snow Goose added. She need not describe the conversation that she'd heard from Gaming Central.

Wait a minute! That wasn't in the original scenario! They're supposed to retreat, find that beached Eskimo canoe, and the dynamite!

Well, Welles had chuckled, *they came up with another approach. Can we handle it?*

Well . . .

More laughter.

Hell, boss, is we Dreams 'R' Us or ain't we?

Then let's give it a shot.

Max looked back at Trianna and Orson, shushed them and pushed them back into the shadow.

They stood on a narrow ridge up around the lip of the valley.

Something was scuttling around the other side of the trail, and he wasn't sure he wanted to meet it without a formal introduction. A tickle of fear stirred in the depths of his stomach. There was only one thing to do, and that was to do what a man had to do.

Max squared his shoulders, inhaled deeply, and said: "Johnny —you want to lead for a while?"

Johnny Welsh's eyes flicked to him and away, back to where a long, horny, hairy leg was coming around the corner.

Earlier, looking up toward the ridge they'd have to reach, they'd seen something that might have been an immense spider, a cross between a daddy longlegs and a tarantula. This could be its leg. There was a sharp, molded tusk fixed to its ankle, anchored by rivets in the chitin.

A second leg came probing, armed with a second tusk. Max was reminded of the fighting spikes mounted on the collars of pit bulls, back before the dogs were bred into animals so vicious they would no longer mate or nurse their young.

The spider's torso emerged, six feet up.

It scuttled backward for a moment, as surprised to see them as they were to see the spider. Its black eyes were multifaceted, and slightly reflective. Max saw his own face in the creature's orbs, distorted with shock and fear. Trianna whispered, "Why didn't you chop it?"

Max winced. "I froze up."

The creature opened its mouth, revealing a black, red-rimmed cavity. It hissed, and charged.

This was like no spider Max had ever studied in biology. Each of its legs seemed capable of bending in either direction. It flickered those leg spikes with disturbing speed.

The ledge was narrow, and Max backpedaled.

Behind him, Trianna said, "There's a wider spot back about fifteen meters."

"Get to it!" He started backing up. He tripped over his feet and fell heavily. "Oh, shit!"

A rifle fired behind him. He glanced back to see Trianna huddled on all fours to give Johnny his chance. Johnny, with carbine to shoulder, was firing into the thing as it advanced.

It slowed, licking at the blood, and came on.

Eviane watched Hippogryph for a signal. Somehow what they were doing, sneaking around to split the attention of the Cabal, seemed vaguely wrong.

They had found a boat, with provisions and dynamite. The canoe was shattered and bloodstained, and . . .

She rubbed her hands against her temples.

There was a fragment of a human foot in the canoe, as if something had risen from the depths and devoured the occupants. But they weren't supposed to discharge the satellite. They were supposed to find the boat, and the dynamite, and blow up . . .

That was a different Game.

Game?

She smiled to herself, even as the confusion threatened to drive her batshit.

Game?

How could all of this be a Game?

And yet . . .

And yet . . . hadn't she seen light shining through one of those monsters? Or a war club sailing through one of them? Yet they crushed physical objects. Or seemed to . . .

Could the whole thing be some kind of monstrous joke?

But why? Who had the answers? Max, dear Max had tried to tell her over and over that it was only a Game . . .

She watched Hippogryph, she looked at Ollie. Damned if it didn't look like Ollie was having fun. He had stuck flares into his bandoleer now. It looked like an editorial cartoon of a Libertarian revolutionary.

Hippogryph (and what kind of a name is that?) wasn't having fun. He was helping them pick their way through a maze of shattered masonry, and doing a fairly good, serious job of it. He was tired, though.

The masonry broke into a wider area here, as if whatever forces had destroyed this island city had found nothing to attack in this one spot. She looked across it. Again, it looked like the huge hieroglyph she had seen from the top of the ridge.

Hippogryph turned to them. "This might not be a bad place to set off the flares. Right out in the middle, there, and then hightail it back to the ruins as soon as anything shows. I think that we can fight a delaying action."

Ollie nodded. "That sounds good to me."

Eviane stared at Ollie. Had she seen his face before? Or Hippogryph's? There was something familiar . . .

"Eviane? Sound reasonable?"

"Sure. Let's do it."

They stared out across the plain. Eviane was watching the sky. Things moved in the shadows, and they hunched close to the ground, suddenly very aware of their vulnerability.

"Ah—maybe this wasn't a great idea . . ."

"The idea," Ollie reminded him, "was to get the Cabal's attention—"

"Preferably with minimal tissue damage."

"—not necessarily to survive."

"Nobody here but us chickens."

Ollie and Hippogryph both had flare grenades. While they prepared to ignite them, Eviane watched the shadows.

Everything was so dizzying. So familiar and unfamiliar at the same time. It was making her groggy.

Who was Michelle?

"All right, we're ready here." They had lashed eight stubby silver flare cylinders together into two bundles of four, and propped them up with snow. The wind that blew from over the great ridge of the plateau herded an eerie howling sound before it.

Ghost riders in the sky. . .

Ollie twisted the fuse ring on his grenade bundle. With a soft *pop* and a burst of incandescently white light, it ignited.

The glow was brighter than the eye could comfortably tolerate. Shielding her face barely helped.

"Come on!" Hippogryph yelled, as he triggered his own. He scampered back for the shelter of the ruins.

She ran as fast as she could, but back over her shoulder she saw the magnesium flares erupting into the sky, shooting fire up and up.

Damned if that wouldn't attract attention! Now what they had to do was—

They hadn't quite reached the edge of the ruins when they saw the first stirrings of movement within. Four of the Amartoqs moved out of the maze, advancing, carrying clubs and spears.

They had attracted attention, all right. Too much, too soon.

Snow Goose saw the false dawn as the first flare went off to what she assumed was the East. She waited for a few moments. According to their timetable, the second batch of flares should be going off simultaneously, but when a minute passed and nothing happened, she could only figure that something had gone wrong.

So Max and his bunch had encountered some obstacles.

Tsk-tsk. How very unfortunate. Ah, well, best not to worry about one's compatriots fighting for their lives against the ghastly minions of the Cabal. Best to concentrate on the job ahead.

Charlene had taken point. Orson stayed just behind her, moving veritably on tippy-toe despite his size.

They had reached the crumbled door of the Cabal's sanctum. They hid behind one of the enormous slabs of fallen rock, watching. Waiting. Yarnall had crawled down from the defile and was poised on the temple's ruined stone roof. Goggles in place, he was ready to warn them of danger.

From the temple mouth came three figures, two male and one female. They were naked. They faced into the driving, frigid wind as if standing on a beach at Maui.

And as the Adventurers watched, the figures began to flow,

changing, shifting shape and color. First they hunched down onto all fours, and then the limbs themselves lengthened and shifted, flowing, flowing. Feathers, fangs, and claws sprouted. Where three human beings had stood, three Wolfalcons nodded to each other and sprang howling into the air. Rapid strokes of mammoth wings lifted them up, up toward the crags and away.

"This is the best chance we're going to get," Snow Goose said. "Some of them are gone, the rest are in deep meditation. Let's move it, troops."

Charlene wrapped the seal fur around her shoulders, and . . .

She began to fade. Her outer clothing seemed to evaporate, and for an instant she stood, unembarrassed, in pale nakedness. Then the skin itself became translucent, and the internal organs pulsed and played against the light.

Charlene's organs slipped away into invisibility, leaving bones. The bones faded. There was just the slightest waver of displacement in the air where Charlene had been, and a ghostly grin, and the sound of a voice delighted beyond all belief. "Oh boy oboy," she laughed, clapping her hands delightedly. "This is great. Have they got a home model?"

"Ahem," Snow Goose reprimanded. "Let's finish saving the world, shall we?"

Charlene entered the temple mouth, with Yarnall right behind. The hallway was cracked and warped by the elements, a lustrous ivory finish obscured by dust and cracked by the elements.

Orson watched the ground. Charlene's footprints appeared with little powdery puffs.

Something with heavy feet moved up ahead, and they flattened against the wall, trying to control their breathing.

They saw the figure now: squatly Mongolian, with beetled brows and heavy, dark skin. His—whoops! Charlene had missed the heavy sagging breasts, the masses of wrinkled skin that were the closest this creature came to secondary sexual characteristics. The bovine nose sniffed at the air, as if trying to scent them.

Charlene's knife rose and fell, and the troglodyte fell to her knees, hands reaching helplessly back for the blade. She pitched face-forward into the dust, twitched and was still.

Orson rolled her over, patted her down.

"Come on," Charlene whispered. In the indirect light she was just a bare shimmering. "We've got to get going."

Orson nodded and got Yarnall to help him roll the body over to the side. The invisible Charlene continued down the corridor.

Ahead was a chamber of some kind. Torches glowed within. Charlene's ghostly hand appeared, and motioned them to come closer.

Snow Goose was the last of them to reach the edge of the doorway.

The tunnel opened up into a larger chamber, with a ruined, cracked ceiling fifteen feet high. At the far end perched a fat Mongol idol perhaps twice the size of a human being. It might have been gold and silver crusted with jewels, but all was scummed with a thick coat of dust. Its thick lips curled in silent, mocking laughter.

A fire roared at its feet. In front of the fire, Robin Bowles's body lay stretched on a rack, partially dissected. In a semicircle around Bowles sat six men and women.

In the center of the temple, shimmering with such force that a preternatural thrill tickled Charlene's spine, was the satellite.

Once it might have been a shining testimonial to the creative powers of the industrial Soviet Empire. Now it was little more than an irregularly shaped heap of slag, an iron-cored meteorite, barely recognizable as something that had been machine-tooled, filled with the most delicate and expensive mechanisms of an advanced culture.

And yet...

Something of the device's original intent still remained in that heap of slag. What had it been? A surveillance device? A targeting system? Had it watched the weather, or found locations and bearings for vulnerable human targets? Had this twisted piece of blackened metal been friend or foe, or, like so many creations of the human mind and hand, had it been merely neutral, reporting back to its masters so that they could make decisions of life and death?

Now it was an object of power. It had been used to throw the entire balance of the world out of control. It controlled the raven, controlled the sun, controlled the fate of millions, *billions*, because it was the balancing point for a world of technology and magic.

Now was a moment of truth, of surpassing importance, and it was all up to them.

Charlene tiptoed closer to the device, carrying the backpacks. Charlene blended into the shadows. She was more a perfect reflection of her surroundings than a truly invisible woman. If she stood still, it was almost impossible to see her. One noted a bit of shimmering, perhaps a slight disturbance in the air. But at the core of her image almost nothing could be seen. At the outer edges there was a bit more. And if you knew exactly where to look, you could see the invaluable pile of backpacks, the magical Falling Angel material—the hope of mankind.

The ranks of the *angakoks* had been thinned. Two women, four men. They were young, perhaps surprisingly so, but withered and pocked and diseased.

One was taller, broader than the others. His voice rose louder, rang with power. His eyes were wide open but blind, corneas scarred and white.

Ahk-lut.

Orson Sands waved at Charlene to move forward.

Robin Bowles, dead but locked into necromantic spells, stirred, and turned to look at Charlene.

Charlene didn't, couldn't look at Robin. Through her peripheral vision, she had an impression of enormous damage to his central body, of skin peeled away and organs laid out or cast upon the fire, but still he was conscious.

He drooled from the corner of his mouth, but his eyes focused on Charlene. From his newfound wisdom, the perspective of death, the sealskin's magic deceived him not a bit.

Charlene paused for a minute, and locked eyes with Robin.

His eyes blazed.

He winked.

Her path took her close enough to Ahk-lut that he could have reached out and grabbed her foot. The blind eyes looked on infinity. Lost in trance and darkness, he sensed nothing.

The firelight cast their shadows against the wall, wild and irregular, as if they were standing and dancing rather than sitting still.

In fact . . .

The shadows were more active, more alive than the sitting figures. They were becoming less and less the shadows of human beings, or of anything normal and sane, and more and more the outlines of horrible things, nightmare things. It was as if that strange flame knew the true shapes of its master's souls and illuminated *that* reality, rather than their mere fleshly disguises.

Quashing a nervous flutter, Charlene edged closer to the satellite.

She could have reached out and touched it now. But dared not.

It's only a Game.

Then why did the hairs on the back of her neck stand up the way they did? Whence came this deep, gut-wrenching fear? Why did the sight of the Cabal, six men and women with ravaged complexions and dead, staring eyes, disturb her as it did?

If she didn't get her mind back on track, she'd never get through this. Charlene unfolded the first of the backpacks and laid it across the satellite.

Orson had suggested it. *Magical objects in this world, in a way, seem to act like storage batteries. They store up power, absorb power by traveling, like an electric motor rotating through lines of magnetic force. They are discharged through the spells or circumstances dictated by tradition. Batteries.*

Now, that's the model that we want to look at. If this thing has traveled around the world thousands of times, then it is a super-charged battery.

And how the hell does that help us? Max was partly irritated, partly fascinated. Orson could do that to him.

A battery can be discharged, Orson said. *If you lay a conductor across the poles, you can force the battery to give up its power more quickly than the manufacturer ever intended ...*

Charlene unfolded the backpacks carefully, with no idea how things were going to happen once the first step was taken. It could be spectacular, it might be lethal.

Five backpacks, reinforced at the edges with Falling Angel cable, single crystal carbon fibers in an epoxy matrix. Almost unbreakable. One after the other, the backpacks landed on the satellite.

At first there was no change. Then the satellite began to hum, and the shadows ceased to writhe in their obscene dance.

But the backpacks ... the backpacks began to smolder. It was as if the magic changed forms, as if the reinforcing filaments in the backpacks were conducting more power than they could safely hold. They began to sputter and smoke.

The Cabalists began to rouse, as from a long, slow dream. Ahk-lut's scarred eyes began to shift blindly. Charlene backed out of the cave. Now the backpacks were melting, actually changing shape, and glowed as if with heat.

The glow shifted and flared with color, like a miniature aurora borealis. Additional small fires raced across the hidden wires within the fabric.

The Cabalists slowly, oh, so slowly began to rouse from their trances. Orson stood, unable to move for a moment; then stepped forward and raised his ivory spear.

Snow Goose caught his arm. "No," she whispered fiercely. "You wouldn't stand a chance."

He looked back at them regretfully. Ahk-lut seemed so helpless, so ready for a killing stroke. He fought with himself, and then agreed. "Let's get out of here."

They turned and bolted. Behind them the satellite's hum grew chillingly loud.

An Amartoq with vast sloping shoulders emerged from the shadows, shuffling in a clumsily hurried gait. Orson jabbed with his spear. The creatures batted it aside almost nonchalantly. It reached out for Orson with blackened claws, and the invisible Charlene struck.

Her spear sank into its back, and for a moment its face took on an almost pitiable countenance as its nails reached back, digging for the shaft. Its death-scream was blood-curdling.

For a moment they were transfixed there by the sound, and then they heard another sound, the sly, deadly shuffle of feet against the bare rock, coming from the mouth of the cave.

Trapped.

Chapter Thirty-Three

WHEN THE SLEEPER WAKES

The second spider came slow-dancing around the ledge on eight long, delicate, coarse-haired legs. It hissed, and the hair on the back of Max's neck stood up and danced as he saw it more clearly. It was five feet tall at the shoulder... or at the thick of the body, if that was the proper way to describe it. He couldn't take his eyes off the jaws.

Johnny Welsh said "Shit!" and backpedaled. He faced the rock wall and tried to squeeze himself flat. "Trianna, get behind me. You too, Max. I'll try a shot."

At its widest the ledge was barely wide enough. Trianna eased past Johnny's back, deliberately lascivious. Fun to watch, but only the corner of Max's eye caught it. He was dancing backward, fending off eight darting horn clubs and spikes as the spider advanced.

He was pushed past the wide spot... and now the ledge was too narrow to change places. The spider, with absurd and disturbing delicacy, crawled around the turn of the ledge and attacked.

Max swung at one of the legs, and was partially relieved when his *usik* passed through it. Then he remembered how little difference *that* made. This thing could chill him pretty damned quick. And if he even *thought* to mock its insubstantiality, the earth was likely to open up and swallow him whole.

The leg flashed red, but the creature had an edge—three of its legs carried clubs. One of them flagged up and down, flashed out at him. It crept forward a little further on the ledge.

Johnny and Max struggled. There was just enough room for one of them to edge around the ledge, and Johnny had the gun. There wasn't enough room for them to change places, but they were determined to try.

They squeezed together, Max momentarily embarrassed by a quick attack of homophobia, quashing it as Johnny's breath warmed his chest.

"We gotta stop meeting like this," Johnny said. "People will say we're in love."

"Har, har."

Trianna screamed, "Watch out!" Johnny turned around in time to yipe and raise his rifle. A club hammered down, striking sparks from the barrel. Johnny moaned, whether acting or serious, Max couldn't tell.

It did look a *lonnnng* way down.

Johnny was past him now, and Max backpedaled as quickly as he could to give Johnny the range and space that he needed. Johnny leveled the rifle and fired.

The creature's right eye flashed red like something in a pinball game, then winked out. Unfortunately it didn't slow down. One of the clubs lashed out in a semicircle, and Johnny's leg went red.

Johnny hobbled backward and fired again, and again. The club lashed out. Johnny hopped back, dodging as best he could on one good leg.

The entire spider-beast was mostly red before it finally collapsed. It pulsed on the ledge and then tumbled over.

The three returned to where the ledge was widest. There they paused to check Johnny's leg. The red flashing was beginning to fade, but hadn't died out.

"Better than a bite." Trianna breathed a sigh of relief. "The flashing probably would have gotten worse as the poison spread."

"What should we do?"

She thought for a minute. "Well, I guess we could bandage it, and then you just be careful, and maybe we'll get through all right."

Johnny slipped his belt out of its hoops, and bandaged his leg with it. "Think this'll do?"

"It better," Max said. "Let's get going."

The Amartoqs were gathering in the forest of jagged slab-crystals. Eviane watched . . . until she felt the huge slab beneath her feet begin to shift.

Hippogryph lowered the point of his spear, confused. The creatures across the divide hissed and gibbered at him, shaking their fists.

"What in the hell is going on?"

"Earthquake?" But Eviane knew different. It felt wrong. It wasn't the random movement of tectonic plates, nor the movement of a melting labyrinth of ice. The motion was deliberate and . . . dare she say it? Controlled.

Behind them a gap had opened that was at least five yards across. Below it was darkness and slow, sluggish coils of sound. Something was *moving* down there, and she didn't like it even a little.

Ollie hung back, looked down. "Jesus Christ!" he screamed. His face curdled with shock, and he staggered back.

The headless Amartoqs attacked.

There were six. They moved with grim sureness. Their arms hung so low that their blackened claws raked the ground. The faces, sunken into those swollen bellies, leered at them.

They were slow, and that was all that saved the Adventurers in the first moments of the attack.

Eviane howled and darted in, her enchanted spear drawing first blood.

Everything seemed to be happening in slow motion—except that the Amartoqs couldn't seem to keep up with the dervish Adventurers. Ice and stone grew neon-red with blood. The monsters fell one after another, and she found herself fighting side by side with Hippogryph, who wielded his spear well.

Her spear was magic indeed! She sliced effortlessly through monster flesh, and with every stroke she slew another.

As the last of them went down, she realized that something was wrong.

Hippogryph was staring at the forest of slabs. The six Amartoqs they had fought were only the beginning. Dozens, perhaps hundreds, were emerging now. Their long heavy nails scratched along the slabs of ice and masonry like nails on a blackboard.

"We're dead," she said, almost matter-of-factly.

The creatures emerged another foot, and then the hideous sunken faces in the bellies looked out questioningly. Something that could only have been fear shone in their misshapen faces. They froze where they stood.

In spite of herself, Eviane turned and looked back over her shoulder . . . and the old recurring nightmare began again.

The slab had opened. The misshapen, octopus-headed thing, the thing from the gulfs, had begun to worm through. It was hideous beyond imagining, and Ollie had time only to scream "Chthul—" before one of the fanged cilia had him, had lifted him into the air, and was carrying him down toward the awful, gaping mouth.

"Ollie!" Eviane had time to scream, and Ollie's eyes met hers. She thought she saw a message there: *I won't die like this!*

The instant before that ghastly mouth would have swalloweo him, Ollie's hands ripped from his bandoleer, the makeshift belt which held flare grenades and sticks of dynamite. With an audible *snick* he pulled a brace of rings free from the incendiary flares.

There was a painfully brief scream of defiance, and Ollie disappeared in a flash of light and thunder that dimmed the auroras. In that light she caught a glimpse of the thing hiding down in the darkness, and wished she hadn't.

It hissed and spit in pain and indignation. The damaged tentacle zipped back into the ground. The slab slammed shut with a thunderous roar.

Sour smoke hung in the air. The ice was littered with corpses. On the far side of the plateau lay something shattered and smoking. She didn't want to go and look.

"Come on," Hippogryph said. "The others need us."

She stared at him. She had foreseen death, but not Ollie's. Now she saw death in Hippogryph's face. Was it real? Was it for him?

He turned, uncomfortable with the intensity of her gaze.

Snow Goose saw it, but didn't really believe it. Orson, protecting Charlene, was a totally different person.

Backlit by the discharging satellite, his bulky figure moved not with grace but with great energy. She heard him mutter, "Here's where Orson the barbarian battles the bloody beast that blocks their path—"

One swipe of the Amartoq's claws, and his left shoulder went red. He gamely transferred his sword to his right hand, stumbling out of the way as its subsequent, slower swipe missed him by inches.

Orson lunged in with the sword in a move that looked like something out of *The Prisoner of Zenda*. It should have stayed there. He lost his balance and stumbled.

The face in the middle of the beast's torso laughed an ugly

laugh. It swung its claws. They came slowly, but they came.

Yarnall, in a movement so swift and sure that it startled her, spun Orson back and attacked in that narrow space, squeezing up from the rear and firing into the Amartoq's rather oddly placed face. Its fighting snarl evaporated in a red mist.

Orson was gasping for air, holding his shoulder and ankle. "Ow! I think I twisted my ankle that time."

Charlene put a sympathetic arm around his shoulder. "I've got some more joint braces," she whispered in his ear. Flickering, nearly invisible, she tried to prop him up. It must have been like leaning on a ghost. "I'll let you borrow one if we can get out of this." She paused, and Snow Goose heard the smack of an invisible kiss on Orson's whiskered chin. "My hero."

Orson glowed, and straightened. "Ready," he growled.

Yarnall led the way.

Something was happening, and Max could feel it. The ground shook, here and everywhere. Fissures divided the giant slabs that defined the walls and canyons. In the distance the bizarre geometry of the alien city was changing shape.

They couldn't move. They had to wait for the others to arrive.

"Over there!" Trianna pointed.

There were tiny dark figures in the sky. Max saw something familiar about those shapes, and he shouted, "Get down!"

The Cabal had taken Wolfalcon form and were hunting the Adventurers.

There was a greater brightness in the sky behind them.

Max's nerves were screaming at him to *hide*! But his curiosity won. He climbed to find a better view.

Did the sun really look a little brighter? Did it really feel a little warmer?

"Max!" It was Orson's voice, and the brother himself came quickly after it, leaning on Charlene, who was flickering in and out of reality.

"We did it. The satellite seems to be on the fritz . . ."

"For how long?"

"Don't know. By the sight of it, I think it's discharging everything. The Cabalists who were there were just wiped out by it. We barely got out with our skins whole." Orson scanned the group. "Where's Eviane?"

"Don't know. I hope they're all right."

Johnny Welsh's shoulder wound had faded to pink. "If they had as hard a time as we did, they may not be back."

There was a rustling behind them, and up through the rocks climbed Eviane. Her hair was wild, her face haggard. "We've got to get out of here," she said. "The entire island is coming apart."

Chapter Thirty-Four

STAR CHAMBER

There were five of them seated in a horseshoe configuration in Harmony's office.

Izumi and Sandy Khresla were at one side of the table. Harmony and Alex were on the other. Millicent Summers was there, and that was it. There was no need for anyone or anything else.

The office vidscreens played a multitude of images.

Down on the floor of Gaming A, the delegates were inspecting various bits of equipment, displays on the subject of Martian exploration and terraforming. From here, from this perspective, it looked like an army of ants. Alex found himself suffering from a peculiar emotional disconnection.

The game in Gaming B was nearing its conclusion. All nine of the Adventurers who remained alive were fleeing across an unstable ice field. Marty Bobbick helped Charlene Dula regain her feet. Ah—on her other side, a beefy guy named Orson gave a hand, helping her up even though Marty clearly didn't need any help. Another complication. Ordinarily Alex would have smiled, but he just didn't have one in him.

On the last screen were images of Kareem Fekesh's offices, images taken by a camera with no metal parts, built into Alex's briefcase, clicking along at a steady five frames a minute. Every inch of the trip was there, from the guard at the front door, to the shape, size, and position of the elevator and its internal decor, to the secretarial and executive offices, to the positions of fire exits and security cameras, to the office where Fekesh received visitors.

Izumi said, "We've seen everything but the inner office. We can map the shape of it by elimination. It's not big. We've got the air system and the private elevator mapped, and magnetic fields gave us a sizable power lead and a sizable computer trunk, which implies a computer the size of a LapCray 20; and since there's only one that size—"

"We're nowhere *near* needing that," Harmony snapped.

Fekesh's face was very clear: smiling, taunting, unrepentant.

Millicent Summers watched Fekesh with a strange expression. Alex recognized it after a moment, and added jealousy to his list of debits against the man.

Harmony said, "So. What is your conclusion?"

Millicent seemed to shake herself out of a stupor and returned to the business at hand. "Based on what you've said and on what we know, we can be fairly sure that Fekesh had a major role in the death of a Dream Park employee, the indirect death of another, the maiming of several, and the corruption of at least one employee who may still be...ah...employed here." She stopped, and looked around. They all knew exactly what she meant.

"Do we have a legal case?"

"I'm afraid not. Not unless we can find the woman, it seems to be just one, who subverted the employee and recruited Tony McWhirter. She's the link. Without her, we have nothing."

Sandy Khresla spoke up. "Dammit, Griff—even if we find her, we can't go to the cops. We're guilty of obstructing justice."

"You don't mean he gets away with it?"

"We can't even be sure he did it," Millicent said grimly. "Or if he did, for how much he's actually culpable. The term 'plausible deniability' was invented to cover situations like this. He may easily have made a bad call on which underlings to trust. He may have already dealt out justice to them. We don't know. And right now, he's helped to put together the Barsoom Project. In a very real way, we have to consider him an ally."

She paused for a moment. "On the other hand, four years ago, there was a major industrial accident at Colorado Steel, during a safety inspection, for Christ's sake. Fekesh picked up a controlling interest at a bargain."

"Hardly conclusive..." Harmony offered.

"*Aw, Thadeus!*"

"But it does suggest a methodology. Alex, in this room he's innocent until we prove him guilty beyond a reasonable doubt. Okay? We're prejudiced. We know it. It doesn't mean we can't protect ourselves."

Griffin brooded, staring at his fingers. He picked up a pencil and rolled it slowly, feeling its textures of wood and thin paint.

"Then," he said slowly, "the way I see it, what we have to do is, first, protect Tony McWhirter. Get him into protective custody now. Reopen his case. Anything. I won't have him killed. Second, find 'Madeleine,' if it is at all possible. She's the link. Third, keep an eye on the Barsoom Project. Get Welles on it as soon as this chubby-Eskimo game is over. Something is going to happen there." The pencil broke in his hand. "I can feel it."

"Anything else?"

"Well, maybe there's another link." Griffin touched a button, and the tape Vail had made in Gaming B went on display. It carried a sidebar of physiological data.

Millicent looked sick.

Griffin cleared his throat. "Dr. Vail has already been reprimanded for this violation of privacy. It won't alter his behavior much, I'd guess. And however distastefully this tape may have been obtained, we cannot ignore its implications. Any disagreement?"

There was no sound from around the table, except for the moment when Harmony softly muttered, "So. I did right."

Griffin looked at Izumi. "Are all of the effects ready? Are you sure that you can pull this off?"

Izumi nodded cautiously. "The prosthetics are excellent. You're risking her sanity, you know."

"We'll take every precaution. There's just something I *have* to know. And after I do—" The half of a pencil splintered, leaving nothing but fragments.

"After I do, maybe we'll have a few more options."

Chapter Thirty-Five

SACRED WEAPONS

The first of the Wolfalcons swooped out of the sky. The human face in its breast gibbered obscenity. Max whirled and swung. The composite-bird wheeled back out of range. Max's *usik* cut a whistling haymaker; he danced to keep his balance on the sea-ice.

The air was warming, wavering.

The island behind them was shimmering with power. The satellite's *manna*, its magical energy, had been short-circuited by the backpacks. It was disappearing into random improbabilities. The aurora had come out of the sky and settled over the island. The light danced and crackled and cast a bizarre, shifting radiance over the impossible angles.

An army of Amartoqs and spider-things were behind them, dots on the ice now, but catching up too quickly. The Wolfalcons acted as flying eyes for the monstrous horde, keeping the Adventurers in sight and urging their pursuers onward.

Orson was panting in Max's ear. "Those damned griffin-things are the leaders. They're the Cabal. Transformed. That's why they're going . . . to let the other beasties . . . do their dirty work."

"What in the hell do we do?"

Eviane looked across the ice field. Far in the distance there was a shimmering, a roiling as of a snowstorm. She pointed.

"That way," she said. "Seelumkadchluk!"

"And if we get across, will we be safe?"

"No," she said, "but we'll be on home turf."

All of them were dead tired by now, and more than a little frightened. It didn't help to know that the deaths of the others were only simulated. It hurt to watch, it hurt to think that it could happen to Max himself. The point was to avoid dying.

"What can we do?" Johnny Welsh was leaning on his spear, panting. "My legs feel like fifty pounds of dead blubber."

Snow Goose looked back across the ice. Like a pack of hounds hunting runaway slaves, the monsters were gaining implacably.

There was a cracking sound under their feet.

"*Now* what?"

"Shit if I know—" Max adjusted his furs. It was getting warm.

Orson slapped his shoulder. "We're dummies! It's getting hotter. The ice pack is melting. The pressure shifts, and the whole thing is cracking up."

"I think you're right."

The sound of the approaching monsters was just audible now.

The ice in front of them burst open with a roar like lightning striking too close. A tremendous blue and white torpedo surged into the air, dropped onto the ice, and slid. A nastily familiar shape, a killer whale blessed with stunted-looking tree-trunk arms, slowed and turned and pushed itself toward them across the ice. Its mighty forepaws gouged furrows.

Max heard Hippogryph's wail of frustration. Hippogryph had spilled his pack across the ice and was reloading in frantic haste, powder, paper, shot—

Yarnall unshouldered and fired twice. The monster kept coming. Yarnall was dancing, trying to keep his balance and his aim; but the ice rumbled and shuddered with every movement of the land whale.

Yarnall paused a moment too long, and it had him.

It was a death deferred, a doom that should have overtaken him two days before. That didn't make it any prettier. He screamed, and its teeth were in him. For a moment there was an expression of almost humorous resignation on his face, and then he was gone, swallowed.

Hippogryph fired his musket. The creature shuddered with the shock, then came on, bleeding red light. Hippogryph poured powder and shot into his musket. He was nibbling on his lower lip, but there wasn't a wasted motion.

"I was too tired. Just too tired," Hippogryph said.

Snow Goose screamed: "Sacred weapons! We need sacred weapons!"

Max looked at the curved *usik* in his hands. *Well?* He ran forward, pubic bone raised on high. The killer whale tried to turn, but Max was faster on land. He brought the *usik* down against a blue-black wall of monster-flesh.

Well, through it, actually. The *usik* passed through the huge head, but where it passed, a wide red swath was cut, and the creature, immense as it was, began to redden. It sank back through the ice.

The ice cracks were spreading, and sheets of ice were sliding up at crazy angles.

The wind howled at them, driving snow even as the sun burned brighter.

"We've gotta make a stand," Trianna screamed against the wind.

Max shouted, "I don't like that idea, but I don't have a better one."

The Gamers scrambled up one of the inclines, taking what could laughingly be referred to as the high ground. Orson said, "Let's hope the landscape doesn't shift a whole lot more in the next few minutes."

The monsters were coming now, fast and hard, across the stretch of ice. At the most, they were a hundred meters away now. The spider-thing was visible in the back. In front were three of the black-taloned horrors, shambling headlessly, heedlessly across the ice.

The Wolfalcons wheeled in the sky.

Max nudged Orson. "Hell of a place to make a last stand, hey?"

"I've seen worse. Ever played Zork? It's an old computer game—"

Trianna hissed at them. "Keep your attention."

She had her sword at the ready, and Eviane, beside Max, had her spear. A wall of ribs . . .

"There are too many of them. I guess we'll just have to die well."

Eviane looked up into the sky. "No. Something will happen."

The spider-thing reached them first. It was slow. It took too long to struggle up the slab of ice. They cut the legs from under it.

The creatures came in waves. Max stood shoulder to shoulder with Eviane, repulsing them one and two and four at a time. At the touch of the enchanted *usik*, the monsters went down. He heard the others grunting and gasping, and Trianna's yell of triumph turn into strangled huffing.

The monsters came in an infinite stream. They swarmed out from the distant shape of the dread island, fought and died until the tide below them glowed red with monster blood.

The Adventurers were gasping for breath, but Max slew on. None of their companions yielded, and as the sky rolled with fire and ice, the Implementors, if Implementors there be, witnessed a battle to warm the blood.

Johnny Welsh lost his footing and slid down the embankment into a mass of ravening monsters, things with arms and clubs and glistening fangs, things which struggled up at them, eyes glaring sulfurous hatred. Max saw Johnny slide down into that vile cacophonous mass, heard Johnny yell, "Hold the mayo—" before he disappeared.

He saw the monsters climbing over each other, struggling—

And then the ice field began to break.

A crevasse opened. Monsters slid into it, screaming and howling. A score of the unholy beasts vanished in a few moments. The Wolfalcons overhead cawed and screamed in rage. A third of their might had died; the crevasse blocked another third.

One of the bird-beasts strayed too close, and Trianna speared it. It flapped in the snow, dying ungracefully.

"Come on!" Orson grabbed Charlene's hand, and they retreated across the ice.

Fissures were opening all around them. They'd reached one they would have to jump. Below them was dark water, and the ice chunks were shifting uneasily.

Max crossed the gap like a great ungainly swan. Eviane leapt across, landed unsteadily on crunchy ice. She waved her arms for balance. Her rifle slipped from her grasp, and slid toward the water, as Max's big hand gripped her parka and pulled her against him. She looked after the rifle as if considering a retrieval effort.

Max retained his grip. "Forget it! I'm not losing you now."

Orson held his breath, and jumped, and missed. He hit the water with a mighty splash. "Help!"

Max said, "Oh, drown it!" and dove in after him. The water was oddly warm—those Implementors were rascals indeed. Also, there seemed to be another layer of iceberg beneath his feet . . . or else it was rather improbably shallow . . .

Ah, well, no time to think.

Something was moving in the water. He saw the tentacle out of the corner of his eye, raised the sacred *usik* on high, and bashed the thing backhand before it could come much closer. Hands reached down into the water, hauled Orson out, then reached down for Max. Blood slick spread around them. If there were predators about, well . . .

Eviane's eyes were glittering at him, and she paused a moment to give him a quick kiss.

"Come on!" Snow Goose yelled. "It's not far!"

Behind them the entire ice field was breaking up. Huge slabs rose and sank, clashed amidst a monstrous spray. In the distance, the Wolfalcons screamed their frustration.

And then . . .

The sun began to change. It was warmer still, and the air shimmered around them, rather like a heat mirage. Nothing extreme, but a sensation of chill ran the course of his body, and he knew—

Seelumkadchluk! Reality lay just ahead.

Chapter Thirty-Six

MICHELLE

The earth rumbled, and then subsided.

There, ahead of them, was the village where they had crash-landed an eternity ago. The burned and blasted wreckage of their plane was a reminder of happier times, like the stripped carcass of last week's Thanksgiving turkey.

A dozen Eskimos, scattered around the edge of the bay, pointed and cried out as the Adventurers ran across the last of the sea-ice. The steadily thinning sheet dissolved beneath their very feet. One by one they plunged into the sea. Eviane's legs burned with fatigue; she hopped from perch to perch, and finally ran out of ice.

Chunks of ice bobbed and clashed about her head as she stroked for shore. Eviane noted how little the freezing water affected her. Her toughness might save her yet.

Snow Goose scrambled ashore to be met by Martin, her father. "My child!" He embraced her warmly. "You have saved us!"

"Daddy, we've still got trouble. The Cabal are coming."

"The Cabal cannot use their beasts or spirit forms in this world, but they can attack as before, with guns. Hurry!" He pulled her toward the trading post. Other Adventurers followed, while Eviane struggled up the strand.

Seven Adventurers remained. Orson and Max, Eviane, Snow Goose, Charlene, Trianna, and Hippogryph. They all looked like something the proverbial cat should have buried in the sand.

Eskimos scrambled to get boxes from the trading post. "Weapons!" Martin the Arctic Fox bellowed. "Sometimes the need is for spiritual weapons, and sometimes for a Smith and Wesson."

Eviane recoiled as an Eskimo handed her one of the rifles. It felt heavy in her hand, and alien, and . . .

A single gunshot set the tired Adventurers to diving behind

buildings. Eviane found herself below ground level in a web of
splintered wood. Something sailed through the air—

"Grenade!" Orson screamed. All heads ducked as one of the
sheds disintegrated in fire and sound. A ragged Eskimo form flew
boneless through the air.

There was firing all around her. Eviane huddled, covering her
face.

Charlene dropped behind the barrier with her. "Eviane! Why
aren't you fighting?" She looked concerned. Eviane had no answer.

She heard the roar behind them. It was not an explosion; it
was the roar of a great beast, and Eviane knew what she would
see even as she turned. She sucked air, hyperventilating, as she
did whenever the nightmare returned.

The thing that rose from the ocean was a form of madness and
nightmare, larger than anything that they had seen yet. It was a
many-segmented worm-shape, with a yawning maw.

Martin walked on stiff legs, unconcerned by the gunfire and
the explosions that had turned the village into a battlefield. He
stared up at the creature, and screamed, "Blasphemy! How much
power did you steal, to manifest in this world! You go too far,
Ahk-lut! I, your father, renounce you! I, your father—"

A sound that could only have been a human laugh emerged
from the titanic shape, and the entire world shook with its evil
mirth.

Martin's magical gestures were evidently inadequate. The
monster humped forward. The shelf of ice supporting Martin
shattered, filling the air with frigid mist and chips of broken ice.
Martin disappeared into the ocean.

Ahk-lut's terrible spirit form dove after him.

"What was that?" Max gasped.

"A Terichik," Snow Goose said, eyes wide. "I'd only heard
about them. Never seen one. It's Ahk-lut, my brother. He's going
to kill us all."

Like a raging mountain, the Terichik rose screaming from a
frozen, nightdark sea. Its many-sectioned, grotesquely wormlike
body reared up; tons of water and ice thundered into the ocean
with a howl like the death of worlds. The night sky swirled
wind-whipped snow through mist that tasted of salt. The Terichik's mouth gaped cavernously. Endless rows of serrated teeth

gleamed as it shrieked its mindless wrath. Its breath was a cold and fetid wind.

The humans beneath it were warrior and wizard, princess and commoner. They were frail meat in the Terichik's path, brittle fleshly twigs tumbled in an angry storm. They scrambled for safety, away from the sea. They fled past the wreckage of the shattered Inuit village: rows of crushed houses, a great stone lodge with its roof stove in, boat hulls splintered and scattered like insect husks.

Max gaped up at the creature, then looked down at the sacred *usik* in his hand. Magic against magic. Why not?

Eviane screamed as she saw Max face the Terichik, remembering another figure who had lost his life while wielding a magical *usik*.

Max died well. He was the greatest warrior among them, but foolish to think that his enchanted *usik*, the pubic bone of the sacred walrus, could stand against the Terichik. Even faced by a beast to dwarf ten killer whales, Max roared defiance and sprang forward.

His magic, his courage, his strength were not enough. The Terichik crushed him, savaged his body with fanged cilia. His screams echoed in their heads long after his body had vanished into its gaping maw.

"No!" Eviane screamed, and ran out. Into the open.

Behind her, Hippogryph yelled, "No!"

She heard. She turned, breathing hard, too hard, hyperventilating.

She took a Cabal bullet through the heart. The electric jolt that meant The End warned her. She saw the red stain spreading over her entire body, and she realized—

I'm not dead! Then . . .

It's a Game!

And . . .

A series of images flooded through her mind, colliding and crashing. She screamed it. "I'm Michelle! *I'm* Michelle."

She turned and began firing at the Cabalists.

One of them flopped back, out of her sight, but directly into Hippogryph's.

• • •

That was no red stain on the man's face! The head had been blown half away, the brain pan leaking onto the snow. Hippogryph jumped back screaming. "No! Oh, no."

And turned around, and saw Michelle staring at him, the gun in her hand, her head cocked slightly to the side.

She stalked toward him.

"You," she said.

He was confused. It was all happening so fast. "Wait a minute. Now. listen to me—"

Michelle's rifle came up to the aim. "Damn you. You're the one who put that rifle in my hand. I never forget a voice. I'm rotten on faces. But if I hadn't been so damned confused, I would have known two days ago. I would have known!"

The other Gamers turned to watch.

"Listen." Hippogryph was licking his lips nervously, staring at the bore of that rifle. "I didn't mean for it to happen like that—"

She fired once, twice, three times. She howled, "Liar!"

Marty felt impacts; he felt his parka twitch. He looked down and saw dimpled cavities ripped through the parka. He could hear the *click click click* as Michelle Sturgeon tried to shoot him again.

Blood filled the holes in his parka and dribbled down. Marty dropped his rifle. Unbelieving and unwilling, he ripped the Velcro apart, pulled open the quilted cloth over his chest and belly, and saw red coils of intestine beginning to bulge through torn flaps of skin.

Hippogryph screamed. He pulled his jacket closed, convulsively, and ran stumbling into the white mist. They heard his screams diminish, then chop off sharply.

Another explosion. Eviane cursed and covered her ringing ears with her hands, then dropped them; she'd need her hands for fighting.

They'd been distracted a moment too long, and the immense figure of the Terichik loomed over them.

Orson shouted and pointed.

The entire sky was blotted out by a shadow which had grown so gradually that none of them had noticed it. Suddenly, with no more fanfare than that, the Raven was there. It filled the sky; its wingspan defined the horizon. It was huge beyond any ordinary concept of size.

It swooped past. The wind from the impossibly huge wings

almost knocked them flat. Cawing, it disappeared into the clouds.

"We're *screeewed*," Orson started. "I thought he came to help us. Why—"

"Look!" Charlene Dula pointed to the horizon.

Striding toward them on legs the size of redwood trees, swathed in furs and carrying a hunting-axe the size of a sky-scraper, came Torngarsoak, Lord of the Hunt and Sedna's lover. Summoned by the Raven and fueled by a terrible mission of vengeance, Torngarsoak came, his round, weather-creased face aflame with rage, black eyes flashing lightning, the aurora bor-ealis writhing about his ears like a crown of glory.

The Terichik squealed in terror and reared back, hissing and swallowing air to increase its size, inflating like an angry cobra.

Ahk-lut and Torngarsoak were matched for size, but the Lord of the Hunt seemed unimpressed by the Terichik's efforts.

In a blur of speed, the Terichik struck, fanged cilia darting out to rend, to tear and grasp.

Torngarsoak sidestepped, his booted feet smashing through the ice, sending a tidal wave of freezing water thundering to shore. Suddenly the hunter was thigh-deep.

It should have slowed him . . . but the Terichik's lunge carried it past Torngarsoak, and now Sedna's lover was behind the beast, thundering through the ocean, every step rending sheets of ice that might have locked a freighter dead.

Ahk-lut turned to strike again, and as he did, Torngarsoak's axe clove the air. Ahk-lut barely snaked his serpentine head out of the way in time.

The mass of Torngarsoak's weapon carried considerable mo-mentum. The Lord of the Hunt spun a little past his target. The Terichik lunged in, and Torngarsoak sprang back out of reach, his awful weight thundering like the detonation of thousand-pound bombs.

The two antagonists circled each other in the shallow sea, probing for openings, weaknesses, as the Gamers watched ashore, mouths open, silent and awestruck.

Torngarsoak swung back with the axe—

And let it fall, lunged forward, grasped the Terichik's neck in both hands, and locked his furred legs around the scaly thickness of its body.

It hissed, it wiggled and writhed, it coiled about him and sought his face and throat with its teeth. Torngarsoak held on, and the two antagonists fell into the ocean together.

The Terichik gouged Torngarsoak's face, fastened its teeth into his arm. The Lord of the Hunt screamed in pain, but never let go, and although blood flowed from the wounds, the Adventurers saw the god's fingers sink into the Terichik's flesh.

With greater and more frantic exertions the monster struggled, but Sedna's lover hung on. They rolled together onto the shore. Adventurers and Eskimos alike fled from their path, and the blackened skeleton of a hypersonic jet was smashed to ashes beneath them.

Finally Torngarsoak sat astride the Terichik, hands crushing out the monster's life. The god threw his head back and laughed hugely, a terrible, primal laugh, the blood running down his face, down his arms, and into the distorted face of the Terichik.

The Terichik spasmed, and then, unexpectedly, began to shrink.

Torngarsoak stood up, shaking the blood from his face, and walked out into the surf. He recovered his axe, and turned, watched as the Terichik continued to shrink. Then he lifted his bloody hand in salute to them, turned, and walked straight out into the ocean.

Far beyond him, a wet black mass burst up through the ice. It was as big as the Terichik, too big to be bothered by bullets. Eviane was ready to fire anyway, before she recognized the face beneath dripping black locks.

Sedna smiled, and submerged. Torngarsoak kept walking until the ice rose above his head.

The Gamers walked toward the dead, shrinking Terichik. It fluxed, changing shape. It was only the size of an elephant now, and assuming the shape of a man—the shape of Ahk-lut.

And finally they stood around the still, naked corpse, the ravaged body of the dead Eskimo wizard. Just a man after all. A dead, defeated man.

For a moment there was stunned silence, and then the Eskimos, men, women, and children, emerged from hiding places around the battlefield, and gaped, and pointed, and (a few) screamed in triumph.

The five survivors formed a group hug and looked at each other. Dirty, grimy, exhausted, and—and ecstatic.

Then the lights came on, and the Game was over.

Chapter Thirty-Seven

CONFESSIONS

Griffin felt sick. He wanted nothing more than to smash or bury the sorry object in front of him, but he had to deal with it, had to question it. He had no idea what he would do with it afterward.

"All right, 'Hippogryph.' How much did they pay you?"

With immense effort, Marty looked up. For the first time in many hours, his eyes focused; for the first time, there were tears. "Griff? I don't understand. I'm dead. She shot me—"

"She had the right!"

Marty waved it off. "Griff. Where did she get the bullets?"

Griffin turned away. Vail said, "You got caught."

"Caught."

"Here." Vail set his tape going. He was still brisk, and it jarred.

Marty's wobbly eyes found the right screen. He watched himself and Charlene in the ice cave . . . brow furrowed, indignation trying to surface . . .

Harmony's attitude seemed to vary: vindication, anger, and apprehensive nausea. Sandy Khresla and Tom Izumi showed barely suppressed rage. Dwight Welles wore an air of almost academic speculation. He doesn't care enough, Griffin thought.

Vail was enjoying the vivisection enough for all of them. "Watch the graphs. You told Charlene Dula you'd never seen Eviane before, *here*. Your blood pressure and pulse rate and skin conductivity all jumped, see? You didn't just lie, you were nervous about lying."

"So you . . . killed me? Made magic?" Marty looked around the interrogation room and knew that there was no hope. He sat on the edge of his chair, his arms hugging his belly, holding himself in. The muscle structure might have been poured into his skin with no concern for rigidity or function.

Marty was a beaten man. He hadn't slept or eaten in at least thirty-six hours, and as far as Griffin was concerned, he might not for another thirty-six. Griffin wanted answers. Legality could be worked out in civil court later, if Marty survived to see a courtroom.

Millicent touched his shoulder, tried to calm him. "Griff— whatever there is to find out, we're not going to get it like this."

"Revenge has an undeserved bad name, these last few centuries. All right, Millie. Marty, what would you *like* to tell us?"

"It wasn't money," he said, and stopped.

They all watched as Marty weighed his options. Then a great shuddering sigh went out of him, and he said, "I know what it must look like. When it all started, I didn't want to hurt the Park."

Nobody said anything.

"You know what was happening. Cowles's relatives were handling business in the Park, and in the company, and everything was falling apart. Then the woman came to me."

"Tell us about her."

"She called herself 'Madeleine,' but I never believed that was her name. She told me that she represented a group of investors interested in pumping some new blood into the company. They needed information before they made an investment like that. So I helped them."

"Out of the goodness of your heart?"

"No—" He was reddening now. "You don't have to talk to me like that. I'm talking to you without a lawyer here. I know what I did, and what happened was wrong. Maybe I've waited eight years for it to come back and settle with me. Let me talk."

"Go on."

"So I got money, and . . . other considerations."

"She was very pretty."

Marty flushed.

"I suppose you thought that putting live ammunition into the Game was just a practical joke?"

"No no no, that came later. But they had me then, Griff, I was in too deep, and besides . . . What was supposed to happen was, the stock would go through the floor and then someone would snap it up. I'd be moved up to executive level. Meanwhile I'd get rich by selling Cowles short. Griff, it was a *monstrous* bribe, and if I didn't take it, Madeleine said they'd publish my unauthorized biography!"

He lowered his eyes. "I did what I thought I had to do. To protect myself, to protect the company from itself."

Alex saw the tension hit Izumi's face, and reacted just a half-second too late. The chunky Japanese moved with startling speed, and his fist took Marty in the face.

Marty's head snapped back, and Tom's hand blurred, formed into the deadly *shuto* position to strike into the exposed throat. But by that time Alex had responded, snatched the smaller man by belt and elbow, pivoted, and threw him into the wall. Tom Izumi bounced, came down balanced on the balls of his feet, eyes blazing.

"No!" Alex said, voice crackling with authority.

"It was an accident," Izumi said hoarsely, hungrily. "Marty and I were just sparring around. It got a little heated. I slipped. Training accidents happen all the time!"

"No," Alex said, the single syllable hanging in the air between them like a shield.

Marty was pawing at the blood on his face, terrified. "I . . . I think my nose is broken." The words were mushy.

"I think you'd better talk anyway," Vail advised warmly. "Otherwise, Alex and I may have to leave the room for a few minutes."

Marty swallowed hard. "I didn't mean for anyone to be killed. I thought . . . I thought . . ."

He buried his face in his hands, and moaned. "I don't know what I thought. They had me. Griff?" Marty's eyes peered over his fingertips. "They didn't lose. I didn't lose. I stuck with Dream Park, and I did get moved up, and I did make money by selling short. And Madeleine's people, they didn't get Dream Park, but they must have made money from the stock they bought. It went up heavy when Cowles got the vacuum subway contract."

Alex was pitiless. He threw a woman's picture on the table. "Does this look familiar?"

Marty examined it: a pretty olive-skinned woman with a sensuous mouth. "Huh! Yes, that's Madeleine! I should have wondered how you knew she was pretty."

"Turn it over." He did. On the opposite side was a picture of the same woman, her throat slashed from ear to ear. "Her real name was Collia Aziz. She was found in Altadena, in a trash dumpster, two days ago. Fekesh doesn't take chances."

Harmony looked sick, but managed to find words. "How did you communicate with this woman?"

"A telephone number." He gave it to them, and Griffin noted it quickly. "To be used only in case of emergency," Marty said miserably. "*She* got in touch with *me*. Always. I never heard the name 'Fekesh' until Harmony tracked him down a year later."

"But all of this time, you've spied for her."

He nodded his head. "And every month an extra thousand finds its way into my bank. I have no idea how it gets there. It's just there."

"What happened with Michelle?"

"Aw, hell, poor Michelle. Griff, I recognized her. Scared the liver out of me. I called the number. I got a voice that told me I'd be called back in an hour. In an hour Madeleine called. She listened to my story, and told me that she'd get back to me in twenty-four hours. The next day they gave me a virus program disguised as a routine watch report. It insinuated itself into the main computer matrix and found the right place to operate. It was almost automatic."

Griffin turned to Welles. "Is that possible?"

"Absolutely. Not just possible, it's one of my recurring nightmares. We're not set up to defend ourselves from our own security personnel."

"All right, Marty, what then?"

"Not much, really. You know all the rest of it. How was I to know you can't kill someone out of a Fat Ripper?"

"Marty, what is Fekesh planning now?"

Marty blinked. "Now?"

"You're small fish. Why would he protect you?"

"I . . ."

Alex leaned close. "Shut up. I'll tell you. He didn't care about a mindless little rat turd like you. You're a distraction. He's got something in mind. It probably involves the Barsoom Project."

Marty went paler. "I don't know anything about that."

"Why would you? All right." He hit a button. Two guards entered. "Take him away."

"Wait. She shot me. Griff? How could she have killed me and—Griff!"

"We switched your parka and vest. Get him *out*!"

Marty was carried out unceremoniously. Alex sighed hugely, and collapsed into a chair.

For over a minute he just sat there, silent, face dark and brooding.

Vail spoke first. "This is a mess. I better go and check out the Gamers. This whole thing has thrown the psychological balance off. Hope to God everyone's all right."

Griffin cleared his throat. "Dr. Vail. Might I have a word with you?"

Norman Vail's bright blue eyes narrowed, and the leathery brown skin around them crinkled tight. "Yes?"

"You recognized her."

"Ah?"

"You had to. You were here eight years ago, in it to your teeth. You must have recognized Michelle Sturgeon when you gave her the psychological tests."

"As unlikely as it seems," Vail said evenly, "no, I didn't."

Sandy Khresla snorted. "Of course you won't admit it, Norman. You're not the type."

"Let me tell you what happened," Griffin said.

"I'm fascinated."

Griffin paused a moment. He gazed up at the ceiling, putting his mental filing cards in order. "Eight years ago, you were just as pissed as Harmony. There was no way to touch Fekesh. You must have tried to help Michelle, and the doctors at Brigham Young told you to butt out. Ancient history she was, and suddenly she's back in the Fimbulwinter Game.

"You had two choices. Expose her, and have her removed, or let her go in and hope it would stir up a hornet's nest. She was the lure. It worked better than you expected." He met Vail's eyes squarely. "How am I doing?"

"Alex, I'd no idea you were so imaginative."

"That's okay. I had no idea you'd risk your professional standing for Dream Park."

"Alex, as long as we're being the omniscient author, why don't we say that she checked out? She was fine. Sane."

"She was a loon. Vail, you're as cold-blooded as anyone I've met. But as you said, where else but Dream Park would you find a home? And just like me, you were willing to risk Michelle's sanity to expose Marty. Jesus, you must have been hiding a grin when I tried to talk you into putting her back in the Game. You couldn't have *dreamed* it would turn out so well."

"If you're quite through?" Vail said politely. "I have business to attend to."

Alex's temper flared, and his voice thundered in the room. "The truth, dammit!"

But Vail was already at the door. Alex wanted to pick him up and hurl him back; his body was ready, poised... but Vail had paused in the doorway. "We all do what we can, Alex," he said. At that moment, he looked every one of his sixty-four years. "You said it yourself. Where else? Where else but Dream Park?"

Then he was gone.

Griffin watched Vail leave, mind racing. There was silence in the room for a long, long thirty seconds, silence that Griffin finally broke.

"Shit," he said in a soft, wondering voice. He turned to face them. "All right. Business." Welles was still watching the doorway. "Dwight, I need you." With seeming reluctance, Welles eased out of his reverie. "All right. Something is happening, and it's happening soon. We don't know where, but it's probably Gaming A. We don't know what." He thought a moment longer, then added, "We don't know when. Lovely. Business as usual."

Chapter Thirty-Eight

SCORE SHEET

Gwen heard Johnny Welsh's voice above the din, strident and tired, but happy. "Hey, Robin! You're looking pretty good, for a dead guy!"

Bowles acknowledged the backhanded compliment with a suitably regal nod. Gwen had to admit, he did look good. Bowles had probably gotten twenty hours sleep since the game ended. He had assumed his former throne in the Phantom Feast, and was surrounded by lovely young things who were watching highlights from the Fimbulwinter Game on a bank of overhead monitors.

"What do you think?" Gwen asked Dr. Vail. She tightened her arm around Ollie's waist. Damn, it was good to be back in civvies again. No more Gaming for six weeks!

Four at least.

Vail smiled thinly. He seemed preoccupied, and even a little worried. "Of Robin Bowles? All indications are that he will do well. But I'd value your opinions regarding the others."

He took her arm. Gwen stood; Ollie stood too. They strolled among the Gamers, their guests, and other visitors culled from the Barsoom Project families. Vail seemed content to be relatively unknown. Gwen wondered how the roomful of guinea pigs would react if she revealed that the tall, well-kept older man so quietly gliding among them was one of Dream Park's maddest scientists.

"On the other hand . . ." Vail said somewhat regretfully.

Here he veered over to the far side of the room, losing Ollie at the bar. Johnny Welsh was holding court, an adoring Trianna on his arm. "And well, hey," Johnny said expansively. "When I saw that the monsters were getting ready to eat me whole I said, 'Hey—'" and here his voice changed as he prepared to deliver his infamous tag line: "'I've had dates like you!'"

On cue, his audience roared.

Vail grunted. "He's the tough nut."

Ollie was back, with three squeezebags of flavored club soda in his big hands. He said, "Johnny? What makes you think Mr. Mirth might be beyond the reach of your insidious mind-bending skills?"

"His defenses are too strong," Vail said reasonably. "He can laugh damn near anything off. With more time . . . or if we'd been able to push him without concern for holding up the others, then maybe."

Trianna kissed Johnny on the cheek and crossed the room to join them. She hugged Gwen and Ollie. "I love you both," she said, little tears glistening in her eyes. "I don't know how, but I feel . . . different somehow."

"It's magic," Ollie said solemnly.

Trianna noticed Vail. "I don't think I've met you."

"Norman Vail," the doctor said, shaking her hand. "I'm with medical services. I'm glad you had a good time." He paused. "You did, I hope?"

"The very best. Even more than that . . ." She took Gwen's arm. "Do you fellas mind if I borrow the lady for a minute? Girl talk."

"By all means."

Trianna took Gwen over to the side of the room, and held both of her wrists. "I just wanted you to know that last night was the first time I haven't had a nightmare for almost a year."

"Terrific."

"And . . . I wanted to say that I know that you were watching over us, every step of the way. I know I act kind of dippy, but you never let it weird you out."

"Darling . . ." Gwen said, laughing. "In comparison to the bunch that I usually work with, you guys have been downright normal and sane."

Trianna laughed until she was crying. Gwen's lips curled in a grudging smile. "Well, you had Hebert and Kevin and Johnny all doing a dance around you, even with the extra weight. I think you better think about getting rid of that armor—it ain't working."

"I guess not, huh?"

"And forgive yourself for that abortion, darling. Don't look so shocked. You dropped enough clues. So you were drop-dead gorgeous, and you got a lot of attention from guys who never saw you, only the face and body."

Trianna's mouth was hanging open. "How did you know?"

"Oh, hush. And one time you got pregnant, and you weren't ready for that?"

Trianna blushed. "Worse. The whole relationship went nasty. And I got rid of the baby to spite him." Her beautiful face reddened with the effort to hold the tears back. "I paid for that," she said in a hushed voice. "Something went wrong, and now I can't have babies at all."

Gwen hugged her, held her. "The hardest thing is forgiving yourself. If you want to thank me, will you do that?"

"I'll try." Trianna snuffled and brushed a long strand of blond hair out of her face. "Anyway, Charlene invited Johnny and me up to Falling Angel, and we accepted."

"We?"

"We."

Trianna looked back over at Welsh. His audience, red-faced, was bouncing on the couches and doubled up painfully, holding their sides and begging for mercy. Suddenly it was difficult for Gwen to remember him in the Game, spear in hand, slaying the dreaded Amartoqs. Unlike Trianna, Johnny still needed his shield.

"Good luck to both of you," Gwen said.

Ollie's warm hand found hers, and they joined Vail. He sat at the rim of a holo stage with Eviane/Michelle, and Max, and Max's brother Orson.

Charlene was there, next to Yarnall, who wore a silly self-righteous smile.

Gwen tweaked him. "What are you so happy about?"

"Welles, that glorious bastard. He liked the Game I played so much that he kept that double bonus going both days. Told me I could play one of his scenarios, anytime."

Onstage was the Island sequence, with various Gamers stalking and skulking about in the shadows.

"Rl'yeh," Orson said. "It's Lovecraft's 'At the Mountains of Madness' combined with his frigging floating island. I never tumbled till I saw it up there on the screen!"

Max snorted. "So wonder boy blew it once. At least you got out alive."

Vail leaned into the conversation. "You know," he offered, "I saw you both play, and I would bet that both of you would play better if you were going for real points. In a Fat Ripper siblings can reinforce each other's habitual roles."

"I think I saw that," Max confessed. "Our act is: he's brains, I'm muscle." Max punched his brother's shoulder. "You know, you did some powerful adventurin' there."

They slapped hands. "Yeah . . ." Orson said contentedly. "It ain't that I don't love you—although I don't—but next time, I'm winging it."

Gwen chuckled, then stopped as she watched Michelle. Vail sat on the couch behind her, too casually. Her face was intense with interest on the holo stage.

"So," Vail said, once again with extreme casualness. "How are you, Michelle?"

"Fine." She looked up at Vail with a face devoid of guile or guilt or trauma. "You don't have to worry about me, Dr. Vail. That nice Alex Griffin already talked to me about staying around for another week. Everybody's worried about me. Everybody can *stop* worrying. I know the therapy I need, and I've got him."

Max grinned hugely. "Taa-dah!"

"And the lifetime Gold Pass doesn't half help, either."

"I only love you for your pass," Max said, and kissed her heartily.

"Just know," Vail said, "that if there's anything we can do—"

"I'll call. I promise."

Vail moved around to Charlene. "How are we feeling?"

She was sprawled on the couch, her feet up in Hebert's lap. He was rubbing the tension out with strong, practiced thumbs. She said, "A little confused, I guess. Nobody will tell me what really happened to Marty. I think that Michelle knows—"

Michelle's eyes were woeful as they met Charlene's. It was Charlene who looked away.

"It was a security matter," Vail said.

"That's what Mr. Griffin says. And Gwen and Ollie say. And Michelle has this funny look in her eye." Charlene sighed and leaned back into her cushions. "Oh, darn. My legs are so sore I'm considering amputation. I guess I won't worry about Marty. Still." A wistful, hurt look flitted across her, then disappeared.

With Vail, Gwen toured the room. At his urging they made notes here, compared opinions there . . . "Only a quick prelim survey, of course. We'll spot-check them for the next few months," Vail said. "What we really want to know is, do we affect the Actors more than the Gamers?"

"Why would you?" Gwen asked.

"Well, in principle it could work like Alcoholics Anonymous.

Get 'em to teach what you want them to learn. Harmony tells me we can put the Actor option in the home Game cassette, but maybe it costs more than it's worth."

They'd made a complete circuit of the room. Vail sighed. "I think that's about it."

Trianna was dancing with Johnny Welsh. Even with her excess weight, she was a woman of such sensuality that half the heads in the room turned to watch. The weight would go when she visited the moon; and then some of the mass would go too. One's appetite decreased in low gravity. Maybe even Johnny would lose some weight.

Eight probable successes.

One cipher: Marty Bobbick. "Hippogryph" had dropped out of the Game most spectacularly. Where he was, and what the conclusion of his story might be, Gwen wasn't sure she wanted to know.

If there were dungeons down below Dream Park, what would the jailers look like?

And the rats?

It had been a good Game. Some of the Gamers had been outrageous enough that she would like them along on a real adventure. Others remained mysteries to her, had never really revealed themselves to her.

That was the name of the game, the war that it always was. All things considered, their success-failure ratio had been pretty good.

Orson and Johnny: failures. (But if Orson joined a real game, he'd have to train. Hmm?)

Robin Bowles, Francis Hebert, Charlene, Yarnall—time would tell, but both she and Vail were confident that progress had been made.

Max, Kevin Titus, Trianna: breakthrough city. And of course Michelle: success beyond their dreams.

Lastly . . . Gwen and Ollie?

She'd had fresh fruit for dessert, and loved it. And salad for a main course, and loved it. And a plain baked potato, and strips of freshly wokked chicken. And no fat or sugar at all. She hadn't felt much of an urge to snack. She had all the catch-phrases memorized, she could persuade herself of anything for minutes at a time . . . but only time could measure how she would use what she'd learned.

She didn't want to lose weight. She didn't need to lose weight...

But what would Ollie think of her in that Y-band monokini at the Blue Lagoon Shop, the scandalous one three sizes too small for her?

She could guess how he would react. And if it didn't work out perfectly, she had every confidence that she could gain the weight back.

Yep, she thought, feeling the contentment expand within her like a warm tide, it had been a very good Game.

Chapter Thirty-Nine

LEVIATHAN

Scratchy-eyed and exhausted, Alex Griffin stood in the security room overlooking the main floor of Gaming A, scanning, watching for...

For what?

For three days after Marty's confession, he had wrestled with the problem, and it just wouldn't resolve. They had scoured Gaming B, had double-checked all of the identifications, had increased security scanning at all checkpoints. It was supposed to make him feel better. It didn't.

He *knew* that something was terribly wrong.

His knuckles were white where his hands gripped the safety rail around the balcony. He was hungry, he was bone-achingly tired, and he continued to watch the crowd.

Ambassador Arbenz and his niece Charlene were in the front row enjoying the closing ceremonies. Everyone around them looked like dwarves. Somebody needed a swift kick for putting Falling Angels between the Japan and China contingents. As many security men as he had walking the floor, surely Arbenz was as safe as a man could be...

Alex continued to scan, verifying for the fourth time what a single glance at the computer printout could have told him.

Fekesh wasn't here.

Some of his representatives were there, but "pressing business" had prevented Kareem Fekesh from personally attending the ceremonies. Extreme regrets, all best wishes, et cetera.

Everything was going fine, everyone was perfectly happy, and Alex Griffin was terrified. He forced his breathing to calm, and his mind back to the job at hand.

Cary McGivvon stood next to him, sipping a cup of coffee. "Sure you won't have some? Caterers just brought it down. Good stuff."

"No. Thank you." He said it through gritted teeth. The aroma was driving him crazy. He had to escape. "I'm going down on the floor. I can't just stand still."

"Okay, Chief. I'll stay on the holovision."

"And treat Dwight Welles like one of the team. We're looking for something very subtle here, and he's got a good overview."

Alex walked down the spiral staircase of the two-story security building erected behind the rows of chairs, the stages, the demonstration areas which crowded the huge dome. Today was the finale, and over twelve thousand guests were watching the final recap of the entire project.

"*All of you have children,*" the narrator said. "*Many of you have grandchildren...*"

Within the dome's illusory black sky a pair of immense, ungainly Phoenix F1 rockets rotated nose to nose around six hundred meters of tether, for the coasting period between Earth orbit and Mars. Two truncated cones with rings of rocket nozzles around the bases. "Aerospike configuration," he had heard someone say. Whatever that meant.

Now the sky was filled with rockets, lightsail vehicles, orbital tethers made of Falling Angel cable, and more. It was a carousel of possibilities, a panoply of mankind's future greatness, served up with soul-stirring music and the finest effects Cowles could create.

Alex moved down one of the side rows, walking lightly, scanning faces, examining badges, nerves afire but still uncertain of the play.

What was Fekesh up to?

"*—and as always, men will be needed. To supervise the machines, test the environment, and reap the rewards—*"

The sky exploded as a comet impacted on the surface of Mars, bringing new life and possibilities. Red and blue light washed over Alex's face, over the room, painting it luridly, and the audience applauded the holographic display, flinched from the stereophonic thunder.

Alex barely noticed it. His ears were deaf to the sound. He scanned the faces.

In time-lapse fantasy, greenhouses and bubble cities sprang up across the surface.

"*—atmosphere by now, enough for airplanes, bubble cities. The question is, and must always be, how can we make money from this at every turn?—*"

As Alex finally reached the front of the room, the narrator was deep into his pitch. At every step of the way, it seemed, there was a fortune to be made. From the mining of comets and the Martian surface, to the manufacture of fusion plants and lightsails; from the design of life systems for the surface of Phobos to the new fashion crazes it would all trigger on Earth. Gaming spin-offs. Edible delicacies for the insanely rich. It went on and on, and they touched enough fiscal nerves to set the room sizzling.

They were ready. After a week of delicate foreplay they were hot, eager, and ready to jump into the metaphorical sack with Falling Angel and Cowles.

The floor rumbled, and for a moment he was startled. Then he looked behind him, at the 300-by-500-foot stage, where glowing mining machines, surface transport vehicles, and other wheeled craft were beginning their circular parade.

The music was John Philip Sousa. Christ, all they needed was to whip out a United Nations flag, and half the room would jump up and salute.

Mitch Hasagawa was standing against a huge hanging curtain, eyes glazed with the spectacle.

"Oh, come on," Alex said to him. "It's not all that great."

"Huh?" The stocky security man shook his head.

Alex must not be the only one on short sleep. "The display."

Mitch smiled, tried to suppress a yawn, and failed. "Yeah. Right, Chief."

Disturbed, Alex walked out of his earshot and touched his throat mike. "Cary," he asked, "how long has Mitch been on duty?"

There was a long pause.

"Cary?"

Another pause. "Ah . . . right here, Chief." She sounded woozy. "Ah—about nine hours, I guess."

"Jesus, have some more coffee, will you? You sound like hell. Send down somebody to relieve Mitch."

"Sure, boss." Cary signed off.

Alex peered through the darkness. Where was the rest of his security force? He spotted one uniformed figure over to the side of the stage, and observed her for a minute before approaching.

She was partially slumped, standing but numb. In her right hand, loosely held, was a foam coffee cup.

The blood sang within him. *Finally.* He triggered the throat mike again. "Cary! How many of our people have had coffee today?"

The pause was even longer this time. "Cary?"

There was a thump behind him, and, sweating now, Alex turned to look.

The Leviathan IV robot mining rig. In some way that he couldn't quite define, it seemed out of step with the other display models.

Was it his imagination? Wasn't it supposed to move in that fashion? The Leviathan was huge, the size of an armored tank, a complete environment for the precomet days, built for three men to roll from home base.

Griffin suddenly had an awful, ugly suspicion. What was it that Fekesh had done at Colorado Steel? An industrial accident during a safety inspection.

And what had happened at Dream Park eight years before? An accident in Gaming B during a proxy fight for control of the company.

And what had happened three days ago?

He touched his throat mike. "Cary!"

"Ah . . . yes?"

"Don't let anyone else touch that coffee, do you understand?"

Dreamily. "Sure . . . boss."

He didn't bother to curse. Alex tapped out Millicent's code on his watch, and was relieved to hear her voice come in crisp and alert.

"Hello?"

"Millie, it's Alex. No time. Get medical over here to Gaming A. Fekesh has drugged Security's coffee—"

"What? Alex, my God!"

"—coffee supply. And find me Dwight Welles."

Alex kept an uneasy eye on that mining rig, offering a silent thanks to his ulcer. His earphone beeped.

"Welles here. Alex, give me a break. I haven't had sleep in two days—"

"And you're not getting any now. Tie in to Gaming A display autocircuits. Hurry!"

"Jeeze." Welles sounded injured, but did it in less than twenty seconds. "Got it."

"Good. Now take manual control of the Leviathan."

"Got you, Chief. Mmm . . . nothing." Welles was talking to himself. "Nothing nothing . . . mmm? Zzzt! Listen, Chief, the manual control is locked. There's something crazy in here."

Griffin was moving, running. In the dark, the luminescent rigs were all that could be seen, not the human being moving to intercept one of them. He dodged robot jeeps, running across a fantasy landscape. "Welles, is there any way into that thing?"

"Wait, I'll get the specs on the screen. Okay... The top is sealed, but there is an emergency exit door on the belly. There's just enough room to squeeze between the treads. I think."

"Great."

It was rolling now.

"Let me know the instant it diverges from its programmed path."

"Got you, Chief. Nothing so far—I just can't take control from here."

Griffin whipped a pencil-light from his jacket pocket, panting now. There was a trillion dollars' worth of juice in that audience, enough to ruin Cowles Industries, to cripple plans for expansion, to foreclose on outstanding loans, to deny access to proprietary technology. The future of Cowles and of the Barsoom Project was in his hands.

"Can you cut power?"

"No, Chief. Power is self-contained."

"Just great."

The thing was lumbering straight at him now, and he had to calm his fears.

He lay down on his stomach, and shone the pencil-light directly between the treads. There—Welles had been correct. There was just barely enough room.

And if it turned to left or right?

His world was filled with the sound of churning mechanicals as the tank began to pass over him.

"And there will be dangers on the surface of the—"

A blast of their damned ultrasonics passed through him, and he blanched. He was too close to the speakers, and his body vibrated like a tuning fork. He floated away on a sea of nausea, overwhelmed, mind lost in agony.

Keep your mind on the job, asshole!

Alex made his hands take hold of the front bumper of the tank as it rolled past his head.

It was dragging him now, and his back was already abraded. He'd only be able to stand a few seconds of this. He climbed down the underside of the tank, sucking air, trying to calm himself as the subsonics roared through his blood.

And then he had the hatch. With trembling fingers, he worked at the latch lever, and was insanely grateful that the Dream Park technos took their maintenance responsibilities seriously. It was well oiled and opened immediately.

He wiggled up through the tight machinery—

What, did they think Barsoom's miners would be midgets? Oh, bloody hell, it was a 2/3 replica, wasn't it? It was going to break his hip. He couldn't quite get through, when—

"Griff. Problem. Something just took over the program."

"What is it?"

He pulled, strained. Skin could give, fat and muscle could give, but not bone.

"It must be a virus. It hasn't shut me out yet, I can still see what it's doing. There's a search program in action on the Leviathan's sensors."

"Search? What is it searching?"

"Oh, shit—it's searching security badges. It's looking for someone. Goddamn! It just locked."

"On who?"

Alex lowered himself. He'd suddenly remembered a story. Something about a monkey who got his fist caught in a jar. If he relaxed his fist, and dropped the candy—

Or, if the Dream Park security man could back out again. The Martian surface savaged his lower body, and there was no way to protect himself.

Bump bump bump.

"It's locked on Ambassador Richard Arbenz. Oh, shit, Griff! It broke out of the circle. It's heading off the platform!"

Griffin heaved himself up into the cabin. There was enough room to move now. But he was sore, and there were muscles and tendons sprained where he hadn't even known he had muscles and tendons.

"Where is the computer link?"

"Should be obvious. Leviathan was borrowed from Rockwell. They were using a manual system—"

"Where? Wherewherewhere?"

"It's just a box chipped into the CPU. Under the main screen—"

There was a horrible bump as the entire mining rig left the

platform. With a crunching sound the barrier separating stage and audience gave way.

Someone screamed.

Too late! Too late!

Angry, sick, terrified, Alex twisted sideways, stretched, still partially caught in the trapdoor, but stretched far enough to grasp the box. He yanked and tore and twisted, cursed vilely, and something gave.

"Chief! Got it!"

"Then take control, dammit!"

Charlene screamed, and Ambassador Arbenz smiled thinly to himself. Even after three days of fantasy role playing, his niece was unused to Dream Park's magic.

Still, as the mining rig came at him, disconcertingly *straight* at him, Arbenz himself began to feel a bit of discomfort. And when those glistening steel claws reached for him—*straight* for him—

The machine stopped, hesitated—

And then continued, reaching out. He felt the claws touch him, gently, close on him and lift him into the air, chair and all, as gently as a mother lifts a baby. It scooped him high into the air and held him there, as triumphant music played.

From his vantage point he could see security men scurrying around the room, and the uncertain faces of the other guests wondering how to feel about what they had just seen.

Ambassador Arbenz brushed himself off, stood in the cup of the claws, and smiled, striking his hands together smartly in applause.

After a moment's hesitation, a confused Charlene did the same, and within a few seconds, the rest of the audience followed.

Chapter Forty

NIGHTMARES 'R' US

Kareem Fekesh was in a frenzy.

By remote camera he had watched the entire fiasco, safe in his San Diego tower. Arbenz should have been dead, the Barsoom Project in chaos. All of the Cowles shares he had bought on margin . . . all of the sell orders . . .

Paying off wouldn't cripple him, but he would feel the sting.

Everything had gone wrong. It wouldn't be long before the California police would want to question him. Let them wait. He wouldn't be available. Freight flights and tanker ships sailed and flew under the aegis of his company. Nothing could keep him in the United States if he didn't want to be here.

But first there was a matter of personal business, of honor.

He supervised the Kismet-126 program as it searched for the fool who had broken him. Who had it been? Dream Park must have many computer technicians capable of the job. How many would Griffin trust with an assignment of such sensitivity?

Kismet-126 had chosen twenty-two possibles. Through penetration of the Dream Park personnel files, Fekesh had access to each of their schedules for the past five days. He should certainly need no more than that.

Thus far he had found nothing. Very well. Outside contacts? Every phone call that Griffin or his assistant had made.

He was still getting nowhere. *Patience. He who takes vengeance after forty years has acted in haste* . . . but circumstances change, and haste was called for. He considered calling a guard for coffee. *Later.*

He set the Kismet-126 program to tracing Griffin's personal identification number as it moved through the Park. As it ambled through the Park. Taking its own sweet— *There*, it intersected with the woman Millicent Summers. She used to be his secretary. Would she know—

There, Griffin had made a call from her office to Chino Men's Prison to an Anthony McWhirter.

McWhirter. Was that name familiar?

Fekesh's finger touched the Return key, about to start a search program. Instead, he suddenly clapped his hands and laughed aloud, delighted with the symmetry of life. He had used McWhirter against Dream Park, and now Griffin had returned the joke upon him. It was almost worth leaving the little fool his life!

But no. McWhirter's death would serve as an *immediate* message to Griffin. Griffin himself could die later, but first he must *anticipate*. Fekesh tapped Return.

McWhirter vanished. Collia Aziz lay dead in a trash dumpster, sprawled head-down in a bed of used printout paper. Her mouth gaped slackly, and her eyes, and her throat. Dried blood crusted her hair.

Fekesh threw himself backward. The chair tipped and he somersaulted and was on his feet before any enemy could have reached him.

It was her. His fingers stabbed the keys, and the screen cleared. What could that have been? Why would he have put a record of the assassination of poor Collia in his files?

He wiped his forehead. His throat felt tight.

He set his chair in place, and sat. Now, then! He could enter the command that would cause the computer store to pass a message for the special security branch. And security would arrange for McWhirter, even safely ensconced in Chino—

At the touch of his fingertip the screen flashed a picture of an Oriental male sprawled against a featureless white background. An Eskimo's fur headpiece lay half-shredded near his outflung hand. The ragged top of his head gaped against snow splashed with bright red. Izumi must have been freshly dead when this was taken.

Fekesh didn't scream.

He pushed his chair back from the screen. He reached forward to hit Return and the image became a corpse torn almost in half by a fallen girder. Fekesh stared for some seconds, but he didn't recognize the man at all.

Irrelevant; distracting. Fekesh stood, snatched up his briefcase, pushed his hand forcefully into one corner. The plastic shell gave, and now he was holding the pistol grip and trigger of a still-concealed spitgun.

They had penetrated him, had found him, here in his private

offices. He was no longer safe. What he had considered to be beyond consideration, he must accept now: Dream Park intended to assassinate him.

Well. On his home ground they couldn't reach him, and they could not know how many ways he had of reaching home ground.

He pushed a button on the wall. A panel slid back to expose an elevator door. Private. Safe. He heard a *shshsh*, the windsong of an elevator moving upward through its shaft, and then the door slid open.

He half-expected to see a crouching assassin. Too melodramatic, too practical for Dream Park. He lowered the briefcase/spitgun. He was about to take that step forward when a wave of fear hit him. In hasty paranoia he tested the floor—

And his toe went right through. There was nothing there. Beyond where he perceived patterned scarlet rug, his foot turned murky, nearly invisible. Then the top and bottom edges of the door began to extrude teeth. Fekesh yanked his foot back, overbalanced, and fell on his arse, without ever taking his eyes off the elevator. Sharp teeth, dripping—

Dream Park stuff, Dream Park's signature, and if they wanted his attention *here*, then *what was happening behind him*? Fekesh gathered himself and abruptly rolled backward, briefcase aimed, *wait. Nothing? Look again. Nothing?*

An empty office, a computer running quietly. That gory photograph onscreen must be one of the men who died in the accident that gave him control of Colorado Steel.

He hit the Escape key with savage force. The screen printed ESCAPE? in block letters across Colorado Steel's torn work foreman.

Fekesh was sweating now, heart thundering in his chest, and his fingers ripped at his tie. He was struggling for breath, and not finding it. What was happening? What was—

He staggered back to his desk, and punched his phone line.

"I am sorry," an operator's disconnected, recorded voice said mockingly. "This line is temporarily out of service—"

The special security number was dead. The fire alarm circuits, dead. The elevator was alive and deadly, but what about the fire stairs?

Too damned predictably, the lock was jammed. Everything was dead, broken, jammed, and now he was gasping for breath. He staggered to the wall vents, sucking for air—

By Allah's Holy Name? The vent was working. He could hear it, but there was no air pressure against his palms.

In fact—

He screamed. It was pumping air *out* of the room.

Air. Air.

He tore off his jacket and held it against the vent. Air hissed through the cloth.

He aimed his briefcase at the picture window, at the San Diego skyline, but he didn't fire. There was a reason . . . what was it? A bullet fired into *this* glass would ricochet. He'd shoot himself. He dropped the briefcase. He heaved a chair up from beside the desk, and hammered once, gaping like a fish now, twice against the shatterproof glass, spots before his eyes, and again—

And it cracked. He swung again and it spiderwebbed, and the crack ran all along the glass—

And down across the floor. The floor was turning crystalline even as he watched, and then everything around him turned transparent, all of the chairs, the tables, the desks turned to broken glass and vanished, and on hands and knees he was suspended above San Diego. Then—

Then!

His clothing dissolved, his skin, his organs and flesh, and then his bones. He was *gone*. He began to understand that there was no more Kareem Fekesh.

There was time for him to say goodby to himself, a discorporate awareness suspended above San Diego. Then San Diego dropped away. Kareem Fekesh rose with the speed of a rocket. The Earth dwindled to the size of a tennis ball, and there was no air, no air. Something passed across the black starscape, flapping vast golden wings.

"Griffin . . ." he whispered. Or thought of whispering.

His vision went black and red, black . . .

And then, nothing.

Chapter Forty-One

EPILOGUE

"'A tragic accident' is what the papers call it."

Seated gingerly on a table near the window, Griffin turned to face Millicent. His back was still terribly sore, and his left elbow was bandaged. "How's Fekesh?"

It was a quarter to nine in the morning. As if sensing his black mood, Millicent had appeared at his doorway ten minutes earlier with a pot of the best damned decaffeinated coffee he had ever tasted. She was seated at his desk now, scanning his computer screen. Like the friend and helper she had always been, she noted his discomfort, but chose to distract him rather than call his attention to it.

"Well," she said slowly, "there was considerable organic brain dysfunction due to oxygen deprivation."

"In medical terms, then, he's a vegetable."

"Not quite. Massive motor dysfunction, recurring nightmares. Memory impairment. Mental level of a ten-year-old, maybe."

Alex tsk'd. "And the final notes, on his computer at the time?"

"How did you know to ask that?" Millicent said suspiciously, scanning the newsfax. "It was a call to arms, asking his followers to stand one hundred percent behind the Barsoom Project."

"Isn't that interesting."

"Fascinating. There's no suggestion here that it might be fake ... if that's what you were wondering. Even more interesting is the fact that he's too sick to leave the country right now. This clinic in La Mesa—doesn't Vail work out of there?"

"A few hours a month." Alex smiled warmly. The nagging pain had him feeling vicious. "I'm certain that Fekesh will get the very best of care."

"Cowles owns a share of the clinic."

"I'm not surprised at all."

"And recently acquired an interest in Fekesh's elevator repair company. Jesus, Alex, I don't know who scares me more: you or Vail!"

"No need to see conspiracy in every little coincidence. Diversification is the wave of the future."

Millicent joined Griffin by the window, sat so close that their knees were touching. "Griff, how much did you have to do with this?"

"Absolutely nothing." His face was all innocence . . . until something slipped. "I only opened the box. And all these things flew out." He looked inside him for the guilt, and found none. Even so— "I don't imagine I'll ever open that box again."

He wondered if she'd pursue it. He was being judged. Alex wondered what verdict *he* would have rendered. He'd been on painkillers, but he'd been lucid enough when he went to the magicians . . . when he turned Izumi and Khresla and Welles and, God help him, Vail loose.

She said, "And what were you doing on the night of June seventeenth?"

The lobster dinner? "The same thing I was doing on the night of June twenty-fifth."

She smiled. "That's tonight."

"Hope springs eternal."

He could see her shoulders relaxing. "What hope was that?"

"Finishing dinner with my beautiful ex-secretary."

"Who was much too good for you."

"Correction. Was much too good to be my secretary."

"Ah-ha."

Her fingers touched a file folder on his desk, and a fingernail flicked it open. In it was a picture of Marty. "Poor Marty."

Alex's attempt at good humor faded. "Nobody intended it. Vail swears he had nothing to do with it. I *swear* it, Millie."

"Not a bite?"

"Hasn't eaten for almost two weeks. If they force-feed him, he vomits. County put him on IVs, and Marty kept tearing them out of his arm. Legally, we can't force him to eat."

She shook her head. "Try the Dream Park diet," she said. "Lose a pound a day, and never be hungry again."

"Jesus," Griffin said. "You've got a morbid streak, don't you?"

Millicent shuddered. "Listen, maybe if one of the other Gamers talked to him—"

The outer office door opened, and a tall, slender man entered. He looked a little pale and wan, but the smile was genuine.

"Griffin," he said, cautiously extending his hand. "You kept your promise."

"Tony McWhirter, you kept yours," Alex said. "You're on work furlough, loaned to the municipality of Dream Park. Ah—as the duly elected Sheriff of Dream Park, I tell you that you are restricted to within two kilometers of this office—" Alex's voice softened. "The only other restriction is that you make up for lost time, Tony."

The two men faced each other, looking uncomfortable. Tony looked around the room. And through the external windows, around the Park.

The Barsoom Project was gone. Dream Park was alight again, ready for the public. It wore its public face. Dream Park was bright and beautiful and flashy.

"I feel . . . so strange," Tony said. "I can't believe that you're giving me a chance like this."

"You've panned out," Griffin said. "Let's start over again. I want you here, in Security. Meantime, until we know exactly what the situation is, you'll stay in CMC, with full protection. Just in case."

"Appreciate that."

McWhirter nodded to Millicent. His eyes lingered on her until he suddenly flushed with embarrassment. He left the office hurriedly.

Millicent watched him go. "Could be the beginning of a beautiful friendship."

"Yeah," Alex sighed. "Based on honesty and trust."

"Based on fantasy," she said.

"Not the worst place to start," he said.

His arm stole around her.

It wasn't his fault. None of the death, the deception, the injury surrounding the Barsoom Project, and the past of Cowles Industries, had been his fault. But his aching back and bruised ribs, and the sight of Tony's hollow face, had reminded him that it was all his responsibility. He had done the best he could. And he had to believe Vail.

Vail just *couldn't* have reached into Marty's head somehow, and *twisted* . . .

He thought of Kareem Fekesh in La Mesa, and of Vail's loving ministrations, and shivered.

He had to let it go. If he could just manage to live with himself for another week or so, maybe he could go on, and do his job.

He felt heavy, and old, and tired.

Millicent kissed him gently on the cheek. "You know what let's do?" she said softly.

"What?"

"Let's sign up, the two of us, as partners in that Shipwreck Game next week." She paused. "I wouldn't mind being your girl Friday again."

"A whole week's Game?"

"Tropical sun, digging for turtle eggs, exploring semi-extinct volcanoes for treasure . . ."

"I don't know. I'm damned busy."

She punched him in the good side. "I happen to know that you've got three weeks accumulated vacation. Harmony would give you three more without a blink. Refuse me and I'll have Vail give you a psychiatric suspension."

"On what grounds?"

She turned his head with palms that were warm and soft. Her lips parted slightly as she pressed them against his. "You'd be crazy to turn me down."

He laughed. Not a large laugh, but it held promise, the first glimpse of sunlight through storm clouds. It was going to be all right. As long as he had friends like Millicent and Harmony, he could survive anything.

They held each other and watched the front gates open.

The crowds would marvel at the effects and immerse themselves in the adventures. For a time they would lose their minds, and most would be the better for it. But if they knew what lay behind the magic . . .

That one question, at least, he could answer. Most people don't really want to see the strings, don't want to see what lurks behind the mirrors. They need dreams. Need magic. Always have.

Alex couldn't hear the sounds of laughter, of gaiety and excitement, couldn't see the individual smiles of anticipation. But he could see the flow, the tide of life as it streamed once more into the streets of Dream Park.

We are the Magicians, Griffin reminded himself proudly. *We bring the dream to life.*

And we're the only ones who can.

AFTERWORD

This was an ambitious project. *Dream Park* was fantasy wrapped in science fiction wrapped in mystery. *The Barsoom Project* is cut from the same pattern. Our intent has been to blend dozens of individual threads of information into one (we hope) seamless tapestry.

In the case of the Fimbulwinter Game, it proved more difficult to trace down data on the spirit world of the northern peoples than we had anticipated. Thanks and acknowledgments are even more appropriate than usual.

The people whom we call *Eskimo*, or *Inuit*, are not a single group, but a scattering of tribes and small nations ranging down from the Arctic Circle, and up from Asia and the North American Indian peoples. There are many lifestyles and many languages. Some of the Inuit are still hunters in the "primitive" fashion of their ancestors. Many are modern professional people. As one might anticipate, the traditional tribal structure is in danger of being destroyed by contact with the forces of Western culture and technology.

Myths are the first steps toward science, an attempt to explain the unknown. The Inuit live in the most unforgiving environment on Earth. They have devised a vast and complex mythology encompassing everything from weather gods to the usual xenophobic tales of cannibals-beyond-the-mountains. There is no unified world view that one can truly call the "Inuit Way."

We needed to find an entry into their world, their way of seeing the universe. Enter Richard Dobson, of the Transformative Arts Institute in San Geronimo, California. An expert in contemporary shamanism, Richard was of integral help in explaining the belief patterns common to all shamanic peoples worldwide. Many hours of lecturing and discussion yielded a framework within which the scattered pieces of data began to make sense.

Harley "Swift Deer" Reagan, a master of the Sweet Medicine

Sundance teachings of the Cherokee and Athabascan-speaking peoples, offered additional insight into the epistemological structures through which the North, South, and Central Native American peoples organize their lives, world view, and cosmology. Additional thanks must be given for specific data on the value and techniques of the pipe ceremony, the Medicine Wheel, and that most amazing tool for spiritual enlightenment and/or masochistic semi-immolation, not to mention native cuisine: the sweat lodge.

Steven was smart enough to choose his father-in-law carefully. Thomas Young, a Texaco engineer who specializes in building ice roads in Alaska, provided books, video, photos, and stories of the Eskimo world. Special thanks.

Of the books on the Inuit peoples, by far the most useful was *Inua: Spirit World of the Bering Sea Eskimo*, by William W. Fitzhugh and Susan A. Kaplan. Also valuable were *The Nelson Island Eskimo*, by Ann Fienup-Riordan, and *Ancient Men of the Arctic*, by J. Louis Giddings.

All of the Game's natural magics stem from Inuit traditions of the people of the north, though not from any single tribe. Likewise with the gods, archetypes, monsters, and wildlife, except in the single case of the Wolfalcons. Here the authors took a general myth pattern, establishing that Inuit shamans can mutate themselves into bizarre bird, animal, and fish shapes, and allowed the Cabal to become creative.

Shaping the Barsoom Project was much easier.

Gary Hudson has wanted to build spacecraft for some decades now. Over the years his "Phoenix" designs have changed many times, following changing technology. Always they have been small single-stage ground-to-orbit craft, truncated cones using the aerospike engine configuration.

Schemes for terraforming Mars generally involve using comet impacts and gene-tailored algae to shape a breathable atmosphere and/or to free the air and water that once carved riverbeds on Mars. It would be cheap and easy compared to the terraforming of Venus.

Skyhook devices are pretty much as described. Every such device would be initially very expensive, but very cheap to run. Each would open the solar system to mankind. Each could be terribly destructive if it failed, and each would be more easily and safely built using Mars as a test bed. Join any of today's space advocacy groups and you need not seek information on skyhooks; it will seek you out.

Dream Park, our first collaborative novel, has achieved some notoriety, and is considered by many to be something of a minor classic. It has never been out of print, has been under film option continuously, and has even spawned a real-life version of the International Fantasy Gaming Society.

In April of 1989, we were invited to the first convention held by the *real* IFGS, in Denver, Colorado. These are bright, energetic, highly creative and infectiously enthusiastic folks, who sponsor and coordinate elaborate costumed fantasy role-playing events. They are literally committed to bringing Dream Park into existence. Power to them, and may their legions increase! Presently they have chapters all over the United States and are building a network overseas. They can be reached at the following address: IFGS, P.O. Box 3555, Boulder, Colorado, 80307-3555.

They were understandably eager to know what we thought of them. Let's just say that, although the FAA would certainly have frowned upon it, your humble authors could have flown back to L.A. without a plane.

Since the original publication of *Dream Park*, countless readers have requested a sequel. We have to confess a certain degree of reluctance, at least partially because it would have been too darned easy.

So we waited until the right idea came along, in the right context, at the right time. (Easy, hell. We don't seem to *get* easy ideas.)

Seven years have passed since the events of *Dream Park*; but Dream Park technology hasn't changed much. We assumed, then as now, that computer technology and hologram technology have become stunningly powerful by the mid-twenty-first century. Within Dream Park, reality has become almost optional. The authors find it fascinating to watch how human beings handle that.

Dream Park is a special place for both of us, a playground in which the collaborative game of "Can you top this?" can be played on a dozen fields at the same moment. If it has been half as entertaining to read as it was to write, then it was indeed worth the wait, and the effort.

—Larry Niven and Steven Barnes
Los Angeles
May 25, 1989